SURVEILLANCE

Other books by Bernard Keane

A Short History of Stupid—with Helen Razer
War on the Internet (ebook)

SURVEILLANCE

BERNARD KEANE

ALLEN&UNWIN
SYDNEY·MELBOURNE·AUCKLAND·LONDON

Allen & Unwin
83 Alexander Street
Crows Nest NSW 2065
Australia
Phone: (61 2) 8425 0100
Email: info@allenandunwin.com
Web: www.allenandunwin.com

Cataloguing-in-Publication details are available
from the National Library of Australia
www.trove.nla.gov.au

ISBN 978 1 76011 385 8

Set in 11.5/16.5 pt Sabon by Post Pre-press Group, Australia
Printed and bound in Australia by Griffin Press

10 9 8 7 6 5 4 3 2 1

To Sam

'It was the day Australia lost its cyber-innocence—a hack that rocked a nation and sent a government into crisis. One man broke into the innermost recesses of the Australian government and went on a rampage with our politicians' deepesh secret—blergh. Sorry I'll go again.'

Kat looked down at her mark on the floor and shuffled her feet, cleared her throat and glanced at herself in the monitor beside the camera.

'Whenever you're ready, Katrina, it's fine,' said the director.

The Kat in the monitor was looking off to her right, of course. She considered the image of herself for a moment, then smoothed her top down over her stomach and straightened her jacket.

'You look great, Katrina,' said a voice from the darkness beyond the camera. 'You comfortable?'

'Yeah yeah, it's fine, Susan,' she replied. Camera Kat was still looking off to the right, perhaps contemplating yet another version of herself that only she could see.

She looked back at the camera lens and cleared her throat. The autocue text had scrolled back to the words *It was the day Australia lost its cyber-innocence—a hack that rocked . . .*

I can't believe I'm saying this, she thought. Cyber-innocence? Seriously? She flexed her mouth.

'Okay.' Pause. 'It was the day Australia lost its cyber-innocence—a hack that rocked a nation and sent a government into crisis.' She was

1

slower this time. 'One man broke into the innermost recesses of the Australian government and went on a rampage with our politicians' deepest secrets. The Cyber War turned white hot as governments were panicked by revelations of who was saying what to whom, almost in real time. They called him an infoman—fuck, sorry.'

'It's good, good rhythm, just go from the start of the last sentence. Your pacing is fine,' the director said.

Kat glanced behind her at the green backdrop, which in post-production would become a blur of digital images. Then she looked at the monitor again. The tip of her nose itched, but she dared not scratch it for fear of ruining her make-up. She settled for trying to wiggle it, which prompted Camera Kat, gazing off into the space to her right, to make a ridiculous face.

'Okay, here goes. They called him an info-terrorist and launched a worldwide hunt for the hacker humiliating the Australian government. But by the time they'd caught their man, there was a new superwarrior in the annals of the Cyber War: Michael Servetus.'

She glanced back at Camera Kat. 'How was that?' she watched herself ask.

'Perfect,' said the director. 'Really nice pace, Katrina.'

'Yep, that was fantastic,' called Susan.

'Can we go one more time, just a little bit slower?' said the director. 'Just so we've got some options when we put it together, some of it will just be voiceover.'

'Okay,' Kat said. She straightened her jacket again. 'Slower. A lot slower? A little slower?'

'Just a little slower.'

'Cool. Okay. I talk too fast, I know.'

'Yeah no no, just a wee bit slower. Couple of seconds. Also, can you put just a little more emphasis on the ending, on Michael Servetus?'

'Michael Servetus,' she said softly to herself. 'Michael fucking Servetus.' She looked into the lens. The autocue had scrolled back. She flicked her gaze to the Kat in the monitor, who was again looking away.

One of these days I'll catch you watching me, Camera Kat, she thought. 'We rolling?'

'Yep, whenever you like.'

'It was the day Australia lost its cyber-innocence—a hack that rocked . . .'

**MONDAY
2 NOVEMBER**

The green, jagged steps lurched downwards, each successively lower, though by seemingly random amounts. Most of these precarious platforms themselves tilted down, although two of them had a small, irregular bulge, in neither case anywhere near enough to arrest the spasmodic descent across the screen.

Mark Chalmers adjusted the chart scale from one week to one month. The drunken stairs vanished, replaced with an uneven slope, considerably smoother but still steadily declining. He moved it to three months. There was now a hump at the start, and then a more consistent version of the same descent, stretching out below the words *NYSE Emergent Technology Systems (ETS) 121.94* ⇓ *17.14 (14.06%)*. He added the Nasdaq for comparison. The new red line began below the green hump but then tracked slightly upwards across the screen—not smoothly or perfectly, by any means, but in an altogether healthier direction than the share price for ETS.

He turned away from the screen, grimacing, and gazed out of the window behind his desk for a moment. Twenty-seven floors below, Hyde Park stretched away. The War Memorial was in sunlight, but it was still early enough that the shadows from the buildings on College Street lay across the area just to the east of it. The sky was clear and it would be a bright, spring Sydney day. He made a clucking sound with his tongue, rose from his desk, picked up a coffee mug and left his office.

'Going up to see Derek,' he muttered to his assistant, and walked around to the lifts.

Veldtech had been, until 2010, the third-largest software company in Australia. In early 2011, American defence tech giant ETS—headquarters, aptly, Marshall, Virginia—had bought it, along with half of Veldtech Scientific, a Perth-based defence contractor. That had made Derek Anderson, who'd begun Veldtech as a cybersecurity firm in South Africa in the early 1990s and moved to Australia in 1996, the twelfth-richest man in the country. At sixty-three, he continued to helm Veldtech (he remained inexplicably proud of the pun), as well as being an ETS board member.

Chalmers's colleagues were already in Anderson's office, seated at his new meeting table, which added a distinctive and rather pleasant scent of jarrah to the room. It was positioned next to Anderson's floor-to-ceiling windows, with a slightly different view to Chalmers's—he could see the very top of the Harbour Bridge and, mostly between the tops of buildings, the harbour around to Rushcutters Bay. Derek liked his harbour views.

He looked around unsuccessfully for a coaster, and produced a neatly folded handkerchief, on which he placed his coffee mug, emblazoned with the National Security Agency logo. Across from him was the other Mark: Rathbone. (Strictly speaking, there were three Marks, if you counted the absent Special Counsel, General Mark Levers (ret.)). Rathbone was COO; Chalmers was division head, Intelligence. They maintained a rivalry of sorts given their respective backgrounds—Chalmers from ASIO; Rathbone a former senior Australian Signals Directorate officer, although he'd been in the private sector for much longer than Chalmers. Beside him was Maria Campanella, head of Defence Solutions, who'd been notoriously 'put in by the Americans'; she was Australian but had worked in ETS HQ in Virginia for a decade. Rathbone, nicknamed 'Basil' by Campanella, had only just arrived back from a trip to Europe on the weekend and looked exhausted. The other current member of the executive team, Jane Webb, Civil and Sustainability Solutions and acting head of Corporate, was still overseas. Veldtech's CFO had recently left for a position at Telstra.

Mark Chalmers is a former senior public servant, businessman and holder of a doctorate from the University of Sydney and a law degree from the Australian National University, ran the blurb in the corporate section of the Veldtech website, alongside a picture of a smiling Chalmers. As several colleagues had pointed out, few had ever seen him smile in real life, and many assumed the image was photoshopped.

> *Prior to joining Veldtech, Mark was a deputy director-general of the Australian Security Intelligence Organisation and spent twenty-six years in both the Australian Attorney-General's Department and in ASIO, as well as a period as an adviser to the Attorney-General. Mark is also Adjunct Professor of National Security at Sydney University's United States Studies Centre. Mark has extensive experience in addressing emerging cybersecurity and cybercrime threats at a national level, while his leadership strengths and extensive relationships with both the Australian and other governments make him an invaluable member of the Veldtech executive and the wider ETS family of companies.*

'That's me,' Chalmers had said when he'd first read it. 'A real fucking family man.'

'Thanks for coming,' Anderson said, walking towards them from his desk some metres across the room. He clutched a glass of sparkling mineral water, which he proceeded to spill as he sat down.

'Oops.' He rose again and fetched a tissue from his desk. 'Good weekend?'

'Would have been if I didn't spend most of it here,' said Campanella, who rarely spoke much above a whisper.

Anderson had a thick shock of grey hair and was thin, almost gaunt, as he had been since his 'oncological difficulties' several years before. He wasn't shy about discussing his bout of cancer, indeed he seemed to regard it as evidence of his capitalist superiority, and often helpfully passed on to interlocutors and recipients of his charitable largesse (the Anderson Fund for Men's Health) the lessons he'd learned while battling the disease, chief among which were 'don't give up', 'stay positive' and 'focus'. He dabbed at the water on the table, then placed his glass carefully on the tissue and sat down again.

The reason for the meeting was notionally a mystery to Chalmers, but he had his suspicions: Veldtech's half-yearly results had shown that revenues were falling and unlikely to improve for the rest of the year. With ETS's share price under sustained pressure, the last thing Marshall or investors wanted to hear was bad news from Sydney. Anderson would be keen to show Marshall that things were on the improve. The prospect of even more second-guessing from Anderson was not a cheery one; he already had a habit of roaming the building, randomly interrupting staff to inquire what they were doing and offer homilies, which staff felt unable to ignore, no matter how inappropriate his advice.

'Look, I wanted to discuss a couple of things early this week. There was an emergency board meeting on Saturday that I teleconned into. Currently ETS is looking at a profit downgrade of about twelve per cent for the full year.'

He paused for a moment. Rathbone whistled quietly.

'But it gets worse. It looks like they're going to miss out on the CBIS contract.'

'Ah, fuck,' said Campanella, unusually loudly.

'What?' said Chalmers, alarmed. 'I thought that was a lock.'

'So did everyone in Marshall. Seems SAIC is going to get it. It's not confirmed yet, but when it's announced, the share price is going to cop a hammering,' said Anderson.

ETS had been confident the Connected Battlescape Information System, an idea the company had helped the Pentagon develop, would be a key new revenue stream going forward. The idea was a system to integrate real-time feeds from sensors on vehicles, aircraft and soldiers' gear into a coherent, easily navigable data stream. The original Pentagon appropriation was over US$10 billion, but that had been cut during one of the Congressional budget standoffs. Even so, losing the contract would be a painful blow for the company.

'So Marshall wants us to slash costs to offset the CBIS news,' said Campanella, with a slight, though thoroughly professional, sneer.

'In essence,' Anderson agreed. 'Tony's last monthly report'— Tony was their former CFO—'had revenue down five per cent, EBIT looking down six per cent. Needless to say that won't be popular in Marshall. They want to see EBIT *up* fifteen per cent next half.'

'Fifteen per cent? That's ridiculous,' said Rathbone. He and Chalmers exchanged meaningful glances.

'Where the fuck do we get fifteen per cent? Seriously?' said Chalmers, almost laughing, half to Rathbone, half to Anderson. 'You know how things are in procurement currently.'

Anderson sipped his water. 'I know better than you, Mark. I had lunch with the defence minister last week. He made it clear.'

'Marshall's being completely unrealistic,' Maria began. 'There's no—'

Derek's phone rang, and the voice of Ethel, his assistant, emanated from the desk. 'Sorry, Derek, I've got Vanessa on the line, she says she needs a quick word right away.'

Anderson sighed and rose. 'Excuse my wife,' he said. He went to the desk and picked up the phone. 'What's up?'

'Typical Marshall bullshit,' Campanella said, below Derek's hearing. 'Fifteen per cent. For fuck's sake.'

Anderson was silent for twenty seconds and then his face broke into a grin. 'Okay, that's fine, I'll reschedule it. Yep. Me too.'

He returned to the table. 'It doesn't matter if they're being unrealistic. Everyone across the group has to pull their weight. The Brits, the French as well. They're getting rid of five hundred people in the US. They're hiring a new firm to get into Congress and lobby for cyberwarfare funding. As you know, the focus has all been back on kinetic in the Middle East.'

Despite its size, ETS didn't do much 'kinetic', in the form of physical weaponry, beyond Derek's own, not very large, company in Perth. A missile arm of ETS had, as was the management fashion of the time, been spun off years before, to be eventually acquired by Raytheon.

'So we need to contribute to the body count,' said Chalmers.

'Well, cutting bonuses won't be enough,' Derek said after a pause. 'They want a big rise in EBIT in the second half. So, yes, we'll have to lose some numbers.'

Chalmers leaned back in his chair and looked out the window. 'Some human sacrifices to appease the gods of the market,' he said, nodding.

'But cutting numbers is straightforward,' Anderson continued. 'The key priority is to book more revenue, and quickly. Doesn't matter how. You have to get out there and shake the tree. We're bidding on everything, and we're underbidding. We can deal with the costs next financial year when we get them to extend the contracts. But Marshall wants more revenue as well as the cuts. Everyone's on the phone looking for business as of now.'

'That's crazy,' said Rathbone. 'It's November, procurement's about to wind down. There'll be a four-week break across the end of the year.'

'Yep,' agreed Campanella animatedly. 'And the federal budget is really tight.'

'I want those numbers,' said Anderson with finality. 'Start looking at who you've got to cut and start telling me what new revenue you're chasing. Pull out all the stops.' He sipped his water again. 'I know it's tight. Marshall knows it's tight. They face the same environment in Washington, only much worse. I don't care how we do it, okay? We just need to lift those numbers; whatever it takes to give Marshall what they want. Get everyone moving.'

'This is fucking crazy,' said Chalmers, once the three of them were in the lift and out of the earshot of Ethel, who sat outside Anderson's office. 'Are they serious?' This directed to Maria.

She nodded. 'Oh hell yeah. This is all about their remuneration packages. If the stock price falls more than fifteen per cent, no one gets a bonus. They're already out of fashion because they don't have things that blow shit up. When the CBIS news comes out it'll take another hit. They want a stream of good news about costs and revenue to announce between now and end of financial in March so there's a floor under the price.'

'Bloody great,' said Rathbone tiredly. 'I don't know about you guys, but I'm not exactly overburdened with staff.'

'Maybe I should have put some extra on just so I'd have a few to sack when shit like this happens,' said Chalmers. He sipped his coffee, which he hadn't touched throughout the meeting.

'I can't believe they fucked up CBIS,' said Campanella. She was more agitated than Chalmers had ever seen her. 'I was there when that started. It was our fucking idea. Then they got the Pentagon interested in it. We had some general on the board who put the whole deal in place. Then he quit last year, and they've buggered it up.'

'So I guess Jane is in for a shock when she gets back,' said Rathbone.

'And I imagine there won't be a new head of Corporate any time soon,' said Maria as they left the lift.

'Katrina Sharpe, what does this say about politicians and social media?'

Kat smiled across the glass desk at the host of *NVR*, Gareth Males. Inside the desk beneath her was a monitor, with a dull green cursor blinking on and off just enough to annoy her throughout the broadcast. She had a pre-prepared spiel, one of her usual lines, good to go.

'Gareth,' (she always made a point of throwing in first names on television), 'it shows that some politicians are still getting to grips with what social media actually is. These are the late adopters. All these new platforms go through a period in which we establish the rules, if you like, of how they should be used and how they fit into the rules we already have. Like the first few years of email, when people didn't fully understand about reply all or didn't realise that things could take on a life of their own once you'd hit send. Same thing with Twitter. Laurie Donahue has just worked out that Twitter is both a one-to-one communications platform *and* a broadcast platform, unfortunately in a highly public way. He might have thought he was justified in lashing out at someone baiting him online, but he was doing it in public, which is the problem.'

'I think there'll be a few media advisers explaining to their bosses the difference between a Reply and a DM tonight,' said Males. He turned back and faced the camera. 'Well, that's all we've got time for. We'll be back with more *NVR* at the same time tomorrow evening.

Thanks to our guests Patrick Lee, Mary Wallace in our Melbourne studio and Katrina Sharpe. I'm Gareth Males. See you next time.'

Gareth held his gaze into the camera as the title music began playing, then relaxed and turned to his two guests. 'Thanks, guys, that was fantastic.'

Kat began undoing her microphone. 'Gee it goes fast. It never feels like forty-five minutes.'

'Tell me about it,' said Gareth. 'Well done, Pat. That was good.'

Lee was a first-timer and had been nervous beforehand. 'Really? Thank you,' he said, waiting to be disentangled from his microphone by one of the techs.

The producer, a young woman in T-shirt and shorts, came onto the set. 'Thank you, thank you,' she said. 'That went well. Thanks, Kat. Loved how you were all over the kids-walking-home-alone thing.'

'All good,' said Kat, moving toward the door. 'Look I've gotta bolt, I'm going to the ANMII awards up the road.'

'Okay, see you next time, Katrina,' called Gareth from the desk.

She was already a little late, but luckily the awards event was only a couple of blocks away at the Powerhouse Museum. She grabbed some wipes from the make-up area and quickly scrubbed her face clean of the TV-level pancake. She headed out of the ABC onto Harris Street and walked quickly up the hill.

A certain amount of psychological prep was going to be required for the event, because Chris was also going to be attending, with Her. Kat had seen them together before—once at another function, and once by chance (the Notorious Supacenta Incident)—but felt like she could handle it with the right preparation. She checked Gmail as she stopped at the lights and waited to cross over to the museum. Just a quick one from Chris: *Love you can't wait to see you even though I won't be able to touch you xxxxxxx*. Then she checked Twitter.

ABC should have @kat_sharpe on more often she's a breath of common sense.

Thank you, @rennywilks, bless you and your mixed metaphors.

Don't approve of @kat_sharpe's new hair. very black makes her look like the junkie girl from BreakingBad #nvr

Thanks @janemajors44, always love unsolicited comments on my appearance.

@kat_sharpe is hot. Brains and looks. #nvr

That may or may not be the creepy stalker guy under a new avatar.

there's that stupid bitch @kat_sharpe on #nvr again ABC lift ur game.

Arsehole. Blocked. She couldn't even be bothered retweeting that. She liked to retweet abuse, especially sexist abuse, but these days it took being called a cunt, or getting some form of physical threat, to earn a Sharpe retweet. Abuse inflation.

She walked across the plaza in front of the Museum, hoping she wouldn't arrive at the same moment as Chris and Her. She knew exactly how she'd react the moment she saw Her. A visceral feeling . . . well, *feeling* was far too weak, far too *innocuous* a word—more accurately, a visceral bolt of unthinking, jealous fury would erupt from deep inside her brain, emerging from some place at the reptile level, the bit left over from when dinosaurs roamed the earth. That part would boil with fury that anyone would have the effrontery, the unmitigated *gall*, to stand beside Chris, posing as his partner, posing as someone significant to him, as someone who shared his life.

She knew all that and was prepared for it, ready to meet it head on and then keep functioning at a level considered acceptable in polite company.

'Katrina Sharpe,' she said to the two young women in black at the desk. One, who had an extraordinarily aquiline nose, watched the other, who had short blonde hair, leaf through several pages then slide her finger down a column.

'Thanks, Ms Sharpe, have a lovely evening,' said the blonde.

Nearby was a man wearing the same sort of outfit as the young women, holding a camera. He glanced at Kat and resumed looking bored. Damn. Still not famous enough to make the photographers' cut.

On the positive side, she was confronted almost immediately by a waiter with a tray of drinks. She selected sparkling wine, with low expectations, but it tasted surprisingly good for Event Liquid.

She looked around: there must have been at least a hundred people present, probably more, in a rather narrow area in front of a tall black curtain, behind which, presumably, the actual awards ceremony would occur. There was Event Food circulating, she could see, but she couldn't immediately spot anyone she knew and to whom she could talk. She decided that the best strategy was to advance purposefully into the crowd, offering smiles of faux-recognition to several people who looked up from engrossed conversations. Then she veered to the left so that she wouldn't reach the curtain too quickly, which meant she almost walked into Mike Jephcott, who'd launched her book a year before. Jephcott was barely a hundred and seventy centimetres tall, and she hadn't spotted him in the throng.

'Hey, Kat.'

'Hey,' she said, delighted at encountering someone to whom she could talk. Jephcott was a British software engineer who'd moved to Australia and launched two start-ups since arriving. Kat had been on a couple of conference panels with him. 'How are things?'

'Oh, you know, not bad. You?'

She looked over at an obese man talking to two quite attractive women. 'I'm good. Did you see our friend Phil over there?'

Phil was Phil Desmond, or Diabetes Phil, a mutual and mutually disliked acquaintance whose regular technology columns were the subject of joking between her and Mike on Twitter.

'I see he's brought *both* his girlfriends,' said Mike.

'Ugh,' she said. 'Mike, that's revolting.'

'They're probably robots he's trying out for his next column. How's work?'

She waggled her hand. 'So-so. I'm a bit desperate for some more writing gigs. I just came from *NVR*. It's mostly consulting at the moment.'

'Why don't you charge more for consulting?'

She frowned. 'Why would I do that? I barely get enough work as it is.'

'You're a media personality. Bureaucrats and HR departments will expect to pay more for someone like—'

She didn't hear the rest of his sentence. 'Oh my fucking god . . .' she said, staring across the room. Near the entrance, the guy with the camera who'd ignored her was capturing the arrival of Amy Dinh. She was wearing a tight, blood-red strapless dress and smiling for the camera as the guest of honour stepped forward to greet her.

'God who?' said Mike.

'Amy Dinh,' Kat muttered. She felt a brief twinge of regret that she had gone for black like just about everyone else. 'And, of course, her arse.'

It was not a comment made with vindictiveness or even, in a sense, jealousy; it was more a statement of resignation in the face of a greater power. Amy Dinh was a model and, until recently, a blogger, prone to putting short films about herself on YouTube; these had invariably racked up hundreds of thousands of hits and as a result she had recently picked up a job with News Corp.

'Ah, the lingerie blogger,' said Jephcott, standing on tiptoes and craning his neck. Among her three blogs, Dinh ran one devoted to her considered thoughts on underwear, and pictures of her in same (always carefully omitting her head). She had a News Corp column on 'Sex and Gen Z' and was a 'social media expert' as well. She'd also, famously, won some sort of internet award for 'best arse'. When she'd heard, Kat had, passive-aggressively, posted a picture of a prize-winning donkey on Twitter, and said nothing more.

She, along with probably a large proportion of men in the room, contemplated the prize-winning flesh as Dinh turned, her tight dress revealing it in all its power. Kat felt like running from the room and going home and doing three hundred squats.

'Wait till she's a mummy blogger—then she'll be completely insufferable,' said Jephcott comfortingly.

'I dunno, if I could get a regular column by posting pics of myself in my undies I'd do it,' she said.

'Hot Geek Girl dot com,' said Mike. 'Did you get invited to AusCERT next year?'

'I did, though just for a panel.'

'They want an address and a panel from me. I don't know what I'm going to talk about. I get sick of giving the same talk.'

'Long as I'm not on a panel with fucking Brandon Butler.'

'Oh god, he's so annoying.'

'I actually wanted to punch him in the face last time I was on a panel with him,' she said, watching Dinh's arse as it made its way across the room, moving slowly and sinuously through the crowd. 'I literally had to restrain myself.'

She sipped her sparkling wine half-heartedly, suddenly not in the mood for socialising. Dinh was a competitor, an unfair competitor, in a limited market. Currently, Kat's main income came from consulting on social media strategies, which was mind-numbingly boring; her book on corporate use of social media the year before had failed to make any sort of splash, although she still got the occasional speaking engagement from it. Every TV and radio spot, however obscure, she was glad to do for the publicity. Maybe, she thought occasionally, she should branch out from social media. Or try for an academic job again. At least there she could write as much as she wanted and not have to compete with a lingerie blogger. She had, when she'd published the book, made some website list of 'hottest IT girls'. She felt faintly disgusted and angry about it, partly because she hated that sort of shit, but also because her immediate reaction had been to wonder if it might get her more gigs. In the meantime, she lectured public servants and bored corporate types on social media while trying to make a living writing.

Sigh. A struggling author. In love with a married man. Good life choices, Kat, amirite?

Speaking of whom, there he was. Oh fuck. Him. HIM. Chris was wearing a blue suit. Shaking the hand of the ANMII president. White shirt, tie. Sweet, sweet Jesus, he looked perfect. Inside his trousers, she knew, would be some black or maybe dark grey tight-fitting boxers, and inside those, the delicious, large cock that she knew so well.

It was her body, in a way. Not in that he was an extension of her, but that it belonged to her, that she was its rightful owner. She understood it, knew how to bring it pleasure, knew how to exploit its own phenomenal pleasure-giving characteristics. She knew how to fuck it, to possess it, and she knew how to submit to it, to be possessed by it, she knew the joy of giving it pleasure and the delight (weirdly almost equal to, and sometimes better than, sex) of lying next to it, sometimes talking, sometimes not, just knowing his body was where it belonged, next to her.

Instead, at that very moment, it was next to Her.

The ice dagger of jealousy entered her, at the top of her skull, and plunged down into her stomach, which contorted violently. She had enough self-possession to remind herself to hold on tight. Her wore a dark green dress, knee-length, a little low cut; shoulder-length red hair, faintly voluptuous, once pretty, now, well, early forties, not too bad.

Hold the fuck on, girl.

Kat couldn't help comparing herself to Her, wondering if Chris had once liked Her body more than he did Kat's, despite the age difference. Her had a decent bust, for a start. Maybe Chris would like it if I got a . . .

Okay, breathe slowly and count to ten, she told herself, watching Her, the impostor, standing where she should rightly be. You've prepared for this. Five, six, seven, eight. It was a desperate effort to stop the thoughts about Her breaking through, thoughts about what would happen if she could never replace the interloper at Chris's side, in his arms, on his cock, in his life, growing old with him.

'Hi, Kat,' came a voice.

She tore her gaze away from Chris and his wife.

'I just wanted to say I'm halfway through your book and I just *love* it,' said Amy Dinh.

**TUESDAY
3 NOVEMBER**

A sharp peal of thunder woke Em right on 5.30 a.m. She climbed out of bed and peered through the blinds at the trees swaying in the wind, illuminated from beneath by the streetlights. There was no rain for the moment, but there was another flash of lightning.

'One . . . two . . . three,' she counted mentally.

When she was growing up in Adelaide, Em would be awoken by storms on summer nights. She'd get up to stare out through the blinds, watching as the sky turned briefly into day and lightning summoned the tree in the park next to Mrs McGorry's place into momentary existence, then dispatched it again to the accompaniment of gunshot-like thunder. She loved storms, especially at night.

The rain began, not especially heavy, as she returned to bed, aware she wouldn't be able to return to sleep. Instead, she lay there, hands on her chest in what she called her funeral pose, watching the ceiling flare with the storm. After ten or fifteen minutes, the rain faltered and stopped, half-hearted, not really in proper storm mode. She stayed in bed for an hour, tired but sleepless.

'Eight thirty, important meeting, go go go,' she muttered eventually, turning her phone alarm off before rising and heading to the shower.

She stood beneath the water, eyes closed, not wanting to leave it, thinking its warm embrace would be a relative high point of the day. She willed herself out and dried off slowly, then stood on the scales and considered the result unhappily. Cheating, treacherous bastard of a body, she thought, returning to the bedroom and donning her clothes. As a token of organisation, she had prepared her work outfit the night before, but now her ever-present internal critic, Dark Voice, started up.

You should really think about a skirt instead of pants. Who wants to see your ever-expanding arse? That jacket won't hide it. No jacket could *hide it . . .*

She hesitated, then glanced at her phone—7.15, shit—and began pulling on her pants. Not enough sleep *and* running late. She hurried into the kitchen, shrugging her jacket on. Her apartment was tiny: one bedroom, shower, kitchen-dining, lounge, a balcony that over-looked the townhouses behind the property, plus a sort of space—not even another room—a three-metre long, metre-wide area (amusingly labelled a 'conservatory' on the plan) that wasn't quite useable for anything, not even drying washing, since it faced south.

You certainly can't afford breakfast, Dark Voice noted as she poured herself some juice. She settled for a slice of toast, then brushed her teeth, got her shoes on, grabbed her bag, then, slamming the door behind her, headed for the lift. It was 7.34; barring misfortune, she would just make the 7.56 train.

The storm had rolled out to the north-east, opening the way for a fine Sydney day, mild and clear, but with an edge of approaching warmth. This was her favourite time of the year. Summer was arriving: in the late afternoon when a warm breeze blew across the city while the sun hung in the western sky; in the evening with the pervasive smell of jasmine throughout the suburbs; even at night, in the light of the full moon that, in the mild nocturnal air, seemed like daytime.

After she'd inelegantly run from the car park, she discovered the train was two minutes late. She found a seat next to a young man with bad skin, a poorly fitting suit and just the faintest, faintest tang of body odour. Daryl, she imagined he was called. Or maybe Harrison.

Ashfield, Summer Hill and Lewisham rolled by, but then the train slowed to a crawl. Her phone buzzed with what turned out to be a text from James, who worked at the Commonwealth Bank; he wanted to come over that night, to which she was amenable. She checked Facebook desultorily as some schoolboys embarked, then noted the time: 8.09. The 8.30 meeting was with her boss, to discuss the Big News going around the company about staff cuts. She took out her book; she was halfway through *We Are Anonymous*. She'd developed an interest in hackers and online activism back when she was at university, at the same time as the Arab Spring and WikiLeaks.

Forget the book, you're gonna be late. How unprofessional, Dark Voice whispered, very softly, but it was enough to make her start worrying. Stanmore. Newtown. Daryl-Harrison rose and departed, trailing his slightly disconcerting does-he-smell-or-doesn't-he odour behind him. It took forever for a bunch of feral-looking people to get on at Newtown. At Redfern, she remembered she'd forgotten to take her Cipramil and cursed herself silently. Not enough sleep, but still running late, and didn't take my meds.

She found that, psychosomatic or otherwise, even missing a day of her antidepressants made her more fragile and downbeat. She normally carried a supply of Panadeine Extras—her 15 milligram friends, as she called them—for such situations; she slid a hand inside her bag and felt the edge of the Panadeine packet. Somewhat comforting.

Central, finally. It was 8.19 as she left the train and joined the throng heading for the station exit, stuffing her book back into her bag. To her dismay, a thick plug of walking flesh slowed her journey; people with no important meetings to attend and no jobs to get to, with nothing better to do than waste other people's time.

Once in the open, she strode up Elizabeth Street. Being tall, Em was a good strider. She could get some serious striding action going. Even Dark Voice couldn't find a complaint about the stride. Purposeful, fast, but not stupid-looking, even a little elegant. Slightly feline, she liked to think; Em on the prowl.

Dark Voice: *Pfffft.*

She reached the lights just as they turned Don't Walk. Glance at the phone: 8.26.

She almost ran the last few yards up Liverpool Street and into the building where her company had the top eight floors. Yes! In the building foyer at 8.29. She was, officially, if some sort of official audit were to be taken, on the premises prior to the start of the meeting. She ran liftwards, any effort to maintain a semblance of elegance abandoned. The lift, bizarrely, failed to arrive any faster despite repeated, and increasingly forceful, pressings of the Up button. She stopped punching it once three people whom she didn't know halted behind her.

At 8.33 she bolted out of the lift on her floor as if ejected by some volcanic force, waved her pass furiously at the sensor by the security doors, and hurried in.

Clear your desk, you unprofessional fuck. Em on the prowl for a new job.

But, thankfully, the meeting had yet to begin when she dumped her bag on her desk; in fact, Tom's door remained closed and her colleagues were staring at their screens. She grabbed her water bottle, hurried round to the kitchen to fill it, then returned and grabbed a Panadeine from her bag. By now her two colleagues were on their feet and Tom's door was open.

Made it.

By dint of a tactical pause in the doorway, she was able to ensure she didn't have to sit next to Craig as they squashed in around Tom's miniature meeting table. Craig was overweight, sniffed constantly and his mere existence made her mildly queasy. Adriana, with whom she was good friends, was oblivious to his personal habits. She sat next to him instead.

Tom rose from his desk and pulled his chair over to the meeting table. He seemed to be In A Mood. Em wondered if she had done something, or failed to do something, that had led to Tom's crankiness.

'Okay, I thought it would be a good idea to address some of the rumours going around,' Tom said. 'Here's what I know so far: first, the company is looking to lose around sixty jobs. That means about twelve from this division. We don't know where yet, but obviously the larger areas have greater capacity to cut than small areas like this one. I don't know any more than that at this point. I'm just as likely as any of you to find myself out of a job.'

Craig sniffed. Then sniffed again.

'Second, as a major priority, every area is going to have to come up with ways to generate additional revenue. This is the key thing. Everyone's got to start thinking outside the box about what we can bid for, and lift revenue. So we need to start coming up with ideas. Obviously this division will be focusing on public sector non-defence products. We've got to bid for everything we can find, and where we can't find anything, we've got to be creative.'

Sniff.

'Third—Emma,' he said.

Em wondered why she was singled out. Adriana raised her eyebrows at her.

'I've been asked to do something for General Levers. He's going to write an op-ed on cybersecurity, telling governments they need to increase spending on it across the board. News Limited . . . News Corp, sorry, are going to run it for us. He'll need some facts and figures to put in. Can I get you to pull it together?'

'Sure,' she said. The task had some interest at least.

Em's background was in marketing, but she'd got the Veldtech job on the strength of a nine-month stint she'd done at the Defence Materiel Organisation, assessing tenders. Her current job was a strange mix of things in which she was lent out to help with various projects across the Intel division. That was how she'd acquired a working knowledge of matters like cybercrime, and hacking, and security, despite having no background in IT. But it was a miscellaneous sort of role, in a miscellaneous sort of area. She had heard about the job cuts already, and had spent the previous day wondering, with considerable encouragement from Dark Voice, if she was going to be employed for much longer.

Another sniff from Craig.

She popped a Panadeine. They were handy for when she felt particularly down; the codeine would give her a euphoric bounce off the bottom that made work tolerable.

'You might even have to write some bits of the article,' said Tom. 'Levers is a warrior, not a wordsmith.'

'Yup,' she said, swigging from her bottle. Levers, a former deputy chief of the Australian Defence Force, was a—sniff—'special counsel' to the company, which translated mostly as in-house lobbyist.

'We'll have to tictac with the government relations area,' Tom said. 'I'll tee that up, there's some guy called Nathan Welles I'll speak to.'

Sniff.

Instead of codeine-derived euphoria, however, a small kernel of nausea had started forming in her stomach, induced by proximity to Craig. Each sniff was like a screech reminding her of the presence of this overweight, unhealthy man who in summer sweated profusely after he returned from lunch.

God, think of something else, she thought to herself. She scribbled 'government relations' down on her tablet.

You know he probably fantasises about you, said Dark Voice. The thought sent a shiver through her. *The only male who fantasises about you. Even James probably thinks of someone else when he's fucking you.*

Now that was a low blow, even for Dark Voice.

'Beyond that,' said Tom, 'we need to workshop some ideas about generating revenue,' said Tom.

Workshop ideas.

Workshop ideas.

If Em had a criticism of Tom, it was his fondness for debate. He was otherwise, she felt, pretty much above criticism—intelligent, pleasant, somewhat humorous, devoted to his family. He was the polar opposite of the arsehole she had endured at her previous employer; good to work for, even fun sometimes.

But he loved talking through things: getting around a table, communicating, brainstorming, bouncing ideas off, teasing issues out, exploring all sides of an argument. And workshopping. She'd forgotten that one. Often he would wander into her cubicle, sit down and begin with a question, usually about a document she had prepared, and she'd know that, inevitably, the next half-hour would be given over to Tom turning something around and around in his head. No thought would be allowed to pass undiscussed, no idea undeveloped, no concept unexplored in such meetings. Initially Em, with the enthusiasm of one anxious to impress, had worked hard to engage in such discussions, rather than following her natural instinct to tune out, but it was becoming increasingly difficult.

Sniff.

Agreeing with him didn't help. In fact, that was downright dangerous. Trying to avoid a prolonged discussion by agreeing with whatever he put forward at any point merely encouraged him to switch sides and start, in effect, arguing against his original proposition, playing devil's advocate, 'stress testing' (that was another one) his thoughts.

The word 'workshop' thus faintly terrified her. She and Adriana exchanged worried glances.

'So I thought the first thing we'd do is review our unsuccessful tenders over the last eighteen months,' Tom continued, 'and bounce around some ideas about why we missed out.'

Bounce ideas around. Yup. It was going to be a long meeting. At least an hour stuck in proximity to Craig. She began thinking about Craig as a superhero, his superpower an ability to . . . what? Make his enemies sick with his presence, maybe. And maybe to suck objects up with his powerful nasal intake.

What would you name him?

Sniffman? Snortman. Yes. Snortman Rises.

Tom passed around a sheet of paper with some tender information in table form.

Captain Inhalia. Avengers—Age of Snortron.

You could play his love interest.

She stifled a giggle. Tom gazed at her levelly. She could feel herself turning red. Quick, think of something relevant to say!

'Sorry,' she blurted out. 'I was just thinking, maybe we should encourage some hackers to steal something embarrassing from the government.' This was the first useable thought that came into her head, probably derived from her current reading. 'That would make the government spend more on cybersecurity.'

'Let's focus on the task at hand, Em,' said Tom sternly. 'We've got a lot to get through.'

WEDNESDAY
4 NOVEMBER

Three faces watched Mark Chalmers, all with expressions varying between dismay and terror. He only knew one of them, Theo T., mainly because Theo never wore a suit. Which was fine, Theo was a good software engineer. The other two were Theo's functionaries and not of great interest.

Uncharacteristically, there was a pile of paperwork on Chalmers's desk. He was good at paperwork, always had been, good at processing it quickly, even if he had to take it home overnight; he'd always found it easy to scrupulously observe his agencies' 'clean desk policy', never got a warning about leaving classified files around. As his partner liked to observe, this was somewhat at odds with his slovenliness at home.

But the tall pile of folders and papers was all of his division's recent bids for work, which he found easier to work through in physical form, a chore at which he'd been engaged since around 6 a.m.

'So this Flexible Networking Platform bid,' he said at length, gazing at a piece of yellow paper.

'Yep,' said Theo T.

'The third party IP is the big cost.'

'Yep.' Theo nodded. He leaned over the desk and pointed to a particular figure. 'And the language development—but after the tender last year for the AFP, we've got some better language expertise. Dave Cuneen and his guy.'

Chalmers lifted his eyes momentarily to the ceiling, trying to place the cited Dave Cuneen.

'Okay. Well, cut it by five per cent.'

'Sorry?' said Theo, eyes widening. The other two glanced at each other. One had glasses and looked like a geek from central casting. The other looked about fifteen—a beardless boy, in Chalmers's parlance—and wore a suit that was far too big for him.

'Cut what? The language development cost?'

'The whole bid. Cut it by five per cent.'

Theo looked vexed. 'But that's more than our profit. There's some serious competition for this. We're not padding it.'

'I know,' he said distantly, and looked at Theo. 'Cut it.'

He scratched the left-hand side of his chin, which tended to itch and go red when he was feeling tired or stressed. Unless he applied some cortisone cream, the skin would eventually start flaking off. 'We need that tender. Cut it.'

Theo gestured. 'Fine. Can you sign off on the revised bid by three p.m.?'

'Sure.' He placed the yellow document to his left, pulled the top folder from the pile and opened it, then yawned. 'Excuse me. Now, the AIR 7000 Phase 2B modelling.'

'Yep. You agreed we couldn't do it last week, after Jane and I spoke with Bill Tyndale.'

'Was I at that meeting?'

'You were in Canberra. Tyndale emailed you about it afterwards and copied us in.'

'Ah okay,' he said, after a moment's reflection. He screwed up his face. 'I remember now. Well, let's bid anyway.'

This caused more silent consternation from beardless boy and the geek. 'But . . . as Bill said, we literally can't actually do that modelling,' said Theo. 'We don't have the in-house expertise on missile maths. It's rocket science. It doesn't come cheap. Maybe the Perth guys—'

'Bid anyway.'

'It closes COB tomorrow.' Theo's tone was more than a little plaintive.

'Look, Theo, I realise I'm being a complete bastard here, but I'm not doing it for fun, believe me, and I don't want to have to keep repeating myself. We need to bid for everything within reason. That's the order from the top, okay? So unless it's fucking running a detention centre or building a submarine, we're on it.'

Theo raised his hands in supplication. 'Okay, okay, sorry. We'll bid, we'll knock it together.'

Chalmers scratched his chin again. 'Mary,' he called, hoping his EA would hear him. 'I really need some coffee.'

He exhaled and went to the next folder. 'Okay, so these are the tenders due next week.'

'Yep,' said Theo with resignation.

'Let's go through them.'

The young public servant was babbling; Kat had lost track of what he was saying before they'd even got in the lift. He'd been tasked with escorting her back to reception after she'd finished delivering the training session on 'Communicating Effectively in a Social Media Environment' to a roomful of bored bureaucrats. They'd had coffee, but it was awful; on her first sip, she'd actually been tempted to spit it out. She was, accordingly, now desperate for some form of caffeine stimulus, desperation deepened by the incessant talking of the young man in the suit.

The talking stopped. She had the impression he had asked her a question, but she had no idea what.

'I'm not sure, but I could kill for a coffee,' she said.

It obviously wasn't a complete non sequitur, as he nodded enthusiastically and resumed babbling. OMFG stop talking you're giving me a headache, she thought. Your voice is migrainegenic. Please stop. The only thing that Kat was registering was his green tie with teddy bears on it. Once they had exited into the foyer and he'd farewelled her, urged her somewhat superfluously to send her invoice and invited her to remove her temporary pass and hand it to the guard sitting at reception, she headed straight for the cafe located in the lobby of the same building. Then she paused. What if this was where they'd got the coffee she'd had upstairs? Surely they hadn't. Surely they'd made it themselves, perhaps out of dried rabbit turds for beans, or some special public service coffee supply deliberately designed to discourage bureaucrats from taking breaks. Still, just to be safe, she headed out onto the street to look for another cafe. She was at Railway Square, a place not renowned as a coffee mecca. She recalled there was a cafe in the new area, or what she called the new area, next to the entry to the Devonshire Street tunnel. She headed up there.

Her next task for the day was an article she was writing for *The Drum* site, which she needed to get off quickly; it was mostly done but she wanted to go through it one more time, being mildly obsessed with producing a masterpiece that would send more writing offers flooding in her direction and smooth the way for her pitches. While she sat and waited for the coffee in the otherwise deserted cafe, she opened her MacBook, checked Twitter and opened Gmail to see if Chris had been in touch. They spoke by phone at least once a day, usually at lunchtime, what she called her daily check-in, in which they talked about domestic matters and everyday banalities. This had to suffice in lieu of sharing their lives, and a day without a phone call was difficult for her to cope with, making her wonder if he had decided to dump her. Gmail was for sex talk, joking, sharing the things each knew the other would be interested in, and generally just being in one another's mental vicinity in a way that made the separation endurable. Now she saw that not only was there a message, but he was actually logged in on Gmail, which was unusual on a weekday. She opened a chat with a grin.

Morning!

Morning to you, beautiful! he replied.

Why aren't you lecturing or teaching or whatever it is you do with all those young women, mistah?

Told you—classes are over. Examination time.

Oh fuck yeah, I forgot. No work for you.

Thank you. REAL work for me. And more flexibility timewise.

Yay! So when are you coming over to my place next?

Kat's coffee arrived. She barely glanced up.

Tuesday?

OK lock it in.

Er, I won't be locking it in, I'll be doing something else with it.

I have a full-on lady boner right now.

She did. Even just organising Chris's visits aroused her, and she usually spent several hours before he arrived unable to work or concentrate. On the couple of occasions he'd had to belatedly cancel, she had been infuriated beyond all reason.

Save it, my love!

It's not going anywhere. God I love you.

I love you too. I'm so in love with you.

Can't come down to Railway Square and fuck me right now, can you? I need your cock. There's no one else in this cafe.

Can I do some marking while I fuck you?

Fuck I love this man, she thought.

They'd met at an IT conference early in the year; he was MCing a panel she was on, on . . . something. Something internetty, whatever. It was a deathly dull post-lunch session, but he'd livened it up considerably. At one stage he'd theatrically pointed at her and yelled, 'Kat Sharpe, comment!' and she'd grinned at what was the most public and cutest flirting to which she'd ever been subjected. Just for once, she decided to attend the dreaded 'networking drinks' at the end of the day, where normally she'd be gawked at and hit on by dozens of IT industry dickheads; luckily, Chris was there too and she'd had a long talk with him. Afterwards, she'd read his articles, and then did something she'd never done before: emailed him on the pretext of wanting assistance on a project, unable to decide whether she wanted him to see through the ruse, or was mortified that he might.

But it was his articles that sealed the deal, oddly. He wrote well and had lots—*lots*—of amazing ideas. She knew he was married—in fact, he'd mentioned his wife during the panel session—but she was smitten, hopelessly smitten.

Hmmmph. All right, you can lie there and marke while I get on your cock.

*Mark.

OK, gotta meeting—are we confirmed for Tuesday? Want to make up for seeing you on Monday night and not being able to touch you.

YES!

OK, talk later today. I love you! xxxx

Love you too, so so so so much.

After that, it was a struggle to concentrate on her article.

THURSDAY
5 NOVEMBER

Freshly Panadeined in anticipation of what would unfold, Em entered the meeting room with a cup of coffee. Tom was already seated, doubtless champing at the bit to start workshopping, brainstorming and teasing things out. This was the 'tictac' that Tom had referred to on Tuesday, a wholly inappropriate term given Tic-Tacs took hardly any time at all to consume and this meeting might well go for hours under Tom's epic chairmanship. She sat down beside him. The meeting room was one of the small ones, and a little airless; on the whiteboard behind them, someone had written, in red marker, the sort of inscrutable terms that only ever make sense to participants of the meeting in which they were scrawled—*revaluate!*, *Monetising eval cycle*, *Incentivate* and *ordinat*, the remaining letters of which, if indeed there were any, had been wiped off.

A short, fat man with a walrus-like moustache entered the meeting room. This was Jim Gibson—inevitably, Gibbo—a former editor of *Guns 'n' Ammo* or *Defence Specialist* or some slaughter-related publication, now the company's hands-on media contact who helped run Veldtech's propagandising efforts. Em had met him a number of times.

'G'day, Gibbo,' said Tom.

'Mate. Hi, Emma.'

Gibbo had company; a forty-something man named Mal, who was painfully pale-skinned, not an albino, but like he'd just spent six months indoors and was ravaged by Vitamin D deficiency. He smiled at Em and Tom when Gibbo introduced him.

That one's fresh off the slab, mused Dark Voice.

Because I could not stop for Death, He kindly stopped for me, she replied mentally, 'The Chariot' being one of her favourite poems.

A short time later, the other attendee arrived. He was a tall, good-looking man, early or mid-thirties, with short hair, wearing a suit without a tie. He sauntered in and sat—or slouched, more accurately—down beside Mal.

'G'day, Gibbo,' he said.

'Well, well, well, you well, Mr Welles?' said Gibbo, looking over.

Keeping a completely earnest expression, the man said, 'I wouldn't be dead for quids, mate.'

Gibbo smirked in reply.

The man turned and looked at Tom and Em. 'Nathan Welles, from Government Policy and Relations,' he said.

Tom nodded. 'I'm Tom Dao, and this is Emma Thomas.'

'Hi,' said Em quietly. She watched as Nathan reclined further in his seat. He was reclining so far she could almost see up his nose.

'Your new boss started yet?' said Gibbo.

'No—Monday,' Welles said briefly.

'Well, thanks for coming,' said Tom. 'Now, Mark Chalmers has asked us to help General Levers out with an op-ed,' he began, leaning forward. 'Something explaining how critical it is that governments ramp up cybersecurity spending. It will run in News Corp, and with any luck there'll be some in-house support from News's commentators. General Levers knows them and they're usually happy to help us out.'

Gibbo and Mal nodded.

'It's a newspaper article. So . . . something dramatic. You know— a little apocalyptic. The idea is to have a former senior military figure really spell out the need to invest more in cybersecurity. So clearly we want Gibbo's input, but I think it's also useful to make sure Government Relations is happy with it.'

'Sure,' said Welles.

'So,' Tom continued, 'Mark's thinking is that this will be seen by the media as a major intervention by an authoritative figure on cybersecurity and its priority, especially given everyone's focused on terrorism again.'

'Yep,' said Gibbo. 'I see what you mean. Just at the outset, we've been thinking in our neck of the woods about using a term other than cybersecurity. We got someone to focus-group it. The word has nerdy connotations; it sounds a bit specialised and people tend to think it means getting a four one nine or a virus.'

'Sorry,' said Tom, 'what's a four one nine?'

'Nigerian scam email,' said Em, without looking up from her tablet.

'We tested "cyber-defence" and it got a much better response,' said Gibbo. 'People understood it better, it sounded more hardcore. So maybe we could give it a trial run in this piece.'

'That sounds really good,' said Tom.

'And then there's a clear link between more spending and protecting people from some apocalyptic cyberattack.'

'A cyber Pearl Harbor,' said Welles, a little cryptically, his fingers interlocked on his stomach.

'Or the cyber-bombing of Darwin?' said Gibbo.

Welles adopted a contemplative expression in response to that. 'Was that our Pearl Harbor? I guess we never got a surprise attack like Pearl Harbor.'

'Cyber midget submarine attack on Sydney Harbour, maybe?' Gibbo offered.

'Digital Bali bombings?' said Welles. 'Not very catchy.'

'And too soon.'

Welles nodded. 'Yep, way too soon.'

Em smirked. The meeting was more interesting than usual.

'Sorry,' said Tom, interrupting, 'what do you mean cyber Pearl Harbor?'

'Oh, it's what the Yanks use when they want to beat up cyber-security. Warn of a cyber or a digital Pearl Harbor,' said Gibbo.

Tom nodded, and looked meaningfully at Em. 'Sounds good.' She took his hint and wrote it on her tablet, wondering if he was annoyed that she hadn't been writing the whole time.

Make sure you get that down, Em, said Dark Voice.

'We did an article a while back, pulled together some stats on cybercrime and cyberwar,' said Gibbo. 'But they'd be out of date. You could get some more up-to-date ones yourself. The ones the government put out when they set up the new Cyber Security Centre are probably out of date now too. But there's always stuff around.'

'You have to be a little careful,' said Welles to Gibbo. He glanced at Em and took in that she was writing down what he was saying. 'You don't want to give Levers something that makes him look an idiot when someone points out it's rubbish. Some of the stuff out there on cybercrime is bullshit.'

Gibbo nodded, watching Welles, picking at his fingernails. He had short, stubby fingers, the sort Em hated as they reminded her of her father's. Short fingers were one of her many physical revulsions about men. 'Yep,' he said. 'People chuck in all sorts of stuff into the category of cybercrime.'

There was a momentary silence. 'A bit like hacking,' Em offered. 'Like, there's always headlines about companies being hacked, but often it's just really poor security.'

What?!

'That's right,' said Welles. 'But you wouldn't want to say that. It's not really the company line.'

Hacking? Em, the adults are speaking. Shut up and take notes.

Gibbo's chest momentarily heaved and his moustache arched, as though he was silently belching. He looked at Mal, who had yet to trouble the scorers with a contribution to the meeting. Mal looked at Tom, who remained unmoved. Em, in turn, looked at Nathan, who was across from her but at an angle so that he was facing Mal. She could thus examine him without his being particularly aware of her gaze, although after a moment he turned and gave her a brief smile, then looked away. He was not bad-looking at all, she decided.

Despite the lack of a tie, he dressed well—it was a nice suit, grey with a faint pinstripe, a plain light blue shirt and a nice silver watch. But his eyes were his best feature. His face wasn't especially attractive, but his eyes were almost hypnotic, with that sort of clichéd brooding intensity that she was a sucker for.

'If we want Levers to make an impact,' said Welles, 'what we should probably think about is trying to offer something a bit different. The cyber-defence thing is good. The government itself has said cybercrime's terrible et cetera et cetera, and set up the ACSC, but we should be saying, "Here's where the real problem is—let's get real and focus on it."'

He said 'real' twice.

Shut up, he's hot, she thought. 'Maybe we should confine it to hacking,' she said suddenly. 'Wouldn't that work with the cyber-defence thing? Actually acknowledge that cybercrime and stuff isn't the big threat, but focus on hacking and espionage as the serious threat to national security and governments and companies and ultimately to Australians.'

Gibbo stopped playing with his fingers or expelling gas, and was looking at her, intrigued. 'So, more about stuff like WikiLeaks or Anonymous than about cybercrime?'

'Yeah.'

'That'd work,' said Mal, breaking his silence. He nodded.

'Em's a bit of a guru on all that stuff,' said Tom. She wasn't clear if he was praising her or apologising for her sidetracking the discussion.

'Not a bad idea,' said Gibbo. 'It'd forestall criticism that we're just whipping up hysteria. Sorry, of Levers.'

Did you see him belch before? He totally like silently burped. Dark Voice was in a fun mood today.

Welles made to speak, then stayed silent.

Gibbo leaned back in his chair, his stubby digits stuck to his chin as he thought, perhaps summoning more gas.

'Okay, well, Em here will pull some material together along those lines and run it past you guys before we send it upstairs to Chalmers,' said Tom, displaying unexpected decisiveness. Unusually, it seemed as though Tom was going to chair a short meeting.

'Sounds good,' said Welles.

Em smiled at him. He smiled back.

'Madwoman.'

'Kathmandu. Where are you?'

Kat had just got off the 373 at The Spot in Randwick. 'Racing home to get to a landline for a radio interview. What's happening?'

'I'm sitting at my desk doing my job,' said Maddy. 'Like what that guy said about you on Twitter?'

'Another angry male. There are so many of them,' Kat said.

The previous evening Kat had got into an argument on Twitter with some unknown male about women in social media. In the end, she'd just retweeted his more annoying comments and let her followers start kicking him, until he'd come back to her with *bitches like u need a good fucking 2 sort you out.*

The comeback was easy: *If someone like you knew anything about fucking, I'd respond to that.*

Watch your back cunt, came the reply, which once retweeted elicited a further round of abuse of her (presumably) male interlocutor. Several had told him they'd forwarded his tweets to the police. A short while later, his account vanished.

Online abuse, of which she received a steady stream, didn't particularly worry her. She had a thick skin and was unconcerned about the views of anonymous people, or even threats, an insouciance that seemed to amaze and sometimes enrage other women with social media profiles. Rule number one of social media, she'd say to them: if they're abusing you, you're winning, and they know it.

'Are we still on for tonight? You haven't got a date with Married Guy or something?'

It was, ever so faintly, a bitchy comment from Maddy. It didn't reflect disapproval that Chris was married, but that Kat had told her very little about him, almost nothing in fact, and certainly had never allowed her to meet him, thereby locking her best friend out of an important part of her life. All Maddy knew about him was his age, what he did—generally, not where specifically—and that he was married with a school-age son. She'd never met him or seen him. 'Not until we're official,' Kat had said, as if she didn't want to jinx the relationship. She knew that Maddy was keeping a series of concerns in check, and she didn't really want to hear them anyway, especially not that Maddy would almost certainly tell her that she didn't think he'd leave his wife for her.

The result was that Maddy normally couldn't refer to Married Guy, as she'd derisively christened him, without making some aside about having a lack of knowledge of what was going on with them.

Kat elected to ignore it. 'See you around eight? I have to go to the gym.'

'Want me to pick you up?'

'Nah, I'll bus it.' She moved the phone from her ear so that she could see the time. She had about five minutes to get to her flat. She jogged across St Pauls Street near the cinema.

'And don't forget my party on the twenty-first.'

'It's booked, bitch. When's your office Christmas party?'

'Um . . . the fourth. Why?'

'Just wondering. I don't get Christmas-party invites. I'm totally outside the whole Christmas-party thing. None of my regular publishers have seen fit to invite me.'

'That is such a fucking first-world problem. Why don't you complain on Twitter to your million followers? You'll probably get a hundred invites.'

'Did I tell you I got another consultancy? Education and Communities. Six training sessions starting February.'

'Cool. What about before Christmas?'

'Nah, it's looking a bit lean. I've got a couple of articles but looks like I'll be holding out to the new year.'

She turned into Lee Street and began walking more quickly, worried the ABC might already be ringing at home.

'In fact, at this rate I'm gonna have to move back in with Mum unless I get some more work.'

As she walked, she made a mental note to call her mother. She hadn't spoken to her for a couple of days.

'Well, you know I'd offer, babe, but . . .'

'But,' indeed. Kat and Maddy had flatted together when they were first out of uni. It had been a disaster, and they had resolved never to live together again. They were best friends, but their personal habits had infuriated each other, especially given their contrasting approaches to cleanliness. Kat still liked to reflect on Maddy's dislike of cleaning and Maddy still readily deployed the term 'anally retentive' about her.

She glanced at the time again. The ABC was due to call in precisely one minute. 'Gotta bolt,' she said.

'Kbye!'

FRIDAY
6 NOVEMBER

The glacial speed of the bus through the peak-hour traffic didn't annoy Nathan. By temperament he was a car user, but commuting was almost ludicrously convenient for him—his home in Kensington was only a fifteen-minute walk from Anzac Parade, where he caught the L94 into the city, alighting literally outside his workplace. The slow speed of the bus journey during peak hour was no annoyance, but instead permitted an extended study of fellow passengers, as well as the parks, shops, motorists and passers-by visible from the bus, although this morning he hadn't managed to get a seat.

He stepped off the bus on Liverpool Street, walked into the lobby and over to the Level 18–28 lifts, where he waited with a dozen other people. The lift stopped at level twenty and Angela entered with a young male colleague. She spotted him at the back of the lift and raised her eyebrows at him while continuing to talk to the young man. They got out on twenty-two, her usual floor. He went up to twenty-three, wondering who the young man was and whether Angela was sleeping with him.

He waved his pass at the sensor at the security doors and, as per Veldtech rules, turned his mobile off. It was already busy on the floor, but he was relaxed. Today was his last day in his current position, and he had already performed the Herculean task he had assigned to himself for the week: to move his stuff from the office back to his desk outside. His stuff, in fact, amounted to a picture of his wife Ree and their daughter Sophie, a coffee mug from *The Onion*, and a drawer's worth of odds and ends acquired from ten years of gainful employment. From Monday, he would be returning to his previous position, which would be as underling to his successor, having competed unsuccessfully for that position in a permanent capacity. Instead, a Mrs Rachael Ambrose would be moving into the office. Because of her name, he already pictured her as a sort of fat, jolly, middle-aged woman.

Nathan's anger about this was of a sullen, slow-burning kind. Revenge was, for him, a dish best served after storage for several months in a freezer. He held grudges for a long time, indeed, carried a collection of them like a backpack, carefully preserved from years or decades before; he could still recall individuals from school whom he would happily, but for the threat of imprisonment, murder. He did not, however, intend to sabotage his replacement. That would be unprofessional and he was never that, no matter what the circumstances. That wasn't his style, if he could be said to have any style. His anger at being overlooked for the job he'd done so competently would instead be dammed up, to flood forth at some future point when it felt most appropriate.

He greeted his two supervisees, neither of whom he much cared for. Brian was a twenty-six-year-old who had graced the company for perhaps twelve months. Brian was convinced of his own genius, and regarded Nathan as a kind of traffic accident blocking the path to his future senior executive position. But Brian's competence only partly matched his ambition, the sort of dissonance that sustained Nathan through many an awkward managerial moment. Eve was a lawyer in her early forties with a young child. She was competent but prone to breaking down if she was given more than two tasks at a time. Together, they constituted Veldtech's Government Policy and Relations unit, which monitored state and federal government activities for their impact on the company.

He opened Twitter once he'd logged on, something the company had recently allowed given the strict rule against mobile devices.

U look hot, Angela had DM'd him.

He did look okay, he thought. Black suit, crisp white shirt, red tie. Very red. He knew Angela loved that combination.

A number of emails awaited his attention. The most significant related to a delegation from company HQ that week. The Virginians were coming, to find out what 'strategic learnings' could be gleaned from the land down under. Or, rather, they *had* been coming; they no longer were. The 'strategic learnings' would apparently have to be acquired at a later time or perhaps via some remote, trans-Pacific delivery mechanism. There was, clearly, an upside to the wave of austerity sweeping both Veldtech and its parent company. The day was, thus, off to a positive start.

The last email arrived while he was reading the others. It was from his group manager's assistant, advising him that the manager wanted to see him 'when you get in'. This necessitated an immediate trip up to level twenty-six. Group Manager had a name, but Nathan merely called him, both verbally and mentally, GM; he ran Nathan's area, among others, and reported to Jane Webb.

He took his time going up to twenty-six. He no longer cared particularly about annoying GM, or at least didn't care anywhere near as much as he had prior to the decision about filling his position. He sauntered, moseyed even, around to the lifts, then ascended to twenty-six, dangled his pass by the sensor and walked along to GM's office, which faced west and had a view primarily of the top level of the building next to their own, across Nithsdale Street. He noticed GM had a new executive assistant outside his office as he went past.

GM was a tall man—he'd been a second-grade rugby backrower for Eastwood some time in the 1990s—now going bald and paunchy. But he dressed, Nathan would admit if pressed, immaculately. His suit, a charcoal number, was elegant and perfectly tailored; the cuffs of his expensive light blue shirt extended the perfect length on his wrists; his tie, made of vague grey and blue shapes, matched the ensemble perfectly. Nathan, who didn't feel sartorially intimidated easily, felt underdressed in front of him.

'Mr Welles,' GM said, rising from behind his desk. He had a high-pitched voice, most inapt for his elegant turnout.

Nathan sat down at GM's meeting table. GM's strangely cheery tone had instantly aroused his suspicions.

'What's up?'

GM closed his office door and joined Nathan at the table. 'I just wanted to have a bit of a chat to you about your job.'

Nathan stiffened. His mind began racing, on the assumption he was to be sacked. Everyone was talking about cuts, but he'd assumed—foolishly as it now turned out—that he'd be immune because of his performance while doing his boss's job. Idiot, he thought. Overconfident idiot. His next thought was whether he'd be able to continue fucking Angela, then what sort of job he would start looking for, given his reluctance to go back to law.

But GM disabused him of the notion before he could go too far with it.

'You must be disappointed at missing out on the position,' he continued.

Nathan instantly relaxed. It was to be a sympathy session. No sacking, not for the moment.

'Indeed,' he allowed. In other circumstances he might have politely demurred, but he was in no mood to cater to executive feelings. He didn't follow up with any additional comment.

'Well, we want you to know that it was no reflection on how you've performed in that position over the last few months.' GM nodded at him, a bright spot arcing back and forth across his scalp as he did so.

We? Who on earth is 'we'? he wondered. GM seemed to be hoping that Nathan would respond, but he remained silent. GM shifted uncomfortably. He had a Windsor knot, Nathan noticed. Of course.

'We were very pleased with your performance in that position,' GM continued redundantly. 'All things being equal, you would've got the job, and we would've been quite happy, but Mrs Ambrose applied and she was a very strong candidate.'

Nathan now nodded. 'Well, I'm sure she's very good.'

'She *is* very good,' said GM, as if Nathan had just put his finger on the nub of the issue and spoken a truth that had so far eluded him. He extended a well-manicured finger to the nub himself, as if encouraged by Nathan. 'Good experience, good skills, and I think she'll really bring a lot to Veldtech. But that doesn't mean your skills and experience aren't valued, and we think—'

'We' again.

'—that you'll be a very good team. As you know, the executive chairman has some plans for regulatory change next year, and we'll need our best resources to work on that.'

'Sure.' The discussion was not progressing anywhere, unless its purpose was to annoy him, in which case it was nailing its KPIs.

GM leaned back in his chair, making it creak under his weight.

'Now, there is another matter which is a bit of a problem.'

Nathan felt himself stiffening again, this time wondering what it would be, given he had just been assured of continuing employment. He elected not to reply.

After a suitably uncomfortable pause, GM went on. 'So, look, when we asked you to fill in for Simon, and didn't give you anyone extra to help you out, we indicated that we'd pretty actively consider the issue of some sort of performance bonus.'

Aha. Actively consider it? They'd fucking well promised him one. He debated how to respond. He settled for, 'I think there was a commitment in relation to that, yes.' He wasn't going to try to get out of it, was he?

'Well, look, I'll just get straight to it: there's been a company-wide freeze on bonuses, as of this week.'

He *was* going to try to get out of it. Right before his eyes.

As if slightly ashamed, GM glanced around, not meeting Nathan's gaze.

'You probably know there're some very significant issues the company has to face over the next six months, and every division has been asked to make some sacrifices. The bonuses are just the start; there'll be some job cuts. They've slashed travel, perks, every-thing. So, I will have to ask you to hold off on that performance bonus for a while.'

GM finally looked at him, searching his face for a reaction. Nathan kept it expressionless. 'Hold off on that bonus,' he thought to himself. Odd terminology.

'You're kidding me,' Nathan allowed himself to say. He felt like yelling at him.

'Um, I'm afraid not. I know this is awful timing—'

'For how long?' Nathan said, interrupting him. He gathered that GM was trying to say he wasn't going to get it at all, but couldn't quite muster the courage to do it.

'Well, for the time being,' he said. 'And I'd ask for your understanding on that.'

'Ask for my understanding', thought Nathan. What did that mean? Was he being invited to listen to and comprehend the words GM was saying with greater concentration than normal, so as to achieve greater insight into the fact that he'd been promised a bonus and was now not being given one? Was there some 'understanding' GM was urging him towards that would somehow erase the company's bad faith? Did GM want him to accept this philosophically, with Buddha-like detachment?

He stared at GM. 'Okay, so I do two jobs for several months, I don't get paid any extra, I don't get the job, and I don't get any bonus.'

'Well . . .' GM laughed half-heartedly. 'That's a very blunt way of putting it.'

'Anything else?' said Nathan.

GM frowned in confusion. 'Anything else?' he repeated.

Is there an echo in here? thought Nathan. 'That you want to speak to me about,' he said, a little slowly.

'Oh, well . . . I thought . . .'

Nathan enjoyed his discomfort. Faintly. Slightly. One-thousandth of one per cent of the enjoyment he would have got from the extra money or the job.

'Ah, no, not at the moment.'

'Well, I need to get on with cleaning out my office,' he said, rising. He raised his hand in apology. 'Sorry—Mrs Ambrose's office.'

'Ah, okay, sure.' GM rose with him, uncertainly, buttoning his jacket. 'Thanks for that, Nathan. We really do appreciate your efforts.'

Nathan stopped by the door, unable to resist the opportunity. 'Oh I can see that,' he said, nodding, blank-faced. He turned and walked out, smiling at the assistant on his way to the lifts. She's quite attractive, he thought.

Chalmers hung up from the call he was on.

'My back is abso-fucking-lutely killing me,' he said to Tom Dao, standing over by the window. It was nearly 7 p.m. and the shadows had almost completely swallowed Hyde Park below, a different version of the shadows that had lain across them when he'd arrived that morning at 6.30.

'You look like shit.'

'Thanks.'

'No, no, really, you look awful,' said Tom. 'The thing on your chin is up.'

'Shut up.'

Tom's easy familiarity with and lack of explicit respect for Chalmers mystified other Veldtech employees, who found Chalmers' seniority, aggression and hail-fellow-get-fucked style quite terrifying. But Tom had worked for Chalmers at ASIO in Canberra for a number of years, and had met his partner Steve several times. He'd left ASIO a couple of years before Chalmers had, but they were firm friends, although few people seemed aware of the connection between them.

'Okay,' Chalmers said, 'let's do it. So you meet any costs you need to, and I'll reimburse you directly. I've got an entertainment budget I can use. Well, I do for the moment, until it gets cut. Fuck knows I never get any time around here to use it.'

'Yep, that's fine,' said Tom. 'I don't think it'll cost much. We just need two VPNs at this stage, and a laptop. That's nothing. There's just the problem of having a broadband connector that can't be traced, for full anonymity.'

'Have a talk to Ewan Mazzoni,' said Chalmers. 'He's Derek's security man. Handles the dark arts stuff. He'll get you an ID. I'll tell him you'll call him.'

'Okay. So the remaining issue is using the back door.'

Chalmers rose and wandered over to the windows. 'There's no risk with that. If they find out, they can't link it to us, and the only people who use it are my erstwhile colleagues.'

'They won't be very impressed.'

'I should think they'll be downright fucking apoplectic, having to share their toy. But they're not really in a position to do anything.'

'You're not going to run it by Derek?'

Chalmers rubbed at something on the glass of the window. 'There are some matters on which the wisdom of our fearless leader wouldn't be useful. And I rather suspect this is one of them.'

'So I just need the back door.'

Chalmers turned and walked back over to his desk. 'Just hang on a sec,' he said, and picked up his phone and dialled a number. 'Mate. Are you busy? Can you pop up?' He paused. 'Ah, okay—no, that's fine, I'll come down. Just need a second.'

'We'll go and get it,' he said to Tom.

'Who was that?' Tom asked, following him out the door.

'Theo Triantifillides. He runs one of the software sections,' Chalmers said. 'His team won the original PICS contract.'

A young woman, carrying what looked like takeaway food, gave Chalmers a wide berth as they walked to the lift.

'Haven't these people got homes to go to?' he said as they got in, loud enough that the woman might have heard. 'So how are you going to release it?'

'You don't need to know that,' Tom said.

'If that's your idea of plausible deniability, it's pretty shithouse,' said Chalmers, after a pause.

'Just leave it to me.'

They exited on twenty-five, swiped in and wandered along a series of darkened offices before Chalmers found the one he was after. One of Theo's minions, the beardless boy, was tapping away at a desk over by the window. The man himself was standing in his office at a tall desk with three monitors, looking gaunt and unshaven. Chalmers walked in without knocking and contemplated the furniture.

'What's this, Theo?' said Chalmers, gesturing towards the desk.

'I prefer standing up,' Theo said, looking at them briefly before turning back to one of his screens.

Chalmers rolled his eyes and closed the door. 'I hate those stand-up desks. They remind me of urinals.'

'Yeah, thanks for that, Mark.'

'Look, this is Tom Dao. We've had something just come up that we need your help with. I think I may be able to lodge a late tender for a big parliamentary project tonight.'

Theo frowned. 'What, after 5 p.m.?'

'Yeah,' said Chalmers. 'I'm calling in a big favour from an old friend. But we've got to get it in by 11 p.m., and we need your help to knock it together.'

Theo's frown turned into a look of obvious dismay.

'So I was wondering if you'll be able to help us get it in tonight,' Chalmers continued.

'Ah, okay . . . I guess I'll have to ring home. I was hoping to see my family tonight.'

Chalmers adopted a solicitous expression. 'How long have you been at work?'

'Well, we had to get these new tenders in and work through all those other changes you wanted, so I was here all night.'

'All night?' said Chalmers, turning to look at Tom. 'Jesus, Theo. I didn't know. I knew you'd be busy but I assumed upstairs would do all the admin stuff.'

'Well, they did, but there was a lot of technical input from us. Anyway, it's fine, I guess a few more hours won't hurt.'

'Well, I guess,' Chalmers said uncertainly. Then his face brightened. 'Oh, but hang on, actually Tom and I can knock it all together—the only thing we need from you is the PICS software. If you can give us that, we can do it all ourselves.' He looked at Tom. 'Can't we?'

'Oh sure.' Tom nodded.

Theo turned away from the urinal desk and faced Chalmers.

'PICS? Full access?'

'Well, it'd have to be if you're not around.'

'That's class six software. You know I need a division-level request to provide access to it. I'd better stay.'

Chalmers shook his head. 'No, I'm not going to keep you here a minute longer than I need to, Theo. We're always talking about work–life balance but we never fucking honour it. If we miss the deadline, we miss the deadline.'

'But PICS is housed in Jane's division, so I need her clearance.'

'Jane's travelling. Look, I'm happy to take full responsibility. Any problems with Jane, get her to call me. And you can go home to your family and we can get this tender in.' He glanced at his watch a little theatrically. 'I hope.'

Theo paused, then looked at Tom. 'He's taking full responsibility, right?'

Mark turned to Tom and raised his eyebrows.

Tom shrugged. 'Sure,' he said. 'Happy to vouch for it.'

Theo watched him in silence for a moment. 'Okay. It'll take me a few minutes to access it.'

'That's great, Theo,' said Chalmers.

'No problem. Thanks for being so understanding.'

'No, no, it's fine. I'm not *totally* devoid of human kindness,' Chalmers said.

'You certainly aren't, Mark,' Tom agreed.

MONDAY
9 NOVEMBER

'Is that your boss, mate?'

Em was waiting for coffee with Adriana and Jayde, who worked on the other side of her partition, when Jayde spotted Tom, hovering weirdly outside the entrance to the cafe. Jayde was short, with long hair and the vestiges of gothdom in her clothes. She was a New Zealander, a 'cheeky little Kiwi' as she liked to declare, who called everyone 'mate' as a default. She gestured out the door, and Em and Adriana looked outside. Tom was standing by the entrance, not doing anything at all beyond occasionally glancing in at them.

'If he wanted coffee, why didn't he ask?' said Adriana.

'Maybe you're in trouble, mate,' said Jayde to Em.

'Guess I must be,' she said, inclined to agree. Their coffees were ready but Jayde was waiting for a banana smoothie for her friend Tim, who worked one down from their level. Eventually the smoothie appeared and they made their way to the door.

'Hi,' Tom said. 'Can I see you for a sec, Em?'

'Sure,' she said. She assumed she'd committed some egregious error; Tom looked deeply unhappy.

'See ya, mate,' said Jayde, raising an eyebrow at Em. They headed for the entry to their building.

Oddly, Tom actually walked away from the entrance of the cafe to be closer to the traffic.

'How's, um, that cyber-defence article coming along?'

'Fine,' she said, mystified. 'In fact, I was going to give you a draft this afternoon so we could send it around to everyone.'

He's come down here to ask that? Dark Voice was as puzzled as she was. *Must be something else that you've fucked up, surely?*

'Cool,' he said. 'Uh, you know last week you said we should try to hack something from the government?'

She stared at him.

'Yeah, I know it was a joke,' he continued. 'But I want to do it, kind of.'

Everything froze. This was straight out, by far, the most peculiar thing anyone had ever said to her in her entire life; an utterance so profoundly incongruous it had a dreamlike quality. That her boss, the conservative, ultra-cautious, decision-resistant, diligent work-shopper Tom was telling her he wanted to do something like that was truly, extraordinarily, bizarre. She'd have been less surprised if he'd exposed himself to her there and then.

Finally she found some words. 'You're kidding, right?'

But she already knew he wasn't. No way. From the look on his face, and his nervous manner, and the fact that he had led her over towards the traffic, she could tell he was perfectly, deadly serious.

He flicked a glance around. 'Look, Em, the company is desperate. Dozens and dozens of people are going to be sacked. Maybe lots more. There's no money in the government at the moment and won't be for ages. We've got to do something to stimulate demand.'

She could only look at him, lost for words.

'Stimulate demand?' she said eventually, incredulously. 'It's illegal. Breaking into the government and stealing stuff? You could go to jail. And anyway, we don't even have that kind of experience.'

'Okay, here's the thing,' he said, moving closer to her. 'What if it didn't involve hacking at all? What if we could get some stuff without hacking?'

'I don't . . .' she began, then stopped. This was ridiculous.

A bus pulled up right next to them, bringing a wave of warm exhaust.

He resumed, louder, to be heard over the bus. 'There might be a way to get some stuff from within the government and then we just need to find a way to *pretend* it was hacked without anyone linking it to us. It'll be embarrassing for the government, they'll spend more money on IT security, we'll swoop in and get the contracts because we'll know exactly what the problem is, seeing as we'd be the ones who started it.'

Em was still finding words hard to come by, so amazed was she at what Tom, of all people, was saying. His brainstorming had, evidently, taken a turn for the weird. 'What sort of way to get stuff? It's still stealing data, whether it was hacked or not.'

Suddenly it occurred to her that this was some kind of ethical test that Tom was running, maybe something designed to catch her out, maybe provide the basis for sacking her.

'If I can get you the data,' he said, 'can you set something up to release it without anyone linking it to us?'

'I'm not going to do that, Tom. No fucking way.'

'I'm saying could you, not would you. I know you're interested in all that Anonymous and WikiLeaks stuff. Would you be able to?'

'Well, yeah, maybe,' she said. 'But that's not the point.'

'The point is,' he said, glancing around again, 'it won't be illegal. The information won't be stolen—not even received from someone who stole it. It'll be from a whistleblower.'

A whistleblower, she thought. She now began to see what he was getting at.

'And what the hell happens when someone finds out?'

'Who's going to find out?'

'Someone in the company I mean,' she said, speaking over the squealing brakes of a truck slowing for the lights at Elizabeth Street.

'It's okay. I've already spoken to someone. They're okay with it, as long as the info isn't stolen, as long as it's from a whistleblower.'

She looked at the traffic for a moment. A car containing a small child waving went past.

'I can't believe you're saying all this, Tom. It's not like you.'

'I don't want to lose my job,' he said. 'If we pull this off, it'll really expand the opportunities for the company. We've got good products in this line. The company that Anderson bought before the takeover, they've got some great stuff. We've got a program with the New South Wales government on information-management plans that would be perfect for the federal government. And it's all going to waste if the bloody government keeps cutting spending.'

She watched him for a few seconds, suddenly conscious of the cars slowing to a halt nearby, as if they could divine what they were speaking about and wanted to hear more. Maybe the occasional cyclist flashing past, too.

'The info won't be stolen,' Tom repeated. 'There's no risk. Just . . . it's not something we can ever keep a record of.'

'If there's no problem with it, why can't we keep a record?' she snapped.

'Because the source of the info might be revealed,' he said, after a second. 'The person revealing it. The whistleblower. We don't want the whistleblower to be placed at risk. If we keep a record and they find out it was us, they can subpoena us, get our documents. If there're phone records, the AFP can get the metadata. Then they've got the whistleblower's identity, throw him . . . throw them in jail.'

'So you've got a whistleblower with information from the federal government and we're going to pretend it was hacked?'

'Yep. Which will help the whistleblower as well, by misdirecting attention away from them. All we've got to do is disguise it. Create some . . . I don't know, dress it up so it looks like a major security breach. That's where you come in. Do it all anonymously, encrypt everything, make it look like hackers, like WikiLeaks or something.' He paused. 'You in?'

'Who's the whistleblower?'

'I can't tell you that. You can never know their identity. But you know how many people here used to work for the government or in defence. What do you reckon?'

'I'll think about it,' Em said.

Around 2 p.m., Rachael Ambrose asked Nathan to accompany her for coffee. 'Be good to have a chat,' she said.

She'd arrived late. Nathan was at his desk, feeling drowsy: Sophie had been ill during the night, and he had spent most of the hours between 12.30 and 3 a.m. helping her to throw up. Ree had taken over later, but he had that drained, one hundred o'clock sensation from the early days of parenthood that he had forgotten. Ah, joy. GM, who rarely graced the lower levels such as Nathan's with his dapper presence, hove into view, his shiny pate signalling his presence. A short, dark-haired young woman—'girl' was the first word that actually came into his mind, but he banished it—was with him. So complete had his conception of Mrs Ambrose as an overweight middle-aged woman become that it took him several seconds to make the connection between his new boss and the woman with GM.

'This is Nathan Welles,' GM had said, 'whom I've told you about.'

'Nothing good I hope,' he'd replied, and extended his hand.

She extended hers. 'Pleased to meet you,' she said, almost tonelessly.

He'd sized her up very quickly, and entirely in physical terms. She was not that young, he thought, now that he saw her up close, probably not much younger than him; early thirties, but quite attractive, in a quiet sort of way. She had a long crème jacket on over a dark top and skirt, somewhat short.

He introduced her to Brian and Eve. She smiled painfully, as though the act of meeting them was a profound source of angst, or even of physical pain. They exchanged inconsequential banter, then she turned and headed for her office. Nathan had found himself watching her as she moved, wondering what she looked like naked, before mentally slapping himself.

Fuck, you're pathetic, he thought. Grow up.

'Long as you're paying,' he said, a trifle clumsily, when Rachael suggested a coffee. Nathan, once a man capable of truly heroic caffeine consumption and possessed of a refined connoisseurship of the substance, was no longer a coffee drinker. He had stopped two years before, not for health reasons or its effects on his sleep— indeed, he had routinely had a cup before bed, so inured was he to its effects—but after it started giving him diarrhoea. This involuntary colonic mimicry of an espresso machine was a good way to keep weight down, he felt, but at the cost of having to use public and work toilets. That was something of which he had a longstanding patho- logical fear, although the men's at the public entrance to Congress in Washington had turned out to be surprisingly clean: Congress might be gridlocked, he thought, but they understood the needs of those who weren't. He was thus now a tea drinker, to which he applied the same smugly unsatisfiable standards as he had previously brought to coffee. The tea at Antonio's downstairs varied rather a lot, but he agreed to Rachael's request anyway.

She had yet to respond positively to any of his normal conver- sational gambits. No smile cracked her stern face in response to his quips; no laugh erupted in response to his dry wit; she didn't grin at some of his particularly amusing and faintly naughty off-the-cuff remarks. Having discovered that his primary means of interaction was failing, he was at a loss.

They walked over to the lift together; at just over six feet, he was seven or eight inches taller than her and it felt odd having to gaze down at her as she spoke. She wanted to know his background.

'I went to law school, legal firm in corporate litigation for three years, left in disgust, did legal work for the state government, came here. You?'

She stabbed G; the lift was empty.

'Lawyer, too. Government lawyer, then government relations at TBF, then at Reardon.'

'The software company?'

'Yep.'

He had googled her ahead of time but found nothing. Now, hearing her CV, he understood why she'd got the job. Reardon was a rapidly growing competitor to Veldtech that had a big non-security software business; its three young male founders were the darlings of the business press. And they had been doing a lot of smart things to lift their profile, much more so than Veldtech.

'Which law school?' she said.

'Sydney,' he replied, looking straight ahead as the lift descended. He could see her nodding out of the corner of his eye.

'New South,' she said.

He felt an immediate, involuntary moment of alumni one-upmanship, but it was not quite enough to banish the faint feeling of intimidation induced by her stern demeanour.

In the foyer they passed Angela, who was wearing black jeans and a white shirt through which he could see the faint outlines of her bra. She flicked him a neutral glance but nothing more, although he could see her hand, the one not occupied with carrying a coffee, reaching for her phone. Officially, he and Angela didn't know each other and didn't speak in public. But she would almost certainly DM him before she swiped in on her floor. He could visualise her thumb moving dextrously over the screen of her phone without her needing to look at it.

They sat down at a table in the cafe after ordering; Nathan, displaying local knowledge, guided them towards the back since the noise from outside would be distracting.

'You don't drink coffee?' Rachael said as they sat down.

'I gave it up for health reasons. And my tastes became so refined that I could never enjoy coffee anywhere,' he said. He noticed a couple of the other male patrons eyeing Rachael. 'I was like the Count Pococurante of coffee.'

'Coco purante?' she said, frowning.

Ugh, he thought. Now I'll have to mansplain the reference and sound patronising.

'There's a guy, an aristocrat,' he said, 'in Voltaire's *Candide* who's so surrounded by all these amazing things, but his tastes are so, like, hyper-refined he can't enjoy any of them.'

'So anyway,' she said, pulling out her phone, switching it on and placing it next to her, 'are you pissed off at me?'

It was, he thought, a reasonable question, and he appreciated her directness. While he was not feeling in a sufficiently sympathetic mood to want to allay all her concerns, he did have a certain sense of fair play. He shook his head, then got out his own phone and placed it on the table.

'No, not at all. I'm pissed off at the whole world, but not at you in particular.'

She smiled, slightly more warmly than the last time she had smiled at him. Very slightly. Progress, he thought. By 2019 she might actually smirk.

'I was told you'd done a very good job,' she said. 'And your hand-over note is excellent. I have to say, I'm wondering why I'm here. A bit.'

Nothing if not professional, Nathan had prepared a long and, he thought, very good handover document, 'exhaustive and exhausting', one that would convey to the person who had taken *his* job how complex it could be but also detailing the best ways of dealing with its challenges.

He ventured into the murky waters of existential jokes. 'You say that like it's unusual to wonder why one is here . . .'

She didn't hear him properly or missed the remark, and continued. 'So I was wondering how you felt about things, whether it's gonna be a problem.'

Something about her voice registered with him. She was quite well-spoken, but it seemed an effort, and occasionally, in the middle of her sentences, almost too quick to notice, something jarred. 'Gonna' had done just that.

'There'll be no problem between us,' he said. 'There's no reason for there to be a problem.' He paused. 'Big ring. If that's not rude.'

He was intrigued by her wedding ring—indeed, amazed—and couldn't help himself. It was huge, with a big purple stone in it, and contrasted greatly with the rest of her jewellery, which was quite understated. She wore a thin silver necklace, almost invisible, and a plain black, presumably very expensive, watch.

She instinctively glanced at the ring, and nodded with a half-smile. 'It is, isn't it. My husband's selection.'

Well, he thought to himself, maybe if I just act naturally rather than trying to be charming, my relationship with my new boss will be a lot easier. He was rapidly assembling a picture of her. She was from a working-class background, had made good via the law degree, and married someone wealthy, maybe a barrister, or maybe a wealthy client she'd met at work. The ostentatious ring suggested someone ethnic to Nathan. But then again, he thought, I'm racist. And my psychological profile of her is probably wrong. I've completely misjudged her.

The coffee and tea arrived; the latter in a small white teapot with the string from the teabag elegantly draped over the side. He emptied the contents of the small jug of milk into his cup, then got up, went over to the counter, and asked for more, checking Twitter as he stood there. As he'd expected, he had a DM from Angela: *You move fast.*

'They never give me enough milk,' he said when he returned.

She watched him with her lips paused at the rim of the coffee cup; she was, he thought, quite attractive. The thought 'pocket rocket' came into his head. He began putting sugar into the cup and stirring it with deliberate slowness, having decided he wanted to impress her.

'So what are our employees like?' she said. He was amused by—but appreciated—her use of the word 'our'. She was saying all the right things for someone in her position.

'Neither of them . . .' he began, but trailed off when she suddenly looked at her watch.

'Problem?' he said.

'No, no, it's just that I have to go up and meet some more executives at three,' she said. 'Now, tell me about Brian.'

'Well, he's a dickhead,' Nathan began.

**TUESDAY
10 NOVEMBER**

'Cock,' said Kat. 'Cock, cock, cock, cock, yes, yes . . .'

'Cock, cock . . . yes, yes . . . I love you, I love you, I love you!'

She leaned forward, breathing hard, resting her head on Chris's shoulder, her eyes closed, for nearly a minute. He brushed her hair back gently. She produced a sort of sob-smile, then exhaled loudly as she eased herself off him. Then she lay on her stomach, her face turned to him.

'Now that's a beautiful face,' he said, as he rolled over and moved between her legs. She widened her legs and he slid inside her.

'Fuck, I love your cock,' she said.

'It fits perfectly in you, doesn't it?' he said. He kissed her ear and began thrusting gently, inducing a sigh from her. She looked over her shoulder at him with an expectant smile. He placed one hand over hers and their fingers interlocked.

'Just hang on a sec,' she said, and awkwardly reached for the pillow Chris had been lying on. He pulled back and she lifted herself up and pushed it beneath her.

'That's a better angle,' she said as he re-entered her.

'Oh yeah,' he said. 'Oh yeah.'

'Oh fuck,' she concurred.

He began fucking her hard, their fingers interlocked again until he pushed her down into the bed, her loud breathing momentarily stifled by the pillow, as he came.

He lay on top of her after he'd finished, a fine sheen of sweat over both of them. Eventually, he slid off her and lay beside her, pulling off the condom before placing an arm beneath her head. She rolled into the crook of his arm.

Neither of them said anything for perhaps three or four minutes, both comfortable in the silence.

'Can't stay here all afternoon can you?' she said after a while.

'I have a meeting at two thirty,' he said slowly, unhappily.

'I've got a fucking radio interview at four,' she said. 'A long one.' She turned and looked at him and blew some hair off her face, succeeding only in briefly dislodging it. 'Have to go into the ABC.'

'*Busy old fool, unruly Sun, why dost thou thus, through windows, and through curtains, call on us? Must to thy motions lovers' seasons run?*'

'What's that?' she said.

'John Donne. I like you looking at me through your hair.'

She stroked some short grey hairs on the side of his head nearest her. He was forty-two, with a healthy proportion of greys, which she actually liked.

'I.e. you like me with bed hair.'

'I love you so much,' he said.

'I love you too,' she whispered. 'I love you so, so much.'

They lay there in silence for several more minutes. She didn't need to talk; she was happy to listen to him breathing, happy just to absorb his presence beside her, everything in its right place. Finally she pushed herself off him. 'I better get a shower. You want one?'

'I'll tag team with you,' he said. He rustled through his clothes on the floor and produced his phone. 'Ah, fuck it, my battery's flat. I need to check my emails. Do you mind?'

'Go for it,' she said, standing naked before him. She loved being naked with Chris. He made her lose all self-consciousness about her body, made her actually prefer to be naked in the presence of the body made for her. She grabbed some clothes off the floor as he went out into her kitchen and brought back her laptop. She watched his body, and especially his cock swinging pendulously as he walked, then she kissed him and went into the shower, where she sang.

Nathan walked out of Governor Phillip Tower, glanced at his watch, and decided walking back to the office would be quicker than any other means of transport. It was a warm spring day, just gone 1.45, and he removed his jacket and folded it over one arm, put his sunglasses on and set off.

The meeting, with a government minister's chief of staff, had been reasonably productive, though the precautionary presence of a senior public servant had somewhat stifled discussion. Rachael had been slated to come along, but had been pulled into a meeting along with other managers by GM, presumably on cost-cutting business. He'd been late, an unprofessional and, for him, unusual error, although he'd still ended up waiting ten minutes while his interlocutors were delayed in another meeting, somewhat ameliorating his sense of self-reproach.

He walked around to Phillip Street amid lunchtime pedestrians. There wasn't much left to do that day, indeed there was something of a lull as Rachael got across issues but didn't move them along. Nathan liked to turn things around quickly and get them off his hands as fast as possible, and had taken pleasure, during his stint as manager, in simply binning requests for input on matters he felt weren't important enough for his time, whereas his predecessor— well, Rachael's predecessor, strictly speaking—took care to give thoughtful consideration to every request that came across his desk, or get Nathan to give thoughtful consideration to them. Those days, it seemed, were back.

Even so, there was no point going home; Ree and Sophie weren't there anyway. Ree worked at a gym in Randwick, not too far from Soph's school, four afternoons a week. She had a communications degree, but she was by occupation a model, having spent much of her teens and early twenties earning money that way. This ostensibly exciting career (if Big W catalogues and *Women's Weekly* fashion spreads equated to glitz and glamour) had left Ree, who had similarly abstemious habits to himself, with a solid asset base from which they drew several thousand dollars a year in dividends. Ree also owned their house in Kensington, although this had not been provided by showing off her body but by the death of her mother some years before, and her being the sole heir. Her lack of any real qualifications—Nathan, an academic snob, regarded her degree as meriting a position somewhere between toilet paper and a cereal-box novelty—and of any great financial pressure accordingly meant that Ree's commitment to employment was less than total.

Perhaps, given the sudden diminution in his responsibilities and dearth of tasks at work, Veldtech would get rid of him, although that hadn't been the thrust of GM's comments the other day. But, having actually given thought to his prospects after GM's cut-and-run on his bonus, he'd got used to the idea of looking for another job. He could live in hope that another round of cuts might see him given a severance package.

Waiting to cross Hunter Street, he noticed a CCTV camera mounted on a pole above him. He was sufficiently well-versed in surveillance equipment to know it was a City of Sydney one, not a traffic camera. Veldtech had unsuccessfully tendered for a facial-recognition software contract for the city's network of cameras. That had been before the tie-up with ETS, when Nathan had first arrived. Veldtech had offered a bespoke solution miles more expensive, they'd later learned, than their two US rivals, but in the end no one had got the tender, because facial recognition was still expensive and tricky to do in the wild rather than in a controlled environment. But the boys downstairs were continuing to work on the software, while the guys in Marshall and Texas worked on database integration. The more he learned about ETS's many and varied surveillance systems, the less he liked it; three months after starting the job, he'd encrypted his hard disk and internet connection at home, right around the time ETS had sold some spyware to some Gulf state dictatorship, with the deal done via Veldtech to hide it from prying US eyes.

As he walked down Elizabeth Street, a tall young woman wearing tight grey pants and a tank top emerged from David Jones just ahead of him and turned to walk down towards the pedestrian crossing to St James Station. Nathan removed his sunglasses and watched her arse from a distance of about four metres, and decided to follow her across Elizabeth Street, on the basis that he was going to have to cross at some point anyway. He was motivated as much by aestheticism, he told himself, as straightforward lust. The girl's backside was splendid, a work of art in motion that would have pleased anyone with an eye for beauty, regardless of their sexual preference. He hovered behind her at the crossing, restored his sunglasses once he was out in the sun again, and followed her across the road, where she turned right and walked to the bus stop nearby. After a moment's indecision, he kept going towards work. He wondered what bus she was going to catch.

After waiting fifteen minutes to get a container of pasta from Antonio's downstairs, he walked into the lobby at work and just missed a lift, but the next one pinged open immediately. He stabbed 23, but a young woman grabbed the door just before it shut and joined him, looking slightly flustered.

'Sorry,' she said.

'Perfectly okay,' he said. 'I have no problem with anything that delays my return to work.'

She smiled and pushed 26, giving away she was a colleague.

'Many cuts in your area?' said Nathan.

'Apparently there'll be five,' she said. 'But I'm not sure. I only started a couple of weeks ago.' She wore a green top and black pants, had short dark hair and was, Nathan thought, quite cute. He glanced briefly at her backside when she was looking away.

'Where in?'

'Civil Solutions. Carrie McGrady's area.'

Nathan nodded sagely. 'Aha. Well, we're neighbours, kinda.' He kept his voice flat, almost dismissive, as though any workplace connection between them was a matter of no moment to him. 'I'm in Corporate. Same division. Nathan Welles, Government Relations.'

She smiled. 'Erica Whitecross.'

'Well, welcome, Erica Whitecross,' Nathan said as he got out. 'Thanks.'

He returned to his desk and immediately googled her, then spent the next half-hour going through her Facebook photos.

The train wasn't too crowded for a weekday evening, and getting a seat was unusually easy. Em found herself sitting behind a young man engaged in a lengthy, though not especially loud, phone conversation. James had been supposed to meet her after work but had been pulled into something at the bank and cancelled on her. She watched the platform slide away as the train left Central.

Tom had chosen the right hook to get her involved in his lunatic faux-hacking scheme by setting her the intellectual challenge of distributing information in a way that would not be traceable to the company, but which would maximise the amount of publicity it attracted. She'd been dwelling on it ever since.

It was plain to her that Tom was driving this, but clearly he had some sort of authority from higher up. However outlandish the idea that Tom was actually serious about this, it was beyond even the wildest flight of fancy that he was doing it without some sort of tick from someone more senior. After all, wasn't every area now expected to come up with ideas to increase revenue? But it was to be top secret: no records were being kept, no emails referring to it were to be written, no discussion of it over the phone, no company IT equipment used for it. Indeed, the preferred venue for discussing it seemed to be the footpath next to the traffic downstairs.

She'd broken it down from legal and ethical perspectives. She would be publishing confidential information from a whistleblower. But she wouldn't know who the whistleblower was, because Tom was going to give her the information, so if anyone found out she was the one who'd published it, she could simply say it had come from Tom, and leave him to deal with the problem. She'd already run that scenario past him and he'd agreed. She decided that withholding the identity of the whistleblower from her was actually the only sensible approach.

'I taught him a fuckin' lesson he'd never been taught before, I tell ya,' said the young man into his phone. Em took out her book, but didn't bother opening it.

Then there was the ethical issue. She wouldn't be publishing the information for the public interest, but merely to create the impression something was wrong with the government's security. In a way, of course, there was, but not of the kind that Veldtech would like to exploit—although she knew Defence Solutions was working on software that used a profile of whistleblowers to determine if someone looked like they might become one. All of this was more problematic. Was this the sort of thing she wanted to do? Invent problems so that her company could make money from solving them?

'I gave him some fuckin' dees,' declared the youth, dropping his voice. 'Nah, nah—some *dees*.'

A bald man in a dark blue suit had got on the train and sat behind her, flicking a glance at the young man as he passed.

And yet there would be a public benefit. The whistleblower was handing over information that he or she wanted to see public. It was plainly important information. If she set up a way to release the information that would be hard to trace, it would be better than if they put their faith in a journalist at a newspaper. She knew how easy it was for police agencies and intelligence services to find out who contacted journalists. And few journalists bothered with encryption or even understood what it was. Veldtech had a program called Inspektor that processed large volumes of metadata and assembled profiles of groups of people, although so far they'd only sold it overseas, not locally. In a sense, the whistleblower, whoever he or she was, would be safer releasing the material this way than any other way.

She stared at the vivid red cover of *We Are Anonymous*, with its headless, suited male.

Maybe Tom just wants you to think that, said Dark Voice.

'Nhhh hhhh hhhh hhhhh.' The youth had a weird laugh. 'Nah, I'm on the fuckin' train.'

The train pulled away from Redfern Station.

And who was the whistleblower? She knew Tom had worked at ASIO. He'd alluded to other people in the company. Then again, it didn't really matter who the whistleblower was, more that they were safe in publishing information. Sometimes, she reflected, it didn't require purity of purpose to achieve pure outcomes.

But that wasn't, she admitted to herself, the thing that really interested her. She actually liked the idea of setting up a pretend hack. The company was going to give her money to pretend to be a hacker, to play at being a cyberactivist. The thought intrigued and excited her, and faintly worried her, given the dangers. It had been a while since she felt any excitement about work.

Or, for that matter, life, offered Dark Voice.

WEDNESDAY
11 NOVEMBER

As Chalmers waited for the lift to close, Rathbone rushed in. Chalmers had gone for a coffee; it was only 7.30 am and his EA wasn't in yet.

'G'day, Baz.'

'How are things?' said Rathbone.

Chalmers made a face. 'Pretty fucking average. We had another incident with Troy yesterday.'

Rathbone frowned. 'Oh no. What happened?'

Troy was the son of Chalmers's partner Steve, from Steve's marriage; he was nineteen and had been living with them for eighteen months.

Chalmers rubbed the spot on his chin. 'He decided to take Steve's car for a drive to Newcastle. Didn't bother telling us, just decided to go to Newcastle. And he didn't charge his phone, so we couldn't reach him. So Steve came home yesterday and the car's missing. He actually reported it as stolen about nine o'clock because we hadn't heard from Troy, but then Troy rings up at about ten thirty from a fucking petrol station because he's got no money.'

'Oh shit.'

'So luckily the servo has a fax,' Chalmers continued, 'and I've still got one for my office at home, so we faxed the bloke credit card details for some petrol. He is just fucking out of control.'

'What does he do? Is he studying?'

Chalmers waved airily with his free hand. 'Oh, he's supposed to be an apprentice chef or something, but I've no idea how that's going. I actually have to lock up my office at home so he doesn't go in there and fuck around with my stuff. It's like living with an addict who's just addicted to making our fucking lives miserable. I don't know what Steve's going to do with him. Christ knows his mother can't control him.'

'At least he didn't get brought home by the police, I guess,' said Rathbone, referring to a previous and more serious incident six months before.

'Yeah, well, small mercies. How are you?'

'Not too bad. Long as I can find some people to sack.'

'Fucking tell me about it.' The lift opened, and they both swiped themselves into level twenty-seven.

'How's your tree-shaking going?'

'We've got a couple of things going,' said Chalmers. 'But nothing that's going to bear fruit immediately. Or shake the fruit off onto the ground. What about you?'

Rathbone glanced around and moved closer to him. 'I fucking gave Derek a list of savings measures in August and he signed off on them, right? Now he wants another round. I told him I can't produce more cuts without it affecting operational budgets. He thinks there's some huge fucking hollow log of, you know, training money, and he's still fucking around recruiting a new CFO. I said to him, "If you're convinced there's all this padding there, then you find it, because I can't." He's like, "Back-of-office stuff, Mark."' The last bit was delivered with a fairly accurate impersonation of Anderson's accent.

'He's an IT specialist,' said Chalmers. 'You might have to produce some fantastic savings that look great on paper to win him over. Something he can wave at Marshall.'

'Well this was a bloody successful company until those fuckers bought it.'

Chalmers lowered his voice as one of the EAs went past. 'We've tendered for a good dozen projects that I'd be embarrassed to win, because we don't have the staff to do them well. I'm desperately hoping we don't get them.'

'I know exactly what you mean.'

They peeled off in separate directions.

The landline began ringing just as Kat opened the door. It was, she assumed, ABC Adelaide. She put her coffee on the kitchen bench and grabbed the phone; the wait for a coffee around the corner at the cafe had been much longer than usual. She'd felt rather under-dressed, having decided she could duck out and back in track pants and an old T-shirt, only to wind up stuck there for fifteen minutes on full public display, sans decent clothing and hair.

While she waited to speak, she slid in front of her laptop. *Waiting to talk to ABC Adelaide about different rules for different forms of communication*, she typed on Twitter, the phone jammed between ear and shoulder. She refrained from making a comment about the hideous song they were forcing her to endure. If I was better organised with this shit I'd have links to the streaming page good to go, she thought. Gotta promote the fuck out of yourself, hon, amirite? Mental note to write down a full list of regular interviews and have tweets prepared for them. She drew the line at retweeting praise, something she despised when others did it, but for a so-called social media expert she often didn't even do the basics of self-promotion well.

She'd been halfway through tapping out an email to Chris on the phone when her coffee had finally appeared, so now she found her Gmail tab and reopened it.

'Joining me now is social media strategist and author of *Social Mania*, Katrina Sharpe. Morning, Katrina!'

She realised she hadn't registered the name of the presenter when the producer spoke to her. 'Good morning!' she said brightly.

Gmail appeared, and looked weird. She realised after a moment that since she hadn't used her laptop browser since yesterday, it was Chris's account still open from when he'd used it. There was a long list of emails from her own account there, plus some others. Idiot hadn't logged out, she thought. As she chatted with the Unknown Presenter on the phone, she shifted the pointer over Sign Out, then got up from her chair and wandered around her kitchen as she spoke, eventually picking up her kitchen cloth and wiping her benchtop down, a reflexive habit she had when talking on the phone at home. She got some of her best cleaning done while talking on radio.

The interview only took a few minutes. She finished her coffee and returned to the laptop, and was about to sign out when she noticed, interspersed with batches of her own emails to Chris, ones from another account called clairebear1995. The first few words of each email were on display. One, with the subject 'xxx', read: *Hate exams, cos I can't go to watch your gorgeous body at lectures.*

The email exchange was at least thirty strong.

An ache, like she'd been hit in the stomach, developed within her. She suddenly became conscious of her own breathing.

She didn't debate very long with herself whether she should open the email before she clicked on it.

The 'hate exams' one was two days old; it was in response to one the night before from Chris. That went: *thought a lot about you last night, about having your body against mine, breathing in your hair, feeling your skin on mine. Want to fuck you, hard, again.*

Her breathing became short and shallow. A wave went through her, half an emotion, half an actual physical feeling, cold, nauseating, shuddering, like the bottom had dropped out of her stomach, or out of her whole existence. She had an overwhelming urge to be sick. Standing up so quickly she knocked her chair over, she bolted for the toilet, where she threw up the coffee and the cereal she'd eaten for breakfast.

Your skin on mine. Breathing your hair. Feeling your skin. He'd used those phrases with her. How many times had Chris told her on email that he wanted to fuck her, hard? How many times to her face?

She slumped next to the toilet, looking into her shower, where there was still water pooled from that morning. She tried to stand, and threw up again, her heart pounding.

She had to go back. She had to go back and read what else Chris had written to clairebear1995.

Chris and 'clairebear' had fucked the week before. At her place. Like he fucks me at my place, she thought.

She read further back. Whoever it was, this Clairebear, this woman, was besotted with Chris. She was clearly a student of his; interspersed with discussions of fucking were anodyne comments about his media law course and what she thought while she listened to him in a lecture theatre.

Her heart continued to pound.

She checked his chats. There, in between their chats, were his and Clairebear's.

Fuck. Ten days before he'd been chatting at night with both of them at the same time.

Her mobile rang. It was another phone interview, one she'd been approached for the previous day. She ignored it. They rang four times, then stopped. She was physically incapable of speaking, or of thinking about anything other than what was on the screen.

An exchange on the previous weekend caught her eye.

Clairebear1995: *I know I shouldn't say it but you have such a special place in my heart.*

ChrisJohnFawkner: *I know I do. Me too.*

Clairebear1995: *You always will.*

ChrisJohnFawkner: *You in my heart, I mean.*

Clairebear1995: ☺

Clairebear1995: *I love you so much. Know I shouldn't say it. But I do, even if I can't ever have it reciprocated.*

ChrisJohnFawkner: *I know you love me. And I love you.*

Clairebear1995: *Love you so so much.*

Kat got out of the chair, walked backwards and sat on the carpet, then lay down on it. Her phone rang again. She curled into a ball and began to cry.

THURSDAY
12 NOVEMBER

Em wasn't sure whether she simply hadn't noticed the woman before or whether she was new, but this was the second time she'd seen her in the kitchen. It was not especially surprising: the floor was large and there were a number of offices, and only two kitchens. The first time, the previous day, Em had come in and noticed the woman using the microwave, and they had not spoken. This time, Jayde was there as well, and greeted her with her customary, 'Hey, mate.'

Em paid a bit more attention to the woman this time. She was short and very pretty, and wore quite expensive clothes, although Em wasn't convinced that what she wore entirely suited her. She was again wearing pants, as she had been previously, pinstriped stretch pants that probably came with a matching jacket, but she had open-toed shoes with bright red toenail polish, which Em did not rate at all. She had two ear-piercings, which Em pruriently considered one too many, but her lemony-coloured knit top was, she thought— trying to be scrupulously fair—quite nice. And she evidently wasn't the Milk Thief, a notorious miscreant who routinely raided the Pura Light Start milk that she, Jayde, Adriana and several other women on the floor all contributed to.

'Hi,' the woman said with a smile. 'I'm Rachael. Just started last week. Government Relations.'

'Hi,' breathed Em, smiling. 'Emma Thomas from Intel Coord.' She realised that this was the new head of Government Relations to whom the disgusting-fingered crypto-belcher Gibbo had referred when Nathan Welles entered the meeting.

'I'm Jayde,' said Jayde, as if that explained everything.

'Nothing much is working round in our kitchen,' Rachael said.

'They're hopeless at repairing stuff. You've got to complain ten times before they do anything about it,' said Jayde, her New Zealand accent breaking through.

Rachael turned and opened the dishwasher and bent over to put her cup in. Em couldn't help noticing that her underwear was showing above the waist of her trousers, along with much of the small of her back. Worse, the tag of her underwear was sticking up. After a second, the bright red underwear and white tag disappeared from view, but she could sense it remained ready to leap out again the moment its wearer swayed away from the vertical.

Hmm, Em thought, tag dag. A bit tarty for the workplace, surely? Not a good look going around flashing your undies. Em herself never risked such exposure, being paranoid not so much about her underwear as the small of her back, which she refused to believe was not too ugly for public display, a view not unsurprisingly shared by Dark Voice, who against all evidence muttered about 'welcome mats'.

James: 'For fuck's sake, you do not have a welcome mat. There is no hair there at all. I will take a photo.'

Dark Voice: *He's just saying that to be nice and will photoshop the picture.*

Rachael's presence reminded Em that she needed to chase up Nathan and Gasman Gibbo for their comments on the Levers article, which was due with Mark Chalmers by COB. Tom was supposed to check the draft but seemed to have been too engrossed in what they now both called, on the rare occasions they discussed it, Project X. She realised, given the presence of Rachael, that Nathan must be on the same floor as her, only down the other end and on the other side, well beyond her usual paths. When Rachael left the kitchen, she waited a few seconds then followed, turning left when she usually turned right. The other woman walked past a long line of offices down towards the western end of the building. Em watched for a moment, then saw Nathan stand up near the windows and lean over a partition to talk to someone. She gazed at him for several seconds, without thinking, then turned and returned to her own territory and sat at her PC.

Hi Nathan, she typed into an email. *Just wanted to check if you had any comments on the article for General Levers. Mark Chalmers wants a draft this afternoon. Thanks!*

Ewan Mazzoni sat impassively in the executive waiting area, wondering if he could be bothered picking up one of the magazines on the coffee table nearby. Across from him Ethel, Derek Anderson's assistant, directed telephone traffic, taking innumerable messages in her harsh, almost guttural voice. After several minutes, he reached out to pick up a five-year-old copy of *Business Review Weekly*, which looked the least boring of the titles available, when the door to Anderson's office jerked open. Two men walked out and the door closed again. Instantly, Ethel picked up the phone. She glanced over at Ewan and resumed typing.

'Gary, he's free.'

Gary was Anderson's senior executive assistant, Gary Crick, a pasty-faced fop of a man universally disliked across the company. Along with everyone else, Ewan had acquired the company-wide habit of referring to him as Gary Prick. Prick appeared after about a minute, his trousers tight and high, wearing a grey waistcoat that matched his pants. He didn't look at Ewan, who continued to recline on the couch, and went over to Ethel.

'We right to go?' he said to Ethel.

'Yes, love,' she growled without looking at him, and pressed a button. 'Executive office, may I help you?'

Prick glanced over at Ewan, who pushed himself up from the couch and followed him. They entered Anderson's office without knocking.

The thing that had most struck him about Anderson was how thin he looked for a man in late middle age. Ewan, in five months' working for him as security manager, had never seen him exercise at all, but knew he worked long hours and had noted that he rarely touched the food he was served at the multitude of functions and meetings he attended every week.

'Morning, Gary,' said Anderson. 'And,' after a micropause, 'Ewan, isn't it?' he said, reaching out to shake Mazzoni's hand. Ewan, taller and wider than both men, nodded, looking slightly downwards at Anderson.

'Now what have you chaps got for me?' Anderson said. He sat down at a large table next to the windows looking out over Hyde Park and further afield.

Ewan had encountered a couple of South Africans while he was in the army, but still had to listen hard to Anderson to make sure he understood everything he said. He assumed Anderson had a similar problem with his own, occasionally thick, Scottish accent. He examined Anderson's hands, which were intertwined on the table in front of him. The fingers were elegantly long. Ewan leaned back and rested his hands on the back of his shaved head.

'Ewan has completed a security audit of the residence,' said Prick, not even looking at him, 'and has some recommendations for you to consider. And Vanessa too, I guess.'

Anderson turned and looked at Ewan. After a moment, he reclined in his chair and raised his hands to the back of his head.

'What have you got for me, Ewan?' he said.

Mazzoni, conscious they were mirroring each other, lowered his hands from his head and opened a blue folder on the table. 'Well, I mean some of this stuff is straightforward. It's a very exposed position, even from that little spot at the bottom of Darling Point Road. For a start, I want a twenty-four-hour security presence, aided by a couple of external cameras. I also want you to start wearing an RFID implant with your health information on it. And that wharf, down on the water—it's very poor security. You should remove it, or at the very least it should be monitored and fenced off.

In fact, the whole waterfront really needs a decent fence. It'd be easy to go there in a boat and walk straight onto the property and up to the house.'

Anderson smiled. 'You know, I think the biggest problem with that place is the bloody block of flats round the corner that looks down on it.'

'That was there when you bought it, Derek,' said Prick.

'We've got that shitty sandstone wall along the water now,' said Anderson. 'I agree that could be replaced with something a little more aesthetic and maybe high security, although the War Office won't like it. Anyway, tell me what you think that'll cost.'

'Probably around five hundred grand, plus ongoing costs of around one fifty a year,' said Ewan. 'Some of that capital expenditure would obviously be recouped if and when the property was sold.' He realised Anderson was referring to Vanessa when he said 'the War Office', but stayed focused on the business at hand.

Back in his soldiering days, Ewan had done an accountancy course, not so much in pursuit of the glamorous career of army accountant as because his own high school education had been confined to some Standard Grades at Cleveden Secondary in Glasgow before he'd joined the army at seventeen. The only thing he'd found easy at school was maths, and he eventually worked out the best thing about the army was the opportunities it offered for him to catch up on the education he'd ignored as a teenager. He also had a mild interest in doing better than his parents. His dad was the son of Italian immigrants and a labourer like them, his mum had been a receptionist. By the time she died, he'd left the army and joined a private security firm; he was in Iraq when he heard she'd passed away.

'What's it matter what the cost is?' said Prick. 'The company can pay for it. It can be written off as an expense. You know ETS's security policy.'

Anderson rolled his eyes. 'That's going to be a bit difficult at the moment, Gary. But you're right about the wharf. I think you should get started on that. I never use it. If I wanted to go anywhere by boat, I'd go next door and catch the ferry.'

'Well, don't do that by yourself, please. Anyway, I'll come up with some options,' said Ewan. 'You and Mrs Anderson can consider them.'

You and Mrs Anderson, he echoed internally.

'There's a change in Derek's travel plans,' said Prick, addressing Ewan for the first time. 'He's not going to Brisbane until Thursday morning now, because the meeting with the American visitors has been cancelled. You're connected up to Derek's email and diary aren't you?'

He nodded. 'I'll change the detail roster.'

'And I'll probably go to the US again in a week or two for an audit committee meeting,' said Anderson. 'Looks like it'll be Aspen, but ETS will take care of that, you don't need to worry about it. And you'll be coming tonight to that function?'

'Yep,' said Ewan.

'I need to talk to you about that thing,' Prick then said to Anderson.

'Okay, thank you, Ewan,' Anderson said, smiling pleasantly at him. That was his cue to leave.

Nathan kept watch just up from the corner of Elizabeth Street, across the road from work. The evening peak was at its height, although traffic was crawling relatively freely and, in places, faster than walking pace. Standing in a large crowd gathered at his bus stop, Nathan craned his neck and spotted, behind an L94—his bus, normally—a yellow Corolla in the outer lane. As he did so, it flashed its lights. He began walking up Liverpool Street, keeping to the edge of the gutter. When the traffic halted, he stepped out between the cars and over to the vehicle, opened the door and got in.

'Afternoon,' he said.

'Hello,' said Angela softly. She drifted the car forward. 'How are you?'

'Good. You?'

'Good.'

Angela had been a new recruit to Veldtech at the start of the year, fresh out of university. She'd done a three-month stint in the area next door to Nathan's, during which time Nathan had assiduously charmed her. He had strong principles: he would never sleep with a woman who actually worked for him, and especially not a young woman commencing her career. Moreover, such behaviour in other men at the company infuriated him. Others not under his direct sway, however, were in his view legitimate targets. Accordingly, he was sleeping regularly with Angela, who would drive in to work on the days when they were going to her place.

She placed her hand on his thigh as she nudged the car across into Oxford Street. 'Good day?'

'Tolerable,' he said. He interleaved his fingers with hers. 'Yours?'

'Boring. I could've done with some more DMs,' she said, glancing in the rear-view mirror. She had dark brown, curly hair, with a face that Nathan thought was quite pretty.

'What's he waiting for?' she said crossly about the car ahead of them. Nathan ran his hand along her left thigh. She glanced behind as a prelude to trying to go around the car in front, but it suddenly accelerated away. She followed it.

'You want some money for parking?'

'No, you can buy me lunch.'

'Speaking of which, how was the area lunch?' he said.

'Why is it,' she said, 'that I always get stuck with the most boring people in the place at work lunches? It's like they gravitate to me.'

'All work lunches are automatically boring. That's why I never do them.'

'I had the OH&S guy sitting next to me. Fuck he's annoying. Seriously, would you want Sophie to grow up to be an OH&S rep? Then again, everyone was talking about the cuts anyway. How's the new boss?'

'Not bad, actually. Not insensitive to my situation.'

'Well that's good.' She braked hard, then put her hand back on his thigh and slid it up into his crotch. 'You going to sleep with her?'

'Oi,' he said. 'I can have coffee with my boss without any unprofessional intentions.'

'No mentoring coffees,' she said, referring to one of the ways Nathan had suborned her.

'As I recall, you quite liked our mentoring coffees.'

'And the funny thing was, I actually thought at the start you just wanted to mentor me, and I was quite disappointed.'

She moved her hand from his leg to the steering wheel as she accelerated through an orange light and turned into Flinders Street, glanced behind her and then changed lanes. He loved the way her curls moved when she moved her head.

'Who was the guy you were with the other day?'

'Which day?'

'When I was in the lift with you.'

She smiled. 'You jealous?'

He shot a glance at her. 'Well, to the extent that I can be as your married lover.'

'That's Todd. He just arrived. It's okay, he has a girlfriend. Is that all right? You approve?'

'Hmmm. Oh, how's your mum?'

She slid her hand onto Nathan's penis through his trousers and began slowly stroking it. 'She came out of hospital this morning. I offered to go up'—Angela was from Brisbane—'but Dad said everything was okay. He's gonna take a few days off.'

'Your brother could always lend a hand, couldn't he?' He had rapidly become erect with her touch.

'You're kidding, right?'

She reached over and unzipped him. 'Now, you know I've just got my period?'

'You mentioned it,' he said neutrally. He ran his hand up beneath her skirt, drawing circles on her thigh. As always, she was driving as quickly as possible and changing lanes constantly, with minimal actual benefit.

'Sorry,' she said.

'Shut up,' he said. 'I'm a father. I understand female biology.'

'Don't say "father".' She grinned. 'Makes me feel like I'm fucking an old guy.' She floored it to get through the Albion Street lights.

'You're not fucking an old guy. An old guy is fucking you.'

'Ew!' she cried. 'Stop it! Fuck!' She'd missed the lights to turn onto South Dowling Street. Frustrated at not being able to keep moving, she slipped her hand back inside his trousers.

'You're going home for Christmas though?'

'Oh yeah,' she said. 'Back home for the big wog Brisvegas Christmas.' He moved his fingers higher up her thigh. 'It's George's turn with the twins and Nan will be there too.'

Nathan had an in-depth understanding of Angela's family as she regularly complained about them and delighted in living thousands of kilometres away. She was now rhythmically stroking his penis, but paused to fly away from the lights. She was heading for Southern Cross Drive; she lived in Botany, two suburbs away from Nathan. 'You?'

'We'll go to Mum and Dad's place. With my sister and her kids. It's nice, actually. I like Christmas.'

'That'll be fun for Soph. Where are they?'

'Putney.'

'Where's that?'

'Oh, kinda just below Ryde, closer to the river.'

He noticed Angela had her crucifix necklace on, although from what he gathered she wasn't exactly a devout Catholic. He called the necklace 'the agony and the ecstasy' given the miniature silver Jesus was suffering the torments of crucifixion while nestled at the top of her cleavage.

The traffic was slowish on Southern Cross Drive, and little faster for Angela's constant changing of lanes, but easier once she turned off onto Botany Road, where she had to abandon his penis in order to drive properly. They briefly discussed work, as Angela's area had been mentioned as one likely to suffer casualties, although she'd been told that as a junior staff member she was less expensive so more likely to be retained. Nathan endorsed that view.

'Now, I'm assuming my flatmate isn't home,' she said as they turned into the street where her townhouse was. The carport, apart from three carefully stacked cardboard boxes, was empty; she pulled in, turned the engine off and they got out with practised efficiency and entered the split-level unit. Her cat meowed in greeting; Nathan avoided him like the plague as the creature had scratched him the first time he'd visited.

'Hey, Felix,' she said, putting her bag down. She walked into the tiny kitchen and got a glass of water. 'You want anything?' she said.

'No thanks,' he replied. 'Well, I mean, not anything from the kitchen.'

She turned and headed upstairs, with him in tow.

'Just hang on a sec,' she said, disappearing into the bathroom. He entered her bedroom and removed his jacket and tie, draping them over the chair by her desk, which was covered in marketing textbooks. Angela was still finishing a part-time commerce degree from her university days. Her bedroom overlooked an unkempt suburban backyard with long, untidy grass. Down the back, an equally unkempt man was standing over a lawnmower. There was a small child with no pants on beside him.

'Renters,' he thought.

Angela closed the door behind him and removed her jacket; the pants of her suit were unbuttoned. Once she'd finished hanging up her jacket he slipped his hands around her from behind and pushed her pants down while kissing her throat. She turned around and undid his belt and pushed his trousers down. 'Chair?' she said.

'Yup,' he replied. She loved fucking him on her desk chair, for some reason, but he was quite amenable to it.

He went and sat down on the chair where he'd placed his jacket. She slid onto his lap, his arms around her waist and they began kissing. He cradled her left breast through her shirt and began rubbing her nipple through the fabric while she pressed herself hard against him, their tongues intertwining. From outside came the sound of the lawnmower being started up. He pushed his finger inside her underwear and began stroking her, making her breathe in loudly.

She began kissing him again but broke off, her eyes closed, panting as he alternately stroked her clitoris and pushed his finger inside her. She relaxed onto him, breathing warmth into his left ear as he continued to touch her, her panting guiding him as to how close she was to orgasm. As usual, she came easily and quickly, her breathing becoming faster and more shallow, until she held her breath for a moment, hugging him tightly. They held the pose for a minute, until she relaxed and began kissing him gently.

'I have never known anyone to come as quickly as you,' he said. She smiled somewhat ethereally at him.

'I think it's the quality of the stimulation.' She reached down and pulled his erect penis free from his clothing. He reclined and closed his eyes, letting her stimulate him, feeling her lips against his as she continued kissing him. Then she moved her crotch onto his penis, still holding it with her hand, and rubbed the tip along herself.

'You're being naughty,' he said, between breaths.

'Uh-huh,' she said, sounding excited again. She moved forward slightly and his penis slid inside her easily.

'Oops,' she whispered, breathing hard. She started rocking back and forth on him.

'Oh, shit, that's nice,' he whispered.

'Sure is,' she said, grinning.

'We should . . .' he began, then stopped. 'That's gonna make me come,' he said.

'Good.'

'Wait, wait, wait,' he said. 'Wait. Condom.'

She stopped, mildly exasperated. 'Okaaaaaaay,' she said, climbing off him and reaching into her bedside drawer. Her shirt lifted slightly as she bent over, exposing her buttocks. He noticed some blood on her thigh as she did so.

'Fuck, you've got a nice arse,' he said, catching the condom she threw him.

'I know, hon.'

He stood up and rolled the condom on. Instead of sitting back down, he pushed her towards the desk. She bent over it, and he slid inside her and began fucking her. She began pushing back and forth on his penis as he thrust away, and after some dissonance, they found a perfect rhythm of movement between them that swung the little silver Jesus back and forth violently from her neck and made Nathan come very quickly.

Next door, the unkempt man was mowing the lawn while the small child pushed a toy lawnmower some metres behind him.

•

It was 7.10 p.m., well after Nathan's normal arrival time, when he got home. Angela had had a quick shower; he thought he should have one too, but it was getting late. It was only when he was putting his shirt back on that he realised some of her blood was on it. Angela, who was meeting friends for drinks, dropped him off in Kensington. His entry and clean-up would require some tactical nous, he knew. Sophie and Ree would greet him when he came in, and he worried that Ree would smell Angela on him. So his first step was to go quietly over to the front garden hose and quickly splash some water onto his face. He rubbed furiously, feeling pathetic, then dried it with his sleeve. Then he walked around to the front door and opened it.

'Hi, everyone,' he called as he came in.

'Hi, Dad!' Soph yelled from the lounge room.

He wandered down the hallway, waiting to be assaulted by females, but none came. He looked into the lounge room. Soph, still in her school uniform, was seated on Ree and they were watching TV.

'Hi, babe,' said Ree, motionless, barely glancing up. He decided to go over and kiss her, as it would be, he thought, the last thing an unfaithful husband would do. He pecked her on the cheek and then kissed Soph.

He turned and was casually wandering from the room when Ree said, 'What happened?'

He stopped.

'Sorry?' he said.

What happened? Had she smelled something?

'I called you at work about quarter to six and they said you'd left.'

'I went to a Social Committee meeting,' he said instantly, without even thinking. 'They've just started one up. I was gonna contribute. Well, I thought I would, until the meeting.'

'Why?'

'The people running it are idiots, really bureaucratic. It was a joke. They were still going when I left.'

She looked at him. 'What were they talking about?'

'Elections for positions. For a Social Committee, for god's sake. You never get enough nominations for those things. Then someone started talking about alcohol in the workplace. Anyway, I'm buggered. I'm gonna take a shower.'

'Okay,' said Ree.

'How was school, Soph?'

'Good!' she said loudly.

Lying was the easy part for Nathan; indeed, it was effortless. The whole Social Committee spiel had not existed prior to its issuing from his mouth, ready-made, a perfect package of fiction. It was a particular skill of his, a natural, untrained talent, to lie convincingly, to create a story that was not merely plausible but eminently believable. The art, he knew, lay in embroidering the story, the lie, with a detail that the recipient would find compelling, or which reinforced the recipient's views or beliefs. The Social Committee story was entirely plausible, but the compelling detail lay in the clownish behaviour of anonymous, bureaucratic-minded colleagues who were still discussing elections even as Nathan had walked out. Lies, after all, were supposed to be threadbare, designed just to cover the truth and no more. But for Nathan, lies needed detail, observation, and a texture that gave them the same appearance as reality, which was rarely as clean-cut and carefully polished as most lies.

He watched himself in the bathroom mirror for a moment as he dropped his trousers to the tiled floor. He wondered, occasionally, whether he should feel guilty, whether there was something missing from him that would have enabled him to feel some twinge of conscience. But then, he thought, with a sort of mental grimace, he would have to decide which behaviour he should feel guilty about— the lying or the infidelity. Certainly not the lying; for Nathan, the issue was not the difference between the truth and what he related to Ree, but how to get from the truth to meeting Ree's need for information. What to tell Ree was an abstract problem, a mental challenge, rather than a moral issue. Nor could he muster any guilt about his infidelity. He had felt guilt the first time, years ago, was horrified at himself, though not enough to stop him from doing it again. But several affairs later, with Angela, he no longer felt a thing, not even a mild twinge.

He wore his shirt into the shower, in an attempt to get the blood off without going straight to the washing machine. Sweat stains, he would complain about, after he placed it in NapiSan. He let the water run on his face for a time, thinking about Angela, then washed his groin thoroughly.

FRIDAY
13 NOVEMBER

She'd read everything. Every email, every chat, going back weeks, from their first tentative forays with each other, flirtatious but unsure, before they'd slept together and spent hours talking about sex. Sex, the course he was teaching her, his wife and son, her family, and stuff. Boring stuff that lovers in the first bloom of passion find fascinating about each other. The same stuff she'd spoken about with him.

Each word was a knife in her, a jagged blade of which she could feel every millimetre. But she had to read it all, to know everything, to obtain every last detail. She'd sat there the whole night, reading through them, unable to stop no matter how intense the pain. She had to know.

At one point, Claire had started a chat. She didn't know if Chris had the account open on his computer at home.

Hey you there? Xxxx, she'd said.

Kat sat there, watching the chat box, overcome by a strange, prickly flush, half embarrassment, half rage. There she was, almost within reach, the fucking bitch, the fucking little cunt.

For a moment she contemplated responding. *Stop contacting me, it's over.* Or, *Leave me alone. Stay the fuck away from me.* But she wouldn't. She didn't want to end Chris and Claire's affair. She just wanted to murder Claire.

Claire Wagner. Claire Alice Wagner.

She had readied herself to do whatever it took to track her down. She was, after all, a social media expert, and this little bitch would have left a digital trail behind her to follow. But as it turned out, early on Claire had sent Chris a job application and asked him to comment on it, then offered him a drink after work as payment.

Somewhere, distantly, she recognised Claire's opening gambit, but ignored the thought.

There was thus no need to track her down, because Claire had offered herself up, a tasty morsel for him, a sexual treat for his selection any time he wanted. She was a PLC girl. She had done high school debating. She had spent a gap year in South America. She spoke French and a little Italian. She worked at a CBD retail outlet part-time. Her BFF was named Susanna. She wanted to be a journalist.

Kat studied her photos on Facebook carefully. She was pretty, in a bland way, with perfect teeth. Seriously perfect teeth. Kat created a fake Facebook profile of a girl two years behind her at school then sent off a friend request and followed her on Instagram, where there were more pics.

She wanted in on the bitch. All. The way. In.

And with every detail she read, Kat's face set harder and harder. Sometimes she felt dizzy. Not normal dizzy or physically dizzy, not the dizzy of everyday life, but dizzy inside her mind—no, inside her *soul*, like she didn't have anything to grab on to and hold to steady herself, like there was nothing left to keep her from floating away into the abyss. But putting together the profile of Claire kept that feeling at bay and gave her some sense of control. She noted every-thing about the girl, her eyes cold, sitting there contemplating how best to inflict a world of pain on her.

Until the photo.

That might have been the lowest point, she reflected later. Claire had sent Chris a photo late one night, weeks before. She saw later, after comparing times, that she and Chris had been chatting at the same time. In one of the email conversations, down at the bottom where she'd missed it first time around, there was a selfie of Claire, very teenager—which she basically was anyway—in her bathroom. Standing there in pink underwear with no top, okay tits, thin, not a great body but cute, staring at the mirror with her light brown hair down over one eye (just the way Chris liked), not smiling, left arm extended and holding her phone so that her left breast was just a little higher than her right. Just in front of the mirror was what looked like a *Frozen* toothbrush.

She didn't sleep. Couldn't sleep. Sleep was a comfort from which she was to be permanently excluded henceforth. She had an article to write by the end of the following day and hadn't even thought about it. She continued to ignore the phone. Maddy rang twice, and she ignored her. Chris emailed her three times, twice innocuous things, the third time, after no responses, *Is everything OK?*

She ignored it. Him. It. That man.

At 5 a.m. she'd thrown up again, then finally slept for an hour. She awoke in hell, her own personal, permanent hell. Whereas until 11.42 a.m. the previous day she had been so happy that, on occasion, she'd found herself singing, there was now, she felt, nothing in her life. Everything had been taken from her. All her plans, all her thoughts, all of it, replaced with a dull throbbing pain floating in a void.

She desperately wished she'd stayed asleep, or could return to sleep, or just be able to not think, just for an hour, to be able to not feel anything. Just for an hour, or forever.

At 8.55 a.m., Chris called her. She stared at 'x', her phone code for him, on her screen until it stopped ringing.

Sometimes she let herself think she would forgive him, that she would confront him, demand his abject apology, demand even that he leave Her, and agree to start rebuilding things if he could convince her that that would be the end of his betrayal. Even in her anger and dismay, the thought was tempting. But how could it be the end? she asked herself. If he's doing it only months after meeting you, why wouldn't he do it far more if you ever ended up together? You'd just be the next Her, being cheated on with some other Kat, some Claire, someone.

Pls call 321, You have 1 New VoiceMail messages

'It's 86 Darling Point Road—right at the bottom of Darling Point Road, on the harbour. I'll be there to let you in the gate.'

An Asian face appeared in Ewan's doorway. He gestured it in.

'That's fine. See you then.'

Ewan put the phone down.

'Mr Dao, I presume?' he said theatrically.

Tom Dao nodded at him. 'Mr Mazzoni.'

'Indeed. Mr Chalmers gave me forewarning, or perhaps warning, of your impending visit to this neck of the woods.'

'He said as much.'

'Please have a seat. You're after a licence?'

'Yeah.'

Ewan liked to collect fake IDs wherever he lived. It was a hobby, almost; he liked the challenge of procuring high-quality forgeries, but also the freedom it gave him to go about his business with less government monitoring than would otherwise be the case. He had, after all, been a soldier in Her Majesty's Armed Forces, and had killed people, and had people try to kill him, in Iraq; the security posturing of pissant governments like Australia's was almost offensive to him. His first fake had been a dodgy UK driver's licence when he was sixteen, which barely passed muster in the dark entry of a Glasgow nightclub let alone anything official. In Germany, he had met a man who did passports and German ID cards; he'd ended up with five sets, all excellent quality, although all were now long since expired. Since arriving in Australia, he had acquired several fake driver's licences, credit cards and Medicare cards, all online, and had opened two bank accounts with them, but preferred real driver's licences obtained from crooked bureaucrats that would withstand a police officer's verification. He had three Queensland licences for that purpose, which had cost him—or, rather, one of his fake bank accounts, and ultimately Veldtech (Prick, to his credit, had asked no questions)—five thousand dollars. He'd also used them to acquire several mobile phones.

'Do you need any other IDs, or just the licence? You can't open a bank account with just this.'

'No, no,' said Tom. 'I don't need to open any bank accounts. I just need to buy a broadband connector anonymously.'

Ewan stuck his bottom lip out contemplatively. 'Tell you what, why don't I just go and buy your broadband connector? That way, we don't have to buy a licence with your photo on it. Save us time and money and it's more secure.'

'That'd work fine,' Tom said. 'How soon could you do it?'

'I'll do it for you this afternoon, if that works for you?'

'That'd be great.'

'Okay, I'll let yer know when I've got it. So, you're a pal of Mr Chalmers?'

Partly for his job of managing security for Anderson, but also partly out of interest, Ewan had done his research on most of the senior people in the company and was aware of Tom's history with Chalmers, who intrigued him somewhat—much more so than Anderson himself.

'Yeah, I knew him at ASIO.'

'What was he like?'

Tom didn't answer for a moment, preferring to scrunch his face up. 'Well, he was very good at playing the role of a senior intelligence bureaucrat. But inside him there was always a sarcastic, foul-mouthed prick dying to get out.'

'Ah,' said Ewan. 'A man after my own heart.'

'And what about you? Where you from? Apart from Scotland, obviously.'

'British Army until I got bored with it, then a few bits and bobs before I was a security contractor in Iraq.'

'When were you in Iraq?'

'From 2005 to 2007.'

'Shit,' said Tom, impressed. 'You saw the worst of it.'

Ewan nodded. 'Yep. It wasn't a fun place to be. Mind you, it's no better now. And a hundred and eighty of my former colleagues died to achieve it. And fuck knows how many bloody Iraqis. Poor bastards. Anyway, I'll give you a ring once I've got your dongle.'

SATURDAY
14 NOVEMBER

'That meowing is driving me nuts,' Em said.

'It's cool,' said James. 'I love this game.' He smiled at her from behind his laptop. He was wearing only his boxer shorts; they'd had quick and, for Em, unsatisfying sex as soon as he'd arrived because they were due to go out with Adriana.

'It plays over and over again.'

'That's because it's a game, babe.'

She walked around to where he was sitting. To the strains of some dinky MIDI-style music, James was manoeuvring a monstrous upright cat around, or sometimes through, a series of obstacles, including the occasional set of skyscrapers that could be knocked down. Periodically, it would issue a noise somewhere between a meow and a Godzilla scream and stretch out to grab nearby objects or flail at the aircraft that were assailing it.

'What is it?'

'*Kittehsaurus Rox*. And I'm fucking awesome at it.'

The cat pawed three times rapidly at a passing jet, but missed, and was obliterated in an explosion of red viscera.

'Fuck it.'

It was nearly 7.20 p.m. and there was no sign of Adriana. While James played his game, Em had been making some notes on how she might release whatever dodgy information Tom was going to obtain.

'You going to get dressed?' she said, worried he might prefer sitting there playing on his laptop to coming out.

He rose and went into her bedroom. She watched his body as he did so. He was a little overweight, but no worse than when she'd met him. He could secks better, was her main complaint.

There needed to be a plausible entity behind the release, Em had decided; someone whom the media and whoever investigated the leak would be distracted by. While waiting for James to finish off fucking her earlier, she'd hit on the perfect distraction: a group of cyberactivists, hackers. A bit like Anonymous, but with a WikiLeaks-like focus on political information. They'd release the information on Pastebin or maybe a few other host sites, then send the links to media organisations. She just had to come up with an identity. After some googling, she'd set up two separate VPN accounts and bought a MacBook with cash Tom had given her. Then she'd loaded Parallels onto the MacBook and set up a broadband dongle Tom had provided via some security guy in Veldtech. All she had to do was log into one VPN, start the virtual machine, then log into the next one. Tom had been suitably impressed when she'd shown him in his office, with the door closed, yesterday afternoon.

'Ring Adriana,' James said, emerging dressed. He was in jeans and a collared shirt and, having done his hair, looked quite present-able. He returned to the game.

'I did. Voicemail. I'm just going to change,' she said.

She pulled on a top and some black jeans, ignoring Dark Voice's taunts, thinking through what sort of identity the group should have. She could still hear the music from James's game, along with occasional meows. She heard the door to the balcony open. James was evidently going outside for a cigarette. 'You fucking addict,' she called. He smoked perhaps four or five times a day.

The alternative, she mused, was a bunch of cyber-anarchists, just doing it for the lulz. But she felt less comfortable about pulling that off.

Back in the lounge room there was a text from Adriana: *5 mins*. She went to the kitchen, opened the fridge and took out a bottle of Riesling.

'Are you okay with your beer?'

'Yeah,' he called back. 'But what have you got?'

'Riesling.'

'What do you mean Riesling?'

'What the fuck do you think I mean? I dunno, I just buy by price.'

She poured two glasses and stood for a second by the kitchen bench, watching the screen of James's laptop. The cat, left by James to do its own thing, was clinging to the side of a skyscraper and kicking it with its hind legs, shrieking.

That's it, she thought.

There were more people than Kat expected at the reserve at North Maroubra. Dog walkers, spring-evening picnickers, a large group having a cricket game, a guy in red running clothes stretching. There was an easterly breeze, in which a man and his two young daughters were flying, or trying to fly, a kite.

She'd spent another day in seclusion, ignoring all phone calls and emails, only tweeting once, retweeting some article she hadn't even read just as a signal she was still alive, in case anyone cared. Chris would have seen it, and wondered why the fuck she was not answering him. Eventually she couldn't stand being inside, and decided to walk to Maroubra.

Mahon Pool was dead calm with the tide out and only a few, mostly elderly, swimmers were paddling about. She walked onto the rocks, just to the left of the pool, then began working her way up to the top of the headland, regularly pausing to watch the waves, the salty breeze whipping her hair about. A dog with a plastic cone around its neck ran past, panting, apparently unaccompanied by any humans. She walked past a couple sitting and watching the water, her head on his shoulder. She and . . . she couldn't remember his name, some guy from first-year uni, had done that in a similar spot, just a few yards away, years before.

Brad? Brendan? Brian? It wasn't Brian. She'd never been out with a Brian. Never would. *Brian?* FFS.

This wasn't her first broken heart, by any means. Fuck no.

There'd been four or five of those. But it felt the worst. *Was* the worst, by a long stretch. Chris had been the real thing. Okay, correction, Ctrl-Z, Chris had *seemed like* the real thing, the one she didn't just love, but the man she was comfortable with for life, the man who had been allocated to her by cosmic design, the one intended to complement her, who finished her sentences and whose she finished for him, whose body fitted together perfectly with hers, like their minds did. Yes, he'd ended up with someone else, that was just the ordinary course of life; in time, that would be resolved and she'd be with him.

Brandon? Brenton? Brenton.

Only, she wouldn't, not now. Not because he'd cheated on her. He slept with Her every night of the week. Not because someone else loved him. She could understand Claire's obsession with him, however much she wanted to obliterate Claire from the face of the earth, to torture the cunt to death. Not even because he told Claire that he loved her, cheapening his love from something that was pure, that existed only properly for her, into something polluted, poured out to some blandly pretty student with perfect teeth and okay tits.

It was because, she realised, Chris didn't exist, not the Chris that she loved. Chris in reality was an ordinary guy, with some wonderful good points, and some faults, some glaring faults. The man she loved wasn't real, and that had now been exposed. Chris was someone else, someone different, more ordinary, more banal.

There was an eruption of cheering from the cricket game nearby, followed almost immediately by the dull thump of a particularly large wave on the rocks below.

The worst part wasn't that Chris didn't love her, that he was lying when he said he did, or that his idea of love wasn't what she thought it was. The worst part was Chris, she knew, *did* love her, probably as intensely as he'd led her to believe, but that didn't change what he was really like, didn't fix his faults, didn't make him stop being the sort of academic who'd fuck his students.

That was the worst, the realisation that hurt the most. It would have been so much easier if Chris had told her he'd suddenly decided he despised her and never wanted to see her again, or that he'd never loved her and was just using her.

She reached the top of the headland and stood there, facing the wind. Nearby, close to the edge, so close the swirling water far below made her scared, was the plaque for Ronald Nelson that she read every time she came here, straining to make out the embossed lettering that had been slowly eroded by the wind and salt. She rocked slightly in the wind and noticed a fisherman on the rock ledge just to the south talking on his phone. She retreated from the edge—she might be broken-hearted, but suicide was the last thing on her mind—turned around and walked around towards Lurline Bay. There was another thud, followed by the sound of spray from below.

But the fact that Chris wasn't real didn't make the loss any less painful. There was still a Chris-sized hole in her life, in her future, regardless of whether the man himself ever fitted it properly. She missed him.

God, how she missed him.

She sat down near the edge, more comfortable when her centre of gravity was lower to the ground, and looked up the coastline, past Coogee and Wedding Cake Island towards Bondi.

And she still wanted to punish him. That was why she hadn't responded to any of his attempts to contact her. He'd called her six times, and she'd ignored him each time. She assumed some of the blocked numbers in her now-lengthy list of unanswered calls were from him as well. She wanted him to writhe with uncertainty, not knowing what was going on, wondering why she had, so suddenly, stopped all communication with him. Maybe he'd figure out she knew about Claire. But she wanted him to wallow in pain and confusion. Let him suffer.

After a time, she rose and kept walking. An elderly woman walking her dog went past. A young couple was getting out of a car on Marine Parade, carrying barbecue things. They seemed to be having a good-natured quarrel about his friends. Up above, in the refurbished units on the corner, a middle-aged woman was standing on one of the small balconies. She nodded and smiled at Kat, who smiled back. She kept going along the path that led down into Lurline Bay.

And she wanted to get Claire. Seriously. Oh, fuck yes. She wanted to do a real number on that bitch, to dig out everything the girl had ever put online. She hated herself for thinking like that, but she couldn't accept Claire as a human being like she could Chris or anyone else. Claire was scum, sub-human scum who deserved the most savage punishment she could devise. Bitch had picked a fight with the wrong woman. Bitch had made a seriously bad move. The worst move. She was going to pay.

She felt a renewed burst of anger just thinking about her. She had plans for—

She froze.

A couple was walking towards Kat, on the steps of the path ahead down to Lurline Bay. It was, remarkably, ludicrously, Chris and Her. She couldn't believe it. It was definitely them. She started to panic and glanced behind her. *Her* wore a cap and sunglasses, *He* was in a T-shirt with sunglasses. What the hell were they doing here? They lived in Five Dock. She was between streets; the only way to avoid them on the path was to turn around and walk away. But it was too late. He'd already seen her, surely. They were advancing towards her, a mere twenty metres away. Would Chris think she was stalking him? Trying to engineer a confrontation? Her heart was pounding. Ten metres. What the hell was she going to do? Chris and Her were chatting quite loudly, though she couldn't quite make out their words in the breeze. A few steps brought them closer. Chris suddenly laughed. 'I thought it was Stephen's,' he said.

Fuck. She breathed out. It wasn't them. They looked kinda similar, but it wasn't them. The man nodded to her as they went past. 'Good evening,' he said, with a slight accent.

'Hi,' she said.

Listening to Ree's breathing in the dark, Nathan lay watching a sliver of light on the far wall of the bedroom, created by the street-light across the road breaking through a tiny gap in the curtains.

Ree was still beautiful, he thought, as much as when he'd met her and she had been funding her way through uni by modelling. But he'd lost interest in sex with her. Once he was close to her, arousing her and making her climax, or beneath her as she made him ejaculate, he loved it, and he enjoyed the post-coital feeling of lying next to her as she drifted off to sleep, contented, as she was doing now, feeling the warmth coming off her, running his eyes and his hands along the shape of her relaxed body, enjoying the sensation of her skin against his. But normally the thought of sex with her did little to excite him.

Nathan reproached himself continually about this, from any number of angles. He watched other men watch her subtly, knowing they were attracted to her. And worse, she wanted only him, found only him attractive, indeed based her whole notion of what was attractive in a man on him, and more or less had done since they'd met, at Frank's barbecue, as they had referred to it ever after.

He sometimes wondered if he'd only married her for ego, so he could boast to himself that he'd married a model, but that was too shallow even for him. He *had* been in love with her; he'd loved her snarky sense of humour, loved how cool she was, loved how he felt when he was with her, how good they were together. They'd gotten married after she became pregnant; both of them, unexpectedly, were delighted about becoming parents. But he'd begun having affairs when Sophie was around eighteen months old, when the reality of being a suburban dad had begun to sink in.

And that was that. He enjoyed having Angela, a pretty young woman who eagerly pursued sex with him. It made him feel more than a husband and dad, more than a domesticated drudge. It wasn't even so much the sex; it was the way Angela watched him, laughed at his comments, looked forward to seeing him; it was the way Erica Whitecross had turned her body towards him once he'd begun conversing with her in the lift, the way she'd smiled when he'd introduced himself. 'Fuck, I love the way your brain works,' a woman had said to him once as they lay naked next to each other. That was . . . he struggled to remember. The girl at the law firm, Kate, one of his first affairs. He enjoyed pleasing women, whether sexually or intellectually or just with his constant banter. That was why Rachael's hard-to-crack facade threw him.

He wondered what Angela was doing. It was late Saturday night, so she'd be out drinking with her mates, enjoying weekend debauchery, while he was at home on domestic duty, helping Ree cook dinner, convincing Soph to go to bed, and watching a movie. Was she with that kid from work? What was his name . . . Todd? This 'Todd'—Nathan mentally spat the name out—was probably fucking her. He imagined 'Todd', whose features he could barely even remember, fucking Angela, probably boring missionary position because he was about nineteen years old.

He got out of bed—Ree was by now asleep—and, after checking on Sophie, fast asleep on her back, as always, went into the spare bedroom and turned on his laptop. He didn't know Todd's last name but would dig it out from the company directory on Monday and then look him up. He opened Instagram and went looking for Angela's latest posts. Not unusually, she'd posted two pictures from earlier in the evening, one of a large beer ('First belgian beer ever, better be good Belgium!!') and one of her with four friends ('Elk is an awesome wingman'). The venue looked like a pub. Three of her companions were female, including one very attractive blonde—possibly the Elk of lauded wingpersonship—but there was a curly-haired male with them, between Angela and the blonde. It wasn't, to the extent that he could recall, Todd. The male looked faintly woggy, which might mean he'd appeal to Angela.

He was undeniably jealous; jealous that Angela had a single's social life, and that she was sexually available to men other than himself. He resented that she wasn't content merely to be his secret girlfriend, as nonsensical as he understood that to be. He kept the resentment to himself, only ever revealing it by queries about men he saw her with. I must pursue the lovely Erica more aggressively, he thought, by way of consolation. He checked Erica's Facebook page, but she hadn't updated it since he'd seen it earlier in the week. But she was also on Twitter, and had Instagrammed a nice pic of herself with a friend earlier on Friday. He wondered what Erica was up to at that moment.

SUNDAY
15 NOVEMBER

'So this is gonna work, right?'

'I dunno. Let's try.'

Chalmers handed Tom a beer as the latter opened a laptop. They were sitting in the back of Chalmers and Steve's house in Paddington, under an elaborate sail. Chalmers sat down beside him, dressed in a T-shirt and shorts, drinking a Corona. Steve emerged from the back of the house, followed by a golden retriever, slid the long glass door shut with his foot and slumped in the hammock nearby, reading a magazine. The backyard was Paddington-tiny, but very elegantly landscaped and more or less an extension of the back of the house.

'Okay, I log in to the VPN,' Tom explained. 'Then I start the virtual machine. Hopefully Emma has got it all up and running. Then I use that to log in to the second VPN.'

He read from a small piece of paper, then typed in the login details and hit enter.

'Okay, virtual machine . . .'

Chalmers swigged from his beer. 'These aren't those fucking free VPNs, are they?' The dog wandered over and sat beneath him.

'No, no, proper ones. Okay. Then we log in to the second VPN.'

He again read from a small piece of paper and typed in the login details.

'So even if the VPNs are secretly logging, they can't link any activity to you,' said Chalmers.

'Yep.'

A thumping *doof doof* sound erupted from an open window upstairs.

Steve looked up. 'Troy, turn it down,' he called.

'But how did we pay for the VPNs?'

'Bitcoins.'

'They can be traced,' said Chalmers.

'We swapped them several times over and changed the amounts each time.'

'Good. And did you get a driver's licence from our Scottish friend for the dongle?'

'He went and bought one himself with a fake ID,' said Tom. 'Okay. Tor.' He accessed the thumb drive plugged into the notebook, and Firefox appeared.

The music hadn't reduced in volume. Steve called again, louder. 'Troy, turn it—'

'*All right!*' came the response from upstairs, screamed at the top of his voice. The music lowered in volume by about five per cent.

'Test your IP address,' Chalmers said.

'Yeah, yeah, yeah, I was gonna do that,' Tom said. He typed: *what is my IP address.*

'Slow,' said Chalmers.

'Yes, that's Tor. Just wait.'

It came up with a location in Germany.

'Awesome. You might keep your job yet, Dao,' said Chalmers, and swigged his beer.

Tom opened the one bookmark in the browser.

'Can you set it to China instead of Germany?' Chalmers suggested. 'That way it could look like Chinese hackers.'

'Well, we could ditch Tor and just use the VPN, but I don't think the VPN we're using has a Chinese server,' Tom said. 'There's an Eastern European one. Romania. We could use that?'

'Russian mafia,' said Chalmers. 'That could work.' He adopted a Russian accent. 'Ivan de Russian hacker stealing Aussie secrets for sale to de highest bidder on de darknyet.'

'But I think it's better if we keep using Tor as well as the VPNs,' said Tom. 'Just in case.'

After a delay of several seconds, a screen appeared with the words *Parliamentary Information and Communication System*, a login box, then the words *Powered by Infratext, by Veldtech* below it. There was a long string of random text in the login name box.

'How's Ash's arm by the way?' Chalmers said. Tom's nine-year-old son had fallen off his bike several weeks ago and broken his arm.

'Cast comes off at the end of the week apparently,' Tom said as he glanced at his piece of paper again, then slowly typed in an extended sequence of characters, and hit enter.

It took a while to load, but eventually a page with a series of tabs down the left-hand side appeared.

'We appear to be in the APH system,' said Tom.

Chalmers poked at the screen. 'Users—there, click on that.'

Tom brushed his hand away. 'Get out of it, you idiot, we're not even in the right area.' He scrolled down and found a link called Administration Options, clicked it, then opened a sub-link called Mail Client. That produced a clunky-looking screen with another series of options. Tom clicked on Users. The result was a list of names, several hundred strong.

'Ooh yes. There are our MPs,' said Chalmers.

'Twenty-five nuns,' Steve said obscurely, looking at his magazine.

Tom began scrolling up and down the list. 'There's the Prime Minister. Let's have a look.'

'Ministers are on separate systems, you dumb prick,' said Chalmers. 'That'll just be the PM's electorate account. Wouldn't be used for anything official. Remember, this is just the GayPH system. It's for non-ministers and everyone else. Start opening them up. Start with government MPs first. More senior ones.'

'Right,' said Tom. 'Let's see what we can find.'

Chalmers took a long swig from his beer. 'This is gonna be interesting.'

MONDAY
16 NOVEMBER

'Here you go,' said Tom, and handed Em a USB stick and a bag containing the laptop and dongle. He turned and went back to his office.

A shiver of fear and excitement ran through her, quite unlike anything she'd felt for a long time. She stood for a moment, almost shaking, then calmly walked around to the lifts, clutching the USB in one hand, which was now feeling slightly clammy, and the bag in the other. She held the bag to herself a little more tightly when two people from level eighteen got in. Down on the ground, she walked out of the building, then went to the pedestrian crossing over to Hyde Park. She glanced around, feeling nervous and under suspicion, while she waited for the Walk sign, then crossed Liverpool Street and entered the park near the War Memorial. In spite of the cloud cover, it was a warm morning, and the air for some reason smelled good. A group of schoolkids was visiting the War Memorial; she skirted them and walked around to the Pool of Reflection and down to the far end, where, deciding she was far enough from work, she sat on an empty bench, pulled the laptop out and opened it.

A couple was sitting nearby; on older man in an unmatched jacket and trousers and hat walked past; over the other side of the pool there was a young mother and her child, a little boy, with a dummy and one of those leash things that made Em cringe.

She started the virtual machine, logged into both VPNs and inserted the USB.

A bald man in a dark blue suit and sunglasses walked past the young mother, smiled at the little boy, and sat down on the bench across from her at the end of the pool.

Tom had put a .txt file on the USB; the only other file was a Tor browser Em had put on there herself. Tom's file contained the contents of an email to 'Donahue, Laurie (MP)' (Laurie.Donahue.MP@aph.gov.au) from Sheena.MASTERS@ag.gov.au.

Hi Laurie—AG asked me to forward draft cabsub to you, expect this to come before Caucus Tuesday week after Cabinet Monday. This is NOT final but close to and guts of sub are there, will send copy of coord comment (assume PM&C/Treas/ Fin support) and brief on key talking points. Not for circulation. Thx Sheena.

There followed a long series of numbered paragraphs with what had evidently been tables but which in the .txt format were now several rows of confusingly formatted numbers. As Em slowly worked through it, it became clear it was about planned cuts to two legal aid programs.

She googled Laurie Donahue. He was a government MP who was, she eventually discovered, chair of one of the government's backbench committees, on social policy.

She looked back at the document. The cuts were worth $90 million; she had no idea if that was a lot or a little of the legal aid budget. But it was a cabinet submission; that was exciting enough. She knew from her brief time working in the DMO that that was a big thing.

She glanced around. The couple had left, so too had the mother. Now there was an elderly woman sitting on the next seat along, and the bald, suited man was still sitting across the other side of the pool, checking his phone.

She went to Pastebin, which opened slowly, and logged in, then pasted in the contents of the submission. She had to spend several minutes tabbing around each table so that they made sense. Once it looked satisfactory, she went back to the top and began typing, slowly at first but then with increasing fluidity. She'd been thinking about what to say and had the outline of her introduction of the online activist group she'd devised already planned.

> *Kittehsaurus Rox is a small, highly mobile irregular force engaged on the frontline of the cyberwar. Our enemies are governments and corporations engaged in asymmetric information conflict: a war where they demand to know everything about YOU but won't let YOU know what they are doing.*
>
> *We state our mission objective simply and proudly: Information is power. KSR is dedicated to rebalancing power in favour of citizens.*
>
> *KSR's first strike is to both share information and demonstrate our power. We have obtained a cabinet document in which the government plans to cut legal aid by 90 million dollars. This submission will be considered shortly. It is time for citizens to tell their government what they think of cuts to assistance to the poor when huge corporations spend billions on litigation.*

'The poor.' Hmmm, she thought. Didn't quite sound right. Never mind.

> *KSR will launch more strikes soon.*
>
> *If you are a government or corporation we WILL look for your information and we WILL find it and we WILL give it to citizens.*

She'd got that bit from a Liam Neeson film. She loved that line. She reread the statement, and was pleased with it. She'd been toying with the words for a few days, running them around her head whenever she had a spare moment. After a moment's thought, she decided to put in a couple of spelling and apostrophe errors to make it look more authentic.

Then she converted the text into all caps, named it 'Kittehsaurus Rox Communique 1', checked to see if that had disrupted the tables, and then hit submit without further pause. She reread through the published document.

Then she logged in to Twitter. @KSRComms was about to produce its first tweet.

Kittehsaurus Rox's first strike: an Australian government cabinet submission #KSR, followed by the Pastebin URL.

She had a list of about twenty journalists whom she'd followed, and she laboriously tweeted the same thing to all of them, in groups of three. The whole endeavour had taken half an hour.

She logged out of everything and cleaned out the browser, then removed the USB from the laptop. As she walked back into work, she couldn't remember the last time she'd felt so happy or excited.

The phone call had been brief, as always, like she was scared to stay on the line too long, on the phone he'd got for her, an old dumb phone he'd bought online, with a SIM purchased with one of the fake licences. If someone else ever found it, she could dismiss it as one she'd lost years before. She only ever turned it on when she needed to contact him.

'One forty-five to two forty-five,' she'd said, and hung up, just like that.

They'd never trace that in the movies, he thought.

In turn, he'd called the usual hotel at Potts Point, but had no luck. He was more successful with some studio apartments near Chinatown, using one of the fake credit cards. Probably smarter anyway, not to use the same place all the time. His place would be ideal, but for some reason she didn't want to go there, and anyway it was in North Sydney, and quite a trip during a weekday. He'd texted her the address, then deleted the text, like she'd delete the one she received.

He'd busied himself for the subsequent two hours, making sure he didn't spend too much time thinking about the looming assignation. Since the hotel was within walking distance, at 1.10 p.m. he closed his door, changed into a new shirt and walked out to the lifts, standing behind three young women chatting as they rode down to the foyer. None of them interested him, given what awaited him at the hotel. He had something altogether better, he thought. His jacket folded over his arm—he liked to dress nicely for her—he walked out and turned left on a path that would take him down several blocks to George Street, where he crossed and then headed for Chinatown. It was a mild day, and a little breezy, so he didn't really warm up despite being unable to resist walking quickly. At 1.35 he reached the 'lobby' of the hotel, such as it was, waited several minutes while a couple of indeterminate Asian origin debated some abstruse matter involving in-room video, then checked in using one of the driver's licences. Hmmm. He'd been hoping to have time for a shower, but it was already 1.41.

Thirty seconds later came a text: *there in a sec.*

He removed his shoes, feeling a nervous expectation, taking the tissues from the bathroom to the bedside table, drawing the curtains across the window, which looked directly across the street into offices, turning the aircon down, fiddling, to occupy himself. Her imminent arrival always induced a state of stomach-churning excitement.

She's late, he thought at 1.50. I had time for a quick shower. He was a little obsessive about personal cleanliness. At 1.51 there was a gentle tap at the door. His heart accelerated.

'Hey.' She was in a broad-brimmed hat and sunglasses, and wore a black pant suit with a red top.

'You're late,' Ewan said softly as she entered.

'Cabbie took forever to find some change,' said Vanessa Anderson, as she removed the hat and sunglasses and placed them carefully on the console next to the television.

'Sorry about the crap room,' he said. 'Usual spot wasn't available.'

She smiled at him. 'I don't care.'

He looked her over. He knew she'd have some extraordinarily expensive lingerie on beneath the suit. She 'loved dressing up for him', she'd said.

Vanessa was thirty-seven and had been married to Derek for just over three years. She had been a lawyer at Veldtech, and she had met him not long after she'd started there, courtesy of her manager being taken ill and leaving her to provide corporate governance support to the then-board. She was slender and blonde and aggressive—much as Anderson's first wife had been, people said. Currently she was supposed to be hosting a Streetscene lunch, at which female business executives were plundered for contributions to homeless kids, but she had cancelled, pleading illness.

They'd met a short time after Ewan had started. He'd been hired by Prick when Veldtech was acquired by ETS; all the ETS board members were supposed to have security, even though Anderson, despite his wealth, had barely any public profile in Australia. In his role as security manager, Ewan not only accompanied Anderson on business but spent a considerable amount of time with Derek and Vanessa in the course of Derek's social and charitable activities, which Ewan would spend standing at the back of the room feeling uncomfortable in a suit, or lurking outside the entrance. After a while, he noticed that Vanessa was frequently seeking out his company during the course of these functions, complaining she was bored. To entertain them both, he'd tell her stories from Iraq, either ones he'd experienced or ones he'd heard, or from his time in Germany, or explain his security assessment of the venue to her. She'd listen, rapt, and demand more every time he finished. During a trip to Virginia taken by Anderson earlier in the year, there'd been some vague threat made on social media and he'd visited their house to check the property, which was woefully unsecure. Vanessa had arrived home while he was there and asked him to join her for a drink. As long as she made the first move, he had no hesitation in responding positively.

'I've been looking forward to this for days. It feels like it's been so long,' she said quietly.

He placed his hands on her hips and they kissed. He instantly slid his hand around onto her backside. She broke off the kiss and stared at him intently for a few seconds, then raised her hand and touched his shaven scalp, not smiling, searching his face. Then they kissed again, much, much harder, and he began to undress her.

Kingsford Girl got on at her usual stop, near Crown Street. She was like clockwork. Every time Nathan caught the 5.40 bus, she got on board next stop.

He called her that because he'd stayed on the bus past his own stop once to see where she got off, and she'd gone around to Kingsford. She was just below average girl height, with black short hair, and was, in Nathan's view, possessed of a beauty rarely found outside art. He was deeply in love with her, or at least that was how he'd justified his stalking to himself. He could stare at her elegant Eurasian features for hours.

When on board the 5.40 bus, Nathan accordingly engaged in extensive and complex calculations as to what positioning would maximise his chances of being close to her. He had no intention of actually interacting with her, but liked the idea of being as close as possible to her to surreptitiously inspect her and glean information about her, to see what she was doing on the iPhone that she spent most of the bus journey staring at and texting on. Intellectually rigorous, Nathan was the first to acknowledge that there were too many variables to deal with properly: the one time the previous winter he had spent the entire journey next to her had been sheer luck, when the bus was unusually full and he'd been standing up right from his own stop, and she'd shuffled her way down towards him, her overcoat against his jacket. Nonetheless, he made the effort to replicate that experience, seeing proximity to Kingsford

Girl as part of an existential battle against an indifferent, random universe.

On this occasion, however, there were a number of people standing between Kingsford Girl and the middle of the bus, obscuring his view of her. To the extent that he could see her, she was wearing the navy suit with a pink top, the suit being a regular Kingsford Girl outfit. Kingsford Girl did not, he figured, have a great deal of money to spend on work clothing. But she looked damn fine in it, he thought. One of his persistent fantasies was undressing her in a hotel room (having lured her there with his effortless charm), where he would remove her top, cradling her small breasts through her bra, kissing her from her mouth down her throat and onto her breasts, running his lips across her amazing skin.

He glanced out the window as the bus went through Taylor Square. A young man in a car in the next lane was using his phone as he drove, with one hand on the wheel. Wonder how long till that guy rear ends someone? he thought. He took out his phone and opened Twitter, idly hoping Kingsford Girl might appear on his Nearby tweets. He tweeted: *Wonder how long till that guy in the Yaris in Taylor Square rear-ends someone?* to his forty-nine followers.

Then a tweet from an IT publication caught his eye. *Mystery group claims Cabinet document hack*. He opened the link.

> *An unknown online activist group has claimed to have hacked federal Cabinet documents and posted them online.*
>
> *This afternoon the group Kittehsaurus Rox posted the text of what it claimed was a Cabinet submission dealing with $90 million cuts to legal aid spending by the federal government.*
>
> *If true, the hack would be a major violation of government IT security as the high-security CABNET system used for distributing classified documents is considered secure and used for the transmission of some of the government's most sensitive material.*

The current CABNET system, based on Lotus Notes, is shortly to undergo a major upgrade that will bring it into the second decade of the 21st century, with mobile device access.

The offices of the Special Minister of State and Attorney-General are yet to respond to the claims.

He glanced up. Kingsford Girl had moved down the bus and was now standing just two metres from where he was sitting, earphones in, looking at her phone. From what he could see, she was on Facebook.

Kittehsaurus Rox is a previously unknown group that claims to be 'a small, highly mobile irregular force engaged on the front-line of the cyberwar' dedicated to 'rebalancing power in favour of citizens'. The group is named after a popular online game.

Nathan was intrigued. Veldtech had actually bid for the CABNET upgrade tender a few months ago. He'd advised an area in Maria Campanella's division on it and gone to Canberra for a couple of meetings about it. Eventually, they'd lost out to the local branch of SAIC, which was a big miss—it was a solid chunk of work worth several million dollars. The current CABNET system, he knew from the tender process, was old and clunky, but as far as he knew no one had ever penetrated it. If they had, it was big news, especially if a group of activists had managed to get in.

He glanced up again and found himself looking straight into Kingsford Girl's Facebook account, hovering about fifty centimetres to his left. Sharon Lee was her name.

Sharon Lee. He managed to see enough of the page to be able to find her on Facebook.

You're an evil stalking bastard, he thought with delight.

'Madwoman.'

'Kathmandu! What the fuck? Where have you been? I've been worried.'

Kat drained the glass of wine she was holding.

'Yeah, I know. Sorry. Married Guy is no more. I've been grieving.'

'Oh, fuck. Babe, I'm so sorry. I'm so, so sorry.'

Silence.

'I'm so sorry. This must be killing you. What happened?'

'I just . . . I was wrong. I was so wrong. I've been killing myself. It hurts like hell.'

Kat felt herself tearing up. It was, she realised, the first time she'd actually vocalised anything about Chris.

'You want me to come over?'

She swallowed. 'No, I'm just gonna . . . I've got too much to do. I've spent two days curled up on the floor ignoring the phone. I need to get my shit together. I haven't answered the phone for ages.'

'I know.'

Kat refilled the wine glass.

'Sorry about that. I haven't answered the phone to anyone for days.'

'You okay?'

She realised she'd repeated herself. Maddy sounded genuinely concerned.

'Yeah, yeah. I'm over the worst of it. I hadn't even got drunk, I was just so smashed into pieces. Now I'm kinda . . . I just miss him so badly.'

Her voice wavered on 'miss'. She drained half the glass in one gulp. 'But yeah, can we get together later in the week? Do dinner?'

'I'm clear Wednesday.'

'Cool, I'll come by work around six.'

'Cool.'

'Cool.'

'I just miss him so badly,' she blurted out again, feeling stupid.

'It's okay, babe. Look, I'll come over.'

'No, no, no, it's okay. Really. It's okay. I'm okay. I'm just . . . five stages of grief and whatever. I'm working through it. Making progress.'

'You sure?'

'Yeah.'

Miss him badly. Badly. Oh fucking god yeah.

He'd torn a piece not out of her heart so much as her whole life, taking away what in the space of nine months had become every-thing she'd aimed for in life. It wasn't that he was all she wanted. She was desperate to make a success of her career, as half-baked as it often appeared to be, and she loved that she could be paid to write, even if a lot of it had to be subsidised by doing bullshit seminars for public servants. But Chris gave meaning to her life, because she was made for him and he for her and growing old with him and writing books that impressed him and raising his children was how she saw that part of her life. And now that was gone, yanked away from her in a few seconds.

What was he doing at the moment? she wondered. It was 6.53 p.m. She finished the glass of wine and poured another. She hated this time of day. He'd be at home, either cooking, because he loved to cook, or getting ready to go to some function with Her.

She briefly contemplated going to her mum's place, taking her car and driving over to Five Dock to watch his house. She then dismissed the idea on the basis that she'd already had too much wine to drink. Otherwise, she'd have done it.

Fuck him, stop thinking about him, she told herself. It was time to get on with the plan. She still had his Gmail account open on her browser; she'd left the MacBook running permanently, and kept opening and closing emails so she wouldn't lose access to it. The previous evening she'd seen they were having a chat, but through a huge effort of will she didn't look at it, indeed at one stage she had reached over to quit the entire browser, which would have closed the account forever to her.

But that wouldn't do. Because she had a plan; a plan for Claire. She sat down at the MacBook and opened a new email.

Hey, she wrote.

I've just had a close call at home. Nothing to worry about, no dramas, but something to get me thinking. What we have is . . .

She paused, thought. Needed to make it sound exactly like Chris.

. . . too precious to be ruined by a simple accident. I want to make sure we're able to play it safe when we need to. So I want to give you the password to this account. It's G3rb1ef3rd3r. If there's some sort of emergency, you'll be able to get access to this account. I trust you completely, as you know.

So store this email away. I know you won't ever need to, but I just feel more relaxed about us if you've got it. Just in case some remote circumstance arises when you need it.

Love,
Me

He'd signed at least two previous emails with 'love', and 'love, me' was a regular sign off from him to Kat.

She drank the rest of her wine and hit send, then contemplated her glass.

Gershwin, she thought. She needed some Gershwin. She wasn't particularly musical, and her tastes were fairly bland, but Gershwin was her dad's favourite and since he'd passed away she'd become more and more enamoured of him; she'd even gone to see a Gershwin performance by the Sydney Symphony Orchestra a couple of years ago. She went and put *An American in Paris* on and stared out the window as darkness began to gather outside. She felt instantly better with the sprightly opening, or the 'opening gay section' as she saw it once described. She returned to the MacBook and contemplated her empty wine glass again.

'Fuck it,' she said, and went and poured the rest of the bottle into her glass. She was drinking too fast, but she didn't especially care.

Claire had replied to Chris, she noticed. Replied almost instantly. She rolled the cursor over to the email and clicked on it.

> *Hi my darling*
> *Is everything OK? You've got me really worried. I had a bit of a panic attack when I got your email. What happened? Did wifey find out anything?*

'Wifey?' Kat spat out loud. 'Wifey? What the fuck, bitch?'

> *By the way the password for my account is #breakingdawn95# if you ever need to use it for emergencies. Can't think what but keep it handy!*
> *I love you.*
> *Claire*

Kat punched the air jubilantly and let out a whoop: #breakingdawn95#. Unbelievably, it had worked.

'Bitch, you have just been socially engineered,' she yelled as she deleted the emails.

TUESDAY
17 NOVEMBER

'Fucking awesome,' said Tom quietly. He was standing behind Em in the coffee queue. 'Everyone thinks it's come from the Cabinet system when in fact it was our whistleblower. Brilliant. I'll have some more in a couple of days.'

Em said nothing. He was right. It was awesome. Scarily awesome. The story was second or third on TV news bulletins and a major story on all the media websites. She'd felt a keen thrill of fear as she watched the morning news programs recount how a group calling itself Kittehsaurus Rox had hacked into the nation's Cabinet system and stolen a Cabinet submission. That was the point when it all became real, the moment when the creature she'd made came to life and lurched into public view, no longer controlled by her, inducing fear and panic. Kittehsaurus Rox was her Frankenstein.

Frankenstein's Monster, you idiot.

The government had initially refused to confirm it was an actual Cabinet document but then said it had called in the federal police.

'*This is a deeply serious leak of confidential information and as a priority we have asked the federal police to investigate,*' she saw a harried Attorney-General say.

AFP is coming after you, said Dark Voice. The thought scared her but she felt undeniable pride, as well.

The Opposition was having a field day both with the hack and the $90 million cuts.

Most of the reports had followed the line taken by the early

146

ones yesterday and assumed the material had been hacked from CABNET, which apparently was the Cabinet system for distributing documents between departments. No one had thought to consider it might have been a whistleblower. Tom's strategy had worked perfectly.

The worrying thing was that federal police were probably right now looking for the leaker who handed over the material, and watching for more activity by Kittehsaurus Rox. But what was there to watch? A Twitter account, operated anonymously, and a Pastebin account. She wondered if Tom knew the identity of the leaker and whether the leaker knew about her.

The mix of fear and excitement she felt every time she contemplated what was happening was by no means unpleasant. It felt a little like going very high on a swing when she was a kid, that vertiginous feeling at the exact moment the swing began its descent.

'Did you see Levers spoke at a conference yesterday?' said Tom. 'He used most of what we wrote for him for that op-ed.'

'I missed it. Where was that?'

'His office is getting a video of it. We should take a look when they can give us a copy. Apparently he went the whole "cyber-defence" thing. It was—'

His phone rang. He stared at the number for a moment, then abruptly walked out.

•

Later in the morning she took the laptop downstairs, logged in to the VPNs and then opened the Twitter account. It occurred to her, sitting in Hyde Park, that someone might be able to time her absences from work with a log of activity on the Twitter account. She had to swipe out of Veldtech when she left and back in again on return. She felt odd doing any of it from within the building—for a start, there was a ban on non-Veldtech devices except outside the lift areas—but decided that she'd make the occasional entry without leaving Veldtech, just to make sure. Still, it felt good sitting outside in the park beneath the trees. Even the roar of the traffic seemed pleasant. The city was alive, buzzing, on the cusp of summer, and she wasn't just another of its millions of inhabitants, but one of the most important, the woman at the centre of one of the biggest stories in the city, indeed in the country. She felt at home, and content, even happy, despite the worry that somehow she or the leaker might be detected. That morning, she'd even entertained the thought of cutting back her Cipramil.

On her way back up, she was joined in the lift by Nathan Welles. He smiled at her. He was wearing a grey suit and a black shirt and looked, she thought, gorgeous. He was also taller than her, which a lot of men weren't. He punched 23 and faced the doors. She was desperate to make conversation.

As if a guy like that is interested in you, said Dark Voice.

'Apparently Mark Levers spoke at a conference yesterday using that op-ed we all did as a basis,' she ventured.

'Ah, okay, cool,' Nathan said, turning towards her. 'Has anyone got a copy of his speech?'

I mean, seriously, the guy is pretty good-looking. Why the fuck would he be interested in some overweight giantess like you?

Fuck you, sixty-six kilos is not overweight, she shot back.

'I think we're gonna get a video of it, if you want a copy?' she said to him.

'Yeah, sure. Drop it down at my desk. Do you know where I am?'

'I think you're on the other side and down the other end of the floor from me,' she said. Then, to cover herself, added, 'Outside Rachael Ambrose's office?'

'That's the one. Just drop off a copy.'

'Sure,' she said, a little gushily.

The lift door pinged open on the twenty-third floor and Ewan pulled his suitcase behind him around to his apartment door. He had accompanied Anderson to Brisbane, with Gary Prick, and spent the day there, then flown back to Sydney. Anderson and Prick were, for reasons unclear, taking a later flight. He'd slept most of the way back. He unlocked the door to his bare apartment.

Bare was understating it. It was spartan. It had a splendid view, looking towards the Harbour Bridge and the CBD—some of his Iraq money at work—with North Sydney Oval just below and off to the left. But Ewan liked a certain spareness in his interior furnishings. He had a black sofa, a black coffee table and a long, low black bookshelf which contained black speakers for his iPod dock (and many books; he was diligent about his reading). The walls were bare and white, like the carpet.

He left the case in the entryway, went over and opened the sliding door onto the balcony, then went to the music dock and scrolled down to his Coldplay playlist. Then he removed an Asahi from the fridge in the small kitchen and stepped out onto the balcony.

It was clear and warm, the sort of weather he could never stop loving after growing up in Scotland and spending most of his army career in the UK or Germany, until he had gone to the Middle East. He watched some figures moving about on North Sydney Oval far below, moving in and out of the shadows, and took a long swig from the beer, thinking about . . . of course, Vanessa. Vanessa. Vanessa. Vanessa. He loved simply repeating her name. He wondered, vaguely, if he wasn't falling in love with her. He'd never been in love, though he'd been engaged to a French girl in the 1990s while in Germany. But the thought of not seeing her for a week or ten days was enough to annoy him.

He realised his phone was ringing inside, and fetched it from the kitchen bench. After a slight pause, there came the distinct Scottish accent of his father.

'Ewan, it's Dad. How are you?'

Even after a long time away from home in places around the world, it wasn't until he'd moved to Australia, where he spent all day surrounded by the nasal accents of Aussies, that he'd realised what a weird accent his father had. His own Scottish accent, occasionally thick, had softened after years of working in all sorts of international environments. But his dad's, a combination of his Italian parents and thick Glaswegian, was occasionally difficult even for Ewan to decipher these days.

'You're up early, Dad—or is it late?' Ewan said. 'Just let me get the computer out and I'll Skype you.'

'Okay, son.'

He pulled his laptop from his travel bag, fished around for the right cables and set it up, then opened Skype.

'Hey, Dad,' he said. 'What time is it?'

His father put his glasses on. He still had all his hair, now steely grey, and was thickly stubbled.

'Quarter to six.'

'You're up early.'

'I couldn't sleep. How are you? How's the job?'

'Good. I just got back from Brisbane with the boss.'

'Where's that?'

'About a thousand kilometres north. It was very warm.'

'Very what?'

'Warm.'

'It's freezing here.'

'I expect so. It's beautiful weather here. You should come visit.'

'Mebbe. Are you coming home for Christmas?'

'I'm not sure what my plans are. It will depend on what the boss wants. He might have Christmas in Europe. If he does, I could maybe come over after that.'

He knew Anderson had no intention of spending Christmas in Europe. If anything, he liked to go to the US. He had a place in New York and a rented place in Vail, Colorado, and he liked to ski. He just wasn't inclined to commit to his father, for reasons associated with Vanessa.

'How's Stephanie?' he said.

Stephanie was a seventy-something woman his dad had met at the seniors' club. Ewan hadn't met her.

'She's a wee bit ill, got pneumonia.'

He pronounced it 'nimoonya' and it took a moment for Ewan to understand what he'd said. 'Pneumonia? Is she going to be all right? That's very serious at your age.'

'Naw, she'll be fine, doctor says she'll come good.'

'Tell her I hope she's up and about real soon.'

'Tell her what? Oh, yer've frozen.'

Ewan waved. 'Working yet?'

'No . . . oh, wait, there you are.'

'Tell her I hope she's up and about soon.'

'I will. Listen, did you settle that legal case you were in?'

Ewan paused. 'You mean the one from Iraq?'

'Yeah.'

'What are you bringing that up for?'

'I just read about a shooting the other day, a different one, that some people, some Yanks, got charged with but they never got put on trial.'

'Yeah, yeah, no, that was all settled. The company settled it. That was a while ago. Before I started here. I wanted to sort it before I came to Australia. What made you think of that?'

'I told you, I read about something similar.'

'Yeah, well, there were a lot of accidents like that.'

Ewan had shot a child in Al-Wahda. Well, it was either Ewan or one of the others with him; there were five of them in all, three of them peeling off shots in all directions, Ewan then screaming to hold fire and identify their target and work out exactly what had prompted Douglas, the idiot Canadian Ewan had never wanted to be near, to start shooting. The driver had floored it, hitting a civilian vehicle and injuring the couple in it. Ewan had fired twice at what he thought was a gunman. In retrospect, he realised he had reacted poorly, but it had only been a week since three of their men had vanished during a similar ride; all three turned up dead months later, presumably taken by militia using police uniforms. Or the police themselves. Douglas must have emptied his entire clip, but sprayed it around so much that, incredibly, the fucking idiot didn't seem to have hit anything—or, more accurately, anyone. Tillot, the Englishman next to Ewan, had fired several rounds before heeding Ewan. The two other guys were in the front trying to see what the hell was happening.

Ewan suspected it was either Tillot or himself who had hit the boy, an eight-year-old, in the leg. He'd learned later that the kid had lost the limb; an inch or two higher and it might have been a fatal outcome.

Still, that wasn't much consolation. Ewan had shot a boy, wrecked his life, for nothing. He'd killed four or five people in Iraq, combatants, proper enemies, bad guys, usually trying to shoot him or his men or blow them up. Shooting a kid, all because he hadn't been smart enough or strong enough to kick Douglas out or sit him down and make him get his act together, well, that was all on him and never going away. Ever.

That was one Iraq story he'd never told Vanessa.

The company had tried to get out of paying anything, except to the Iraqi officials investigating. Ewan demanded they pay the boy's family a lump sum and then set aside regular payments for the kid until he was twenty-five, and that the couple in the car get money as well. And Douglas was sent packing. He turned up later with some amateur American outfit, when things had got to the really bad stage, before the surge. Eventually, Ewan heard, he'd had his head cut off in Mosul, which wasn't a bad outcome, in his view. 'Stupid bastard never used it anyway,' Ewan liked to reflect afterwards.

Odd that his dad had brought it up now. He hadn't thought about it for a while. He used to obsess over it; for at least a couple of years he never stopped thinking about the boy, Mohammed al-Barak, and his missing leg. Then he'd left Iraq, with his money, and it lost its sting, but slowly. Up until a few months ago, he still dreamed about Mohammed occasionally. The company had been sold earlier in the year, and Al-Wahda had fallen to ISIL ages ago, so he doubted whether any money was reaching the boy.

After he'd finished talking to his father, he sat at the kitchen bench, drinking the beer in silence, then opened another one.

'Here we go, here we go. Let's see if you're even dumber than you look, bitch.'

Kat typed Claire's email address into the Facebook login box, then pasted *#breakingdawn95#* into the password box. Enter.

Circle, circle, circle. Fail.

She tried *breakingdawn95*.

Circle, circle, circle. Fail.

She was set to click Forgot Your Password, but then tried *#breakingdawn#*.

Circle, circle, circle, success.

'All too easy, bitch.'

She went into Claire's Facebook page. Claire had over two hundred friends. Lots of messages, but none from Chris that she could see. Lots from uni friends. Today was Andy Torpy's birthday, whoever he was. Another male, Stuart Ross, was apparently an ex- or semi-ex-boyfriend; he and Claire still exchanged messages about sex. Then there was her family; her dad was a friend, as were her older brother and younger sister, still in Year 9. Her grandmother, on her mother's side apparently, was on there too. Kat sipped her wine and continued to explore the account.

Oh yeah did I ever mention I hate exams?!!!!!!! STRESSED was her most recent posting.

How the fuck Chris found this child, this mental toddler, appealing was a mystery. She must've been a seriously good fuck.

Ten likes, and a comment from Nanna: *I know you'll do brilliantly Claire xxx.*

Ha! Claire was indeed about to do brilliantly.

Kat had the topless photo and she was going to post it: tits, pink undies, *Frozen* toothbrush and all. The only slight problem was trying to work out what comment to accompany the photo with. *LOL here's a selfie what do you think?* was a bit bland, but would do.

That should fix the bitch up. Sip of wine. That should fix her up really fucking good. Her two hundred family and friends on Facebook, her dad, siblings and Nanna, were about to see a side of Claire they had never seen before.

Hey, be accurate Kat, they were going to see a *front*, amirite?

Wonder what Nanna will think. She'll be shocked. *Shocked.* Her treasured granddaughter, little Claire, showing her tits. Kat laughed aloud at the thought. There was a photo of Claire and Nanna, actually, in her Photos, Claire hugging her, both grinning. Nanna must love her very much. She was going to be so, so, *so* disappointed in her pretty little granddaughter.

Life's a bitch, bitch, Kat thought. You'll have the tiniest inkling of what my fucking world of pain is like. You might even work out that you fucked up, seriously fucked up, when you went near Chris, you cunt.

She clicked Add Photo/Video, then linked to Claire01.jpg on the thumb drive to which she'd saved the photo.

What do you think of my selfie, bitches?! she wrote when it had uploaded.

She hovered the mouse over the post button, her fingertip starting to press down. It would be hilarious, Claire's semi-nude selfie, sent out to family and friends.

She went back to the photo with Nanna. The woman must be in her seventies at least. Kat didn't have grandparents. Her dad had died when she was fourteen. Her mum's parents had stayed in Canada and were both dead now anyway; Kat had never known them. She'd known her dad's father, he'd been a presence in her life until she was eight; Nanna Sharpe had died about five years ago. Claire was lucky to have a grandparent. Clearly her grandmother felt lucky to have her. And Kat was about to subject both of them to an exquisite agony.

A germ of uncertainty infected her. Bitch deserved it, she thought. *Deserved it.*

But how? If Chris was like that, not only cheating on his wife with me, but cheating on me with Claire, and maybe cheating on all three of us with some other compliant student via some other email account, who the fuck knew, then it didn't matter that it was Claire. All Claire was guilty of was falling in love with her uni tutor, and Kat herself, and plenty of her friends, had been guilty of exactly that.

Besides which, evidently the girl had good taste in men. 'I know, right?' she might have said to Claire. 'He's fucking awesome. And has a great cock.'

She pushed the mouse back over to Post, trying to will herself to do it.

Since when did I become evil? she wondered. Since when do I do this sort of thing?

Since this cunt slept with the man I wanted to spend my life with.

My rage and jealousy have turned me into someone who breaks into people's private accounts. Is this really me?

She closed her eyes, hard.

She couldn't do it. Claire was just an ordinary young woman. She hadn't done anything wrong, well, certainly not anything that Kat could criticise her for. Kat was twenty-eight, had more than half-a-dozen years on Claire, and was also having a relationship with a married man. She'd fallen in love with Chris. She couldn't exactly blame Claire for doing the same.

Fuck it, this is wrong. I hate myself being like this, she thought. After a moment, she closed the Facebook page, closed the browser with Claire's Gmail page open in it and closed the browser tab where all the pain and rage had started, with Chris's Gmail. She resolved to shut the computer down for a while, go offline, get some perspective back.

She pushed away from the computer, went into her room and lay on her bed, face down, feeling like crying, partly in anger at herself, partly in dismay at what Chris had turned her into.

In Kat's dream, she didn't know Chris, but she'd met him. Or perhaps he was someone else, a mixture of Chris and some other lover from her past. This Pseudo-Chris was living with someone else, but not Her, another woman, unidentified, to whom she was speaking about the Pseudo-Chris. Non-Her was explaining how wonderful Pseudo-Chris was, how he'd got her pregnant. He was nearby and could hear every word. Then the woman's phone began to ring, except it wasn't her phone, it was Kat's, and it was ringing outside the dream, IRL, in meatspace. She slowly reached for it in the dark on her bedside table. It was, according to the phone, 4.47 a.m. It was a private number, but she answered it anyway, not thinking until a second later that it might have been Chris trying to catch her by surprise.

'Hello?' she said groggily.

'Is that Katrina Sharpe?' said a female voice.

'Yeah.'

'Oh, hi, it's Emily from *Sunrise* here. I'm *really* sorry to call you so early. Look, we wanted to talk to someone about this Kittehsaurus Rox thing this morning and wondered if you were available. I know you've been on with us before a couple of years ago. Are you across Kittehsaurus Rox?'

Kitty saw what? What the fuck?

'I'm not fully across it, I've been a little busy,' she lied.

'That's okay—we wanted to talk about hacking in general and

what this means and what these hackers are all about, because this is a pretty big hack.'

Kat reached for her MacBook on the floor, flipped it open and began typing furiously into Google.

'Look, sure, I guess I'm available, I'll just need to make sure I'm fully up to date on the latest about it.'

'Great,' Emily said. 'Any initial thoughts?'

'Well, hacking is always a mixture of things, it's never one simple thing and I think it's a bit of a mistake to always assume one particular motivation for something like this,' she said by way of filler. Despite her entering 'kitty saurus', Google still produced a *Sydney Morning Herald* article, which she hurriedly scanned.

'But I think in this case,' she continued, 'it's pretty clear that this is a quite deliberately political group who are offering a pretty specific challenge to the Australian government, so it's a bit of a first in Australia because we haven't seen the kind of aggressive hacking and denial-of-service attacks that have been almost par for the course in the US.'

'Okay, that's great,' said Emily. 'Well, we're aiming to do the segment at around seven fifteen, so if you can be at the studios at around twenty to seven for make-up that'd be great. I'll send you an email to confirm this with my contact details—and we're happy to cover a cab fare to and from, of course.'

'Sure thing,' Kat said. 'I'll see you in a couple of hours.'

She hung up.

Kittehsaurus Rox. Fuck The What? What was this shit? She reread the article. They'd hacked Cabinet documents. Holy fuck, she thought. That was pretty impressive. She switched to Twitter and went looking for the account. Then she recalled the dream, but pushed it out of her mind.

A moment of panic seized Ewan, kneeling on the bed, erect, watched by Vanessa, lying beneath him. He cast around, then bent over to where his clothes were on the floor. He reached into the pockets of his pants and came out empty-handed.

'Fuck it,' he said, distraught. He turned and looked at Vanessa, who stared back expectantly then snapped her legs shut.

'You forgot them?' she said incredulously. 'Don't tell me you forgot them.'

He gave a wan smile. 'I think so. Fuck.'

'Or no fuck, in fact,' she said. 'You know I can't have any lying around.' She looked down at his penis, which was rapidly deflating, along with her mood.

'Hang on,' he said suddenly. 'Hang on.' He reached for his pants again, pulled out his wallet and opened it. 'Aha!' he said, and pulled out a condom. He checked the packet. 'Yep, still okay.'

'That's lucky,' Vanessa said with a smile. She reached out and flicked his penis. 'Only problem now is that.'

'Well I'm sure it's not gonna be a problem for too long.' He ran a finger along her thigh and then pushed it easily inside her. She closed her eyes and half smiled. The mere fact of her arousal was sufficient to excite him again, and he adeptly opened the packet one-handed and then rolled the condom onto his penis. She opened her legs, smiling, and he pushed himself between them and, guiding himself with his left hand, entered her. She closed her eyes and sighed, and he began thrusting. Then his phone rang.

'Oh for fuck's sake, Ewan!' said Vanessa, annoyed. 'I thought you turned it off.'

He listened to the ringtone. 'Fuck, it's Derek,' he said. He withdrew from her.

'Don't answer it!' she said, suddenly whispering, as if her husband could hear.

He looked at her plaintively, saying, 'I have to.' He heaved his legs over the side of the bed and raised the phone to his ear.

'Ewan Mazzoni?'

'Hi, Ewan; Derek here.'

'Hi, Mr Anderson, how—'

'Where are you?'

'I'm . . . I'm just seeing a contractor about the fence down by your wharf.'

He turned and made a 'what can I do?' expression at Vanessa. She glared back.

'Listen, I've just decided I'm bringing forward the trip to the US to late tonight. Can you talk to Gary about how that affects next week, please.'

'Sure, I'll call him.'

'He's right here. I'll put him on.'

He looked helplessly at Vanessa.

'Hello, Ewan?' came Prick's well-modulated tones.

'Hi.'

'Okay, we're going to move—'

Ewan's attention was distracted by another phone ringing. He stood bolt upright, as if electrocuted. Vanessa jumped as well.

'Have you got another call?' said Prick.

'Ah no, it's the contractor . . .'

Vanessa was stretching out of bed, legs splayed awkwardly, reaching for her handbag to get her phone. 'Fuck it!' said Vanessa in a loud whisper. 'That's Derek too.'

Ewan panicked a little, jumped over the bed, his penis flapping up and down as he did so, while Vanessa, equally inelegantly, was plucking her phone from her handbag. He found himself watching the way her breasts were hanging as she reached for the phone, and walked into the chair by the desk, stifling a cry of pain, then made it into the bathroom and closed the door while Vanessa took the call from Derek.

'Hi, Gary? Sorry about that.' He contemplated himself in the bathroom mirror, standing there naked with a condom slowly sliding off his penis.

'You got a pen?' said Prick.

'Ah, sure, let me just get it.' He looked around, then reopened the door to hear Vanessa engaged in a discussion about domestic arrangements with Derek. He grabbed a pen and hotel stationery off the desk and returned to the bathroom.

'Okay, go ahead,' he said.

'All right,' Prick began.

Vanessa had finished her call when he exited the bathroom, and was sitting up on the bed.

'Okay?' he said.

'Derek's moved the trip to the US forward to tonight. Wants to get some skiing in.'

'I know.'

She slid off the bed and began pulling her underwear on. 'I've got to get going. There's stuff to do.' She glanced at him. 'You look ridiculous.'

He looked down, then pulled the condom off himself with a snap, wincing.

She clipped her bra in front and then rotated it about and put her arms through the straps. 'This US trip fucks everything up,' she said, almost angrily.

'Tell me about it.'

'I'm sorry, hon, but I've got heaps to do before we go. Just heaps.' She looked at the time on the clock on the black bedside table.

Ewan sat on the bed, unmoving.

'I'll make it up to you,' she said, rising and heading into the bathroom. 'Promise.'

'I know,' he said. He began picking up his clothes. 'I wish that bastard of a husband of yours would stick to his plans.'

'Don't get nasty,' she said. She reappeared, collected her handbag and returned to the bathroom, leaving him to pull on his clothes. 'And what happened to you coming to the US with us? Wasn't that the plan?'

'The company has people over there.' He walked over to the bathroom, carrying his shoes.

'Not that it would've been any good,' she said, adjusting her hair. 'We would have spent all that time together and not been able to do anything.'

He stood watching her, marvelling at her transformation from the woman he had been fucking minutes ago to the elegant, businesslike woman fixing her hair in the mirror.

'Do they ever ask questions when you check out two hours after you check in?' she said.

'Two hours? I don't think we've ever managed two hours.' He watched her body, wanting her, feeling the urge to move behind her, encircle her in his arms, then slide inside her from behind. But her manner was such that he wondered what else had transpired while she was on the phone to Anderson. She began applying lipstick.

'Does your lipstick mean I don't get a goodbye kiss?'

She turned and walked over to him, and kissed him lightly on the lips. 'I'll see you at the airport tonight? You can at least see me off.'

'I'll try,' he said, feeling foolish.

'Make sure you wait a bit,' she said, heading to the door.

'Make sure you wait a bit.' Not 'I'm going to miss you.' Or 'Goodbye.' He thought, occasionally, about what exactly it was in him that she found attractive. Not due to any lack of self-esteem on his part, but Vanessa was not exactly your average woman, given she was married to an immensely wealthy man. She could be extraordinarily passionate about him, but could also be very offhand, which he found disconcerting. Circumstances did not help, either; the coitus interruptus had left him deeply annoyed.

He left the room and checked out, saying, 'I've had a change of plans,' as he always did, and went down into the car park below. He was actually intending to go see the contractor he'd contacted about Anderson's wharf, and so had brought his vehicle. He returned to it in a foul mood, and headed out onto New South Head Road. He drove slowly, methodically even, but as he had to slow down once he reached traffic, he grew angrier about the change of plans. 'Fucking arsehole!' he muttered, punching the steering wheel in frustration.

At the intersection with Darling Point Road—Vanessa and Derek's road—he halted the car at a red light, and when he moved away with the green, a car in the left-turn lane accelerated past him, trying to get sufficiently far ahead to change into his lane and avoid a truck parked about ten metres beyond the intersection. Ewan had moved smartly away at the light, and the other vehicle almost struck him as it moved into his lane. He pressed the horn hard, and then lost his temper altogether. 'Fucking prick!' he screamed, then pulled into the right-hand lane and accelerated until he was level with the car. Still leaning on his horn, he aimed the car leftwards, and the driver was forced to brake hard and let Ewan go ahead of him. He glared in his mirror and accelerated to get through a yellow light at the intersection with Mona Street, leaving the miscreant behind.

He hadn't seen the police car, of course, although it may not have tempered his response if he had. The first inkling he had was when he saw flashing blue in his mirror. Attention from the police didn't normally distress him, but he was in a truculent mood. He immediately pulled over in a bus zone, which he knew would annoy them, and watched them pull up behind. A tall young man in blue, who looked no older than eighteen, approached him.

'Excuse me, sir,' he said loudly, 'but do you realise you were speeding back there?'

The vehicle that had cut in on him went past, and sounded its horn as it did so. Ewan looked at the numberplate and memorised it. He was going to find the bastard and kill him.

He eyed the officer, waited several seconds, then replied so softly he could barely be heard above the traffic, 'Sorry?'

'I said you were speeding back there when you went through that intersection.'

He looked back at the officer. 'Yeah. I probably was.'

'Sorry, sir?'

'I said I probably was.'

'Why was that?'

'Well, another vehicle cut me off.'

'So you went over the speed limit.'

He frowned, as though he didn't quite understand the question. 'The speed limit?'

The policeman rolled his eyes in exasperation.

'Can I see your driver's licence, sir?' he said.

Ewan was quite happy to show him his driver's licence. He wasn't even going to bother wasting one of the good ones, just one of the fake ones would do. Nor did he mind them knowing the registration of the car. He'd made sure the car wasn't registered to himself or Veldtech, but to a randomly selected Queensland address, as was the spare pair of plates that he liked to carry around.

'My driver's licence?' he said to the officer in an astonished tone.

'Yes, sir,' said the policeman, now more irritated.

Ewan shifted in his seat and pulled out one of his driving wallets, from which, making sure he only gripped it by the edges, he extracted one of the fake licences. He handed it to the officer.

'It wouldn't be any good if everyone who got cut off did what you did, would it?' the policeman said, taking the licence.

'I think that depends, officer,' Ewan said, in a rather different tone of voice to the confused one he'd been using.

The officer turned and walked back to his car. Ewan observed him in his side mirror, watched one car go by, then quickly started the engine and accelerated out of the bus stop, just ahead of an oncoming stream of traffic. He drove rapidly down to the next corner and turned left just as the police car began flashing its lights, then left again. The police would have no chance of finding him after they pushed their way into the traffic and around the corner, though he rued the waste of a pair of numberplates, which he'd now have to change.

Still, it had improved his mood considerably.

It was a gorgeous day, Em thought. The weather was spring-perfect, the people on her train were inoffensive, there were no hold-ups or delays, the queue for a coffee seemed a little shorter and the coffee itself tasted nicer. And Craig was off sick, probably for the rest of the week, doubtless from some nasal-related injury. Everything was right with the world.

While bolting a cup of coffee and twenty milligrams of Cipramil—breakfast of champions—she'd watched Katrina Sharpe, whose book she had bought and devoured last year, talking about KSR on *Sunrise*, which felt very, very cool. '*It seems that Australia has lost its cyber innocence,*' the *Sunrise* host had declared, which made her laugh aloud.

'*We don't know who this group is, but its mission statement is similar to that of other online activist groups, obviously like Anonymous, but also like WikiLeaks and other more clearly political actors in this area,*' Sharpe had said. '*And from what I can tell, they appear Australian. I mean, like, normally you can tell when some of these overseas groups do stuff here like denial-of-service attacks on government websites, they don't really understand how our government works. But this seems more like the work of a local group.*'

@KSRComms had over two hundred mentions and several hundred retweets and its follower count had gone over two thousand. Among the mentions were a good twenty or more requests for interviews from journalists, including one from @kat_sharpe.

Without bothering to tell Tom, who'd purposefully given her a free hand with creating the image of a hacker group, she decided that a little publicity wouldn't hurt. She wanted to talk to Sharpe. There were lots of mainstream media journalists and TV shows wanting to speak, but she liked the idea of just using one person to communicate with the outside world.

She followed Sharpe—so far the only other account @KSRComms followed—and DM'd her.

D @kat_sharpe Happy to conduct i/v via Twitter We respect your work and will only talk to you.

Then added:

Tomorrow 1pm.

Kirsty from Mark Levers's office called her as she was closing the account. Kirsty was a target of particular vehemence from the normally easygoing Jayde, who'd had some sort of run-in with her in the past and insisted Kirsty was an attractive airhead employed purely because of her looks and impressive bust.

'Hi, it's Kirsty from General Levers's office, Emma. Just ringing to say we've got that video from Mark's address to the conference on Monday? If you want to come up and get it?'

She couldn't help imagining Kirsty sitting at her desk, wearing her usual short skirt, 'flashing her high beams at every guy in the place', as Jayde immortally put it, hunting and pecking at a keyboard. Jayde could be forensically mean when she wanted to be.

'Sure, Kirsty, I'll be right up.'

She took the elevator up to twenty-seven and went around to Levers's office. Kirsty—dressed rather soberly and contrary to her reputation in a jacket and high-necked top—handed her a USB.

Em took it back to her desk, loaded it on to her PC, then copied it onto another USB from her desk and left the original on Tom's desk, before walking around to hand the spare USB to Nathan Welles, slumped in his seat like he had been in the meeting, but with his elbow resting on his chair and his hand on his chin staring at his screen. James had stayed over last night and she'd endured— or enjoyed, she couldn't be sure which—his rather tepid efforts at lovemaking. Her mind had wandered while he was fucking her, and she'd found herself, out of the blue, thinking about seeing Nathan in the lift, about his gorgeous eyes, what he might look like naked and what he might be like in bed.

The mildest of thrills went through her when he greeted her. He gave her a smile and thanked her, but she couldn't come up with any way to extend the conversation.

THURSDAY
19 NOVEMBER

Rachael had a habit of wiggling her pen between her teeth while thinking. She also, occasionally, poked her tongue out slightly when she began to write something, like a small child. Nathan thought it was unbearably cute, especially for such a serious woman.

'I brought some sugar,' he said. 'I didn't know how much you liked. They usually put it in down there.'

'What is *with* that? I hate that. I put my own bloody sugar in. I'm not a child.' She scribbled on a piece of paper with her tongue momentarily poking out.

He removed the lid and sipped his tea with a smile. He'd spotted Angela with the man-child 'Todd' again on the way down to Antonio's. She'd raised an eyebrow at him, instantly knowing what he was thinking. 'Todd' was Todd Brown—could there *be* a more boring name?—from Sustainability Solutions. Nathan now hated him. Actually, *hate* was the New Age, caring and sharing utopia-disturbed-only-by-the-steady-singing-of-'Kumbaya' description of how he felt. He wanted to thump the little shit. But he'd also bumped into Erica Whitecross the day before and secured her agreement to have coffee one day.

Rachael proceeded to add sugar to her coffee and stir it with her pen. Having had some time to settle in, she had loosened up quite a bit, and even laughed at some half-baked quip he'd made earlier in the week.

'Now, you've got that corporate plan meeting at lunchtime. Can you wing that or do you want me to take you through it? Last one was about a month ago but it was just preliminary stuff.'

'No it's fine, I'll wing it.' She glanced out the door of the office. 'Close the door?'

His immediate, involuntary thought, as he reached over and pushed the door shut, was that he could fuck her on the desk with the door closed, preferably from behind, like with Angela, pushing her skirt up.

Fuck, you are sad, he told himself.

'Brian wants a reference,' she said.

'For where?'

'Some promotion in Intel.'

'That's good.'

'It's not good,' she said. 'I don't know the first thing about him.'

He gestured. 'Yeah, but I mean it'd be good to get rid of him.'

'You might have to help me draft it.'

He shrugged and sipped his tea. 'No probs.'

'Can we afford to lose him? They won't allow me to replace him.'

'At the moment we can afford to, as long as you can manage Eve all right.'

'Hmmm. Can you do something up for me and send it? About Brian, I mean?'

'Sure. Oh, by the way, apparently General Levers gave a talk the other day based on the op-ed we inputted to. I've got a copy. I suppose we should watch it to see how he played it.'

'You can give me the greatest-hits version can't you?'

'I'll go watch it now.'

'Okay. Thanks for the coffee.'

Nathan opened the door, went back to his desk and sat down, a trifle bored. He picked up the USB stick the Amazonian girl from Tom Dao's section had given him, plugged it in and opened it up. There was a large .avi file, a text file and what looked like a browser. He opened up the text file. There was a string of letters and numbers, followed by another string, then the letters '@KSRComms' and

'%kcatta%', then what looked like the text of an email to 'Donahue, Laurie (MP)' from Sheena.MASTERS@ag.gov.au.

> *Hi Laurie—AG asked me to forward draft cabsub to you, expect this to come before Caucus Tuesday week after Cabinet Monday. This is NOT final but close to and guts of sub are there, will send copy of coord comment (assume PM&C/Treas/ Fin support) and brief on key talking points. Not for circulation. Thx Sheena.*

He began reading through the text below, and instantly recognised it. It was the material that had been leaked by that Kittehsaurus Rox outfit.

He sat back for a moment and stared at the screen, then went looking online for the Pastebin file that had the original KSR release and, after a moment, pulled it up. It was immediately clear that the material released by KSR didn't have the email part. All it contained was the rest of the document.

'That's odd,' he said, to no one in particular.

He re-examined the text, looking for what he was missing. There was an email, followed by the text that had been released by the hackers. Nothing else. There was no mistake, no context that somehow cancelled out the fact that he had a thumb drive with the original version of a document the leaking of which had caused huge controversy.

He shut the document hastily and glanced around.

What the fuck do I do? he asked himself. What is this? That blonde giantess, what was her name . . . Emma. She looked too absurdly timid to be responsible for something like the leak. But maybe that was her cover. *It's always the quiet ones.* And if she *was* leaking to a hacker of some kind, where was she getting the material from?

It didn't make any sense. They'd be found out, for sure.

He copied the contents of the thumb drive onto his PC then ejected it, thinking it would be better not to draw suspicion. He pulled it from his PC, stood, and walked up the floor. Emma had said she was on the same floor, up the other end. He wandered around until he saw her long blonde hair. She saw him approaching and gave him a broad smile. Fuck, he thought. I'm going to have to play a very straight bat here. He tried his best to affect insouciance, despite worrying that his expression was giving away that he knew something he evidently wasn't supposed to know.

'Hey,' he said neutrally. 'Just returning this. Thanks.'

'Cool, thanks,' she replied brightly, still smiling. She paused, and he was about turn away, when she suddenly spat out, 'What did you think of Levers's speech?'

The question threw him a little. He hadn't even started watching the video. 'Er, I only got partway through. He's not the most compelling public speaker. I'll watch the rest later this arvo.'

'Cool,' she said, still with the smile.

'Anyway, thanks.'

'Anytime!'

Em placed her coffee carefully next to the laptop on Tom's table, angled to ensure no one walking past the office could see the screen, started the virtual PC, logged in to the VPNs and then went looking for the browser to log in to Twitter, and realised she hadn't put the thumb drive in. She went outside to her desk and retrieved it, and hurried back; it was 12.59.

At 1.01 p.m. Kat Sharpe DM'd her.

We still on for an i/v? Kat

We're good to go, she replied, after waiting about thirty seconds.

OK, who's we? Who is Kittehsaurus Rox?

Em had diligently prepared the cover story of KSR, and found it surprisingly enjoyable to craft a complete lie, then think about which parts weren't realistic and fix them.

We're a group of like-minded individuals of different talents who believe in the need for transparency.

How many?

That's classified. But we're not a large group. Large groups can be a problem, some of us have found.

Where are you based? I mean location wise?

Most of us are in Australia.

How do you work? By consensus? Who controls the Twitter account?

There are a couple of us here in a room and a couple of others are participating via IRC. 1/2

We operate by full consensus, even if that means sometimes it gets frustrating and slow. 2/2

Why did you attack the Australian government?

Em sipped her coffee. This was good, she thought. She was having fun. And Kat's questions were good.

Like all governments the Australian government is committed to a surveillance state. 1/2

We intend to subject the Australian government to the same surveillance that it wants to impose on its citizens. 2/2

How did you hack into the government's CABNET system? That's quite a feat.

We have some very talented individuals.

There was a pause. Sharpe was evidently waiting for some more information, which wouldn't be forthcoming.

When will the next release be?

A few hours. I'll DM you before everyone else if you like.

Tom had told her that morning that he had a new release ready to go. She was about to send the message but realised she'd made a mistake. She replaced *I'll* with *We'll* and sent it.

Sharpe replied instantly. *That would be fantastic. What do you say in response to the Attorney-General saying you should be jailed?*

She paused a bit longer than usual. Tom came into the office. She had only caught the tail end of the Attorney-General's comments on television.

We haven't seen the Attorney-General's comments. What did he say?

That the AFP was investigating the leak, would find the perpetrators and they would be jailed.

The response of the surveillance state is predictable. We are monitoring the AFP's investigation.

You mean you have hacked into the AFP as well?

We are everywhere. Everywhere and, as the AFP will discover, nowhere.

Em decided that was a rhetorical high point on which to end the interview.

That's all for now. We will be in contact.

OK thanks for the interview really appreciate it, and if you DM me the next release that'd be great.

'Are you working on Project X?' said Tom.

'Yep.' She began shutting down everything. 'I was just . . . Actually, don't worry.'

'Okay, I'll give you the latest document. Leave the laptop set up. Is that your thumb drive or mine?'

She looked at the thumb drive. 'Ah . . . that's mine.'

'Okay, leave it in and I'll transfer what the whistleblower got me onto it.'

'Cool,' she said, rising. She went out to her desk. It was at that point she realised the thumb drive was the same one that she'd given to Nathan Welles.

The boy was apologetic. There'd been a mix-up in heaven, some sort of bureaucratic bungle. He shouldn't have died when Ewan shot him. Someone had erred and marked his file for death. The thing was, they couldn't simply reverse the error. Death was death. But what they could do was allow him a short time to come back and say goodbye to his family and friends.

They were delighted to see him again, naturally. He looked splendid, and happy. All was well on the other side, he reported. But he did miss them, and was pleased to have the chance to talk with them one more time, to say farewell. They gathered around him.

It may have been because they were so happy to see him again that they ignored Ewan. They had nothing to say to the man who had killed the boy. He'd been asked to attend as well, in acknowledgement of the error; there he stood, uncomfortable in the role, while the boy's family and friends formed a tight circle around the dead child.

He turned from the gathering and looked outside. It was early morning, the first streaks of sunlight stretching across the road outside the house. Then he saw them, one or two at first, then a large group: men, women and children, clad in black, walking backwards, their long shadows stretching like black fingers towards him. He forgot the gathering around the boy and watched half in fascination, half in fear.

When he awoke, it was with the conviction that the boy had died. He sat up in bed. It was nearly midnight. The boy was dead, wasn't he? Surely he'd died. He heaved himself out of bed and walked down the short corridor that led to his lounge room, where he had left the light on. He had a thing about total darkness, always had, and couldn't sleep unless there was a light on somewhere. He filled a glass with water in the kitchen. It took a moment for the dream confusion to dissipate. The boy wasn't dead, he told himself. He'd lost his leg. He wasn't dead. The room was partly illuminated by the lights from the city, even at this distance. He stood there and watched them. The boy hadn't died, he told himself. It was only a dream.

He wanted to tell Vanessa about the boy, for some reason, to explain himself. What would she do? She might reject him. But he wanted her to know, to fully understand the sort of man she was sleeping with. The sort who shot kids. What else should he volunteer about himself? That he used to use prostitutes? What about the man he'd beaten half to death in Germany in a drunken rage? Or the insurance scam he'd pulled off, worth ten thousand pounds? Ah, Ewan. So much to reveal.

The boy wasn't dead, surely. He'd lost his leg. Yet the dream had been convincing. Didn't dreams offer some truth beyond normal everyday experience? Maybe the boy had died, somewhere in Iraq.

'He's not dead,' he said aloud to reassure himself. 'He lost his leg. He's not dead.'

Why did Vanessa bring out the urge to confess, to spill all his darkest secrets, the moments when he'd been at his worst? He wandered over to the door that led out onto the balcony, looking at the Harbour Bridge and the city beyond.

Because he was in love with her.

Em lay in bed, in darkness, turning the day's events round and round in her head. She hadn't said anything to Tom. Surely Nathan hadn't seen anything. He could hardly have returned the thumb drive to her so casually.

He knows all about you.

Dark Voice was having a field day, conjuring all sorts of visions, repeating how all her careful security measures had gone for nought because she was so keen to impress a man, a man who barely knew she existed.

Oh boy, did it not want to let her forget that.

So anxious to impress him you gave away the whole thing. Why didn't you just go up and tell him about it to his face?

She'd put aside her worry long enough to put up the second release. Tom's whistleblower had secured an Opposition email involving a note from a staff member of the shadow defence minister on the briefing he'd had from the US Assistant Secretary of State for East Asian and Pacific Affairs. Em had scarcely bothered to read it through before posting with a preamble that KSR was a non-partisan organisation dedicated to transparency of all elements of government, particularly dealing with the US military–industrial complex. This time she ended the preamble with the phrase she'd used in the interview with Kat Sharpe, *we are everywhere and nowhere.*

Except that's not really true. Nathan knows where you are.

She'd DM'd Sharpe, who had the kudos of revealing the new leak on Twitter. The account had been bombarded with renewed requests for interviews, but she was happy just with Sharpe for now, particularly given what had happened with Nathan. In fact, at the moment she didn't really want to talk to anyone.

What if Tom finds out? He's gonna kill you.

Oh, god. She put her hands to her head.

Literal face palm.

James shifted next to her, sound asleep.

Tom won't find out. Surely. There's nothing to find out. Nathan doesn't know anything. She shifted position in the bed, listening to James's breathing. FUCK. Everything was going just fine, she thought. And I fucked it up completely.

You fucked it up all right.

I fucked it up.

Distantly she could hear a . . . something, just on the edge of audibility, either someone talking or a television. It wasn't, fortunately, the woman who lived upstairs whom she could sometimes hear fucking.

I screwed it up.

She felt the urge to cry coming on, and then pushed herself out of bed with determination. She was not going to wait quietly while she was overcome with misery. She went over to her handbag and pulled out a blister pack of Panadeine Extras.

Just half, she'd decided. Just half of one of my fifteen-milligram friends. This isn't a major emergency. These things need to be used in moderation otherwise they lose their potency. And it would help her sleep.

She pushed out a tablet, broke it in half and went to the kitchen sink and swallowed it with a glass of water.

Instead of returning to bed, she went and lay down on the couch. Besides, she thought darkly, if Nathan really did know anything she could use it as a pretext for offering him sex. 'You could destroy my life and put me in jail! I'll do anything if you won't—particularly anything involving sex.'

That'll make him more eager to turn you in.

Maybe when they were both working back late. She could go around to his area, past row upon row of empty workstations, no sound but the distant stir of the aircon, to discover him in his boss's office. That would be nice, to fuck him on the desk of that stupid boss of his, to undo his belt and push his trousers down and feel his dick, to kiss him, to feel his lips on her throat, on her ear, to feel his kisses on her breasts. She slid her hand inside her pants and began rubbing her clitoris gently, imagining taking Nathan inside her.

You're about to go to jail and you're fapping?

Fuck off, I'm distracting myself.

The clock ticked over to 1 a.m. There wasn't a sound to be heard. She pushed her pants down and glumly masturbated, thinking of Nathan.

FRIDAY
20 NOVEMBER

'Diplomatic immunity!' cried Derek.

'It's just been revoked! How are ya, Derek?'

Steve Lydecker was short, but intensely muscular; his suit barely seemed to contain him, as if he'd been shoehorned into it. He pumped Derek's hand in a way Derek found slightly painful. To save time, he had taken to anticipating Steve's jokes about his South African accent in order to get them out of the way.

The conference room overlooked the outdoor pool, which was covered in deference to the weather and, in particular, the six inches of snow that had fallen in the last three days, an unexpectedly early start to the season that Derek had been keen to exploit.

'Where are you guys?' said Lydecker, once he'd released Derek's hand from his iron grip. They stood next to the fireplace, in which three logs were steadily burning.

'Presidential suite,' Derek replied offhandedly.

'The one with the butler? Fuck, man.'

'Well, Ness and I are travelling on our own dime.'

'Where is she?'

'Snowboarding, I assume. Or sleeping off the jetlag.'

Frank Zwingli entered. Unlike Derek and Lydecker, he'd dressed down and wore a casual shirt under his jacket. He rolled his wheelchair towards them.

'Hey, guys,' he said. He tossed a folder from his lap onto the long table that occupied the centre of the room and then gestured to the black-clad young Asian woman standing next to the table on which two ornate coffee jugs and assorted necessities were placed. 'Black with two. And keep 'em comin', okay?'

'How 'bout that fuckin' snow, huh?' he said, rolling over to the fireplace. He shook their hands.

'What, it never snows in LA?' said Derek.

'Only in the mountains,' he said. 'How long you been here?'

'We flew in yesterday. It's only a short visit. We've got a few things on in Sydney at the moment.'

'Fuckin' tell me about it,' said Zwingli. 'See the stock kept above a hundred and twenty yesterday?'

'If it falls any further, I'm gonna put my wife's inheritance into it,' said Lydecker. 'A hundred and twenty and change is great value. Where's, ah, Mikey?'

Mike Armstrong was chairman of ETS, and a former deputy Secretary of State under Dubya. He was also head of the board's audit subcommittee. He'd had a fundraiser for some Republican pal in Aspen and had scheduled a subcommittee meeting to coincide with it.

The young Asian woman approached Zwingli with a coffee.

Zwingli looked a little out of sorts, most likely because of the RTSAD debacle, which had accelerated the share price fall. Zwingli had long championed a combat helmet with a live data feed capacity, a project that had sucked in tens of millions in developmental costs because of problems in aggregating and distributing data. ETS had eventually won an $850 million contract for what was called a 'real-time situational awareness display' helmet, designed to operate, as far as Derek could tell, like a military version of Google Glass. Only, ETS hadn't been able to get the unit to function effectively. Instead, they'd hired a game company to put together a video of how 'Ratsads' were intended to function in combat. Somewhere along the line, the Pentagon had been told it was actual footage of a working prototype rather than a mock-up. A whistleblower had revealed that it wasn't.

This, and the follow-up at a Congressional hearing, had been somewhat embarrassing, partly because ETS actually owned a game manufacturer and no one had thought to use them to fabricate the video, instead of an outside firm.

Armstrong entered the room. He was in his sixties, deeply tanned with white hair, wearing a dark grey suit and green tie. He was trailed by another man in a suit and a woman with glasses, long hair and a navy suit.

'Hello, fellas,' he said in a rich baritone with a New England accent. 'You know Gene?' He gestured towards the man in the suit, Gene Langford, the CFO. 'And this is Candy Mellon, the new head of audit.'

Candy Mellon shook hands with each of them, saying, 'Delighted to meet you.' Anderson noticed she had a strong New York accent.

'Cream and two sugars please, Amy,' Armstrong said to the Asian woman, glancing at her nametag. 'Derek, it's wonderful to see you. How are you? How's Vanessa?'

'We're good, Mike,' said Derek genially. 'We don't usually get down to Aspen. We're normally at Vail.'

'Vail's too expensive for my simple tastes,' Armstrong said absurdly, smiling.

'Not because you never forgave Ford for losing to Carter?'

Armstrong laughed. 'Gerry was actually a great skier. Had this reputation as a klutz, but he was a great footballer and skier. Anyway, well, let's get down to it,' he said, taking a seat. 'I'm sure we've all got some snow sports we'd rather be doing.' He waved apologetically at Zwingli. 'Sorry, Frank. Candy, on my right, please.'

Candy was already positioned to his right, and slid into the chair next to his. This seemed to give credence to the rumour, which had reached Derek all the way across in Sydney, that Armstrong was having an affair with her.

'How was the fundraiser, Mike?' said Steve.

'Oh, good, good,' he said, nodding. 'You know, Bob is a good man. A sound man. He understands our priorities. Tough race, though, no matter who the Dems pick. They've rigged that district. There were some goddamn protesters at the event too. Something about Bob's record in Iraq. Tried to disrupt it.'

'That's a direct assault on free speech,' said Lydecker. 'We should drone those sorts of assholes.'

'Urban Ordnance has a couple of products coming onto the market in the new year that can be drone-mounted,' said Zwingli, referring to a start-up that ETS had recently acquired in an effort to bolster its 'kinetic' credentials. 'They're already bidding for contracts with, uh, San Francisco and . . . Seattle, I think. Low-impact ordnance for use in built-up environments.'

'Needs Environmental Control's cellphone-shutdown system,' said Lydecker. 'Otherwise you just get a lot of phone-camera imagery of human–ordnance interaction that can look bad taken out of context and in social media.'

'You always fret about social media,' said Zwingli.

'How are things down under, Derek?' Armstrong said.

Derek sat down and began removing a thick pile of papers from a brown leather portfolio. 'Well, I'll be honest, Mike, it's tough. We're letting some good people go.'

Armstrong nodded. 'I appreciate that. These are tough times right across the company. You all see the stock price. Down a little more this week, although not so bad against the Nasdaq. But you know,' he said, looking around the group, not just at Derek, 'I really think this is a critical time in more ways than one. We've prospered when the going has been good. Now that times are more challenging, this is when we make our mark. The lessons we learn now will stand us in good stead for the future. So, I know it's tough. There are a lot of fine people clearing out their desks in Marshall, and Dallas, and Sydney, and in Vienna and Birmingham.

'We're working hard to try to source more revenue, we really are. Agencies are anxious to make sure no one finds out about their programs. No one wants to look like the NSA and have their PowerPoint slides produced in the press. So they're spending more money on trying to stop leaks, which is good. There are some opportunities in that space, but we do have to be much more innovative. Anyway, let's get to work.'

Kittehsaurus Rox was all Kat's. She was now the official expert on the crisis roiling the government. After the second release, Fairfax, with whom she'd already agreed terms for a piece on the interview, had rung her to ask her to bring it forward a day, so she'd spent the previous afternoon writing the interview up into an article. She'd also doubled her price for it. Kittehsaurus Rox was regularly trending on Twitter in Australia. She'd done two interviews overnight with the BBC and done two morning TV slots and had an evening news interview booked. In the cab on the way into the ABC she'd fielded two more calls for interviews in the same timeslot. She'd agreed to one from 2GB and then accepted a Skype interview with a Canadian TV news bulletin and had to call back 2GB and beg off.

'Christ,' she said in frustration between calls. 'I'm turning into a fucking public intellectual.'

The second release, if anything, was bigger than the first. It wasn't a Cabinet document, but it had some confidential material conveyed by the Americans to the shadow defence minister, including lobbying on behalf of Boeing and Raytheon. 'Australia must pull its weight when it comes to the task of developing new weapons systems. Our defence industries can't be left to lie fallow,' an American diplomat was quoted as saying. And best of all, the diplomat had made some snarky comments about the foreign minister. 'Sometimes seems a bit out of his depth' and 'not particularly well known in Washington'.

'A private conversation that should never have been revealed,' the US ambassador had said in response that morning. 'Nonetheless, the comments, while reflecting the frankness and directness that two close friends such as Australia and the US are able to use with one another, were not appropriate. Assistant Secretary Fearnley will be calling the foreign minister today to discuss the matter and clear the air.'

There was speculation the Secretary of State had called the Prime Minister to apologise to her as well.

The release was thus an embarrassment bomb that had inflicted maximum damage on everyone. A national security journalist in *The Australian* had demanded long prison sentences for those responsible for the hacking. 'They are rapidly making public policy impossible,' he'd thundered. 'The security of the nation and the viability of the public policy process is at stake.'

Taskforce Gideon had been established to hunt down the hackers, involving a range of law enforcement and intelligence agencies. Given that the Cabinet distribution system had been hacked, the Australian Cyber Security Centre was leading the investigation into how the government's systems were being breached. It was the ACSC's first big case since being established in 2014.

'Kat Sharpe, who is Kittehsaurus Rox and what do they want?'

She had the answer to that down pat, so often had she been asked it. Fuck yeah, rote interviews.

Having done ABC News Breakfast from a booth at Ultimo and then gone upstairs to do a radio interview, she was now sitting in the cafeteria in the ABC, monitoring Twitter and checking emails. Among Kat's tweets was one from what appeared to be a newly formed 'Support KSR' group, which wanted to know if she'd speak at a rally. The boy public servant with the teddy-bear tie had emailed her asking her out 'for a catch-up over coffee'. She admired his courage, and deleted the mail. She had trended on Twitter at 7.20 a.m.; some haters were starting to complain about her ubiquity on the subject, which she herself mildly agreed with. But everyone else was playing catch-up; Amy Dinh seemed to have become confused and thought the Opposition used CABNET as well; the political junkies were piling in on her about it on Twitter.

Your amazing arse won't save you now, Kat thought.

Awesome dump of material. This is huge, she'd DM'd KSR, anxious to keep the dialogue going. She needed another coffee, badly, given she'd had only a couple of hours' sleep, and went over to order one, clutching her phone. While she stood behind someone she vaguely knew from TV in the queue, the phone rang, from a blocked number. Doubtless another media request, she thought. If it was radio, she'd knock it back.

'Kat, it's Chris. Don't hang up.'

Looking back later, she decided her reaction hadn't been that bad. Not her conscious reaction, when she opened her mouth to reply, but her true reaction, the moment she processed that it was his voice. Yes, her heart jumped. Yes, she froze, felt a body-wide wave of cold. Yes, there was that same jagged ball of tension in her stomach as she'd had when she first saw the emails. But, maybe because she'd been preoccupied with everything else, she recovered quickly.

Breathe, she told herself, wait, don't rush.

She knew what she was going to say to him. She'd decided days before that, should she ever have to speak to him again, she'd say something very simple and hang up.

And she knew her resolution would be tested, that it was easy enough to decide in advance what she'd say, but when the moment came, when he was actually speaking to her, it would be hard. And there he was, his voice, *him*, the voice that she loved to listen to, eyes closed, forever, wrapped up in it. And suddenly it was hard, too hard, impossible, to say what she had told herself dozens of times, what she had rehearsed dozens of times, to say.

'I don't know why you've done this, but I want you to know I love you Kat, so, so much.'

She closed her eyes. Her breathing was surprisingly slow, she thought, but her heart was pounding.

'I,' she began, faltered, then picked up again. 'I don't want to talk to you. Don't . . . don't contact me again. Have fun with Claire.'

She listened for a moment, and as he began to speak, she made herself, forced herself, through a ferocious effort of will, to hang up.

Everything was still for a moment.

Then: Holy fuck, I did it, she thought. HOLY FUCK! I fucking did it!

She'd expected, while gaming all the scenarios, to feel terrible after she'd done it, but she felt elated. More than elated, better than elated. She felt strong, and in control, like she'd been subjected to a long-feared ordeal, a test that she'd known was coming for a long time, one she'd dreaded she would fail, and she'd come through it, survived it, intact.

Then she realised she'd been asked twice for her order and was holding up the ABC coffee queue.

It was Em's turn to hover outside Antonio's, waiting for Tom. She grabbed Tom's arm as he came out of coffee shop and steered him over towards the road.

'I need to tell you something.'

'What?' His face screwed up in concern.

'Okay,' she said, steeling herself. She'd resolved when she woke up that she had to tell Tom, no matter what, that that was the only responsible course of action. She also felt slightly better about everything, partly because she'd had a delayed response to the codeine and felt quite happy when she got up. 'I'm so sorry about this. We might, *might*, have a problem. The other day I gave that guy from Rachael Ambrose's section'—she wanted to suggest Nathan was barely even known to her—'a thumb drive with the speech by Mark Levers on it. And it was the same thumb drive I've been using for Project X.'

Dark Voice was still having a field day with this, repeating incessantly that she'd either go to jail or lose her job.

Tom's face didn't change expression. 'Shit,' he said eventually, his gaze flicking away for a second. 'Shit. What did he say?'

'He didn't say anything. I don't know if he saw it or whether he just looked at the video file.'

Think of it this way, at least you might be able to lose weight in jail, Dark Voice offered helpfully.

'This is Nathan Welles?'

The name sent a thrill through her, in spite of her predicament.

'Yep.'

You are so sad.

'Fuck,' said Tom. 'Fuck. So . . . we don't know whether he knows anything.'

'No. Sorry. I fucked up. I'm really sorry.'

'So you bloody should be, Em. Fuck. This is a disaster.'

'I'm sorry,' was all she could say.

'So he's still got the USB stick.'

She stared at him for a moment. A truck went by using air brakes, drowning out any attempt at conversation.

'No, no. He gave it back to me.'

Tom's shoulders slumped, but in relief. 'Okay, so we have it back. Okay. That's good . . . that's . . . what did he say?'

'Nothing, he just gave it back. Said thanks.'

He turned and gazed at the traffic, thinking. 'Okay,' he said. He rubbed his forehead. 'So we might be all right.'

'Yes. Or not,' she said, devil's advocate against herself. 'He might have seen the first file your whistleblower got.'

Tom looked at her oddly for a second. 'That's all that's on it?'

'No, there's the browser, and there're the account details for the Twitter account.'

'But there shouldn't be any history on the browser.'

'There's not. There's just the email we put up and the Twitter details, I guess.'

'Okay, let me think about it.'

'I'm sorry, Tom.'

'It's all right, we'll work through it.'

She went upstairs, dispirited, although Tom's matter-of-fact approach to the problem comforted her; he had always had a cool head in a crisis, with an almost unnatural calm, even during periods of maximum stress. He had a way of breaking down crises into manageable components that could be worked on one at a time, a skill she was impressed by and had made herself study.

She unlocked her desk drawer and took out the USB stick, determined to see exactly what Nathan would have seen, to see whether there was something she'd missed that might exonerate her, that she could offer Tom as a way out. On the USB stick there was the huge Levers .avi she'd wanted to give to Nathan as a conversation starter, and there was a .txt file and the browser. The text file had the full email that had provided the basis for the first release, as well as the log-in details for the Twitter account. It would have been obvious if he'd compared the release to the text that there was more there than had been put out by KSR. And if that didn't confirm it, the Twitter account did.

But for the moment the worst was over. She'd confessed to Tom, and he didn't think it was an absolute disaster. Apart from her tiredness, she felt significantly better than she had in the middle of the night.

Jayde stuck her head over her partition. 'Are you coming or not?' she demanded.

Em stared at her for a moment, perplexed. 'Of course,' she said, remembering and leaping up. There was a divisional meeting up on level twenty-five to discuss the staff cuts, and everyone from Corporate and Marketing was expected to attend. She followed Jayde over to the lifts, where Jayde's boss David caught up with them, so the three of them filed into the meeting room together and sat down at the end of a row in the middle. She could see Adriana and Craig two rows ahead, but thankfully Craig was well out of sniffshot. At the front of the room, barely visible above the audience, were the heads of each of the divisions, chatting among themselves, the head of Research, boyish, tieless, looking slightly out of place.

'So what will we hear, boss? I hear all middle managers are going to be sacked,' said Jayde. She refused to take David seriously at all, and he was seemingly powerless to compel her to show him the slightest respect. He turned and looked at her.

'I'm sure there'll be some staff reductions, Jayde,' he managed. 'Is your CV up to date?'

'You think working for you is something to boast about?'

'Putting up with you sure is.'

'And who'll get your coffee when I'm gone?'

The room's seating was rapidly taken up, and latecomers were having to stand at the back and along the sides. The head of Marketing entered the room and walked quickly to the front of the room to join the other executives, her distinctive red curls bouncing as she walked. Then Nathan and Rachael walked past, followed by a young man, looking for seats. They stopped about three rows along from where Jayde, David and Em were sitting, and then Nathan turned and whispered something to Rachael, who smirked. The two of them then retired to the wall behind them, with the young man next to them. A couple of women walked past them, one of whom, an attractive girl with short dark hair, said hi to Nathan, who returned her greeting. Em noticed he instantly looked at her arse once she was past him. The women ended up standing a bit further along.

Jayde and David were now arguing over how often Jayde got him coffee.

Nathan had dressed down today, Em observed. He wore a blue shirt, with the sleeves rolled up just below his elbows, black trousers and black runners. He leaned back against the wall, arms folded, his head tilted towards Rachael. She still didn't look quite right, in Em's view. She had a thin-lapelled white jacket with very low-cut matching pants and a brown, wide-necked top. Wide necks were, Em acknowledged, currently In, but there was no way Rachael, with her short neck and lack of height, should've been wearing one, as it just seemed to draw attention to her short stature.

She looks a damn sight hotter than you.

'Thanks everyone for coming,' began the head of Marketing. 'We've called this meeting to keep everyone informed of issues that might be arising in the new year, especially relating to the half-yearly results and the rationalisation process. Traditionally, this sort of thing has been done via email, but we've decided it's time to talk face to face.'

'Must be serious,' muttered Jayde. 'Hasn't Curly lost weight?'

'Stress,' said Em. 'The best way to get weight off and keep it off.'

How would you know?

She hadn't been worried about her weight lately, not since she'd started the KSR thing, and had been surprised the previous morning to discover she'd lost nearly half a kilo. Today, however, she'd felt hungry all day despite having a pastry for both morning tea and lunch. Hungry and guilty, about the Nathan thing and about eating so much.

'Now it's clear from the numbers at this point,' said the Marketing head, continuing her spiel, 'that we will be looking to reduce costs in the second half of the year. Let me say that upfront. There will have to be cost savings. But the magnitude of those savings will be determined by—'

You have so little discipline.

I was bloody starving and it was distracting me from my work.

The work you fucked up by trying to impress Nathan Welles?

When death came to her, Em had often thought (because she could not stop for Death, he'd kindly stop for her), when the Grim Reaper reached her name in his diary, whether it was sixty years hence or next week, whether she died quietly in her sleep or violently at the hands of a murderer, it would be a considerable consolation that, at that moment, Dark Voice would be finally, permanently, silenced.

I'll be bagging you for getting yourself murdered as you die.

She noticed Craig looking around the room with an expression of supreme stupidity. If she concentrated hard enough, she could probably see his nostrils flare with each sniff, as several litres of air were vacuumed into his ample frame. How could Adriana stand to sit next to him?

He's probably a nice guy, just a little shy and overweight.

Funny how you give the benefit of the doubt to everyone else but me.

Benefit of the snout.

She stifled a giggle, thereby producing a quiet snort, and looked up the front. By now Jane Webb, who was acting head of Corporate, was speaking about the redundancy process. Webb was a youngish, rather plain woman who'd moved from Optus two years before and who was said to be future CEO material; there'd been a profile of her in one of the business mags earlier in the year. Bored, Em looked over at Nathan again. She very rarely fantasised about work colleagues, but in regarding him leaning against the wall nearby, she decided her desire was entirely justified. He had his eyes closed, oblivious to the fact that a number of people, including executives, would be able to see him. She could see his chest rising and falling, and his face was completely still, until he suddenly opened his eyes, looked at Rachael, who was standing there listening intently, and whispered to her; she whispered back, and he nodded and replied, then returned to sleeping upright. He looked, she thought, like he didn't give a fuck about anything. And very cute, even though she couldn't see those lovely eyes. She kept watching him, discreetly, noting the outlines and creases of his trousers. She wished he'd turn a bit more side on. He had a really nice arse.

She lost track of what Webb was saying, but she seemed to be, somewhat redundantly, preparing everyone for a program of cuts that would continue into the new year, emphasising that the reductions would, if needed, occur at all levels, including in senior and middle management.

They threw the floor open for questions. There was that awkward post-request-for-questions silence for quite a time, sufficient for people to begin shifting nervously. Finally a hand went up in the front.

'Yes, Phil?' said the Marketing head.

'What will be the specific process for identifying surplus staff?'

'Well,' Webb began, 'I'll field that one. Look, no one here, in my view, is surplus to requirements. We're not carrying any fat.'

Well you are, Dark Voice slipped in.

'What we may have to determine is what our surplus functions are, and act on that basis. I don't expect that we will go on doing the same tasks with fewer people. I don't think there's many of us who have any slack to pick up.'

'So what sort of functions will be surplus?'

'We haven't considered that yet,' said the Marketing head, running her hand through her luxurious hair. 'That's a decision that the executive will have to deal with.'

'But we're all being told to find more revenue as well. You want more revenue with fewer staff to generate it.'

'Resolving that will be part of the process,' said Webb. 'I appreciate there's a genuine tension there. We're alive to it.'

'Alive but brain-dead to it,' whispered David.

'Janine?' said the Marketing head.

'Why don't they rent out level nineteen? It's been vacant for six months.'

'Ah,' said Webb, breaking in again, 'we've just signed a contract on that, the sub-tenants will be moving in in the new year. Oh, and I forgot—my apologies: we've decided that the transition to subcutaneous RFID chips instead of access passes that was scheduled for 2017 is to be indefinitely suspended.'

This statement prompted widespread and happy murmuring. The proposed chipping of every employee (it was compulsory to add 'like dogs and cats' whenever anyone discussed it) was very unpopular and had already been delayed once pending 'consultations'.

'Can you at least say what sort of levels the cuts will be at?' came a high-pitched male voice from down the front. It sounded to Em like Gavin the Weirdo, a software guy from level twenty. He was well known throughout the company for his eccentricity and dislike of female colleagues, but was tolerated for his brilliance. An obsessive Trekker, he was said to have occasionally wandered his floor saying, 'I am Nomad, I am Nomad, I am Nomad,' until some Scottish guy who worked on that level had yelled, 'Yeah, well shut the fuck up, Nomad,' at him.

'Will they be impacting on senior management as much as on the shopfloor?'

Shopfloor, thought Em. Fuck. Did he think we were in a union?

'Well, as I said,' Webb responded, 'the cuts will follow functions, so that will have structural implications. Just as an example, purely hypothetically, if it was decided to cease the entire Research function, then Terry would be looking for a new job,' indicating the head of Research beside her.

'Yes, but they're not going to cease the entire Research function,' muttered David.

'They would if you were running it,' said Jayde.

'I think the key,' said the Marketing head, 'is that we intend to consult very widely and very vigorously with staff over any cost reductions. We feel it is crucial that staff understand, and participate in developing, the framework for these reductions. We want a viable company going forward in which staff have confidence in the way we take decisions.'

There was silence again, for a bit longer this time. Then Nathan shot up his hand. Em turned to watch him.

'Yes, er, over there?' said Webb.

Nathan folded his arms again. 'So every other time we've had cuts management assured us they'd be undertaken in a logical manner and then they just cut arbitrarily and randomly to hit targets. I assume that'll happen this time as well?'

Em stifled a giggle, as did Jayde and a number of others. The three heads looked at him expressionlessly.

'I don't think that's very helpful, Nathan,' said the Marketing head.

It was only when Em noticed Jayde watching her that she looked away from Nathan.

The nondescript office faced west, and the afternoon sun required the floor-to-ceiling length shades to be pulled down, though Peter could see through them down into Pyrmont below.

'Coffee, mate,' said Spitaleri, placing a white cup in front of him.

'Cheers, mate,' said Peter. Spitaleri sat down beside him as Deputy Director-General Guy Collin entered the room. The corridor lights began flashing outside to indicate the presence of an unsecured visitor. One of the junior staff entered, followed by a man in an AFP uniform, bearing a moustache and a folder. Another staff member hovered outside the door.

'Unsecured visitor,' the first man said.

'Thanks, Tim,' said Collin. 'Fellas, this is Jack Calvin.'

'Paul Spitaleri,' said Spitaleri, rising and shaking hands with the visitor. 'And this is Peter Christian.'

'G'day, mate,' said Peter, extending his hand.

Calvin shook it. 'Mate,' he said.

'Commander Calvin is being seconded to Taskforce Gideon,' said Collin as they sat down.

'Well, I will be, mate,' Calvin said, smiling. 'Once it's up and running.' He adjusted the visitor's pass around his neck.

This was the first time Peter had been in a meeting with a deputy director-general. He'd never met Guy Collin until a few minutes previously; normally Collin was based in Canberra at the

Lubyanka on the lake. Calvin placed his folder on the desk and sat down.

'So what are the reporting arrangements on Gideon?' said Collin.

'Okay,' said Calvin. 'So the lead agency is the Australian Cyber Security Centre, obviously. That has its own dedicated agents who are lead on Gideon.'

'Who used to be AFP,' said Spitaleri.

'Yep,' the policeman nodded. 'In fact, who still are AFP, because there's been no legislation setting up the ACSC yet. We're also providing some supplementary support to ACSC for this exercise, due to resource constraints, but formally everything has to go through ACSC.'

'And that'll be up and running early next week?'

Peter watched the two men talking back and forth. Collin was very stiff, spoke quite softly and appeared not to move unless strictly necessary. Some people had complained that he'd been passed over as Director-General in favour of the former DFAT Secretary, appointed earlier in the year, who'd never worked in ASIO or domestic intelligence. But others said Collin was still relatively young and was being groomed for the top job down the track. Calvin, on the other hand, was like a copper from Central Casting, especially with the moustache.

'So Gideon is purely focused on identifying the source of the Kittehsaurus Rox leaks and stopping them,' Calvin was saying. 'That's the ACSC's priority as of this point, and we're working with them on that. So what are you blokes looking at?'

'We've been looking at the broader national security threat of online activism for some time, obviously,' said Collin. 'We're not directly tasked to look at cybersecurity issues, as you know, as that function is one for ACSC. But we've commenced an investigation of our own that's not intended to cut across Gideon but which may have some crossovers. Our concern is the way the internet permits people to absorb unfettered ideas and information and be radicalised, and we very much have a watching brief on that threat.'

'And there are some ASIO blokes who are now with the ACSC?' said Calvin.

'That's right. Like the AFP. They're from what used to be our cybersecurity area. Different area to us. They report to Alan Phillips.'

Calvin paused, then nodded. 'Ah, okay. I know him. So do you work with them?'

'Well,' began Spitaleri, 'that's a bit complicated because, as you say, the ACSC has no formal existence, so the reporting and information arrangements are a little unclear. There's a bit of silo thinking going on just at this point. We've had some informal discussions with our people who are co-located with ACSC, to both keep them in the loop with what we're doing and to find out what they're doing.'

'I talk regularly to Alan to try to stay in touch with what they're doing with ACSC,' said Collin. 'It's because of this confusion that I'm quite concerned about things falling between the ACSC, ourselves and the AFP in this whole space. We don't want to end up with left-hand/right-hand miscommunication.'

Calvin nodded. 'Good. Very happy to work with ASIO on that. And one of the reasons we're keen to keep in touch with you is to make sure we're all fully in the loop on these leaks.'

'Anything so far on last week's leak?' said Spitaleri.

'Well, look, it's early days,' said Calvin, running his fingertips through his moustache. 'We haven't ruled out any possibility. You know these things—it might have even been a minister. But judging by the reaction of the government, it doesn't look that way. They don't go ape shit like this when it's one of them. The version that ended up on the internet was slightly different to the version that was in CABNET, which is interesting, so that's helped us narrow it down a little. Might suggest someone in the department did it.'

'But then there was this leak yesterday,' said Collin.

'Yeah. Again, we're not ruling out that was someone inside the party. Obviously they don't use CABNET.'

Brief silence.

'We're moving fairly quickly,' said Calvin. 'There's a lot of pressure for a quick outcome on this. The FBI have been in touch.'

'They're concerned about this latest leak?' said Spitaleri. 'The FBI?'

'Oh yeah, very much so, mate,' said Calvin. 'Absolutely. The Americans are pretty embarrassed and want to know they can talk to us without it leaking. They're really exercised. They've raised the possibility of extraditing whoever is responsible to the US so they can be charged with espionage.'

Peter finally ventured his hand. 'And we don't know anything about this hacker outfit?'

'Well, my guys and the ACSC blokes have never heard of them; they're not on our radar at all, completely new. We've been checking in the IRC channels and on forums to try to find out about them, but they're a mystery. There's a lot of speculation but nothing definite. We've asked Twitter for the account metadata, and maybe you have too, but we haven't heard back. I don't reckon it will be useful anyway. We've emailed Pastebin but haven't received a response from them. We found out what the name means, though.'

'What is it?' said Spitaleri.

'One of our officers found out from one of these forums that it's a reference to a sex toy available online,' said Calvin. 'It's what passes for humour with these sorts of people.'

There was silence for a moment. 'I thought it was an online game involving a giant cat,' said Peter, who had been aware of the game before the use of its name in the current sense.

'That's not our understanding, mate,' said Calvin, with a twitch of his moustache.

Peter felt chastened, despite knowing he was right. Someone online had been trolling the AFP, even if they didn't realise they were policemen and women. 'What was some of the speculation about the group?' he said, deciding there was no point in pushing the issue.

'There was a rumour that some American hacker moved to Australia or New Zealand a couple of years ago and that this is all his doing. We're looking into that.'

'Okay, well if we could keep in touch through Paul here, that'd be useful,' said Collin. 'Now, a final thing, just stepping back from the immediate circumstances of this case I think it's fair to say that both the AFP and ourselves, while acknowledging the priority of dealing with the situation, probably have the same perspective: that this merely reinforces the already strong case for more intelligence-gathering, surveillance and enforcement powers.'

'Absolutely,' said Calvin. 'This perfectly demonstrates the limitations of our current powers, in our view, and of course the problems with an inefficient and bureaucratic data-gathering framework.'

'I think we should consider some sort of joint letter to the Attorney-General reiterating our concerns on this front and urging him to bring forward appropriate amendments to the relevant legislation,' said Collin.

'That sounds very sensible,' Calvin said, nodding. 'I'll advise my Assistant Commissioner to that effect and we'll liaise further with you. There might even be some benefit in seeing whether some other agencies want to join in.'

'Excellent,' said Collin, with a note of finality.

'We'll be in touch, mate.' Calvin rose. The group shook hands again. Collin opened the door. The two men who'd brought Calvin in were waiting to escort him out. Peter could hear their calls of 'unsecured visitor' fading away.

'That'll be a good outcome, if we can get the government to revisit some legislative amendments,' said Spitaleri.

'Definitely,' said Collin. 'This is a good opportunity to go a lot further on online surveillance. Best one in years, really. So any initial thoughts on where to go with our work?'

'Peter had some thoughts,' said Spitaleri, finishing his coffee.

Peter had his spiel ready to go. 'Okay, I think we need to move quickly and get in early on whatever support group or network is established to support this outfit. If this mob stay around for a while, they're bound to generate some sort of online or real-world support network, which will give us access to the wider online activist community. And who knows? We might pick up some info that could help ACSC track down who's responsible.'

'So get involved with a support group?' said Collin gravely.

'Yep, right at the ground level. And look, there's probably strong crossovers between the people who'll support this and other groups we're monitoring, your anarchists, WikiLeaks types, hackers. Even if nothing comes of this Kittehsaurus Rox outfit, we might pick up some useful stuff on other targets.'

'You were working in some green groups down in Victoria before this, weren't you?' Collin said.

'Yes,' said Peter. 'Did that for a couple of years.'

'What do you think?' said Spitaleri.

'It makes sense,' said Collin. 'The ACSC aren't going to be too focused on the wider group, they just want to get whoever's stealing this stuff as quickly as possible. We've got the luxury of doing it properly. But I haven't got much in the way of resourcing to spare at the moment with the terrorism work. You should probably check in with the section who were running the WikiLeaks monitoring; they had an officer working in the support groups, I think, who might have some background. But start the paperwork.'

'Sure,' said Spitaleri.

'I need to see you about something, Paul,' Collin said as Spitaleri turned to go.

Peter returned to his desk, carrying his half-empty coffee. There was a message from his wife on his landline. Collin's endorsement was good news. He was already halfway to creating an identity for the sort of covert operation he'd pitched to Spitaleri. An open-source intelligence outfit that worked for the organisation had a number of social media profiles religiously maintained for use undercover, to which they'd add an actual name once a handle was taken from the Dead Kid List, as it was colloquially known, approved and documented. He'd selected 'Peter Armitage', an appropriately anonymous Anglo name that some luckless infant had briefly had in the early 1980s. He didn't particularly like it, but it was useful that he shared a first name. Do I look like an Armitage? he asked himself. And what do Armitages look like anyway?

'Footy tips, mate,' said someone, passing behind him.

'Yep, I'll shoot 'em through soon,' he said.

Peter was thirty-four, and had been with ASIO for nearly five years; before that, he'd been a policeman in Melbourne. He'd spent his first couple of years in Canberra, which had been enjoyable except for a manager who couldn't cope with his ideas and drive. The switch to Sydney and the good luck in getting into Spitto's area, however, had made it all worthwhile. Getting on to the Kittehsaurus Rox case was, he thought, an amazing opportunity, although ideally he would have preferred to be working in the ACSC going after the hackers themselves. Those sort of online vigilantes were, in his view, not merely criminals but a genuine threat to democracy—terrorists, in a way, but worse than most terrorists because they didn't have any particular agenda or goals.

He picked up the phone and dialled his wife and got voicemail.

'Hey it's me. I'm gonna head to the gym at around five thirty and then I'll get some stuff on the way home. Let me know if you want anything.'

The gym session would be light; he'd injured his leg playing Oztag the previous evening.

He went over to the internet access computer and logged in to the Twitter account he'd be using; he'd need to establish a Facebook page and stick some photos on it, as well as setting up a LinkedIn page once he had the name confirmed. There were some specialist guys in IT who'd help him with that.

Peter Armitage.

'I love this shit,' he said to no one in particular.

SATURDAY
21 NOVEMBER

Ewan sat upright and looked around wildly, then realised it was the phone. It was nearly 5 a.m., and he had only been asleep for an hour. He found his phone on the bedside table and answered it.

'Mazzoni.'

'Ewan!'

'Vanessa?' He smiled broadly. 'How are you?'

'Okay. What time is it?'

'Ah . . . nearly five.'

'Oh, I'm sorry to wake you up, babe.'

'No, no, it's okay, it's okay, it's great to hear from you.'

'Derek's busy. We're about to go out to lunch so I thought I'd take the chance.'

He paused. 'What's Aspen like?'

'Really nice. We're having a great time. But I'm missing you.'

'Yeah, I'm missing you too,' he said. He got out of bed and wandered out to the kitchen, where a light was on. 'Can't wait to see you when you get back.'

'What have you been doing?'

'Just the usual stuff. Thinking about you a lot.' He stared at his fridge.

'We're going to spend an extra day skiing and cut down on the time in San Francisco before we come back.'

'Cool.' His eyes rested on the fridge magnet his mother had given him many years before. It was a picture of Jesus, below whom there was a caption: *Defend me everywhere.*

'Are you—'

'Did you—'

'Sorry, you go, babe.'

'No you.'

'You busy at work?'

'Yeah, there's lots to do . . . I can't wait to see you.' He realised, as he said it, that he was repeating himself.

'Only see me?'

'Well, I hope more than just see you. Hopefully I'll get to touch you, and kiss you, and fuck you.'

'God, I can't wait for that. I'm missing you so much. We're having a good time, but I'm missing you.'

He didn't like hearing that she was having a good time; what he really wanted was to know that she was deeply unhappy, miserable at being separated from him. It tainted the rest of their brief conversation, terminated when Derek suddenly reappeared at the other end with a hasty 'Talk to you soon.'

What had been playing in his mind was a vague urge to punish her for going off to the US with Anderson, however reasonable such an action was, however unreasonable, irrational, such an urge was on his part. Vanessa was his, he felt; she didn't belong to that old man. Accordingly, he had developed a sort of proprietorial jealousy about her going away with Anderson. But when he had the chance to speak with her, his delight overcame any thoughts of saying anything or sulking. Just hearing from her, knowing she'd made the effort to contact him, pleased him.

He kept looking at the Jesus fridge magnet for a moment. His mother had given it to him when he moved out of home. Perhaps she had thought, in her own naive way, that it was a suitable imprecation for a soldier. *Defend me everywhere.* It had always bemused him, but he had kept it, taken it with him wherever he'd moved since then, because it was from Mum. Jesus gazed back at him, his heart on display (in the centre of his chest, unobscured by ribs), bearing a faint smile; evidently he was untroubled by his cardiopulmonary peculiarity. *Defend you everywhere?* He had never understood that. Jesus was God. He was omnipotent. Defend him? Why? Jesus needed defending like an ocean needed pissing in.

He returned to bed and lay there, replaying the conversation with Vanessa over and over, looking for subtle signs in her voice and in her words, thinking over the three minutes of idle chatter in which they'd engaged, and he turned the whole thing around and around in his mind, how Vanessa, despite missing him, despite making the effort to call him from the other side of the planet, would never be his, how the ridiculous thing they had embarked on would inevitably cease. Her absence, he realised, lent an air of dullness, of irrelevance, to wherever he was or whatever he was doing, an aching sense that what was exciting, what was fun, was where she was and nowhere else.

'Oh, Lieutenant Ewan Mazzoni, what have you got yourself into?' he said aloud.

It had been some time since Nathan had been to Newtown. Having done arts/law, he had spent a considerable part of his studenthood in its crowded pubs, cafes and side streets. None of this time, he recalled, was particularly well spent, even by his own fairly low standards: much of it was devoted to lusting after unobtainable girls, playing the clown while they overlooked him for more suitable matches; a lot of the rest was devoted to throwing up, or sipping bad coffee and solving the problems of the world with friends. In the end, the only thing of lasting value to him that he had extracted from all that time was a prize-winning third-year essay on Lincoln's approach to habeas corpus ('Habeas Corpus: Producing the body in an era of mass killing') and his Tim Gelmetti Anecdote. He had seen Tim Gelmetti—then lead singer of the Thongs, these days international superstar with Agonistes—playing at the old Sando one night, and the proto-rock god (back before he'd adopted his trademark eyeshadow) had foolishly yelled, 'No applause, just money,' at the end of a song. Nathan had pulled out a fifty-cent piece and hurled it from across the other side of the bar. Usually incapable of even elementary, barn-door accuracy, his throw was perfect, arcing across the smoke-filled interior of the pub and onto Gelmetti's skull, with a crack that could actually be heard above the babble, inducing a cry of pain from the man now worth $20 million. That was his Gelmetti Anecdote. 'Should have thrown a glass/full bottle/chair/brick at the cunt instead,' most people replied when he related it.

After eventually pulling off the remarkable achievement of finding a parking spot and making his way to King Street, he found himself taking a nostalgia trip, if a disorienting one. His favourite bar, Swahili (a name apparently selected at random, for nothing African in theme or faint connection had ever been present, except perhaps for the underrated West African restaurant a block down), was now gone, replaced with Laotian restaurant. The Pub of the Living Dead on the corner where he had got into a fight with an engineer had been replaced with, of all things, a hair salon. Only the cafe Oslo's remained, tucked up between the Red Emperor and the chemist's on the western side of King Street, still with its two tiny wooden tables and rickety chairs—not the same chairs, surely?—on the footpath, just in case you liked bus exhaust, eighty-decibel traffic noise and the faint smell of garbage with your Newtown Fair Trade coffee experience.

He crossed over and peered inside for a moment; like the street furniture, the decor inside seemed more or less the same as he remembered, and even the clientele appeared similar to that of his own era—young men and women, poorly dressed, some older people who looked like the perpetual uni students they probably were, all nursing coffees and talking over the racket from the radio, which was evidently still permanently tuned to Triple J. Four booths down, on the left Sandra had admitted she'd been sleeping with Harry (Harry? Who the hell was called 'Harry' anymore? was his first thought, before a wave of jealousy overcame him) and suggested they not continue their relationship. Across the other side, towards the back, where a door opened out into a jungle-like garden, he had triumphantly collected on his bet with Matt over the outcome of the 2001 election, and gorgeous, amazingly sexy Carol (now a mid-level New South Wales public service manager—he'd Facebook-stalked her) had smiled so sweetly at him he had briefly thought he was in with a chance with her.

Similar, trivial victories, defeats and delusions were doubtless being lived out at that very moment in the melodrama and pinchbeck angst of student lives, interrupted by lectures, essays and shit jobs.

One felt so much more deeply at that age, he thought to himself, and about things of such little significance; luckily, in his case that had been balanced by near-complete detachment about even the most important things as he grew older. He resumed walking, looking for a cafe called Cylabic, where he was to meet Jeremy Steel. It turned out to be on the corner of Hordern Street, not too far past the Chinese restaurant where he, Sandra and Sally Branch had had dinner one warm autumn night in 2000.

Nathan had worked with Steel on several occasions and knew he lived at Randwick; they had seen and nodded to each other on occasion at Bondi Junction. Steel was somewhat reluctant to accept Nathan's invitation to discuss 'a matter that can't be discussed at work', but Nathan had kept at him, cajoling and encouraging him, and finally extracted a reluctant commitment to meet, perhaps more to get rid of Nathan than any other reason. Cylabic, apparently, was Steel's preferred breakfast venue on the weekend.

It was quite pleasant, as it turned out. It was composed of one room, long and narrow, with the bar along the right wall near the front. Aside from the bar, the place was filled with black vinyl couches and black coffee tables, currently unoccupied, a raised area at the end with two pool tables, and an area with tables and chairs near the bar. Along both side walls, at different points, were large TVs, showing a Marx Brothers film, with the sound up. There was no music. The floor had an odd sort of astroturf-type surface, somewhere between carpet and that rubber stuff they used in kids' playgrounds. The bar was closed but there were probably a dozen people in there eating. Steel, a Koori wearing jeans and a hoodie, was the only one sitting by himself.

'G'day, Jeremy,' he said. 'Thanks for coming.'

Steel stood up from the table and shook Nathan's hand; he already had a plate of bacon and eggs.

'Nice place, this.'

'I like it,' Steel said, returning to his food. 'So what did you want to speak about?' His tone was definitely businesslike.

Nathan glanced at the screen nearby and recognised the film as *A Night at the Opera*.

'Look, you're presumably aware of this Kittehsaurus Rox stuff—the leaks from the hacker group?'

Steel nodded.

'Okay, well, I have reason to think it's coming from inside Veldtech.'

Steel's expression didn't change. 'Why?' He pushed a piece of toast into his mouth.

A man approached the table with a menu. 'Just tea, thanks,' Nathan said. 'Darjeeling, or Earl Grey.' He'd already had pancakes at home, made with Sophie's 'help'.

'Someone gave me a file on another matter and the thumb drive they used had some of the leaked material, plus, um, details for the Kittehsaurus Rox Twitter account.'

'That's interesting,' said Steel, between mouthfuls. 'But what does this have to do with me?'

'I'm wondering what to do about it.'

Steel sipped his coffee and thought for a moment.

'Do you have any actual proof that someone in the company is stealing information? Or just this? Who did you get it from?'

Nathan was reluctant to dob in the blonde giantess from Tom Dao's area. 'Some young woman in the Intel group. I'm sure she's not responsible for it. I figure she's just used a thumb drive that someone else used.'

Steel put down his knife and fork. 'Okay, well, you don't *have* to do anything. It's not clear who had this material or for what purpose. Taking my legal hat off, I'd ignore it.'

'And with your legal hat on?'

'Same,' he said, after a pause. 'Look, really, who knows why they have it? Maybe they're investigating this mob themselves. I mean, imagine the coup if the company was able to find out who was doing the leaking before a government agency.'

'True, true,' said Nathan. 'But if someone outside the firm found out, it would look terrible. There'd be all sorts of questions. Like where they got the material from.'

'And where did they get the material from? Any ideas?'

Nathan shrugged. 'Don't know.'

Steel picked up his knife and fork again. 'I'd ignore it.'

'You reckon?'

'Yep.'

Nathan looked around. 'I love the stateroom scene in this film, when they're all crowded in the cabin and then Margaret Dumont opens the door. It's one of my favourite all-time movie scenes,' he said, nodding towards one of the television screens.

'And two hard-boiled eggs,' said Steel, in a perfect Chico Marx accent.

'Yo, bitch.'

Kat kissed Maddy and handed her a bottle of Cattier.

'Hmmm, real stuff,' she said, contemplating the bottle.

'Don't go wasting those champagne cocktails on anyone but us, thank you.'

Maddy was short, overweight and had very curly brown hair. Her preferred party form was DIY cocktails, with tonnes of hors d'oeuvres painstakingly prepared over the previous twenty-four hours. Her apartment looked north from a high-rise on Goulburn Street, with a half-decent city skyline view if you stood on the balcony and looked east. Otherwise, even from the thirty-second floor, the view was obscured by the office and apartment high-rises around them. Kat wandered straight from the entrance hall into the kitchen, ignoring the other guests, and took a bottle of mineral water from the fridge.

'How was the drinks thing last night?' Maddy asked.

The previous evening Kat had ventured out for the first time since Chris; she'd had an invite to drinks with a law firm that had employed her earlier in the year. She'd mainly gone because they were located on level fifty-eight of a building down near the Quay and had an awesome view. It hadn't been too bad, though the Event Liquid wasn't exactly top-notch.

'Not bad. I only stayed an hour.'

'Okay, you have got to meet Duncan,' said Maddy.

220

Oh great, she thought. Maddy playing matchmaker again. It was not unexpected, however; Maddy had not been privy to the full extent of her obsession with Chris and didn't really understand just what his . . . departure? loss? absence? . . . what his absence meant.

'I don't have to meet anyone, babe.' She swigged from the mineral water bottle.

Maddy glared at her. 'Don't drink from the bottle. This is why I couldn't live with you.'

'Sorry.'

'Now you have to finish it off. The whole lot.'

'What, right now?'

'Duncan is gorgeous. European passport. Consultant.'

'Well, good for him. I have an Australian passport and I'm a social media expert,' she said.

She followed Maddy out into the living area, where the dining table had been pushed against the wall and now held an array of bottles. That area opened onto a lounge room and, beyond that, to the balcony through glass doors. There were about twenty people. Maddy's improbably named Spanish flatmate Graham rose to greet her, grinning beneath his salt-and-pepper moustache.

'Katrina, my love, how are you?' He hugged her, a feeling that she unexpectedly enjoyed. She momentarily felt teary; she liked Graham a lot, and felt he had a kind of unconditional affection for her. He also had a thick accent and was, as her dad used to say, as camp as a row of tents pitched on Oxford Street.

'All the better for seeing you, Gra,' she said.

He yelled out, his arm around her shoulder, 'Davo! Davo!'

Davo, his current boyfriend, disengaged from a tall, good-looking guy in a suit and skivvy and came over.

'How are you, luv?' he said, kissing Kat.

'Good, thanks. What have you two been up to?'

'We're off to Tuscany!' said Graham exultantly.

'Fuckers,' she said, with vehemence. Maddy handed her a cocktail glass filled with, presumably, a champagne cocktail.

'I see you've been all over the TV of late,' said Davo, raising his glass to hers.

'Yep, no escaping me,' she replied, clinking with him and then with Graham. 'I'm the queeeeeeeeen of the screen.'

A redheaded woman, taller than all three of them, joined them.

'Katrina,' she said expectantly.

'Hello, Cam,' Kat responded. 'How are we?' Cam had been a professional netballer but had retired with a dodgy knee and was now a development officer for Netball Australia.

'I'm okay. Why are you on TV so much?'

The question sounded insulting, but Kat knew Cam well enough to know it was an innocuous query. Cam had the interpersonal skills of a panicked cat; Maddy like to suggest her role was as netball's 'alienation officer'.

'Oh,' she said dismissively. 'This hacking thing. I'm the expert.'

'Kittehsaurus Rox?' said Gra, pronouncing the syllables individually. 'I love that!'

'They're desperate to lock them up,' said Davo, who was a policeman. 'It's bloody hilarious. All those politicians must be so pissed off.'

'Yeah, good for you,' said Cam.

'Now, Kat,' said Maddy, intervening and grabbing her by the arm. 'You need to mingle, babe.' She dragged Kat in the direction of the guy in the skivvy.

'Duncan,' said Maddy, 'this is Katrina. Isn't he gorgeous?'

Duncan smiled without embarrassment. 'Hi,' he said.

Katrina disliked him instantly. There was no transition, no wavering. It was binary. One nanosecond she was neutral about him, the next, she loathed him. Not because Maddy introduced them. And not because she was coping with the Chris thing and still essentially held the view that she'd had the best when it came to men and was now left to try the rest. It was because he wasn't at all embarrassed when Maddy declared him to be gorgeous, and because of the 'hi'. And the skivvy, too—an expensive-looking (to the extent that skivvies could look expensive) brown one—put her off. But the greeting really needed to work if she was to move on from the skivvy and his apparent belief in his own gorgeousness. Instead, the 'hi' was almost oleaginous, offered with a deep-throated English accent.

'Hi back,' said Kat.

'I need a drink; I'll be back in a tick,' said Maddy, slipping away.

'How are—' he began, but Kat cut him off.

'How do you know the Madwoman?' she said.

'Madwoman?' He frowned.

'Madison,' she said patiently. He looked quite nice, she thought, but his manner annoyed the hell out of her.

'Oh, right, yes, I met her a few weeks ago. You?'

'Same,' she said. She didn't feel like revealing that she'd known Maddy since university.

He nodded. 'Ah, okay. I think she mentioned you were close friends.'

Her turn to nod. 'Well, she makes friends fast. You're not from around these parts, are you?' she continued. It was a line from something, some film or other.

He allowed a gracious smile. 'No, from the UK.' She noticed a sort of sheen in his dirty blond hair. She decided to troll him, and frowned.

'And where's that?'

'The United Kingdom. England.' He gave her a slightly puzzled look.

'Oh,' she said, nodding. 'Cool.'

'And what do you do?'

'Oh, this and that,' she said. 'I'm a bit between jobs currently.' She looked around.

'Madison said you were in the media.' He had realised he needed to work hard to get the conversation back on track.

'Oh, I've dabbled a little bit, you know,' she said. She took a big gulp from her glass. Maddy had made a particularly strong cocktail. She began twirling some hair at the back of her head. It was the rescue signal she and Maddy employed when either was trapped.

They were obligated to drop everything and rescue the other if it was seen, even if it meant social disaster for themselves. 'You?'

'Consultant. Used to work in finance.' He half smiled and arched his eyebrows. 'Decided to take a risk on my own.' He watched her, a trifle nervously, hoping to detect a positive response. 'It's paid off,' he added, as if she might be wondering, which she most definitely wasn't. She was only wondering how long it would take Maddy to rescue her from this fuckwit.

'Cool,' she said.

'Beautiful weather,' he said. 'Sydney's got great weather.'

OMFG this guy is shitting me to tears.

'What part of England are you from?' She twirled her hair a bit more quickly.

'Ah, London, but I grew up in Liverpool.'

She decided on more trolling.

'You must've picked up the accent quickly then, if you grew up in Liverpool.'

'Sorry?'

'Your English accent. Presumably you didn't have that when you were in Liverpool.'

'Oh, ah, sorry, Liverpool in England.' He smiled patronisingly.

She frowned, faintly incredulous. 'Wait, there's a Liverpool in England?'

His smile grew broader. Where the hell was Maddy? She twirled still more furiously.

'Oh yes. I think it's the original.'

'Wow, that's an amazing coincidence,' she said, nodding. She was very good at keeping a straight face, although she realised she might have been pushing her luck with the Liverpool thing. 'I—'

Maddy appeared, finally. 'Sorry, Dunc, can you excuse me? I need Kat's help for just a second. Back in a moment.'

'Of course!'

They headed into the kitchen.

'You took your fucking time!' Kat snapped in a snarl-whisper once they were out of earshot.

'I came as soon as I saw!' said Maddy, in the same tone. 'God, I didn't know you'd start signalling as soon as you met him.'

'He's a dickhead,' said Kat.

'Oh, give me a break. He doesn't measure up to your married guy, right?'

'That's not it. He's just a dick.' The crack about Chris hurt. Maddy had hit the sore spot with unerring accuracy.

'He's a sweetie. Give him a chance. He gives a lot to charity.'

'Oh, for fuck's sake. So does the Pope!'

'Fine, have it your way.'

'I need another drink after that.'

She went back out, having observed that Duncan was safely locked into conversation elsewhere. She chatted with an older couple whom she knew lived next door about the nearby units with too many Chinese students in them, then with Graham and Davo properly, then she decided to go out onto the balcony to look around in the afternoon sun. It was only when she was stepping through the glass doors that she realised there was a man out there already. He had closely-cropped dark hair and wore rather loose clothing—a black top, grey pants and black shoes. He was using his phone.

'What's happening on Twitter?' she said.

He looked up and looked back down again. 'Actually, I'm just pressing the buttons so it looks like I'm on Twitter. Beats standing in the kitchen not talking to anyone.'

'Not by much. I'm Kat.'

He put his phone away and picked up a beer bottle he was drinking from. 'Luther.'

'How do you know Madison?'

'Oh, I don't,' he said, rapid-fire, as if surprised by the question. 'I just abseiled down here. She used to go out with my brother.'

She laughed, something that she realised hadn't happened for quite some time.

'Not Phillip?'

'That's the one.' He spoke quickly.

'I remember Phillip,' said Kat. 'He was nice. Where is he now?'

Luther frowned in concentration for a moment. 'Ahhhh . . . somewhere in the Middle East, last I heard. He's not very good at keeping in touch.'

'That's no good.'

'Well.' He shrugged. 'I don't particularly like him.'

He watched her neutrally.

'Ooooooooookay. So what do you do?'

'Well . . . if you really want to know, I'm a professional musical plagiarist,' he said.

'And that means?'

'I write music for television and films.'

'A composer?' She was feeling like an interrogator.

He cut her some slack and extended his answer. 'I wouldn't go that far. I teach music and do some musical composition for TV. Usually I recycle stuff so that it's not immediately obvious that it's a rip-off.' He gazed off across the space between the balcony and the office building over from them, its western side bright with the late-afternoon sun. 'Then they use it for dramas.'

'Do you like that?'

'Well, put it this way: it makes me feel like I'm part of a great musical tradition, going back through other soundtrack composers, classical composers, right back through the centuries, of ripping off other people's music. And it pays well.'

'What TV have you done?'

'You know *Lawmaker*?'

'Yep.'

'That's mine. Pity the series was so shit.' He slowed down for a moment, then speeded up again. 'All Bernard Herrmann cues. And that documentary series on Curtin?'

'Oh, yep. I didn't watch it.'

'Nor me. That was mostly Dimitri Tiomkin. Although,' he said, screwing up his face in the first real emotion he'd displayed, 'you really can't tell, because he's so eclectic. I'm doing a new series now, *The Streets*. Mostly Angelo Badalamenti, but that's more because the producer wants it. I don't rate Badalamenti too highly.'

Kat didn't know any of the composers to whom he was referring. She looked over the edge down at the street thirty-two floors below.

'What about you?' he said, after sipping from his beer bottle.

'Oh, I write stuff. Mostly about social media. Do some consulting too. And the occasional bit of media as well,' she added. She suddenly realised she was trying to impress him.

'I hope you're not a social media expert?'

'Fuck no!' she spat. 'I hate that phrase. It's my schtick, not my expertise.'

He smiled. She studied him as he too leaned over the balcony and looked down. He was quite thin, and she could see why, because he had a nervous energy about him.

'So do you like being a rip-off artist or would you prefer to be writing your own scores?'

He chuckled. 'No, not at all. I'm not really good enough to write proper music, you see, not music I think is any good, but I'm good at playing around with other people's. And it's fun thinking I'm exposing millions of cloth-eared simpletons to the great film composers, even if they've been channelled through me. Would you prefer to be writing on something more worthwhile than social media?'

She smiled at his question. 'Nup. I'm happy with my thing.'

This guy was interesting, she thought. He had definite potential.

'I'm empty,' she said. 'Would you like a drink?'

'Not particularly, thanks. I'm driving.'

'Okay. I'll be back in a sec.'

Adriana thrust another Pulse at Em, who was very drunk. She'd joined Adriana and a few of her friends, while James went on some sports-related outing with a bunch of guys. Someone called Alan, whom Adriana knew from a previous job, had joined them at the pub. She'd taken a photo earlier of the three of them and Facebooked it, for no particular reason, and made some feeble attempts to engage with him, but he hadn't been overly interested.

Another spectacular failure in your long history of male relations, Dark Voice had offered, but had since gone quiet. When she was in this sort of miserable mood, it left her alone. She didn't get this drunk usually, in fact was somewhat abstemious in her alcohol consumption; her father had been an alcoholic when she was a child, albeit a functional one. But she'd also been alternating alcohol with energy drinks, which she didn't normally consume.

If only they knew, she thought dully. I'm Kittehsaurus Rox. Her ears and eyes were now hypersensitive to the phrase, capable of detecting it in a distant conversation or spotting it in acres of text. Twice that night, courtesy of this new superpower, she had heard people discussing it. Two men some distance behind her at the bar were speaking about how easy it was now to hack 'into anything'. 'They'—meaning hackers, presumably—'can get into everything, no matter how secure it is,' one said. Nowhere was safe, you needed to stay 'off the grid' the other averred. 'These Kittehsaurus Rox guys, that's some serious shit, man.'

'That's fuckin' cool, eh?'

She rose, and realised just how drunk she was, and walked a trifle unsteadily to the ladies, resolving that she should go on a new, proper diet, and maybe get a different hairstyle, to put her misery to good use. James had texted her a couple of times but she'd responded only perfunctorily. When she returned from the ladies, she threaded her way through a crowd of people standing and watching a sporting fixture of some description on the television, and then had to squeeze past a tall, bald man to get back to her seat.

'My apologies,' he said loudly over the noise. He was dressed in a jacket and jeans, and must have been in his forties, at least.

'You're right,' she said.

'I always pick the wrong place to stand. It's a talent of mine.'

She smiled. 'It's the being tall thing. We can't help it.'

Quite how that sentence made sense she didn't know, but Dark Voice remained dormant. Adriana was engrossed in a conversation with one of her friends from outside work.

'I've got your Kittehsaurus Rox letter,' the man said.

She turned and stared at him. She wasn't sure she'd heard him correctly over the noise.

'I'm sorry, what did you say?'

'I said I wished I saw the box better,' he said, gesturing at the TV.

She looked around. The TV was, indeed, slightly at an angle from them. She wasn't quite sure that was what he'd said, but she wasn't thinking clearly.

'It's only a sporting fixture of some kind,' she said after a pause. The words seem to come out slower than she assumed they would. She must have been really drunk.

He smiled. 'True. We're really looking for hackers.'

What the fuck? said Dark Voice, aroused from its slumber.

She stared at the man, slightly panicked, trying to read his face. 'You're looking for hackers?'

'Sorry,' he said, leaning in. 'I said I feel like we're in Macca's.'

She wasn't sure he'd said that at all.

'I think the food's better here,' she replied after a moment, swaying slightly. The conversation was creeping her out. She was also feeling faintly nauseated, either from too much alcohol or too many energy drinks, and was starting to sweat.

The man continued to watch her. She could see a slight discolouration on his scalp, and he hadn't shaved particularly well beneath his lip. His nose was a little bulbous and quite red. She was having trouble working him out.

'We'll find a way to make the link to you,' he said, continuing to watch her.

She watched him back, not replying, wondering if this was really happening.

He leaned in closer. 'I said, can I buy a drink for you?'

Is this guy actually hitting on you? He's like fifty, said Dark Voice. *How desperate is he?*

'Um, I'm okay, thanks; my friend just got me one, and I think I'm gonna head off soon. No offence.'

'None taken.' He smiled. 'Maybe next time. Have a good evening, hmmm?' He turned away.

Had he said 'have a good evening' or 'have a good evening, Em'? It sounded like he'd called her 'Em'.

He called you Em, said Dark Voice.

She sat back down in her seat.

'Y'okay, Em?' Adriana yelled at her drunkenly across the table.

'Cool,' she lied. She glanced back at the man to whom she'd been speaking, but he'd vanished from sight.

That guy has seriously weirded me out, said Dark Voice.

Something that even Dark Voice was scared of. It took a lot to do that. She decided she needed to go home right away.

**SUNDAY
22 NOVEMBER**

Closing his gate behind him, Derek crossed the bottom of Darling Point Road, walked across to the black Lexus SUV and opened the passenger-side door. There were a number of people near the entrance to McKell Park, possibly a wedding party, though no one looked at him.

'Welcome back,' said Chalmers. Anderson's plane had got in at 5 p.m. He'd only been home for an hour.

'What's with all the secrecy?' said Anderson, closing the door.

Chalmers stared straight ahead and chewed the top of his finger. 'This meeting never happened. My phone is at home. I'm out getting a cheesecake and some grog for the barbecue we're having tonight.' He gestured into the back of the car. On the rear leather seat was a Cheesecake Shop box and half-a-dozen bottles of wine.

'Sounds serious.'

'Kittehsaurus Rox,' Chalmers said.

'That's a game,' said Anderson after a moment. 'An online game. You steer this cat . . . or a kitten, I guess, and . . .'

'How did you know that?' said Chalmers, impressed. 'It's also the name of a hacker outfit that has caused a storm here in the last few days by breaking into government information systems and stealing quite important data. Like Cabinet submissions.'

Anderson nodded. 'I saw something about that while I was away.'

There had been a controversy that day with a report that the government was going to ban public servants and defence personnel from reading material released by Kittehsaurus Rox. The Attorney-General had appeared on one of the Sunday-morning current affairs programs and, in a car wreck of an interview, had clumsily justified the decision, saying that the material released so far was confidential and it was 'highly inappropriate' that bureaucrats and anyone else working for the government should read material to which they would not normally have access as part of their duties. He had declined to release the legal advice on which the government's decision was based.

Social media had, predictably, gone ballistic.

'Okay, so there are two problems,' said Chalmers. 'First, Kittehsaurus Rox is actually us.' He felt Derek stiffen, even though he wasn't looking at him. A man in a dinner suit came into view, walking down towards them. Clearly there was a wedding in the park.

'Two people in my division,' he continued. 'They used a back door in the software we sold to federal parliament a few years back that's used for information and email management.'

'So,' Derek said after a moment, 'we're breaking into the federal government's information system using a back door in one of our own products?'

'Federal parliament, not federal government.'

'Who the fuck approved that?'

'Me.' Chalmers had never heard Anderson swear. He was clearly deeply angry.

A small child ran up the street carrying a balloon. A few seconds later, a concerned adult male in a blue suit followed.

'And what's the second problem? God knows that's bad enough.'

'Someone in another area found out about it. And he went to one of our lawyers to ask him about it.'

'How do we know this?'

'The lawyer went straight to Jane yesterday. She came and told me.'

Anderson was silent for a long time. Eventually, he said, 'Why the hell are we stealing things from our best customer, Mark?'

'To make them realise how poor their security is, to cause a scandal so they spend more money.'

Anderson put his head in the palm of his right hand.

'Oh, we are so in trouble. This is bloody *illegal*, Mark,' he said, yelling the word. 'I don't understand how you could have been so incredibly stupid as to approve this.'

Chalmers had his response ready.

'I'm doing what you asked for. You wanted us to drum up revenue any way we could. Shake the tree, you said.'

'I didn't mean something like this,' he snapped.

'Look, this will work. It might be difficult, but it'll work.'

Anderson laughed incredulously. 'But it's *not working*, Mark. Someone's already found out. And how long till the AFP or ASIO find out? All they have to do is check the fucking logs.'

'It's fine, Derek. I've got it under control.'

Anderson looked at him, frowning. 'How is this under control? If any of this gets out, we're ruined.'

'Nothing will get out. I can guarantee that.'

'How?'

'The back door is also used by ASIO to monitor MPs. It had just become available when I left. They use it to spy on politicians. They can't ever let that become public. If people find out ASIO has been using that to keep an eye on people like the Greens, they're finished. The whole damn place will be closed.'

'So ASIO uses this thing too?'

'Yep. That's how I know about it.'

'Are you absolutely certain?'

'Of course.'

Anderson sat thinking for a moment. Another man in a suit, older, walked past.

'I hate these bloody weddings in that park. All the damn time, weddings, weddings, weddings. People always here. It's a huge nuisance.'

He resumed after a moment. 'I think you're missing the point. Why on earth is the government going to ever give us another contract if we've been spying on them?'

'Mutual self-interest.'

Silence.

Chalmers continued. 'There's already talk of more money being pumped into ACSC. Making it bigger, more like a cyber secret service, an actual agency. Imagine kitting out that sort of outfit. That must be thirty or forty million.'

'You should have spoken to me first. There's no way I'd have approved this.'

'That's why I didn't speak to you, Derek. If it all went bad, it was my idea, you'd have complete deniability.'

'That's no help. And when I said "shake the tree" I didn't mean "go and commit crimes".'

'Well then what the fuck did you mean, Derek? Did you think there was an actual money tree somewhere we could go shake? You issue these orders even though you've never done anything but run an expanding company and expect us to find painless ways to save money and get more sales. There are no painless fucking ways, so I found a way that involves pain for the government, not us.'

He opened the console between the front seats and withdrew an envelope and handed it to Derek. 'That's a signed, undated resignation letter. I'll theatrically fall on my sword whenever you like.'

'And what about this other fellow, the one who spoke to the lawyer? What about the lawyer?'

'Oh, the lawyer's fine. He contacted Jane straight away. The other guy is an issue. His name is Nathan Welles. Works in Government Relations. Apparently he actually worked on the tender for this particular piece of software. He was recently passed over for a promotion.'

'Oh—that Ambrose woman, that the one?'

'Yes, that's the one.'

Derek was silent for maybe a full minute. 'You sort it out,' he said finally. 'It's your problem. If you need to, talk to my Scottish fellow. This is his bailiwick.'

'Sure, okay.'

'Now if you don't mind, I want to go and sleep for twenty hours because I couldn't sleep at all on the plane.'

MONDAY
23 NOVEMBER

The Telegraph can exclusively reveal the identity of the hacker behind the amazing breaches of computer security that have plunged the federal government into crisis.

Kat had a mild panic attack when she read the story online. This was *her* story. Kittehsaurus Rox was *her* hacker outfit. She was the expert, with the direct line to the group. What. The. Fuck?

Amy Dinh had somehow got in as well. The bitch.

According to sources in the hacking community, a legendary US-born hacker known only as Servetus is behind the attacks that have seen Cabinet documents, confidential emails and US military secrets released online.

Except. But wait. Hang on. She read the story.

Hackers say Servetus, famous for his exploits in the United States, has never been photographed, but was strongly rumoured to have moved to Australia to escape increasing FBI attention in recent years.

'This is definitely Servetus,' said one experienced 'white-hat' hacker. 'There's only one person with the skills to break into these systems and the attitude to simply dump the documents out there rather than sell them, and that's Servetus.'

'Servetus is a legend,' said another hacker who declined to be named. 'He just doesn't care. It's all about the challenge, for him.'

Australian Federal Police, now engaged in a major operation to track down the leaks, declined to comment.

The attacks have rocked the government, with . . .

That was it.

She reread the article. It was thin, very thin. Indeed, it was Amy Dinh's usual quality. Dinh's portrait gazed at her from above her byline. Arse of the year, and Kittehsaurus Rox expert, allegedly. There was more substance in Amy's recent blog post about the cool new Agent Provocateur underwear range. Fuck yeah, women should celebrate and enjoy their sensuality!

She'd seen the Servetus story too, online. It was bullshit. No one had any idea. Servetus was a half-mythical character anyway, as far as she could tell; a story that circulated among hackers, on fora and in IRC channels, a kind of hacker fairytale, a game-end boss hacker beyond the reach of the law because of his—of course, it had to be a him—amazing skills. One story was that he had created an identity for himself as an FBI agent, breaking into the FBI's system and creating an entire career history, then feeding bogus information about himself to the agents assigned to locate him. It all sounded like rubbish.

She DM'd KSR about the story, not expecting to hear back. But she felt more relaxed. Amy Dinh didn't have anything she didn't have, except a better butt. She *was* annoyed at how people were discussing the story on Twitter, as though it was a major revelation, as though Dinh knew what she was talking about.

Servetus. Pffft.

Luckily, however, it had been overshadowed by the continuing controversy over the Attorney-General declaring that anyone employed by the government was banned from reading material released by Kittehsaurus Rox if it was government material to which they wouldn't normally have access. There was much debate about whether the government had the power to demand that, and extensive mockery on Twitter.

She was in bed with her MacBook on her stomach, waiting for a phone interview with the ABC. Her mobile rang a little earlier than she was expecting. She sighed and grabbed it from the end of the bed.

'Kat Sharpe?' she said, slumping back on the pillow.

'Oh hi, Ms Sharpe, um, my name's Simon Berg, how are you?'

She rolled over onto her stomach. 'Ah . . . fine thanks, Simon.'

'Look, sorry to call you out of the blue but I tweeted you the other day about a support group for Kittehsaurus Rox.'

'Yep,' she said, not having any idea what he was talking about.

'Look, we've had a really good response to our proposal for a rally in support of the group and to protest the attempt to shut it down by the police. We're very concerned that the sort of transparency that the group is bringing to politics is being demonised as a crime. We're wondering if you'd like to come and address a rally we're going to hold outside AFP headquarters on Wednesday.'

Kat recoiled at the thought. 'Wednesday? Let me check my diary.' She paused for a moment, as though consulting her calendar. 'I've got commitments all day, Simon,' she lied.

'Ah . . . well, that's a pity, because it'd be fantastic to have you there. I know you're obviously very busy.'

'What time is the rally?' she said, out of politeness, stretching out on the bed.

'Six p.m.'

'Okay,' she said, anxious to be rid of him, 'I'll try to rearrange things and see if I can get along. I might be a little late if I manage it.'

'No, no, look, that'd be fantastic, doesn't matter if you're late. We're going to—'

'Sorry, Simon, I'm just waiting to do a radio interview, I need to go.'

'Sure.'

'Like I'm gonna go near those lunatics,' she said aloud, after hanging up.

She returned to her Macbook to discover a DM from @KSRComms. There was going to be another release.

She opened up her Date and Time, then went back to Twitter. *I understand another release from Kittehsaurus Rox is imminent,* she tweeted, and watched the seconds. It took two seconds for it to be retweeted, and within two minutes it had been retweeted over seventy times. She opened up the @KSRComms profile and then opened up Word and began preparing some text for a piece on the new release.

The landline rang, and she reached over and picked it up.

'Hi, Kat Sharpe.'

'Hi, Kat, it's Kelly from the ABC here, how are you?'

'Good, thanks.'

'You right to talk to Jacinta?'

'Yep.'

'I just saw you tweet there's going to be another release.'

'Yep.'

'Okay, you've got about a minute, we're just in a song.'

'Okay.'

She recognised the song immediately even though it came in halfway through, in the instrumental break, and she closed her eyes and screwed up her face. She'd only known the Pet Shop Boys for their recent stuff, and Chris, a big fan of theirs, had urged her to 'check out the early, funny songs'. She had rapidly devoured their entire output and loved telling Chris about the songs she liked, especially the one she was currently listening to, 'Jealousy'. It didn't particularly apply to her situation with him, but it summed up the intensity of her feelings perfectly, like a detailed topographical map of her agony over not having him. Now, hearing it made her feel ill, sufficient that she held the phone away from her ear as if disgusted. She didn't want to hear it, didn't want to hear any Pet Shop Boys song; they were now tainted, defiled, ruined by their association with Chris, their merits irrelevant, their qualities meaningless to her. She made a mental note to delete them from her iPod, another stage in the process of editing Chris from her life.

'*Joining me now is social media expert and journalist Kat Sharpe. Kat, I understand there's been another hack?*'

'You right?'

Nathan looked up from his PC at Rachael.

'Ah, yeah, sure.'

She handed him a piece of paper. 'That just came through from upstairs—would you speak to the Sustainability guys about this? This is the first I've heard about it.'

Nathan looked at the piece of paper, but didn't really register what was on it.

'Sure,' he said.

'Ta. You want to grab a coffee soon?'

'Um, I'm okay just at the moment,' he said.

'Okay,' she said resignedly. She turned away and returned to her office.

He went back to staring blankly at his PC, then looked at the piece of paper and tried to read it. Was he right? Not really. A very great distance from right, in fact. Nearly as far from right as it was possible to be. Ree had called at lunchtime, and after some discussion of domestic matters, had said, casually as anything, 'We have something to discuss when you get home. We need to talk about your little affair.'

His affair.

'Affair?' he said nervously.

'Yes,' she said, her voice sour. 'But we'll talk when you get home.'

Little affair.

Her words had set his heart racing, and when he hung up his hands were already shaking. Ree knew about Angela.

REE KNEW ABOUT ANGELA.

He was not right, not by any stretch of the imagination.

The afternoon thus far was a write-off. He had gazed at his PC, not really seeing anything, feebly tapping away at some task, barely even pretending to work, feeling faintly sick. He was preoccupied with two issues: how she had found out, and whom he could tell.

Because he had to tell someone. The only relief from his looming fate was to share it with someone, to unburden himself, to blurt it out to some sympathetic listener. It was a strange, but very strong, compulsion, the irrationality of which did nothing to lessen its appeal. But there was, unfortunately, no suitably qualified recipient available. He did not dare inform Angela until after he had gauged Ree's likely reaction, and no one else knew. Still, he desperately wanted to tell someone that his life, as of approximately 6.30 tonight, was fucked.

He and Ree had never really discussed infidelity, but his assumption was that it was a send-off offence, that she'd walk out, with Sophie—or, rather, kick him out—unless persuaded otherwise. He was going to have to talk his way out of a marriage breakdown. Could he deny it? She seemed coldly sure of herself, but he couldn't know until they'd spoken. It would all hinge on how she found out, what her evidence was, how it could be explained away. Every time he thought about the issue, his skin started to crawl, and it felt like an abyss was opening up inside him.

My marriage is fucked, he thought over and over.

The afternoon dripped by in a supremely slow agony, until he dragged himself downstairs and onto the bus, shuffling down to the middle and remaining standing. How had she found out? he asked himself, turning the issue around and around in his mind. Someone *must* have told her. His stained shirt had been immaculately cleaned by NapiSan. And they'd had only one session in Angela's flat since then. But who could've told her? No one knew. How had she found out? He barely noticed the ponderous progress of the bus up Oxford Street and along Flinders Street.

Jesus, he thought. This is serious trouble. He couldn't even think properly, couldn't marshal his thoughts or plan his response, so great was his fear.

We need to talk about your little affair.

He got off the bus, shoulders slumped, a condemned man. He walked up Todman Avenue feeling as though he should be counting down his last steps as a married man, the last moments of his life as he knew it. He'd have to move out, go and stay in a cheap motel somewhere, maybe a pub, stay in a shitty pub room to keep costs down, walk through the bar when he came home from work, gaze at the regulars, the alcoholics, the old men watching the Dapto dogs on Sky, and reflect that at least their lives had some meaning, unlike his, which used to have a point, but which now had nothing, because he'd so casually thrown it away on sex with an ethnic girl from Brisvegas.

He stopped outside the front door, fumbled with his keys, then got ready to open it.

Well, this is it, he thought.

Ree was waiting for him in the hall, obviously prepared to begin the process of ending things.

'Hi, hon,' she said. She pecked him on the cheek. Sophie ran from the lounge room and hugged him. He stared at Ree glumly, and she smiled, then turned away.

It was a little confusing. Evidently she was waiting until Sophie went to bed, he thought. Retaining the semblance of normality for their child's sake. And, yes, that was reasonable. That made sense. No need for Sophie to see this. God, the little girl's domestic world was about to fall apart and she didn't know it.

But the thought of further waiting felt like an even greater torment.

He changed, almost mechanically, put his suit away, and then went out into the kitchen. It was his turn to cook, and he had taken some fish out of the freezer that morning and put it in the fridge. He removed the fish, then stopped, put it on the kitchen bench and went into the lounge room where Ree was watching the news. Sophie was in her room. He couldn't wait. It was killing him.

'So,' he began, 'you wanted to talk about . . .' He stopped, barely able to say it. 'My affair.'

'Your affair?' she said, frowning. 'Oh, yes. I'm really sorry, hon, but I've buggered it up. I told Felicity I'd look after her kids on Saturday arvo.'

Confusion. Profound confusion.

Saturday arvo?

Felicity?

What?

He stood there looking at her dumbly.

Ree had the wrong end of the stick. More accurately, she had a completely different stick, from a completely different tree, in completely the wrong forest. On some other continent. He was fucking *Angela*, not Felicity. He'd never have an affair with Felicity, not in a million years. Christ. He didn't even find her attractive. Nor, for that matter, would she have an affair with him.

His affair.

Ree watched him, looking concerned.

His affair . . .

Then it came to him, almost literally in a flash, with a sudden surge of delight. She was talking, he realised, about the Christmas barbecue they'd planned for Saturday afternoon. He'd emailed the invites to two other couples two weeks before.

His affair. His party. Not his affair, the affair with Angela.

He suddenly felt lightheaded, dizzy with the unexpected delight of reprieve.

He nodded. 'Well, that's okay. I'll just let everyone know.'

'I'm really sorry, hon,' Ree said, looking a little upset. 'I stuffed up.'

He smiled at her. 'I'm sure we'll cope, beautiful.'

It was 6.30, and Tom Dao's call came straight through to Chalmers. Mary had departed an hour before.

'You free? I need to speak about something,' Tom said.

'Come on up.'

Chalmers was looking intently at his PC when Tom arrived. He closed the door behind him, but before he could speak, Chalmers began.

'If you're here to talk about Nathan Welles, don't. It's being taken care of.'

Tom froze. Chalmers, eyes still on the screen, began to type.

'You don't need to worry about it. Just keep up the good work.'

'You mean . . .' he began. 'How did you know?'

Chalmers finally looked at him. 'There are certain reasons, my friend, why I reached the exalted level of deputy director-general of our domestic intelligence agency while you never got beyond acting Band 1. Anyway, you don't need to worry about it.' He looked back at the computer, then at Tom again. 'Is there any other problem at your end? Everything's okay with that young woman who's been doing it?'

'Er, no. It's all fine. She still thinks I'm getting the material from a whistleblower in Canberra.'

'Is that your cover story?'

'Yeah.'

'It's fucked.'

'Well, I've encouraged her in that belief. Gives her deniability if this all goes to shit. I don't want anything to happen to her.'

'Nothing will happen to her, Tom. It'll be you and me, old china. We'll be the ones hurling ourselves on our swords. But it'll never come to that. Anything else?'

Tom was somewhat nonplussed. 'No.'

'Good. Now, I'm pleased you came up because you reminded me I've got one for you. Levers has just been invited onto some GayBC show on Thursday to debate someone on cybersecurity. We need a full brief for him by around ten a.m. Thursday. The usual stuff. Can you pull that together?'

'ABC?'

'Yeah.'

'Sure,' said Tom. 'No problem.'

'By the way, splendid release this afternoon,' Chalmers said. 'There'll be hell to pay.' He turned back to his computer, which was Tom's signal to leave.

It *was* a splendid release; the best yet, Chalmers thought. Derek's reaction to KSR had been predictable. He was continuing to fulminate about it, but nothing more. In any event, he couldn't control how Derek felt, so he put it out of his mind, preferring to concentrate on matters over which he had some control. Tom had got better at hunting through accounts for the most likely sources of material that wouldn't give away too readily where he'd obtained them. There had been media stories about how public servants could be banned from reading the Kittehsaurus Rox material, based on legal advice. The government, following standard practice, had declined to publicly release the advice. But Tom, bless him, had gone looking for it in PICS, and found it. The Attorney-General's office had sent it to the chair of the Joint Committee on Intelligence and Security, who only had a Parliament House email account.

The girl who worked for Tom had crafted a wonderful KSR release from it. He had thoroughly enjoyed reading it.

No information is beyond our reach. We are privy to even the worried consultations of the government as it tries desperately to find and neutralise the threat of transparency and account-ability. Kittehsaurus Rox is happy to release the legal advice many have sought in relation to the government's attempt to ban its officials from reading what we are doing. You're welcome.

'You're welcome.' The young woman was brilliant, he thought as he read it. As a result, the media was now talking about a 'government in crisis'.

The best part about the release, however, had been missed by Chalmers initially, because he hadn't read it through fully. The government's advice, crafted by the Solicitor-General, had relied both on the standard public service legislation, and on something a little older.

Statutory background: Parliament has traditionally held the power to regulate forms of information consumption, going as far back as 1543 when the Act for the Advancement of True Religion banned the reading of the Bible.

That single sentence was only the start of a long paragraph on the power of parliaments in England and Australia to prohibit reading of certain documents, most of which cited twentieth-century cases and explained, in detail, Parliament's power to regulate access to confidential material. The opening sentence had plainly only been included for the sake of being completely comprehensive in establishing the relevant legal authority. But, unsurprisingly, the invocation of an act from Henry VIII's time had been what had caught the media's eye.

HENRY VIII SAID WE CAN STOP YOU READING LEAKS was one headline that afternoon. On Twitter, thousands of jokes had erupted. Some wag's 'Government quotes Henry VIII on its new domestic violence policy #HenryLeaks' had received over a thousand retweets. Chalmers burst out laughing when he saw it. To his delight, Kittehsaurus Rox was now a full-blown crisis.

Ewan sprawled on the pew, checking his emails on his phone, ignoring the look from the old woman along from him. It had been some years since he had been inside a church, but he felt relaxed, if annoyed to find that there was a queue for confession.

After reflecting on his desire to tell Vanessa about his past, and especially about Mohammed al-Barak, he'd decided it might be sated by enacting a rite he hadn't undertaken since he was seventeen or eighteen; he would confess properly, in a church. This one had the same elements as the one he recalled from his childhood. The Stations of the Cross were around the walls; the ones near him were of the actual crucifixion—the fun bit, as he remembered it—with small bas-relief Roman soldiers looking on at the violence being inflicted on Jesus. None of the figures looked particularly like what they were supposed to portray, and had rather elongated features.

Jesus walks into a crucifixion. Roman says, 'Why the long face?'

Confession, or 'reconciliation' as it was officially called, had always puzzled him. God, of course, knew what you did, observed everything; he had you under permanent surveillance. Confession had thus the air of a show trial, a self-criticism session in which you had to put into words your sins before an audience as the price for forgiveness. Still, he could recall how as a child, when one's sins were innocuous, he had left the confessional with a pleasant feeling, freshly purged of sin, lily-white for however long he could manage. Maybe, he thought, even if he wouldn't achieve the same feeling as when he was eight years old, it would address the nagging feeling about Vanessa not knowing what he'd done. And thus it would, however indirectly, remove one possible impediment to being with her.

His phone rang, but he was quickly able to answer it. 'Hello?'

It was someone from Corporate, wanting to check on his travel allowance.

'Look, I can't talk right now,' he whispered loudly. 'I'm in a meeting, sorry. Sure. Okay. Call you back then.'

The old woman glared at him. But the door of the confessional opened suddenly, and a young woman came out. He switched the phone to silent, put it into his pocket and went over to the door, noting how thick it was, just like the confessional door in the church at Wyndford. What he wasn't prepared for, however, was that here he would sit across from the priest, without any screen or curtain, with nothing to provide the sort of faux anonymity he remembered from his childhood. Evidently they had altered things a bit in his absence, or maybe they did things differently here in Australia. He had heard that churches in the US offered drive-through confessions, and that the church was considering offering online reconciliation. But what threw him even more was that the priest was Indian, a bearded Indian, not at all his conception of a Catholic priest. There was a laminated card on the chair, which had the rite on it, what to say, seemingly intended for those unfamiliar with things, like him.

'Hello,' the priest said, with only a mild Indian accent.

Ewan sat down. The chair was still warm from the previous occupant. He smiled and glanced at the card. 'Ah . . . bless me, Father, for I have sinned,' he began, which was a familiar part. 'It's been . . . um, a couple of decades since my last confession.'

He waited for the priest to react.

'Well, it's good that you've returned,' he said, smiling genially.

Ewan looked at the carpet.

'I have a . . . fairly lengthy list of sins,' he said uncertainly. Rather a contrast with his childhood, when the problem was what to make up by way of sins rather than what to omit to keep it short.

'Unsurprisingly,' the priest said.

'Okay,' he began. Then he stopped and laughed. Having to actually face the priest was unexpected and difficult for him. 'Ah, I've, uh, I've got some . . .' He looked the priest in the eye. 'Okay. Well, I used to be a soldier. British Army. And a security contractor. I worked in Iraq. I killed at least three or four men, combatants, and shot a child, who lost his leg. I was part of a company that did, well, some pretty appalling things. I ripped off my insurance company while I was living in Germany. Um, I used to use prostitutes when I was in the army. I'm . . . sleeping with a married woman.' It all tumbled out, at once, though he'd saved the best until last.

The priest didn't react.

Maybe he doesn't believe me, Ewan thought. He tapped the card on his knee.

'Well, that's quite a lot to untangle,' the priest said eventually. 'Hmmm, let's see if we can work through that a bit. The men you killed in—obviously a conflict situation?'

'Yes, yes, we were, well, shooting at each other.'

'Did they deserve to die, do you think?'

Ewan looked at the priest, slightly confused. Confession as practised in Scotland had not involved an interrogation. 'Well, we were fighting them. They were trying to kill us.'

'But you don't think it's that simple.'

Perceptive, Ewan thought. 'Well, I mean . . . yeah, it was Iraq, during the worst of the insurgency . . . they were Iraqis. Well, I assume they were; there were a lot of foreign fighters there in the insurgency as well. Al-Qaeda in Iraq, and so on. I guess maybe my sin was being there at all. I went for the money.'

The priest didn't speak for a while, evidently thinking. 'Well, I wasn't in Iraq, all I know about it is what I read in the newspapers and saw on TV. And all I can offer is my subjective take on it. There's no official church position on what happened in Iraq. The church is always for peace, as you'd understand, although we don't rule out circumstances where individuals and nations may be justified in defending themselves. It's about what *you* feel, rather than what I feel. I can absolve you of your sins, but only to the extent that you feel they're sins. Otherwise there is no contrition.'

This was not going in any way like Ewan had thought it would.

'What about the child you shot? A boy, you said?'

'Yeah. He lost his leg. We were driving somewhere and my men started shooting . . . one of those panicked things, for no reason . . . it happened a lot because we were all so paranoid. This kid was just in the wrong place at the wrong time . . . I don't know if I was the one who shot him, but I was responsible. He lost his leg because of me.'

'Okay.' The priest was nodding. 'And you were in the army when this happened?'

'No, no. I was in Iraq with a private firm.'

The priest nodded. 'You take responsibility for that, even though you may not have been the direct author of that boy's fate. That's good, it's appropriate. So we have that, and then, it seems, we have your experience in actual military or, well, military-like conflict, where you killed people who may have been trying to kill you, and then we have your simple presence in such a morally questionable situation. We'll just leave aside the other things for the moment.'

This guy is pretty sharp, Ewan thought. 'Yep, that makes sense.'

'You know,' the priest continued, 'I think that if you want to properly complete the act of reconciliation, then you need to be clear to yourself about how and why you sinned. I'm not sure you're necessarily at that point, but you've made a start. I don't know, I'm not a counsellor, I'm just a priest, I can only absolve sins, not work through the psychological issues that they can cause.'

Ewan nodded.

'That's a little above my pay grade,' the priest said, smiling. 'You need to be clear to yourself about what you did wrong, and go from there. I can forgive your harming a child. I can forgive your sleeping with a married woman or defrauding a company, as long as you cease to do so and make reparations. The rest needs work from you.'

'Okay,' said Ewan.

After a pause, the priest went on. 'I think that you should return next week. In the interval, I want you to consider what exactly you want to take responsibility for, and maybe what penance would be appropriate for what you have discussed. I'll do some thinking as well. Then we'll complete the rite.'

'Uh, okay,' said Ewan, further thrown. 'I wasn't aware you could . . . book in for further consultations.'

'Well,' the priest said, arching his thick eyebrows, 'it's not every day I hear a confession out of *The Hurt Locker*. Good thing I don't charge an hourly rate.' He smiled pleasantly. 'Go in peace.'

TUESDAY
24 NOVEMBER

Em stared enviously at Jayde's risotto, and by an effort of will focused her gaze on her cappuccino, which had to serve as lunch, following her renewed resolution on Saturday night to lose weight. Adriana and Jayde's friend and sometime flatmate Tim had joined them; he'd ordered his usual, which was a banana sandwich and a banana smoothie, which always flummoxed the cafe staff. He had a tight bandage around his wrist where he had sustained an injury while lifting weights. They had planned to go further afield for lunch, but the weather had suddenly turned hot, and they'd only gone as far as Canopy next door.

'Katie heard them talking in the lift the other day,' said Adriana. 'There is definitely something going on there.'

'Which woman is this?' said Tim. 'I don't know the one you mean. On your floor?'

'She's just started. Short, short hair, pretty hot,' said Jayde.

'Oh, okay, Brian's new boss. I've seen them down here getting coffee. What were they talking about?' said Tim, between sips of his drink.

It was Jayde who had conveyed the 'news' about Nathan Welles, that he was having an affair with his new boss, Rachael Ambrose. Friends of Jayde's from Nathan's side of the floor had been the first to spot what was going on, and were wondering whether Nathan was a very fast mover or they already knew one another. The idea of their liaison put what Em had seen in context: the two of them seemed more than professionally close.

'She told him she couldn't meet him at lunchtime, and could he delay it till after work. All very conspiratorial,' Adriana said.

Em scoffed. 'That's hardly evidence of anything.'

'They are *always* down here together. And have you seen the way she looks at him?'

'Does anyone have any actual evidence that they're having an affair?'

'Fuck,' said Tim, in his deep bass voice, like a chilled-out Darth Vader. 'What the hell does she see in him? She could do much better.'

'I think he's quite cute,' said Jayde. 'And so does Em.'

'I do not!' she snapped, too quickly.

Jayde smiled, vindicated by her reaction.

It was partly unfair. She was in depressed-irritable mode, which was one step above the times when she struggled to drag herself out of bed, but it made her awfully snappy. In that mode, she could function even when major dramas were happening. But trivial things, like Jayde's goading, made her lose it.

'He's okay,' said Tim, leaning back in his seat and tugging at the triangular tuft of hair beneath his bottom lip. 'But not really a great body.'

'Well, women have different interests than homersimpsuals, Tim, in case you didn't know,' said Adriana.

Em indulgently consumed a spoonful of froth. She had had a brief crisis when deciding whether to get skim or lite milk. This is how shit my life is, she thought to herself, that lite milk is an indulgence.

'Well, so, Emma,' said Tim. As usual he was wearing a shirt about three sizes too small. 'How are you and James?'

'We're fine.' She didn't want to discuss her relationship with Tim, or anyone else for that matter. Indeed, she was regretting coming to lunch at all. Sitting upstairs and starving might have been the less-worse option.

He bit into his sandwich, squeezing a slice of banana out the side. 'I know some hetero guys, if you want to move on,' he said with a mouthful of banana.

Em watched the slice of banana break free of the sandwich and fall onto his plate.

'She's saving herself for Nathan Welles.'

'Fuck off, Jayde.' She tried to say it lightly, but failed; she was too annoyed at how Jayde had—either accidentally, because she was a bloody stirrer, or through an acute reading of her—worked out her feelings about him. Jayde lapsed into silence, possibly offended by Em's vehemence.

The fact was, since having him enter her fantasies, she had been unable to stop thinking about Nathan. Seeing him on the floor at work, of course, hardly helped things. She had noticed that he went downstairs for coffee in the morning, usually with Rachael Ambrose (*his lover!*), and also in the afternoon at about 3, usually by himself. At first she had thought that, if she could catch him alone on the afternoon run, it would be a splendid opportunity for a meet-cute down in Antonio's, or, if she timed things perfectly, to share a lift. But she was strong. She was not going to pursue that, she had decided. The previous afternoon, after she had talked herself into indulging in a pastry (Dark Voice: *'talked yourself into'—are you kidding? Ha ha ha ha!*), she had seen him walking to the lifts just as she set off. She had immediately stopped, turned around, dropped her wallet on the desk and sat back down again, determined not to give in, and proud of herself for her strength. She sat and stared at the PC for nearly ten minutes, irritated and impatient, unable to do any work, then decided that that was sufficient time for him to have got his beverage and returned. She had walked out to the lifts, waited an eternity for one to arrive, and then found herself almost colliding with him as he left the lift. Only a dramatic swerve by Nathan saved her from wearing his beverage.

'Sorry!' she said (shrilly, in Dark Voice's view).

'No, no, my fault!' he had said, smiling charmingly, then lowered his cup and kept going. She had leaned over slightly and watched his arse walk away from the lifts as she waited for the doors to shut.

'Go for it, Em,' said Tim.

'What?'

'Go for it.'

'Go for what?'

Then there was the nagging issue of what he knew about KSR, although nothing seemed to have eventuated from that. But she didn't dare let herself think that she had, against all probability, escaped from her mistake without consequences.

'Ask him out.'

She sneered at him. 'You ask him out,' she said. 'Maybe he's heir to a banana farmer.'

Zing!

'You should ask him out, Em,' said Jayde, staring at her malevolently. Where the fuck did Jayde fit all that food? She didn't go to a gym, so she said.

'Yeah, right. He's screwing his boss,' she said, using Jayde's own claims against her. 'I've got a boyfriend, thanks. What would that Ambrose woman do when she heard about it? Even if I was interested, I wouldn't even think about it.'

Liar! She had thought about it—thought about it a great deal. Most recently, from 4.55 until 6.10 a.m. that morning. Approaching him. Talking to him. Moving jobs and working with him. Doing something, creating some chain of events, that would lead to them having sex.

Ha! Impossible! said Dark Voice.

She had thought it through.

It was not impossible. Not in the sense of what might or might not plausibly happen, but not impossible in the sense that in a universe of unlimited possibility, two living humans on the same planet, in the same country, working in the same building, could interact in some way without breaking the laws of physics; Nathan and Em could sleep together, in a way that, say, Em and Henry VIII could not. Now, work back from there: if it was possible, there must be a chain of events that could lead to it, that could create that event, no matter how improbable. Scientifically speaking, all she had to do was find out that chain of events and make it happen. Scientifically speaking.

At the moment, however, actually asking him out was not one of the ways she envisaged bringing about the fact of physical inter-action between them. Especially not given she was seeing James.

'He's definitely got a nice brooding face,' said Adriana. 'Nice eyes.'

The mere statement sent a thrill of jealousy through Em. Then she looked up and realised Adriana was no longer talking in the abstract. Over at the counter stood Nathan and Rachael: he wearing a dark green shirt that wasn't fully tucked into the back of his black trousers; she wearing a jacket with a ridiculously wide collar (Em knew it; it was a Carla Zampatti number) and expensive-looking pants with those open-toed shoes again. They stood in line, leaning in to talk to each other, doubtless about when they would next fuck.

As Nathan and Rachael collected their cups and turned to go, Rachael glanced over and noticed them, and waved with a smile. Em waved back.

Predictably, Vanessa overfilled the glass, and champagne flowed over the brim and onto the benchtop.

'I can't believe that a woman married to a multimillionaire can't pour champagne properly,' said Ewan.

'Purr champagne prop-lay,' she said in mockery, and turned and kissed him, grinning, an action she was rarely caught performing.

They were both naked, their clothes littered about the room, which looked down on the Opera House and across the harbour. Vanessa had insisted on an expensive hotel room; she'd managed to secure nearly two and a half hours with him, ahead of a dinner in her role as CEO of the second of Derek's charities.

She handed him a glass and they returned to the enormous bed. Her face was a little tanned, and he could see a trace around her eyes of where she'd worn sunglasses while skiing. She was the happiest he'd ever seen her. And, he knew, happy because she was with him. In turn, that made him happy.

'So what did you do while I was away?' She kissed him again and ran her fingers over his chest.

'Not much. Kept the security running at your husband's company, mainly. Missed you.'

She kissed him yet again on the cheek, smiling.

'Missed fucking me, I hope,' she said.

'Oh yes. Definitely missed that. Not just that though.'

It was the first time he'd seen her since she returned from the US, and he desperately wanted to tell her he loved her, that it wasn't just about the sex.

She took a gulp of champagne. 'I don't know why. I don't get why you actually bother with me.' She put the glass on the bedside table.

'Are you kidding?' He stroked her thigh and ran his finger up to her breast.

'I'm a lawyer in my late thirties who married the boss. You're like James fucking Bond. You could have anyone you wanted.'

'Well, one, I don't think I could and, two, I only want you.'

But that was as close as he was going to allow himself to get to telling her he loved her. 'Anyway, James Bond, huh? I've no idea why someone like you would be interested in me.'

She watched his eyes for a moment. 'I'm *interested*, as you put it, because I've never met anyone like you. You've had an exciting life, you've seen some terrible things, you've been in terrible places, but you're smart and have a sense of humour and a great body and you're cool. Really fucking cool. You make me feel like a teenager.'

'Well don't stop!'

She grinned again. 'Oh, and of course there's that elegant Glaswegian accent.'

'Elegant, eh? I guess I'm like James Bond if he joined the army and did exciting things like accounting and supply-chain management courses. Then went off and was a mercenary in a really shitty war.'

She kissed his chest.

'And shot . . .'

He wavered on the brink of saying he'd shot a child, but couldn't quite do it.

'Shot people.' He placed his glass on the bedside table on his side and slid his hand between her thighs.

'You want to go again already?'

'Uh-huh.'

Vanessa giggled, a most un-Vanessa thing to do. He had never heard her giggle before.

'This time . . . I was wondering . . .' she began, a trifle uncertainly.

'What?'

She watched him for a moment.

'What?!'

'I want you to come on my tits.'

'I think I can manage that.'

Great North Road was busy despite the hour and it being a Tuesday evening. Kat was unfamiliar with the area in real life, although she'd examined it on Google Earth many times while cyberstalking Chris. Her mother's rather ancient 323 was a manual, and her long gaps between driving meant she kept messing up gear changes; she stalled at the lights at Garfield Street and was tooted for her sins. She was looking for Henry Street, which was probably the next block up, which would eventually lead her to Scott Street: 4 Scott Street, Five Dock.

The words induced a strange feeling in her, a combination of nervousness, queasiness and excitement. She didn't quite believe she was doing what she was doing. She had to stop behind someone wanting to park outside a place called Bar Rizzo, then resumed, over-revving the engine. A 492 bus went past the other way, just like on Google Earth, then she braked for a pedestrian breaking into a run between traffic.

This was Chris's world, his suburb. These were the restaurants Chris and Her probably ate at, the shops they visited, maybe the hairdresser where Her went. The whole place was imbued with him. With them.

Henry Street. Her nervousness grew. It was smaller than she expected, almost a lane. It ran past Five Dock Public School, where their son Stephen—named after Her father—went. It was so narrow she had to pull over to give way to someone coming the other way, then squeeze between two parked cars, so close she could have reached out the window and tried the door handles as she edged by.

Scott Street. She slowed down to turn, and stuffed up the gear change again. Her heart was thumping. But, oddly, she felt a kind of mental distance, as though she was merely watching herself do this absurd, deeply scary thing. It was as if her body was reacting to it, but her mind wasn't.

Number four was immediately on her right as she turned. She desperately hoped Chris wasn't out the front, or arriving himself. She drove past, not too quickly and not too slowly. A narrow double-storey house with an old metal carport out the front; replacing it was on Chris's to-do list. His car was in the carport. The southern side of the house had virtually no windows, except for a tiny one she assumed was a bathroom window; otherwise, it was just a huge blank brick wall. The mature tree next to the fence had been removed a few months ago. Chris had told her all about his labours in taking it out.

This was where Chris and Her lived.

She went down a block to Newcastle Street. A large boat on a trailer was positioned halfway down the street, pulled onto the kerb. Nice boat, she thought, as she did a U-turn and drove back past the house again. It wasn't quite sunset, but she could see lights in both the lower windows. She did another U-turn at Henry Street and parked, probably twenty metres from the house, next to a large house with bars on the window. She switched the engine off.

Her heart was still pounding, though more in terror of what she was doing than in fear she might be discovered. What now? She didn't especially want to see Chris, or Her. She just wanted to watch the house, to have some sense, however brief and remote, of being part of his life, even if she no longer wanted him to be part of hers. She lowered the window, letting in some traffic noise and, she realised after a moment, the sound of some children in the pool of the house she was parked next to. Maybe Stephen was across the road having a splash with the neighbour's kids. It was a warm evening; the temperature was expected to climb into the mid-thirties for the rest of the week.

After a while, she wasn't sure what she was looking at, or for, beyond the suburban banalities of Chris's house. The feeling that she was observing herself from a distance had grown stronger, that she was a tiny version of herself, inside the head of the real-world Kat Sharpe—Kat Sharpe, Social Media Expert and Hot Geek. She was watching the giant, human-sized woman that she was controlling through some portal, a tiny screen inside the woman's head, ordering that woman to lower the window, telling her to gaze at 4 Scott Street, Five Dock, to consider the rather rundown carport and the tail end of Chris's CX-5, to note the slowly fading light, to contemplate the occasional shrieks of delight from the pool.

And is there an even smaller Kat controlling the little Kat inside my head, she wondered, herself controlled by a still smaller Kat, and so on, to the atomic level?

You can't fool me, young woman. It's Kats all the way down.

Whatever she was doing—watching, or watching herself watching—it wasn't working. The feeling of being completely unmoored from everything, that horrible sensation from when she'd first learned about Chris, the feeling of no longer being connected to anything solid, had returned. She was sitting in someone else's car, staring at someone else's house, in someone else's suburb, trying to feel a connection to a married man she'd pushed out of her life. On a warm evening in a strange street, there was nothing familiar or loved within reach, no sense of comfort or sanctuary, nothing to give her a feeling of being grounded and safe, no thought that she was where she belonged. Driving to Chris's house, in fact, was a trip into the void, so completely and cleanly had it severed her from anything comforting.

Indeed, she thought, she was right where she didn't belong; this was the one place on the planet that she couldn't belong and never would. And this sense of not belonging sprang not merely from the normal standards of the world, by which men's lovers didn't have any right to trespass in the family home. Nor, any longer, did it spring from her own needs and desires, her mourning over losing Chris. Chris and Her may as well have been two randomly picked strangers, like the Faux Chris and Pseudo Her she'd seen at Maroubra, for all their relevance to her now. It was more that there was nothing here for her, there never *could* be anything here for her, and there never was, despite her illusions. There was just some academic who slept with his students, and his oblivious wife and small child who went down the road to the public school in the CX-5 in the old carport of 4 Scott Street, Five Dock. Chris and Kat, as a meaningful conjunction of people, was a silly fantasy, a debunked theory, a hypothesis completely discredited, but here she was, still acting as though it had once had some credibility.

She started the engine and drove down the street, past the house one more time, then turned into Newcastle Street. Bunny-hopping and revving the car back towards Great North Road, she decided she never wanted to visit that suburb ever again in her life.

WEDNESDAY
25 NOVEMBER

The phone rang just as Nathan was about to head to afternoon tea. Once a month, the division gathered for an afternoon tea on Wednesday at 2.30. In the absence of attractive young employees, Nathan found the gathering intensely tedious, but he attended for the food.

He paused, then decided to answer the phone, although that increased the risk he'd miss out on the sausage rolls. 'Nathan Welles,' he said.

'Oh, hi, Mr Welles,' said a Scottish voice. 'It's Ewan Mazzoni from Security here—how are you?'

'Good thanks, Ewan. Yourself?'

'Oh, fine, fine. Listen, ah, we've got a bit of a problem down here, I just wanted to talk to you about it—can you drop down for a second? It won't take long.'

'Sure,' Nathan said cheerfully. 'Where are you?'

'Okay, you take the lift down to level twenty, and turn left when you come out of the lift. I'll be waiting for you.'

'Right. Come down now?'

'Yep.'

'Okay, see you in a tick.'

He contemplated asking Eve if she'd save him a sausage roll, and decided to risk missing out. He wandered over to the lift and pressed the button, then took the lift down, yawning, and walked out onto level twenty, which was rarely more than half full. He looked around for a moment, slightly disoriented. There was a tall man off to his left, muscular with a buzz cut, but Nathan didn't associate him with the voice he had just heard. Then the man waved at him. Nathan waved back and walked towards him, swiping himself in.

'Hi,' said Ewan Mazzoni. 'Thanks for coming. This way.'

He turned and led Nathan around a set of partitions towards a row of offices. Apart from one containing what looked like an engineer, his appeared to be the only one currently in use in that area. He opened the door and held it for Nathan.

'Well, it ain't much, but it's home,' said Mazzoni. 'Take a seat.'

'Ta.'

Mazzoni smiled at Nathan and walked over to his desk. 'How are things? Busy?'

'Oh, it's not too bad currently.'

'Yeah, it's a bit quiet in my neck of the woods too.'

'Anyway, what can I help you with?'

'Ah, yep. Now, okay, when you go back to your desk, you'll have a new computer. The one that you had, which has that leaked email on it and the other material, that'll be gone.'

A hard knot of fear formed in Nathan's stomach.

'You with me, Nathan?' The tone was sharper.

He didn't reply. He stared at Mazzoni, examining the man's face, unsure of what he was doing.

'That matter, the Kittehsaurus Rox matter, is now being investigated. Your involvement'—he pronounced it 'yoor'—'your interest, your *memory* of that ends at this moment. You will not speak to anyone else about this ever again. Let me repeat that: you will not speak about this ever to anyone. You with me, Nathan?'

Nathan swallowed uncertainly.

'I said are you with me, Nathan?' Mazzoni repeated loudly.

'Yes,' he whispered, almost choking on the word.

'If you mention this to anyone, ever, you will breach the conditions of your employment with this company, and we will sue you, and we will win, and'—Mazzoni's tone became slightly lighter—'we will take your house and whatever other property you and your family own. Because we take confidentiality very, very seriously.'

'I . . . I . . . only mentioned it to someone from Legal . . . I didn't do anything else,' Nathan managed to stammer out.

'Indeed,' said Mazzoni, leaning slightly forward. 'You're very lucky you only mentioned it to one of our lawyers, or we'd be having a very different chat right now. You need to be very careful, Nathan. The government is desperate to find who is responsible for these leaks. And here you are, with incriminating material on your computer.'

'Now hang on,' began Nathan in a panic. 'Hang on, you don't think I'm the person behind this?'

'No, not at this stage,' said Mazzoni. 'But others, other people less well-informed and more determined to find a culprit, might not be so generous in their assessment.'

Nathan was silent. He lifted his left hand up and looked at it. It was shaking wildly.

'See, Nathan,' Mazzoni said slowly, 'everyone has secrets, including this company. We're in the secrecy business, as you should know.'

Nathan made to speak but his mouth didn't seem to react.

'And if you don't protect our secrets, how can we protect your secrets?'

Nathan stared at him, confused. 'What do you mean?'

Mazzoni sat there with a faint look of bemusement. 'What do I mean? I mean, everyone has secrets, and if you can't protect our secrets, well, your secrets are naturally harder to protect. Not exactly my taste, but she's a pretty girl. You've not got bad taste in girlfriends. But I'm sure your wife wouldn't be too impressed if we showed her all those tweets you send Angela on work time. So, are we clear, Nathan?'

'We're clear,' he managed to get out.

'Good. I thought this would be easy to clear up. Thanks for your time, Nathan.'

Nathan sat there dumbly for a second, then rose, turned and walked over to the door, paused again, then opened it.

'Are you gonna stand there all day?'

Nathan felt disoriented and sick. He was being tumbled about by events far beyond his control, like being rolled around inside a wave at the beach and then hurled onto the sand. He walked, in a daze, around to the lift. There was a woman inside, holding a coffee. He must have looked terrible; she stared at him and then tentatively asked if he was okay.

'Ah, yeah,' he said. 'Thanks.'

He walked slowly around to his workstation. Luckily, most people were around the other side of the floor at the afternoon tea. He noticed he had a new PC on his desk. He grabbed his bag and walked over to Rachael's office. She was in there, pounding her keyboard furiously, a slice of cake on her desk.

'I have to go home,' he said.

She looked at him and frowned. 'Are you all right?'

'No,' he said quickly.

'What's up?'

'I can't talk about it. I'll call you . . . later.'

'Oh . . . Okay . . . Someone just came and gave you a new PC,' she said, but he was already walking away towards the lift. He went down to the lobby and outside into the heat, almost wanting to run in order to escape the building. It was hotter than he'd expected, which only added to the nausea he was feeling. He walked over to the crossing on Liverpool Street and crossed the road to the bus stop on the Hyde Park side, hoping no one from the company could see him from up above. The smell of exhaust from a passing bus made him feel, for a moment, like he was going to vomit. However, he only had to wait five minutes before a 394 appeared, and he rose, numbly, to get on it, along with an old couple and some young student types, and sat down on one of the last double seats as the bus jerked into motion up Liverpool Street. Nathan leaned against the window, sweating, still feeling ill, his elbow resting on the thin ledge. After a moment, however, the bus's air conditioning began to take effect, and he stopped feeling so feverishly hot. The bus stopped up on Oxford Street, and a young woman carrying a bag and wearing what seemed like gym clothes got on and sat down next to him. He found his thigh touching hers and jerked away, mortified at the thought that she might think he was touching her deliberately.

The thought, such as it was, seemed to set other parts of his brain in action. He began to try to make sense of things, to sort through the questions that began to occur to him. How the hell had they found out? Had they been monitoring his computer? Or was it Jeremy Steel? Perhaps Steel had dobbed him in. And Angela— how had they found out about Angela? They'd accessed his Twitter account, for fuck's sake. They must have a keylogger on his PC, or had installed one once Steel had put them on to him. The bastard. And they were *investigating* Kittehsaurus Rox, Mazzoni had said in that cold, terrifying Scottish accent of his. In what way, exactly? Did they think someone else in the company was behind Kittehsaurus Rox? His thoughts kept returning to Angela, how he had managed to drag her into this, into getting his marriage threatened. Jesus, he thought to himself. Is all this trouble worth an ejaculation every couple of weeks? Angela's nice, but . . .

The bus suddenly lurched to a halt to avoid hitting a taxi that had swerved into its lane, and the momentum pushed the young woman into him, inducing an apology from her.

'That's fine,' he muttered. Anytime, young lady.

What was he going to do? He didn't have anything anyway, not now that the PC had been replaced. The woman next to him, her thigh safely unmolested by any part of him, got off the bus near the Sydney Cricket Ground, allowing him to relax more as the bus sped along Anzac Parade to Kensington.

What if someone else in Veldtech really was Kittehsaurus Rox? Evidently someone in the company thought so, if an investigation was underway.

He got off the bus at his usual stop, with four blocks to walk in the heat. When he reached home, amid the high-pitched drone of cicadas, he was sweating copiously again. Soph and Ree wouldn't be home for another hour at least. He took his shoes off and dropped onto the bed, and lay there, watching the wall, for some time.

Paragraph after paragraph of legal advice scrolled by. Ewan couldn't make any sense of it, but he instinctively understood it was the sort of thing governments hated to see revealed. This Kittehsaurus Rox outfit was the real deal.

Or, in fact, not.

When Chalmers had explained to him the basics of what had happened, he'd been appalled. First, he thought it was a seriously bad idea, one that could blow up terribly for them if there was some sort of slip-up that revealed who was behind the 'hacking', just like what had happened with Nathan Welles stumbling on to it. And, second, Ewan hated hackers and hacking with a passion. Useless cunts sitting in their mothers' basements living off pizza and thinking they were changing the world by breaking into computers. As someone who'd actually been in a war zone and had people try to kill him, he was offended that such troglodytes seemed of fascination to the media. Indeed, one of the reasons he enjoyed his current job was because he saw firms like Veldtech as the answer to fat cunts in basements stealing people's information.

Now they were pretending to be exactly those people. That was why some guy had come looking for the driver's licence the other week.

'You're fucking kidding me,' he couldn't help himself from exclaiming when Chalmers told him.

In any event, he had done the job required of him, which was to scare Nathan Welles into shutting up. It hadn't taken long to get what was necessary on him, with some help from the internal security section in Corporate. The fact that he was fucking some girl in the company was a bonus, and gave him a little more leverage than a direct threat. All straightforward, albeit a little distasteful. In retrospect, he wondered if he'd gone too hard on the bloke, but that was his military philosophy in action—go hard early. Still, given what he was doing with Vanessa, he wasn't in too strong a position to judge Mr Welles's workplace affair. Indeed, he could see himself on the receiving end of a similar conversation, and felt some mild sympathy for him.

In any event, job done. He rose from his desk and went around to the gents. Despite it being on a half-empty floor, when he walked in, all three cubicles were occupied. Ah well.

If he had his way, Kittehsaurus Rox would be shut down quick smart, before there were any other fuck-ups. But then again, the damage was already done. If it was ever linked back to the company, it'd be a disaster.

He stood at the urinal, then heard a flush from one of the cubicles and groaned inwardly. Ewan had a shy bladder. Despite being a trained soldier who had killed people in combat, who had survived war zones like Iraq when they were at their worst, he couldn't urinate if someone else was present, and had never been able to. He immediately seized up: a flush meant someone would be coming out. Now it would look weird, his standing at the urinal doing nothing. The cubicle door rattled as it was opened, and he saw in the tiles above the urinal what looked like one of the IT guys go to the tap. He stood there, penis in hand, waiting, watching the dull reflection of the guy at the sink. The man pumped at the soap several times, and began to wash his hands, then he pumped the soap again, adjusted the tap and resumed washing.

For fuck's sake, thought Ewan, what's taking so long? He was feeling more and more foolish. What was the guy's problem? Either he was a fucking surgeon or he'd shat all over himself.

Eventually, the man turned the tap off and moved across to the paper towel dispenser, from which he plucked three towels and slowly wiped his hands.

Is Pontius fucking Pilate there doing this deliberately to humiliate me? Ewan wondered.

At last, the man was done. He walked over to the door and opened it. Finally! thought Ewan, relief at last. He was on the verge of urinating when he heard another toilet flush.

Oh, fuck it, he thought, tucking himself back in. I'll go piss in a cup in my office.

Feeling profoundly foolish, Kat paused across the road from the AFP building on Goulburn Street, outside the Macquarie Hotel, not very far from Maddy's building. In the area just to the right of the absurdly crass AFP entrance awning was a small knot of people, maybe a dozen of them, or a few more. This was the protest, such as it was, in support of Kittehsaurus Rox. A couple of attendees held placards. It was still hot, though it was nearly 7 p.m., and she could feel a small, unpleasant trickle of sweat forming on her back beneath her top. She'd decided it might be worth seeing who showed up at the rally, although she had no intention of saying anything. But this turnout looked laughable. Still, she'd come into the city for it, and if she was going to be the official Kittehsaurus Rox expert there was a price to be paid. The ABC had invited her onto *NVR* on Thursday to debate some retired general over cybersecurity.

She crossed the road and reluctantly headed towards the gathering, knowing she was going to regret it.

As she got nearer, its composition became clearer. They were nearly all men. She didn't know which one was Simon Berg, but he wasn't the guy in T-shirt and shorts who was addressing the group, explaining that (she heard as she drew closer) Kittehsaurus Rox was a key weapon in the fight against the Zionist World Order. Two rather bored-looking policemen were also in attendance, loitering near the AFP doors.

'They faked the War on Terror. They caused the GFC, the global recession, all to impose Zionist control. The only weapon we've got against them is information. That's what they're scared of, that people will find out the truth.'

The speaker paused uncertainly for a moment.

'Thanks, Terry,' said another man, who, judging by the sound of his voice, was this Simon Berg character. He was a short, slight man in blue trousers and a red polo shirt, slightly balding, the sort for whom she instinctively felt pity. 'Is there anyone else who'd like to say a few words?'

One of the attendees was wearing a Guy Fawkes mask, under which he—assuming, almost certainly, it was a he—was doubtless sweating torrentially.

Another man, in faded jeans and a black shirt, shuffled forward. Kat stopped at the back of the group.

'I think the reason why . . .' he began softly, then spoke more loudly. 'I think the reason why they are so determined to shut down this group is because what they're really scared of is that they'll discover the truth about how 9/11 was faked. That's what worries them more than anything else, you see.'

Kat found herself trying to stifle a giggle.

'When they engineered the collapse of the Twin Towers, they were able to suppress the truth for many years. Yet slowly but surely, we have been assembling the evidence that 9/11 was faked. Well, not faked, but it was an inside job.'

The man next to whom Kat was standing snorted. She shot a sympathetic glance at him. 'This is soooooo embarrassing,' said the guy quietly.

Kat laughed. 'Shhhh,' she said. 'I'm waiting to hear the Vatican mentioned.'

The speaker continued, something about chemtrails. She listened silently, hoping that no one would recognise her behind her sunglasses. The man next to her was becoming impatient. He looked around.

'These people are a joke,' he whispered, leaning towards her. He seemed to be in his late twenties or early thirties, well-built, and wore black chinos and a T-shirt. 'Who organised this?'

'The guy next to the truther,' she whispered back.

The truther had yielded the floor, as it were, back to Simon Berg. She watched the two AFP officers for a moment; they reminded her of bored Roman guards from *Life of Brian*. Near Berg, Kat spotted the one other woman at the gathering: she looked to be in her thirties, and was wearing a floral dress.

Berg said something that was drowned out by the traffic, then: 'We were hoping that Katrina Sharpe, who's done such a great job of covering this, would be joining us, but unfortunately she's not been able to make it.'

The guy turned to her. 'That's you!' he whispered, amused.

'Shut up.' She grinned, startled and yet a little pleased to be recognised.

'I can't think why you wouldn't want to speak at this gathering,' he whispered.

'Me either!'

Simon Berg continued to speak about KSR, explaining how important it was that the group be supported in the face of government efforts at censorship. In contrast to the two previous speakers, he didn't seem demonstrably insane.

'Fuck this, I'm going to get a drink. It's too hot. Want to come?' the man said. 'Someone's got to organise this shit better.'

She didn't reply for a moment. Something in his manner suggested he wasn't merely trying to pick her up. He was carefully scrutinising everyone at the gathering.

'Okay,' she said.

They turned and headed back across the road to the Macquarie.

'I'm Peter Armitage,' he said as they entered the cool of the bar.

'Kat,' she said.

'Yep. You're famous.'

'Well, kinda. What do you do?'

'Telstra mobile,' he said. 'What do you think of this Servetus story?' He pronounced the name 'serv-uttus'.

'Bullshit,' she said.

'Just a Coke, please,' he said to the girl behind the bar, 'and whatever the lady is having.'

'Have you got a, um . . .' She scanned the fridge. 'Hmmm. Gin and tonic?'

'Sure,' said the bar girl.

'Gin and tonic,' Peter said redundantly. 'Yeah, me too,' he continued. 'Still, I was thinking, since no one knows anything about KSR, people will naturally want to create some sort of image of who they are or who it is.'

She got in first and paid for her drink, but he didn't seem to notice.

'Did you see the thing about Henry VIII? Well, of course you did, you're Kat Sharpe. Wasn't that hilarious?'

'Yep. I did CNN and the BBC on that. It was amazing. Just amazing.'

They went and sat by a window.

'But I reckon I could have done a much better job of organising that,' Peter said. His sunglasses were perched on the top of his head. She noticed he had a slightly receding hairline. 'That was just embarrassing.'

'How would you have done it?'

He waved airily. 'Well, first of all, hire some sort of space. Not just tell people to assemble outside the AFP, for god's sake. And then book some proper speakers. I'd get you. Maybe some academic lawyer who knows the legal stuff. Maybe even ask the AFP to come along. They'd say no, but you could say you'd invited them. Even the Attorney-General. I dunno. And then advertise it properly, do a Facebook page for the event, go to like-minded events like Politics in the Pub and hand out some fliers. I mean, it's really not too hard, is it? Just telling your hundred and forty followers on Twitter about a protest is useless.'

Kat found herself intrigued by his manner. He had just reeled off any number of good ideas about how to better plan a protest. He sounded like he had experience in protest action. But he lacked a hardcore activist's earnestness.

'Sounds like you've just volunteered to organise a proper KSR meeting.'

He appeared to mull over the idea for a while. 'Did you say that Simon Berg guy is in charge? I actually found out through the woman who was there. Well, the other woman: Nicola. Hmmm.'

'I get the impression Simon isn't much of an organiser.'

'Would you come along if I tried to organise something?' He sipped his soft drink. 'You're the KSR expert. Your coverage has been brilliant.'

She thought for a moment. A properly organised campaign might generate some more publicity, and further secure her position as the go-to expert on KSR.

'Sure,' she said.

'Okay. I'll give it a go. By the way, how did you get so close to them, if you don't mind my asking? It seems like you're the only person who has actually dealt with them.'

'Well, I haven't really. I did an interview over Twitter. I don't really know much about them.'

He nodded. 'Cool,' he said. 'Fuck, they've got balls. It's brilliant. How about that bloody anti-Zionist?'

She shook her head and laughed. 'Don't remind me, please. It was all I could do to avoid laughing.'

He leaned forward and tried to look out the window. 'Are they still going?'

She bobbed up and down briefly. 'Yep.'

'Bloody hell. I hope the guy in the Anonymous mask doesn't pass out.'

He produced a card and handed it to her. It said, *Peter Armitage, Mobile Network Services, Telstra*, had the Telstra logo, an email address and a mobile phone number. She pulled her phone out and texted his number with 'Kat'.

He looked concerned for a moment. 'Do you think this Simon Berg guy will be too upset if I just barge in and take over?'

'Nah,' she said briskly. 'And anyway, who cares if he is?'

The G&T was surprisingly good, possibly because it was so hot. She was faintly conscious she was still sweating under her top, despite the air conditioning.

'We should establish a group,' he said. 'Friends of KSR. Or is that a bit bland?'

'Kittehsaurus Army,' she said idly. 'No, that sucks.'

He pointed at her. 'No. Perfect. You've done this protest movement shit before. I'll tell Simon I'm going to set up a group. Can I say I'm doing it with your blessing?'

'Yeah, sure.'

'Right,' he said, raising his glass. 'Here's to the Kittehsaurus Army.'

They clinked glasses. He drained his. 'Right. I better be going. It was great to meet you. I'll be in touch, Kat.'

Peter dumped two bags on the kitchen bench. Kylie appeared from the study. 'Hey.' She grinned, and kissed him. 'How was work?'

'Work was, surprisingly, quite good,' Peter said, removing groceries from the bags. Kylie knew where he worked, and only ever asked about it in generalities. 'There's a really exciting opportunity coming up, I reckon. Could be big. You?'

'Same same,' she said. Kylie worked at Parramatta Council. 'You still okay for my Christmas party?'

'Fuck yeah,' said Peter. 'Friday, isn't it?'

'Yup.'

'We'll have to pace ourselves, we've got househunting on Saturday.'

She grimaced. 'I know.'

They had been married for three years and Kylie, who was thirty-four, wanted to start a family, which would entail moving out of their apartment in Parramatta at some point.

'Are we having leftovers from last night?' he said.

'I assumed so.'

'That's cool. It's a bit late to cook. You busy today?'

She went into the room they used as a study. 'It was okay. Helen's being a bitch again. But she's on holidays from next week so I can hold out till then.'

She reappeared and handed him some mail.

He glanced through, tossed it onto the kitchen bench, then took a light beer from the fridge and wandered over to the couch in the lounge room around the corner. The rally—and 'rally' was dignifying it—had been staggeringly, hilariously bad. It was so utterly inept that he'd seen his entire plan of joining a support group dissolving into mockery and stupidity before his very eyes. But Kat Sharpe's arrival had got him thinking. There was someone who had actual interaction with KSR, who might be encouraged to reveal what she knew. Plus, she might be encouraged to help him re-establish the support group on a more successful basis.

'Oi, one for me?' said Kylie.

'In the fridge.'

'I mean, you could've got one out.'

'Sorry.'

Even though she was closer, he got up and went to the fridge, took out a beer and handed it to her, then slipped his hand inside the back of her pants and gave her buttock a squeeze.

The support group would be a good mechanism to get ongoing access to Sharpe and to anyone else who might know a little bit more about KSR than the 9/11 truthers or leftie wingnuts who'd come along to the rally. Then they could set about harvesting information about them. But he'd have to do the work of establishing the group himself, which was not something he had planned or discussed with Spitto. That would require further approval. He'd hoped this Simon Berg guy would do the work of establishing a group, but as Kat correctly implied, he couldn't organise a root in a brothel.

On reflection, he decided, that wasn't surprising. Environmental activists, among whom he had spent quite a bit of time, at least tended to get outdoors and do things, and had well-established networks to organise events, and people who were experienced in coordinating various forms of protest. Theirs was a hands-on activism, well-versed in the minutiae of getting people to show up at particular places and particular times. Online activists were keyboard-bound clicktivists whose idea of agitation was a tweet or Facebook post, or maybe an online petition if they were particularly organised. Real-world agitation, getting out and doing stuff, wasn't quite their thing. That didn't mean they were any less dangerous, of course; they were capable of inflicting serious damage if they tried.

Moreover, in Peter's view—and this was a theory he'd developed himself—organised crime, foreign powers and perhaps even terrorists exploited online activism as a cover for their own activities. Online activists were the useful idiots—he'd picked up the term from a great Wikipedia article—of cyberspace, shielding people with more sinister agendas, like Chinese and North Korean hackers stealing information and the Russian mafia stealing credit cards. That was one of the reasons he was so sceptical about this 'Servetus'. It was much more likely that someone capable of doing the sort of damage KSR was doing was motivated by ideology or criminal instincts, and wasn't just some kid in a basement looking for the 'lulz', as they called them.

He'd made a mental note to look up Servetus, but had forgotten until just now. He found the laptop in the study, returned to the couch and googled him.

Kylie sat down next to him and slipped an arm around him. 'What are you looking up?'

'A guy called Servetus.'

He found the Wikipedia page.

'Who's that?'

'I'm about to find out.'

They both looked at the Wikipedia entry for someone called 'Michael Servetus'.

'What's paedo-baptism?'

'Like, they get baptised with an old priest's jizz?'

Kylie hit him and laughed. Peter scrolled through the entry. Little of it made sense to him.

'How's the leg? You playing this week?'

'It's better. You've got netball tomorrow night, haven't you?'

'Yep. Semi-final. Eight thirty.'

'Good, I'll be home with heaps of time to spare.'

'Any work to do tonight?'

'Just a little,' he said. 'Gotta quick file note to write and some paperwork to do, then I'm sweet.'

He wanted to get the surveillance warrant on Kat Sharpe started as quickly as possible.

Chalmers peered into the fridge, contemplating its contents. It was nearly 8 p.m., and he wanted a cup of tea, but his office fridge was out of milk, a circumstance that often drove him to take milk from the kitchen fridges on his or other floors. Such dramas were the lot of the mighty, he mused to himself, then plucked out a carton marked with *Gio* in red biro, splashed some milk into his cup, returned the carton to its spot with a faint feeling of having got away with a major crime, and kicked the fridge door shut with his foot. Halfway back to his office he heard his phone ring. He picked up his pace.

'Chalmers.'

'Mark. Guy Collin.'

'Mr Collin! What an unexpected pleasure. How's life there?' He sat down at his desk, and swung his feet up onto it.

'All the worse for the gaping hole you left on your departure, Mark.'

Collin had been appointed Deputy D-G two years before him. Everyone, including himself, had always thought that Guy was a future D-G. Guy played the internal politics better than Chalmers, even though he'd never worked in an AG's office like Mark had, but, and more importantly, Collin wanted it—far more, certainly, than Chalmers, whose idea of hell was the top job. But Collin had been passed over when a former DFAT Secretary had been moved over to ASIO. That had caused Major Ructions within the ranks. Every piece of bad publicity for ASIO was now blamed, internally, on the Director-General.

'Sure, sure. How are Julie and the girls?'

'Very well. Amy's going to ANU.'

'She's finished school already?'

'They grow up quick. How's Steve's boy?'

'Oh, don't start me on him. What's up?'

'We're taking a look at this Kittehsaurus Rox thing,' Collin said. 'In a broad sense. Not the specific investigation.'

'Uh-huh, thought you might be,' Chalmers said. He ventured a sip of his tea.

'Can you talk? Now?'

The tea tasted odd. Not like the milk was off, but odd.

'Sure.'

'Downstairs? In a few minutes?'

It was an unusual request from Guy. He sounded more serious than usual, a state that meant he was well beyond the normal human capacity for seriousness.

'Okay. See you over at the War Memorial.'

Maybe it was the latest release, which had come out only an hour or so before. Tom had dug out the ideal leak. The defence minister had forwarded, from his ministerial account to his own parliamentary email account, a copy of the draft minutes of the National Security Committee of Cabinet meeting on Monday morning. It wasn't clear why, but Tom suggested it was because of some restriction on his Defence account, or because he was unable to access the document on the machine he had with him. Maybe he just wanted to print the damn thing off. As Chalmers knew from experience, the best leaks or hacks often came because people were annoyed by pissant restrictions required by security.

But it was what they'd discussed at NSC that made the release. The committee had talked about Kittehsaurus Rox and the previous leaks, resolving that the Australian Cyber Security Centre would upgrade Taskforce Gideon with more resources from the AFP and the Australian Signals Directorate, and ASIO would be asked to brief the committee regularly on the progress of its own investigation of the threat of online activism. The Attorney-General's Department would also be tasked, along with the Departments of Communications, Defence and Prime Minister and Cabinet, with bringing forward a Cabinet submission early in the new year for a new Department of Cyber Security, which would have its own legislation and funding, and be granted full intelligence-gathering and law-enforcement powers. It would also house a 'cyber offensive capability to pre-emptively disrupt threats to Australia's online security'. That would almost certainly put the wind up ASD, whose task that currently was. A nasty little turf war over this new department was almost certainly about to erupt.

The girl who worked for Tom had crafted another beautiful statement.

We watch with great lulz the efforts of a desperate, discredited government to combat the threat of transparency, the sad panic of a government terrified of its own citizens.

Chalmers had laughed aloud himself when he'd read it. She'd caught the tone of online activists note-perfect. If he didn't know it was a fake, he'd have been utterly convinced by it.

He took the lift down, alone, carrying his cup of tea. He nodded to the desk attendant in the lobby, who was packing up to leave, and went outside. It was getting dark, but it was still uncomfortably warm. Chalmers hadn't bothered to put a jacket on.

Collin had evidently called from downstairs. He was standing near the War Memorial—in a suit, as always—waiting.

'Thanks for coming down.'

'It's always nice to see you, Guy.'

Collin removed his jacket. As usual, he was wearing a singlet beneath his white shirt.

'As you'd be aware, there's a top-level admin access to the parliamentary email system outside the control of Department of Parliamentary Services.'

'Indeed. It's Veldtech's system.'

Collin nodded. 'Well, we got to wondering what these Kitteh-saurus Rox releases all had in common, and we wondered if they'd all been documents sent via the PICS system, not CABNET.' Guy's face didn't change expression as he spoke, something Chalmers knew he had trained himself to do.

'Uh-huh,' Chalmers said. He sipped his tea.

'We checked, and all of the documents that were released had been sent, usually in breach of relevant security guidelines, via PICS.'

Chalmers nodded, thinking partly about why the tea was off, partly about how to handle Collin.

'Would you know anything about that?' said Collin.

Chalmers shrugged. 'We're in the dark like everyone else, Guy.'

'This has gone too far, Mark,' Guy said slowly, in a slightly different tone. 'The government is hysterical. They think their entire system has been infiltrated.'

'I'm not sure what you mean, Guy,' Chalmers said, equally slowly.

'I just want to know what's going on, Mark. I'm not having a go at you. Or at the company. You do what you have to do. But I just want to know what's going on so I know what we should be worrying about and what we don't need to worry about. That's all.'

Chalmers chose his words carefully. 'There would have been other accesses using that login, from other addresses, wouldn't there, Guy?' he said. 'From ASIO.' The tea, in the heat, had made him sweat slightly.

Collin watched him, and didn't reply.

'You might have just come back from DC at the time, but I was there when Veldtech won that tender, Guy. I know we gave the access to ASIO then and I know for a fact it was being used. So if you're thinking we might be the ones responsible'—he paused a beat—'you might look in your own backyard first.'

'You could have come to us,' said Collin, more animatedly than usual. 'We could have worked together on this. Made it less messy. We have similar concerns and goals to you. It could have been done much more . . . cleanly.'

A group of four young men walked past. Two of them were shirtless.

Collin had an excellent poker face, Chalmers knew. And he had used it quite effectively. He thought there was a ninety per cent chance Guy was trying to get him to admit to KSR. But also a ten per cent chance he really did think they could have done a better job together. Guy always left that element of uncertainty out there.

Collin loosened his tie. 'It's warm, isn't it?'

'Mmmm. Any progress in the investigation?'

'Well, we're not investigating the leak. ACSC is doing that. I gather from our lads at ACSC they're looking at everyone in the Department of Parliamentary Services.'

'Do they know about the access?' He finished his tea, despite the odd taste.

'I . . . can't go into that. But it would be unwise to assume a full investigation won't reach the same conclusion as we did, even if they take longer to do it.'

He nodded. 'That's a fair call.'

'Look, Mark, we're loath to have to disable that login, or see it closed. Particularly given it won't be our fault.'

'Well, Guy, a lot of people know about that login. Only a few of them work for us. I can account for all of them, and we watch what they do. But there are plenty of people in your neck of the woods who know about it, too. A lot more than in my company. I wonder if this got passed around to more people than it should have, or even if . . . someone lent it to someone outside the organisation.'

Guy stared at him. 'I don't think so, Mark. I think I know exactly what the problem is.'

Chalmers ignored the comment. 'And of course there's the issue of what you're going to tell the AG if anyone finds out.'

Collin glanced around. 'Yes. That looms as a fairly serious problem. The DG is actively engaged on that.'

'I can imagine.'

Collin was quiet, as if waiting for more, but Chalmers was content to watch Collin's poker face in the gathering gloom.

'Okay,' Collin said at length, 'well, I think it's time to go home. Or at least to somewhere where there's air conditioning.'

'So you're based in Sydney for a while?'

'Until this is resolved. We've got a place at Rozelle. It's small but quite nice. Julie's telecommuting.'

'That's very twenty-first century.'

Running across the ground floor of the ABC building, Kat almost tripped, but retained something approaching balance, if not dignity. A few metres away, a young man emerged from behind the security barrier and waved to her.

'Sorry I'm late. Sorry!'

'It's okay,' he said, swiping her in. 'You've just got time for make-up.'

'Okay,' she said, as he took her into the lift. 'That'll give me a chance to catch my breath. The cab got caught in traffic.'

They exited a level up and walked through a glass door around the corner.

'Hi, Irena!' She knew the make-up artist from previous appearances, and sat straight in the chair in front of the mirror.

'Okay, so we're going to do five minutes of news and then Gareth will come straight to you and General Levers. You'll have about fifteen minutes.'

'Yep,' she said as Irena got to work, ignoring Kat's concern about whether sweating would affect the make-up. She'd been stressing out for the last five minutes of the cab ride, thinking she wasn't going to make it to the studio in time. Thankfully the taxi's air conditioning had been going full bore.

'So we'll start off with KSR,' the young man said, 'and then talk about cybersecurity more generally. Maybe talk about what yesterday's release contained.'

'Yep.'

'Okay, come straight in to the studio once you're done, the general's already there.'

'Sure.'

He moved away and then came back. 'Have you and the general met before?'

'Ah, no,' she said, glancing at him in the mirror.

There'd been another onslaught of KSR attention from around 4 p.m. the previous day, with the release of a National Security Committee minute detailing what the government wanted to do about the leaks. On top of the previous release of the Henry VIII legal advice, the government was being humiliated. The issue had been mentioned in a Congressional intelligence committee hearing in the United States, and there was talk that the US was going to shut off intelligence-sharing with Australia until the leaks were somehow plugged. There were calls for the Attorney-General to resign if he couldn't find a way to resolve the crisis. At a media conference that morning, he had grown red-faced and angry at the insistent questions of journalists about the leaks.

All of which, of course, meant still more TV for Kat. She'd started knocking back radio requests unless they were prime time on metro stations.

Once Irena had finished preparing her, she went around to the studio door and entered, feeling more settled. Gareth Males was sitting there, with another man, in a suit, next to him. That, she assumed, was General Levers. He had a grey moustache, closely cropped hair and, literally, a rather military bearing.

'G'day, Katrina,' said Gareth. 'How's it going?'

'Good, Gareth.' She took a chair next to Levers.

Levers appeared innocuous, a boring ex-soldier unlikely to be too threatening in arguing the usual case for, she assumed, more money to be spent on cybersecurity and defence. She'd done some googling on him on the way there, and found out he was an adviser to a big US-owned defence contractor. She wondered how long it would take him to say 'digital Pearl Harbor' or 'cyber 9/11'.

'Mark Levers,' he said, turning to her. He had a certain air of patrician politeness as well as the martial bearing, but didn't come across particularly forcefully. She was feeling good about debating him.

'Kat Sharpe. Great to meet you, Mark.'

She shifted on the chair. It was, more accurately, a shaped stool; there was no back on it, which she always found annoying.

A tech approached her from behind to mike her up. 'If you could just feed this through so that it comes out up top,' he said from behind her, offering her a clip mike. She pushed it inside her top—she'd picked a button-up top precisely for that purpose—and then pulled it up inside, and clipped it below the second button, with the tiny mike pointed downwards. She put the transmitter in the pocket of her pants, then the tech guy gave her an earpiece to push in, and clipped it at the back to the collar of her top.

'Perfect,' the tech said, moving away.

She glanced at him as he moved around the desk, and froze. It was Chris. Or if not Chris, then a perfect replica of him, right down to the healthy smattering of grey hairs. He strolled off across the studio, oblivious to her. She watched him intently.

He looked exactly like Chris. And he'd just been touching her.

All at once, she wanted to cry. She wasn't sure if it was because the guy so reminded her of Chris, or because she was so distraught that Chris was still capable of disrupting her thoughts, whether she wanted to cry for the man who had betrayed her or for how her heart had betrayed her instead.

'Kat?' said Gareth.

'Sorry?' she replied. She forced herself to focus on him.

'Have you met Mark before?'

'No,' she managed to get out, barely stifling a sob. She could feel a tear in her eye. I can't fucking believe this, she thought. 'Sorry, can I get a tissue?' she said, to no one. 'I'm suddenly a bit hayfevery.'

Faux Chris rushed over with a tissue, which didn't help.

'Sorry,' she said. 'I thought I was over it. Weird.'

'You okay, Kat?' said a voice in her ear. It was the young man who'd spoken to her earlier, from behind the glass across the studio.

'Yeah, I'll be fine,' she said, with maximum self-control.

'It was a really bad hayfever season this year,' the voice said in her ear.

'I thought I got off pretty lightly, but apparently not. Great timing.'

She dried her eyes, but could still feel a lump in her throat. Get a grip, bitch, she told herself. Get. A. Fucking. Grip. This is going to ruin your make-up. She felt a little panicked; in fact, very panicked. She was struggling to talk clearly and she was only a couple of minutes away from doing fifteen minutes on television.

Irena came in with some tools and checked her make-up, retouched her slightly, and pronounced herself content, Faux Chris hovering behind her, looking faintly worried, as though he had somehow worked out it was his fault.

Get a fucking grip NOW. F-U-C-K-I-N-double-G-R-I-P, she screamed at herself.

Levers had a mole on his right cheek, which must have made shaving problematic. She tried to concentrate on it, while Gareth stood up and did some links for Perth. Then she noticed a tall, well-dressed blonde woman standing across the studio.

She's hot, she made herself think. What's her name?

'Okay, I'll just do a rehearsal,' said Gareth, returning to his seat at the desk. The *NVR* theme played. 'Hi, I'm Gareth Males, welcome to *NVR*. Tonight, the Kittehsaurus Rox crisis—General Mark Levers and social media expert Katrina Sharpe debate cyber-security. Then, is health reform having any effect in our hospital system? We talk to health economist Frank Ditka. But first, the news headlines with Karen James.'

Ah, Karen James was the newsreader. Kat hadn't encountered her before. Would I turn for Karen James? she made herself consider. She's wearing a lot of make-up. She's not actually hot, more cute. But of course she's got a lot of make-up, she's on TV. I've got a lot of make-up on as well. I wonder what she looks like naked? She began trying to assess Karen James's bust. She and

Maddy used to talk about which female ABC journalists they'd turn for. Would Karen James do me? Does she like the hot nerd look? I'm the hottest nerd social media expert in Australia, with my black hair and glasses and my Twitter following. And I'm going to eat this old military clown up, and impress Karen James, who will want to fuck my brains out.

She stretched out her top lip to mobilise her mouth a bit.

Is Chris watching? she found herself wondering, and then cut the thought off. Fuck Chris, she told herself. She was going to need maximum mental discipline or she risked having a breakdown on 'national television'. She concentrated on her breathing, trying to drive away the thick wedge of emotion that had seized her throat. Breathe. She stretched her mouth once more.

Males had found a speck of something on his suit and was trying to remove it. 'Yep. Yep,' he said in response—presumably—to a voice in his ear.

'Thirty seconds.'

Breathe, she told herself. Slowly. If she could get the first few syllables out she'd be fine, it would give her momentum. The lump in her throat seemed to have diminished.

'Okay,' he said.

The theme music played again, and Gareth repeated his introduction, before Karen James read the news headlines, Kat focusing on her intently. Gareth started reading from the teleprompter; she could see the words in the alternative camera facing her.

'Well, the Kittehsaurus Rox computer hacks have become a fully fledged crisis for the government, with the activist group seemingly stealing crucial government *and* Opposition documents at will. A high-level taskforce has been set up, the FBI has offered to help amid US concern about the security of its communications with Australia, and there is speculation about the identity of the mysterious super-hacker said to be behind the group, Servetus.'

He pronounced it ser-ve-tiss, as the teleprompter told him to.

'To discuss the crisis, I'm joined by former Vice Chief of the Defence Force, General Mark Levers, and journalist and social media expert Katrina Sharpe, who's been covering the Kittehsaurus Rox story from the outset. Welcome to both of you.'

'Pleasure,' they both said simultaneously. Snap! Kat swallowed hard. This was it.

'General, if I can start with you, how serious is what we've been seeing in recent days in terms of national security?'

'Well, it's unprecedented,' said Levers crisply. 'The ease with which this group has been able to penetrate the government's most confidential systems is, really, quite terrifying. If this is what a group of hackers can do, just imagine what the Chinese government or the Russian government or major organised crime groups are able to do. Even terrorists. We know for a fact that terrorists are increasingly working online to cause disruption, reduce our counter-terrorist capacity, even use the internet to launch potential mass-casualty attacks . . .'

Bam. He was straight into it, thought Kat. This bloke's got the full spiel down pat. It was good, though, because it was concentrating her mind and giving her time to collect herself.

'Katrina, do you agree? Is this a major crisis?'

Breathe!

'Um, no it's not, Gareth.'

So far, so good.

'I think we need some context here. Nothing that's been released so far has done any real damage to anyone. There's been embarrassment, sure, lots of embarrassment, but what specific damage has been done? Remember when the Chelsea Manning cables were released by WikiLeaks and there were all these claims about people dying and serious damage being done, and it all turned out to be untrue? The reason we're talking about a crisis is because we're used to this idea that governments should be allowed to operate in complete secrecy, whereas if you stand back, you can see that transparency isn't quite the great evil that it's made out to be . . .'

'I disagree completely,' said Levers, interrupting her. 'This has inflicted major damage on this government and on Australia. No one can have any confidence in this government. Business, other stakeholders, our allies, foreign governments of any kind, they now can have no confidence that anything they say to our government will remain confidential. Transparency is one thing, but governments do need a basic level of secrecy behind which to operate in many areas.'

'What do you think the government should be doing in response?' said Males.

'Well, this group must be hunted down. These people are, literally, terrorists, digital terrorists. They are inflicting major damage. They must be stopped by any means possible. And a new specialist cybersecurity agency with its own laws and dedicated agents is an absolute must. In fact, we have to stop talking about cybersecurity and talk instead about cyber-defence, because that's what it's really about: defending ourselves. And, Gareth, we have to change the culture. These people are being called "hackers" like this is some sort of game. It's terrorism.'

Kat was champing at the bit (or 'chomping at the bit' as her mother always said, regardless of correction) on that.

Males turned to her. 'Katrina, is this terrorism?'

'Well that's silly, Gareth. Calling something "terrorism" is just a way of shutting down debate about this issue. And it's a bit of an insult, really, to people who've been the victims of real terrorism, which comes with tragic consequences. It's clear—'

Again Levers interrupted her. 'With respect, it's all very well idealising some online nirvana, but governments live in the real world. This is cyberterrorism and the government has to respond. We need to go after these so-called hackers and lock them up with the sort of penalties that we give terrorists . . .'

I'm not managing this too well, Kat thought. Doubtless on Twitter she was being castigated for letting Levers get away with so much bullshit.

'You see, people criticise governments for being too willing to go to war. We saw that with Iraq and Afghanistan. But if people want governments to talk their way through to solutions that don't involve wars, there must be trust between governments and within governments. And when there's this sort of thing happening, it destroys trust and it reduces the capacity of governments to achieve peaceful solutions.'

'Katrina, tell us a little bit about this group. You're the only journalist so far who's managed to speak to them. Who is Servetus?'

She wasn't going to give any credence to that story, and refused to follow Gareth's lead. 'I don't know who Servetus is. There's a lot of speculation about that name, but as far as I know there is no evidence pointing to who anyone in the group is, Gareth. Maybe other journalists have access to better information than I do. They claim to be Australian-based, and it looks like they are, but even that isn't necessarily guaranteed—'

'My sources within the national security community,' said Levers, again interrupting, 'say that this Servetus character *is* behind the hacks, and it's a pseudonym for a well-known American hacker. He'll be high on the list of targets for the AFP and ASIO.'

He'd pronounced it serv-ay-tas.

'Well, I—' she began, but this time Males cut her off. What the fuck? she thought. Males was doing nothing to give her a fair go. She felt herself starting to tear up again, and bit the inside of her lip to distract herself.

'Now, apparently the government is considering a specialist cybercrime agency that would focus exclusively on these sort of threats. General Levers, is that a good idea?'

'It's critical. We really need to pour significant resources into this threat, to take it seriously. It's not always the case that a separate agency can deal properly with a new threat, but this current arrangement with the Australian Cyber Security Centre clearly isn't working. It does seem clear that our intelligence and law-enforcement agencies are struggling to cope and to communicate among themselves effectively. Really, the government has no alternative. The alternative, ultimately, is a digital 9/11, a cyber Pearl Harbor that could one day cost us mass casualties.'

Holy fuck, thought Kat, he said *both phrases in one sentence*. This guy is a robot vomiting out cybersecurity clichés. If robots vomited.

Levers paused to take a breath and Kat decided to leap in. This time she was going to talk until she ran out of air.

'If there's one phrase that is more idiotic than any other in this whole debate about cybercrime and cyberterrorism and cyber-security,' she said, before Males could say anything, 'it's "cyber Pearl Harbor". Here we are, talking about hackers revealing some documents from within government that have caused some embarrassment, and all of a sudden we're hearing about "cyber Pearl Harbor" and terrorism. Where's the terrorism?'

'The terrorism is right—' Levers began, but she had purposefully asked the question so she could speak over the top of him.

'The only reason the general here keeps talking about terrorism is because it scares governments into spending more money on this stuff because no politician wants to be seen to be soft on terrorism. And where does all the money that politicians end up spending on cybersecurity go? It goes straight to companies like the one the general represents.'

She pointed at him as she continued.

'His company, Veldtech, is owned by one of the world's biggest defence contractors, and if a new cybersecurity department is established, they'd be the sort of company that would get millions and millions of dollars in funding to fit it up.'

She realised 'fit it up' didn't make sense but she kept going.

'All because we've seen some embarrassing documents from a hacker group. Most of this is hype from companies like the general's.'

Males tried to get a word in, but she talked over him, too. 'The general here would love nothing more than a "cyber Pearl Harbor", so that governments around the world would throw more money at his company. But Kittehsaurus Rox isn't going to create anything like that; they're just going to embarrass a few politicians and spies and impose a little bit of transparency on a government that hates it.'

'That's an outrage!' Levers spat.

•

By the time she'd managed to finish up, remove her make-up, go out and get a cab from the ABC entrance, someone had already uploaded her rant to YouTube and had tweeted the link. It had been retweeted twenty-five times and she had one hundred and forty mentions.

There was a DM from @KSRComms, which read, simply: *you're amazing.*

Just for a moment, she was inclined to agree.

In deference to the heat, Em was still at work, having watched Kat Sharpe on the TV in Tom's office. Her apartment had no aircon, and had a west-facing wall, so work was the place to be for the moment. She had, however, spent most of her time reading news sites rather than actual work.

It had been, for once, a good day. The reaction to the KSR release the previous day had dominated the news; she'd had orange juice for breakfast, three coffees, and no lunch or snacks, mostly because she had been busy all day. As much as she despised being busy at work, there was no doubt it allowed her to cope with her depression more easily.

At around 6.45, after she'd DM'd Sharpe, she decided to have yet another coffee to address her now intense hunger. On the way to the kitchen to investigate if the Milk Thief had left any milk, she noticed that the lights around the other side of the floor were out, so she walked around and had a look. None of the offices were illuminated, and there was no telltale sound of keyboard tapping. Given there was no one else around, she decided to indulge herself; she was, she rationalised, at work after 6.30, so she deserved a little treat. She knew where Nathan's workstation was on the other side of the floor; she would have a surreptitious look at it. She walked towards it slowly, nervous, but with a sense of anticipation. Then she rounded a low partition and found herself facing his desk.

So here was where he sat, she thought. There was a large white coffee mug on the desk, inscribed with *Fuck off I'm reading* The Onion, which still had some discoloured liquid in the bottom of it; a poster on his partition of a hand hovering near a gun in a holster, which looked like it was from some western film; and a photo of a woman and a little girl. Who were they? she wondered. He wasn't married, as far as she was aware—he didn't wear a wedding ring— so perhaps she was his daughter by a previous marriage, or a niece. Other than that, as per company policy, the desk was empty except for a newish-looking PC. She looked it over for a bit longer, then turned, glanced around, and walked back over to the lifts. She was faintly ashamed, but excited by having gained an illicit entrée into Nathan's life, even such a limited one.

Nathan. She liked saying his name to herself.

She returned to her own workstation, wondering how she could make contact with him, strike up a conversation of some kind, whether she could manufacture an excuse for doing so.

Psycho bitch.

Every time Jayde made some crack about Nathan and Rachael being an item, she felt a pang of jealousy. She could handle it if she knew Nathan had no interest in her, but not if there was a possibility that she could supplant Rachael. Maybe she could email him again about work. Or actually try to bump into him downstairs in Antonio's when he was alone.

Of course, there was the Kittehsaurus Rox issue to complicate things. She might be pushing her luck, even in the unlikely event Nathan didn't think she was a psycho bitch, as Dark Voice so eloquently put it, and was actually receptive to her overtures.

She slumped down in her chair.

'Fuck it,' she said aloud, and packed up. She didn't care about the heat now, and she was starving. Time to go home.

The lift stopped a couple of times in its descent; she had not been quite as alone in Veldtech as she'd imagined. In the end, several people exited into the lobby with her. The doors produced a waft of heat as they all left. 'Jesus,' said someone.

'Hot enough for you?' said another.

She stood in the heat near the entrance to Museum Station, tempted for a moment to use the City Circle line to get to Central, then turned left and walked down Elizabeth Street. Crossing Nithsdale Lane, she almost collided with a tall, bald man in a blue suit.

'Excuse me, I'm sorry,' he said, lifting his hand to avoid her. She thought vaguely she'd seen him somewhere before, but couldn't place him.

She walked down to Central without the usual Em stride, which would make her even sweatier than she was becoming. Annoyingly, James had called her, something that she'd only discovered after she'd switched her phone on in the lobby; he knew that her mobile wasn't on while she was at work but called her on it anyway.

What? she texted him.

It's OK don't worry, he replied, just as she was reaching Central.

Fuck that's annoying, she texted back, furious.

She felt gross by the time she reached the train platform, which was almost unbearably hot; she could feel the back of her shirt clinging to her. She just wanted the train to arrive so she could get home and out of public sight and get her bra off. Finally, a hot gust that might have emanated from the mouth of hell signalled the arrival of her train. She pushed on board and went upstairs. It was not until after she sat down that she noticed the tall, bald man in the suit was already sitting nearby, reading the paper.

FRIDAY
27 NOVEMBER

'You've gone viral, girl,' said Maddy. 'Have you seen how many hits that video has got?'

'Forty-seven thousand by last night. And now I've got thirty thousand followers.'

'Not that you're counting.'

Kat was walking up Martin Place. She had an interview at Seven and was a little early. Between that and wanting to avoid sweating, she was walking slowly.

'Half the comments are about how hot you are,' Maddy said. 'You'll have groupies next.'

'Nerd groupies. Obese IT nerd groupies. I can't wait. Speaking of which, that bloody Luther never called me.'

'He didn't call?'

'Nope.' She paused at the lights on Elizabeth Street.

'Well,' said Maddy noncommittally. 'That's weird.'

'Weird?' she said, in an aggrieved tone. 'How does he not call me when I give him my number?'

At Maddy's party, she had done something unusual and actually suggested to Luther as he was leaving that they 'do something . . . maybe a drink, sometime', and given him her phone number. He had not called on the Sunday or Monday—doubtless, she thought at the time, because he didn't wish to appear too interested; much as she hated that sort of game, she recognised that Tuesday was more likely to be when he would contact her. But Tuesday had come and gone, as had Wednesday, then Thursday. She hadn't even considered the possibility that he wouldn't oblige by ringing her. She was, after all, Kat Sharpe.

'I mean, he's a bit of an odd guy, you've got to remember . . . not odd in a bad way,' Maddy hastily corrected herself, 'just, well, he does his own thing. He's occasionally just upped and gone overseas on a whim, a bit like his brother. Maybe he did that.'

'Well he could've rung me first,' Kat said. She began crossing the road, heading over to the Seven entrance. A couple, both young, both quite overweight and dressed in black, were coming the other way. The man gestured at her as they passed, saying, 'That's Katrina Sharpe.'

Such third-rate celebrity moments, as she labelled them, would previously have been fodder for much joking between herself and Chris, lying naked next to each other, or just chatting on Gmail, where the millions of dumb things that annoyed or amused both of them, could be endlessly teased out. But now, the black-clad star-struck couple would go undiscussed, as would all the other dumb stuff that she saw or happened to her throughout the day. The family across the road whose visitors always, *always*, tooted their car horn twice—*beep beep*—when they were leaving, as if they worried that the acts of saying goodbye, climbing into their vehicle and driving off were not sufficient to make clear to their hosts that they were, in fact, leaving. The way men spread their legs on public transport, either as an assertion of male privilege or because their crotches needed airing. The remarkable manner in which even a millimetre of rain in Sydney suddenly reduced the entire population's capacity to drive properly by thirty per cent. The list was endless, and ever-changing, and now she had no one to point out such stupidity to.

Damn you, Chris. Damn you.

'I'm a fucking third-rate celebrity now. He has no excuse not to call me.'

'Well, my love,' said Maddy, in a tone that indicated to Kat she was grinning broadly, 'welcome to the world of ordinary people, where rejection is the norm.'

'Fuck that,' she said. 'Some help you are.'

'You want me to call him?'

'No thank you,' Kat said. On these issues, at least, she trusted Maddy to be discreet—she wouldn't call him and ask why he hadn't called her friend Kat (and hey did you see her on TV?), but simply make contact and find out what he'd been up to. But she was inclined against the idea of anything artificial. She'd expressed her interest to him, and he had failed to do anything about it, so that was that. Fuck him. Fuck men.

It was a parking nightmare near Derek's place at the bottom of Darling Point Road. Ewan parked about three hundred metres up the hill and walked down to the end of the street; there were four uniformed security people at the gate, all picked by Ewan, and an assistant marking off guests as they arrived. A marquee had been erected on the tennis court that was just off the entry to the drive, but, not unsurprisingly, most people were down on the lawn by the water's edge; Derek and Vanessa were doing welcoming duties at the top of the steps leading down to the lawn.

'Ewan, good to see you, Merry Christmas,' said Derek. 'You know Vanessa, of course.'

Vanessa was wearing a shimmering, full-length blue dress and a small silver necklace. She smiled politely.

'Of course,' said Ewan.

'Nice to see you,' she said, shaking his hand. 'Thanks for coming.' She kept perfectly in character, her eyes immediately flicking to the next guest behind him. Expertly done, he thought.

It had been a more pleasant day, still warm but nowhere near as hot as the previous couple of days, and by the water it was even a little on the cool side. It was only down on the lawn, right on the water, that the smell of the harbour, one of the things that Ewan loved about Sydney, was noticeable. With the view, which encompassed the bridge over Garden Island, and the salt tang of the water, and the clear evening, and Vanessa in her stunning dress, Ewan felt as happy as he could ever recall. About thirty people, men in black tie, women in expensive dresses, were scattered about the lawn, where a string quartet was playing, four young men and women—senior music students, he knew, because he'd vetted them—dressed in black. He had yet to resolve the problem of how to aesthetically block off the wharf that led from the lawn out into the harbour, and was increasingly of the view that it should be removed, since Derek never used it. He took a beer from one of the waiters and approached a couple nearby.

'Ewan Mazzoni. Happy holidays.'

Rhonda, whose father turned out to be a Scotsman who'd migrated in the 1960s, was a banker with HSBC, which handled Derek's private capital. Doug was her lawyer husband. Another man, who apparently knew Rhonda, joined them to discuss Clark Island, directly across from them. The sun was beginning to set and lights were coming on. Being a Friday evening, there were a number of party boats already making their way around the harbour, producing a distant *doof doof* that occasionally reached them on the breeze.

He was well into one of his standard anecdotes about Iraq when somehow, by operation of pure loathing, he sensed the foul presence of Gary Prick. He turned around and saw him, stuffed into a dinner suit and looking ridiculous, making his way down from greeting Derek. The thought immediately crossed his mind of pushing Prick into the harbour, or at least the pool down the other end of the lawn. Prick, inevitably, made a beeline for Ewan.

'Can I borrow you for a minute?'

'Of course,' he said reluctantly.

He accompanied Prick down the lawn to where Mark Chalmers was standing talking to an elderly man. Chalmers broke off with an apology and they walked over to the pool.

Ewan didn't know the fabled Chalmers particularly well beyond his involvement with the Kittehsaurus Rox business. Suspecting the matter could yet become much more troublesome, he had wiped the PC taken off Nathan Welles without getting approval, and then had the hard drive destroyed. Though, just as a precaution, he had first made a copy of what was on it for his own insurance purposes.

It was Welles that Chalmers was eager to discuss.

'What's the situation with this Nathan Welles bloke?' he said quietly. 'You spoke to him.'

'It's sorted,' said Ewan. 'He got the message.'

'How well did he get the message?' said Prick.

Ewan ignored him and addressed Chalmers. 'You won't have any problems with him. He's clear about his obligations to his employer.'

'Does he know about the backdoor access to Parliament?' said Chalmers.

The question surprised Ewan. 'Not as far as I know. I thought he only saw the stuff that was leaked and that Twitter login. Did you want me to ask him about it?'

'No.' Chalmers screwed his face up slightly. 'Some people are wondering about that login and whether it's the basis for the leaks. Some other people don't know about the login but might find out about it.'

Ewan rolled his eyes. Chalmers's clumsily coded language did nothing to disguise his point. This was looking worse and worse.

'We need to make sure no one finds out about this fucking back door,' Chalmers continued. 'So we're okay with Nathan Welles for now?'

'He won't be a problem. I've had a good look at him. He'll cooperate. I found out he's having an affair with one of his colleagues.'

'I—' began Gary, but Chalmers cut him off.

'Yeah, I heard rumours about that. He's a fast mover.' He clucked his tongue for a moment and looked around. 'Okay. We'll just have to sit tight and hope none of this gets out to the people actually investigating the leaks. There'll be terrible trouble.'

'Well, yeah, using our own product to steal information from the government.'

'What?' said Chalmers, frowning, as though Ewan had said the most idiotic non sequitur. 'I didn't mean that. There'll be terrible trouble for my erstwhile colleagues. They're the ones who use it to spy on MPs.'

This was news to Ewan, quite shocking news: ASIO had been using the login as well. Chalmers's relative insouciance about Kittehsaurus Rox suddenly made more sense.

'Still, I know it's not my place,' said Ewan, 'but it'd be a smart move to shut the whole thing down right now.'

Chalmers nodded. 'Yeah, I've got a brainwave about that, mate. Don't fret.'

There were now about fifty-odd people on the lawn and the lights in the garden and the house were on. The Andersons had ended their greeting duties and joined the guests, and waiters were now circulating with canapés.

'I'm gonna get another beer,' said Chalmers, walking away.

'Great view,' said Prick after a moment. Ewan ignored him and walked off.

Chalmers spotted the Attorney-General arriving, and made his way towards Derek, who broke off from talking with General Levers to greet his new guest in the marquee. Chalmers took up a spot within hearing distance of Derek for the set piece they were about to perform.

Ever since he'd told Derek about Kittehsaurus Rox and Derek had reacted with such fury, Chalmers had been thinking of ways to bring it to an effectual end. Eventually, he'd suggested that it might be useful to demonstrate to the government they could halt the leaks while the AFP and the ACSC and every other acronym in the Commonwealth were manifestly failing to. It had been Derek who'd suggested the Attorney-General's attendance at his own party might be a good opportunity.

'Merry Christmas, Minister,' Derek said. 'Thank you for joining us. Are you going to have a break over the holidays?'

'I had planned to take two weeks,' the AG said, accepting a proffered mineral water. 'But this bloody Kittehsaurus Rox thing might ruin that.'

'Nasty business,' said Derek. 'Unfortunately, this is what the future looks like. All sorts of non-state actors engaging in this sort of behaviour. Makes one long for the old days when the only enemies were the nice chaps from the Soviet Union and the occasional Chinese spy. At least we knew they were spying on us and why.'

'Life was rather simpler back then,' the Attorney-General said. 'How are things at the firm? I hear there have been some big cutbacks in the US.'

'Indeed,' said Derek, leaning closer. Anderson struggled to hear well in noisy environments. 'They've cut back quite a few jobs and they're keen for subsidiaries to increase profitability. I suspect the same thing is happening with Boeing and Lockheed and Raytheon.' Derek paused, then steered the conversation unsubtly back to Kittehsaurus Rox. 'Just on Kittehsaurus Rox . . . Mark, can I borrow you for a second?' he called out.

Chalmers detached himself from the group he had been loitering near and joined them.

'You know the AG, don't you? Or did you work for his predecessor?'

'No, we haven't met,' said Chalmers. 'Mark Chalmers, Attorney. A pleasure to meet you.' They shook hands.

'Mark's one of my division heads. I was just discussing this Kittehsaurus Rox business with the minister. I think you were saying yesterday that you'd been speaking to some of our US colleagues who thought they could bring the attacks to a halt *tout de suite*?'

Chalmers nodded sagely. 'I ran through what's been happening with one of our units in Dallas, where we've got offices. They think they've got some tools that could enable us to neutralise the attacks, a thing they've been working on for the DHS. We have access to systems and information that aren't available to intelligence and law-enforcement agencies yet: cutting-edge code that our parent company has been developing in the US. Very secret stuff, but the Dallas guys'—and at that point he turned and looked at Derek—'are very keen to try them out in the real world.'

'What sort of tools?' asked the Attorney-General.

'Well, that's our intellectual property,' said Chalmers. 'But this is a new area of cyber-defence, real-time heuristic algorithm-blocking, developed to neutralise whistleblower sites, that we could deploy around pattern recognition, isolating web pages, denial of service attacks, making it hard to access them while they contain certain content. I think we could stop the release of any further material within a couple of days, or at least make it very difficult for anyone to access. Now of course finding who it actually is might be a little more problematic, but we could certainly curtail access to the releases.'

'Really?'

'I'm not a technical expert on these things—my expertise is on the intel side, and I don't understand fully what they propose—but they tell me they're ninety per cent certain. They can't give a one hundred per cent guarantee because it's a heuristic approach, but they say ninety per cent.'

'And how much will that set us back, Derek?' the AG asked.

'Oh, I think given the national interest in stopping these attacks we'd be quite happy to do it without any cost to the taxpayer,' said Derek. 'These damn hackers need to be stopped. And there'd be no connection with the government; it would be a completely informal arrangement. Naturally, we'd hope the government wouldn't forget our good deed when time came to look at any new bespoke cyber-security agency.'

'Well,' said the Attorney-General, 'that's a different matter. But if your company found some way to neutralise these attacks, the government would certainly be very grateful.'

'Of course.'

'You should give Commissioner Thorne a call at the AFP and let him know what you can do.'

Derek flicked a glance at Chalmers. 'Once we've deployed the systems and we think we've stopped the attacks, we'll let you know,' said Derek. 'Anyway, enough talking shop. I must introduce you to my wife.' He looked around. 'If I can find her. There she is. Vanessa!'

Ewan had purposefully avoided Vanessa throughout the evening, keeping some distance from her at all times in order to make sure there was no awkwardness. As the temperature had dropped and a breeze had sprung up off the water, most of the guests had moved into the marquee, requiring extra vigilance from him in observing a *cordon sanitaire* around her at all times. But while he was talking to a small group near the entrance to the marquee and she was engaged in a conversation with the Attorney-General, he found himself in her eyeline. As she nodded and smiled in response to some bon mot from the politician, she flicked a glance at him. After a moment, she gave him another, longer look, unlike any he'd ever seen before, one that suggested deadly earnest lust.

She broke off from the minister, Chalmers and her husband with some remark that prompted laughter, and headed over to Ewan.

'Sorry to interrupt, Ewan,' she said to him, 'but while you're here can we have a quick word about the wharf?' She turned to the group. 'Ewan wants to take our wharf away because it's an alleged security risk.'

Ewan gestured helplessly. 'It's true. What can I do?'

'Fight the good fight, Vanessa,' said one of the group.

He followed her back down to the lawn, where she gestured at the wharf. The string quartet was still playing nearby, their music sheets and instruments illuminated by soft lighting.

'You know the way to my bedroom?' she said softly. 'Take the main staircase, turn right, turn left, turn right. Five minutes.'

He gestured at the wharf as well, as if explaining something. 'Isn't that a wee bit risky?'

'Not if we're quick. I can't stand seeing you and not being able to touch you.'

He nodded, trying hard to keep from smiling, and she left him. Vanessa's words sent an erotic charge through him, generating a palpable excitement, not just a physical arousal but an emotional arousal, an intense wave of love for her and a delight that she was willing to do what she was doing, that she couldn't stop herself thinking about him even on a night like this. He watched her walk up the steps in the poor light, lifting her dress slightly as she walked.

To give further credence to her story, he went over to the wharf and contemplated it until he judged sufficient time had passed, and then he ascended the steps, walked past the marquee, where most of the guests were now gathered, nodded to one of the security men, and went into the expansive entry hall of the house, decked out in thick crème carpet. He walked up the main staircase, not inappropriately labelled as such given it was about three metres wide, and followed Vanessa's directions. He knocked softly at what he hoped was the right door.

'Yes?' she said.

He opened the door and entered. The room was enormous, with a walk-in wardrobe and ensuite off to his left and on the right, judging by the floor-length curtains, a wall of glass looking out onto the harbour. He closed the door behind him. Vanessa was standing next to the bed, pantyhose and shoes beside her on the floor.

'You can lock it,' she said.

'Oh, right.' He did so. 'This is very dangerous,' he said, walking towards her.

'Why do you think I want to do it? We'll have to be quick though. Derek gives his speech at nine thirty. What are you like at quick performan—?'

She'd barely got the words out before he took her hand and pulled her over to the wall between the wardrobe and the ensuite, forced her back against it and kissed her hard, pulling her dress up as he did so. He effortlessly lifted her legs up, making her gasp in surprise. He reached down past the bunched fabric of her dress and pushed his fingers around her underwear and inside her.

'Oh, fuck,' she said, breaking off the kiss and closing her eyes.

'I'm pretty good,' he said.

Sophie, on walks at least, was like a wind-up toy, bouncing about exhaustingly until she ran out of puff, at which point she settled for walking quietly beside them or even pleading to be given a ride on Nathan's shoulders. It was on top of Nathan where she was currently perched, as they walked along the back of Kensington Oval. She occasionally grabbed for leaves overhead.

'You might be okay to walk by yourself now, Soph,' said Ree, 'and give Dad a rest.'

'Soon,' she promised.

'It's okay,' said Nathan, clutching her ankles and returning his sunglasses to the top of his nose. 'You still weigh not much more than a fairy's wing. Just don't kick.'

It was early evening and still warm, but tolerable enough for a walk.

At the cricket nets, a man was bowling to a boy, presumably his son, who was fully kitted up in cricket gear except for shorts beneath his pads. Nathan watched them for a moment, then resumed walking.

'Did your dad ever bowl to you down the park?' said Ree.

'I was a bowler, so I didn't do much batting practice. But no, he never did much practice with me, not outside the backyard. I'd go down to the park with Cory Johnston, who lived a couple of streets away and played in my team.'

'What about David?'

David was Nathan's brother, who'd suicided around ten years earlier. Ree rarely mentioned him, given the manner of his death, especially in front of Sophie.

'Well, he was three years younger, so I couldn't bowl to him. Not fast. I hit him on the elbow once and got into huge trouble with Mum. He wasn't allowed to practise with us after that, poor bugger.'

Sophie by now had decided she was up to walking again, and clambered down from him. 'Did you play cricket on the TV, Daddy?' she said.

'No, princess. I played Under Eighteens in 1998. That was as far as I got. Although I took a hat-trick in the Under Fourteens.'

A dog wearing one of those plastic cones around its neck wandered past them, heading onto the oval.

'Hi, dog!' yelled Soph.

'Did you ever bowl a maiden over?' Ree said, adjusting her sunglasses, as they reached the corner.

'Not enough of them,' Nathan said. 'Didn't there used to be a grandstand here?'

'Yep,' she said. 'They replaced it ages and ages ago with that building.'

'I'm sure I played footy here once and there was a grandstand here in the corner.'

He held back and let Sophie and Ree get a couple of paces ahead of him.

'What are you doing?' Ree said, looking back over her shoulder.

He smiled at Ree. 'I'm admiring your shapely form.'

It was true, for once. Ree was dressed in shorts and a T-shirt and Nathan had been watching her legs. He caught up to her. Sophie had skipped away for a moment, having apparently found a second wind. 'You've got a great arse,' he said softly.

'Rude bugger. You don't appreciate me enough,' she said, smiling, and took his hand.

He was still mildly rattled by the incident with the Scottish psycho, and felt a stab of fear every time he thought back to it, especially over the threat to tell Ree about Angela. But, with the passage of time, he also felt angry about it. He'd done nothing more than talk to Jeremy Steel about what he'd found, and that Caledonian nutjob had invaded his privacy and threatened him. He kept going over the encounter in his mind, as painful as it was, thinking he should have responded differently, but Mazzoni had terrified him.

As for Steel, he was now on Nathan's personal shitlist. That had no immediate ramifications, but Nathan was a stickler in that regard. Once a person had done something to get on his wrong side, there was no coming back; they were a sworn enemy for life. In the event Nathan should ever have the opportunity to take revenge on Mr Steel, he'd do it, even if it were decades hence.

The real target of his anger should have been Mr Ewan Mazzoni, highland thug, but Mazzoni scared him in a way that he hadn't been since childhood. Nonetheless, the fact that someone in the company, someone very senior, had decided that he needed to be intimidated, rankled. More than rankled. He just had to work out quite what to do about it. He wondered who had ordered the Scotsman onto him. Maybe Derek Anderson himself? Maybe that Gary Prick, Anderson's leech-like assistant, hated throughout the company? Nathan had never actually met him or dealt with him, merely knew him by appalling reputation. If he were being fair, he'd have admitted this was no credible basis for despising anyone, but he was a long way past being fair.

Then again, in Angela, he'd given them something with which to intimidate him. He'd decided it was too risky to continue seeing her. Risky for him, and maybe even risky for her, if only in terms of her future status at Veldtech. He just had to work out a way to tell her.

He leaned in and kissed Ree. 'Love you,' he said.

That still left Veldtech itself. The previous evening he'd lain in bed thinking about switching jobs, about getting out of there as quickly as he could, leaving Rachael and GM to cope without him. Rachael was a nice woman, and bright, but not up to speed yet, and she didn't yet have the sort of relationships across the company Nathan had; he was able to call up virtually anyone up to division head level and get their help. If he left suddenly, a lot of the coordination work they did involving contact with governments would fall in a hole. And given there was a major push to try to secure more government funding, that would be particularly poor timing for the company. With government relations on his CV, he was no longer confined to legal jobs, but could slot in at most large companies in corporate affairs.

He resolved to start looking, and maybe send his CV around; if he found something attractive he could pursue it, knowing it wouldn't be resolved before the holidays anyway. That would give him time to evaluate his options. But the idea of walking out on those arseholes at Veldtech was currently immensely appealing.

SUNDAY
29 NOVEMBER

Gazing idly at Clark Island, Chalmers jumped when Anderson splashed him.

'You should have brought your swimmers,' Anderson said.

'I hate swimming,' said Chalmers from his chair in the shade of the pool house. He removed his sunglasses and dried them. 'You do realise, don't you, that when the sea levels rise you'll be completely fucked?'

'It's okay,' Anderson said as he hauled himself out of the pool. 'All my Republican friends tell me that there's no such thing as climate change.'

He stood there dripping on the artificial turf, lean with white chest hair, wearing old-fashioned Speedos, and reached for a towel. He walked past Chalmers and into the pool house, drying himself. 'Beer?' he called.

'Love one.'

There was a warm westerly breeze that made it slightly uncomfortable even down by the water. Chalmers would have preferred to stay inside the house with the air conditioning.

Anderson donned a bathrobe, opened the fridge and, after some rustling about in its innards, removed two Coronas and opened them, then pulled a phone from next to the fridge over to the small wooden table behind Chalmers. Chalmers rotated and shifted his chair to face it.

'You got the number?'

'Yeah,' said Chalmers, pulling a phone from the pocket of his jeans, opening it and handing it to him. There was a faint squeal from some children swimming in the harbour just off McKell Park. Derek put his phone on speaker and dialled the number, looking at Chalmers's phone, then handed it back to him. The call went straight to voicemail, although the voicemail message didn't say whose phone it was.

'Attorney, it's Derek Anderson. As discussed on Friday, I just wanted to have a very quick chat about the Kittehsaurus Rox business. We may have some good news for you. I think you have my home number.'

He hung up and took a swig of beer. 'We're thinking of painting the house.'

Chalmers knew exactly how to annoy him. 'Good idea,' he said, 'as long as it's not white.'

Anderson frowned in consternation. 'That's exactly the colour we were thinking of.'

'It's boring. It's so . . . I-don't-have-any-aesthetic-judgement. Can't you make it purple?'

'Purple?' Anderson wasn't sure if he was being serious. 'How about salmon pink?'

Chalmers nodded and drank from his beer. 'That'd be good, actually. Very retro. Very gaytees.'

Anderson fiddled with the tie on the bathrobe. 'I wouldn't know; I was still in South Africa in the eighties.'

'When you were murdering all them black people.'

'Yup. Then I thought I'd move to a country that has no racial issues at all.'

Chalmers took another sip of his beer.

'No, it'd be preparatory to selling the place.'

'You want to sell? Really?'

'Yes. I've got a bit sick of the block of flats overlooking us. It really is quite intrusive. We might get somewhere across the bay.' He jerked his thumb eastwards. 'Point Piper. Although it might be a little pricey for us.'

Chalmers watched him with some incredulity. 'I didn't think anywhere was pricey for you, Derek.'

'Well, we might have to sell the apartment in New York that we never use.'

'The Central Park West one?'

'I've told you, it's not quite Central Park West. It's one block further west than Central Park West.'

'I really don't like New York. Much prefer Chicago.'

Anderson scoffed. 'Chicago's got no history. It's only about twenty years old. And you freeze your balls off in winter.'

Chalmers shrugged. 'I just like Chicago, to the extent I like any American city.'

The phone rang. Anderson waited until it was between rings before picking it up.

'Anderson? Hello, Attorney. Can I just put you on speaker? I have Mark Chalmers with me. You met him the other night.'

He switched the phone to speaker.

'Can you hear me?'

'Yes,' came the Attorney-General's high-pitched voice. 'I've got my chief of staff here as well.'

'I just wanted to let you know that we got some of our friends in the US to do some work for us and, after speaking to them this morning, we're reasonably confident that you won't be hearing any more from Kittehsaurus Rox. They told us they'd got some code up and running that should be able to neutralise further publications from them.'

'How have they managed to do that?'

'Look, to be honest, we'd rather not say. It's a bit of a prototype put together by the boys in Dallas, and this has ended up being a test for it. But we'd prefer that no one know we're working in this space.'

'How confident is reasonably confident?'

'We'd put the probability at nearly ninety per cent, Attorney-General,' said Chalmers. 'And because it's a heuristic system it's designed to learn as it goes, so that figure should improve. Personally, I'd put it close to a hundred per cent, but the technical people who tell us these things always prefer to be a little conservative. And this is the first time the system has been used in the wild. So I'd wait a few days before saying anything, then maintain a conservative approach.'

'Well, see, that's what I'm asking,' the Attorney-General said. 'If I make any public statement about this and it turns out these pricks are still active, then I'll be in serious strife.'

'We appreciate that,' said Derek. 'That's why our advice to you is that there's a near ninety per cent probability that you've seen the last of these attacks.'

'And what about who these people are?' came another voice, presumably the minister's chief of staff. 'Do they know who they are, given they're able to stop them?'

'That's a more difficult issue,' said Chalmers. 'Without going into too much detail, this has mainly been about sophisticated pattern-recognition algorithms relating to material the group has been leaking and then attacking the particular sites they use. The identities of the perpetrators wasn't a priority for our colleagues in the US in the process. But we're happy to work with the ACSC on their investigation, of course.'

'It's not just about the government, Derek. The Americans want to know this is going to end. They want to get their hands on whoever is doing this, too. They want them sent to America when we've finished with them. We can't afford to muck around anymore.'

'Sure.'

'Okay, thanks for the update, Derek,' the Attorney-General said. 'Anything else?'

'Not at this point.'

'Okay. Let's hope we really have seen the last of this.'

'Indeed, Attorney. Goodbye.'

Derek hung up. 'Heuristics and sophisticated pattern-recognition algorithms? Goodness me.'

'Sounded good, didn't it?'

'Just so long as this brings our little adventure to an end,' Derek said.

'Don't worry, Derek,' said Chalmers, returning to his beer. 'I'm the one who's misled you and prevented you from knowing what's really happening if this goes wrong.'

'Indeed.'

'Why do you do that thing with the phone rings?'

'What thing?'

'You wait till it's between rings.'

'Do I?'

'Yep.'

Anderson shrugged. 'I never realised.'

The website, Peter had to admit, looked perfect. One of the IT guys had set it up based on Peter's instructions, and had caught the desired tone—of half-arsed self-important radicalism—pitch perfect, on a site that didn't look amateur, but didn't look brilliant either. Simon Berg had proved a pushover, ceding control unhappily to him based on Peter's pitch that he could get a stronger online presence going. The woman who'd been helping Berg, Nicola, had proven far more competent and they'd struck up a good organisational partnership. He'd put together dossiers on both of them, and there was already a file on Nicola anyway, as she'd been actively involved in supporting WikiLeaks in Sydney. He'd prepared a fair amount of text on transparency and online radicalism and the importance of Kittehsaurus Rox, and it had been worked into the site, along with copies of each of the KSR leaks, enabling them to boast of being the one consolidated KSR document site. He'd also taken over the Twitter account, @supportKSR, from Simon and established a Facebook page, which had already attracted seventy likes. The business liaison section had been in touch with Facebook, which was happy to help, providing information on everyone who'd liked the page, including where else they'd been online, using their tracking software. He'd also booked the Gaelic Club for a Support KSR event the following Monday. And the open-source intelligence firm they used had begun collating as much data as it could on the people who'd followed @supportKSR and liked the Facebook page.

Spitto was delighted with this progress and eager for him to keep going. How much he'd told Guy Collin wasn't clear; hopefully Collin had a firm grasp of what good work he was doing in profiling this clutch of cyber-anarchists. He figured he was making far better progress than the plodders working at the Australian Cyber Security Centre; in fact, he still thought there was an outside chance he'd be able to track down who was behind KSR before they did.

How good would it be if he was able to break the KSR operation himself before ACSC? And how good for the organisation? It would show a lot of critics where the real talent lay in the intelligence community.

'Who's the girl?' said Kylie. She was curled up beside him on the couch watching a movie, while he was using the laptop. He had a picture of Kat Sharpe open on it, what looked like her standard headshot given the number of times it appeared online at conference websites and next to bylines. Her headshot was okay in a hot nerd sort of way, but she was more attractive in real life, he'd decided.

'A minor celebrity we've having a look at,' he said. He'd been reading Sharpe's coverage of KSR and then, going back further, what she'd had to say about Anonymous, WikiLeaks, hackers and the rise of social media. Much of it was the usual anarchist crap about online freedom, the sort of stuff people who spent their lives on the internet, rather than in the real world, believed. The first recordings from the wiretap on Sharpe's phone and internet connection had arrived that morning, and he'd driven into work for an hour to look at them, which had turned out to be a waste of time. Sharpe had had innumerable calls from radio and TV producers asking her to do interviews, several interviews conducted by phone, a call to her mother and two calls with a Madison Enright, who seemed to be her closest friend. Nothing had been discussed in relation to KSR, although Sharpe and Enright had discussed someone called 'Married Guy', with whom Sharpe was apparently in a relationship, or more likely had been in a relationship with until recently. He'd made a note to get her phone data going back a couple of months to identify the individual and determine whether he was of any relevance to the investigation. The identity of another individual discussed, one Luther, remained unclear. Peter was keen to track him down.

Her internet browsing was even less interesting. Her Twitter messages back and forth with KSR revealed nothing she hadn't already put in her articles. Even so, given she'd had direct contact with KSR, he was convinced she was the best chance of finding out who they were.

'What sort of celebrity?'

'An internet journalist celebrity.'

'Not that Amy Dinh? Isn't she Asian?'

'Um, no, it's not Amy Dinh; it's someone called Katrina Sharpe.'

'Never heard of her. I'm gonna head to bed.' Kylie uncurled herself from him. 'You staying up?' She'd got horrendously drunk on Friday night and spent much of Saturday's househunting nursing a hangover, and was still complaining of tiredness.

He was inclined to keep reading about Kat Sharpe, but knew Kylie didn't like it when he didn't come to bed with her. He turned off the laptop. 'Nope, I'll come to bed too.'

MONDAY
30 NOVEMBER

Em walked into the lobby and removed her headphones, and ended up crowding into a lift with at least twelve other people. The lift doors pinged open at twenty-three, where she exited to swipe in, only for Tom to appear on the other side of the glass doors and point her liftwards. They waited, wordlessly, for a return journey to the ground floor, then went, in silence, around to Antonio's. Em's heart was sinking. Clearly something was amiss.

'Everything on Project X is to stop immediately,' he said quietly, almost tersely.

'Okay,' she said.

'As in everything. Don't even log in to the Twitter account. Nothing.'

'Okay. Is there a problem with whoever's leaking to you?'

'No. It's fine. Just taking precautions.'

'Is it the Nathan Welles thing?' She assumed she had to be at fault somehow, that it was some screw-up of hers that had caused the shutdown.

'No, no, it's not that. There's no problem there. Do you want a coffee?'

'Ah, I think I'm fine.'

'Okay. I've got a meeting.'

'Sure.'

They both turned and headed out of the cafe, but instead of going back into the building, Tom walked up the road to the crossing towards Hyde Park, despite his 'meeting'.

Something bad has happened, said Dark Voice as she took the lift up again. *Someone's found something out.*

Dark Voice had a point. Tom's manner was quite peculiar. Who had found something out? It had to do with Nathan Welles, surely? That must be it. And where was Tom going for his meeting offsite?

Nathan Welles has reported you to the police.

God, shut the fuck up, she thought as she headed back to the lift. KSR had to stop immediately. *Immediately*, she thought in dismay. They'd taken away the best thing in her life, suddenly, without notice. She stood at the back of the lift while three people from outside Veldtech got in.

It was never going to last very long, she realised, though she hadn't thought it would be over this quickly, especially since Tom had ruled out the Nathan Welles issue as a reason to shut it down. She loved being Kittehsaurus Rox. She loved being the secret author of so much chaos. She loved being at the centre of the biggest story in Australia. She loved just sitting on Twitter watching people attack, scold, pour love on and admire it.

At first the sheer scale of the furore around the leaks had dismayed and worried her, but now she was hooked on it, thrilled by the way the country went berserk every time she uploaded something. She loved the sense of power it gave her, even if she wasn't the one risking her neck to get the material, even if it was a giant game of pretend. Nor did she any longer feel the desire to reveal her role in it, to unveil herself as the mysterious figure behind it all, to show the world it was her, Emma Thomas, pulling the strings behind the events that had rocked the country. Now she *preferred* it to remain secret. It was enough that she knew.

The lift stopped at eighteen and disgorged the other occupants.

And now it had been taken from her. She would return to being an ordinary functionary, a junior member of the Veldtech team, nobody.

When she got to her desk, she immediately went and took two Panadeines.

'Telecon, mate,' said Spitaleri as he walked past.

'I'm there, mate,' said Peter, picking up a notebook and pen. He followed Spitaleri around to Collin's office, where he was sitting with a cup of coffee, his phone placed in the middle of his desk and his usual hangdog look. Collin ignored Peter as he sat down, while Spitaleri closed the door, then leaned over the desk and, looking at a piece of paper, dialled a number.

A recorded voice said, '*You are now in secure conference mode. Please enter your six-digit administration code, followed by the hash key.*'

Spitaleri entered a pin number. 'Hello?' he said.

'G'day,' came a voice. 'It's Jack Calvin here.'

'Hi, Jack; Guy Collin here,' said Collin, leaning slightly inwards towards the phone.

'How are you, mate?'

'Good. Paul Spitaleri is here with me and, er, Peter Christian. Are our ACSC colleagues there?'

'Yes, Guy, it's Ashley Wilson here. I've got Tim Mowbray here too.'

'Hi,' came another voice, presumably Mowbray's.

'Jack, I'm assuming you know Ashley?' said Collin, with a faint smile.

'Yep. He used to be in the office next door to me.'

'Good times,' said Wilson, to general bemusement.

'Okay, look, as per the agenda that Paul circulated yesterday, we just wanted to touch base with you on how ACSC's investigation is going and update you on the status of our ongoing investigation of online activists,' said Collin.

'Sounds good,' came a voice; it was unclear whose it was.

'Paul, do you want to take us through where we're at here?'

'Sure,' said Spitaleri, clearing his throat. 'Our understanding is that there's an extensive level of online support for KSR, but it hasn't really coalesced into an active community of support yet. When it does, it will probably draw strongly on existing streams of online activism and in fact much the same people. We're gathering information on an extensive number of people who've expressed support for KSR and obviously if we find any data that will shed some light on who is actually behind them, then we'll be in touch very quickly. Peter?'

As Spitaleri had just summed up Peter's prepared spiel, he didn't have much to say. Moreover, he was reluctant to tip his hand about the possibility he might find out more on KSR than the ACSC investigation.

'Peter Christian here. I've been doing some covert work with the groups involved in supporting KSR. Nothing to add, Paul, you've summed it up pretty well. These are people on the cusp of becoming an organised support network and we intend to monitor them closely every step of the way both for our own purposes vis-a-vis ASIO's brief and, of course, to the extent that it can assist any other ongoing investigations, including your own. We've got phone and internet surveillance warrants for Katrina Sharpe, a journalist who seems to know a lot about KSR, and Simon Berg, who was the head of the KSR support group, and, ah, a woman called Nicola Franks, who's also involved.'

'Who's this Nicola Franks?' said a voice. It might have been Calvin.

'She's an online activist who's already on file with us as a supporter and organiser re WikiLeaks and Julian Assange. She's got involved in this KSR thing too,' Peter said. 'Nothing useful yet on the surveillance warrants on any of them.'

'How's the investigation progressing on tracking down this outfit?' said Collin.

Wilson spoke. 'Okay, we've identified that all of the breaches have occurred through an administrator login on the parliamentary email network. It's a login that has been accessed via several addresses in the last three weeks, for long periods, a couple of them Tor exit nodes. One was a Romanian address as well.'

He paused. Collin looked at Spitaleri, who grimaced back at him.

'Romanian address suggests they might be Russian hackers,' said Calvin.

Peter rolled his eyes but stayed silent.

Wilson continued. 'Now, for some reason—' The beep of someone joining the conference call came across the line, silencing him.

'Who's that?' said Collin.

Silence.

'Anyone just drop out and dial back in?'

There was a small chorus of 'no'.

'Hello to our Australian Signals Directorate friends who've just joined us,' said Spitaleri, to laughter from all of them.

Wilson resumed. 'The software is not logging anything about these accesses except time in, address and time out; there's no indication of how much data has been downloaded or uploaded, or which pages have been accessed. We think it might be a feature of the software that it doesn't log this activity.'

'Who supplied the software?' said Collin neutrally.

'A company called Veldtech. The software is about four years old—a little more actually; it's been updated a couple of times. Parliamentary Services are in the preliminary stages of preparing a tender for a replacement system, but the rollout of the next system won't be for a year or two at least, probably longer given the budget situation.'

Spitaleri broke in. 'Could the software have a flaw that allowed normal users to get access to the back end?'

'Not that we're aware of.'

'Did ASD . . . or, sorry, did DSD as I guess it was then, did they vet that software after Veldtech won the tender?' said Collin. 'Presumably they did.'

'Yes, that's correct,' said Mowbray. 'I was at DSD back then and was actually involved in the vetting. Obviously there was a login for installation and the beta stage, and there are ordinary admin logins. We didn't see this other login during vetting and we're now going through the code to try to see where it is and why there's no logging. We'd also like to look at the data going right back to the installation to see if this access that has been used in the last three weeks has been used previously.'

Peter noticed Collin and Spitaleri again exchange glances. Collin silently gestured to Spitaleri. 'Would ACSC be able to copy us in on those records, please?' Collin said. 'It might have some wider significance for our own investigation. I'm just thinking, if this login has been around for a while, it may have been used by other groups without any of us knowing.'

There was a brief pause. 'Sure, that'd be fine.'

'Have you spoken to Veldtech?' said Spitaleri.

'Not yet,' Wilson replied.

'Actually, we're talking to them about a separate issue,' said Collin. 'We're happy to talk to them about what they know about the software and relay that to you.'

'That'd be much appreciated,' said Calvin. 'We're a bit stretched on the resources front.'

'Obviously we'll need to talk to them about fixing that login,' said Wilson, again drawing a grimace from Spitaleri. 'But that's not a priority currently and of course we want it to remain open for the moment so we can monitor whoever is using it, as best we can.'

'So ACSC isn't close to making an arrest, I take it,' said Spitaleri.

'Not at this point,' a voice said, probably Calvin's, with some finality. 'But we're talking to the FBI about Michael Servelus; they're sending their full file on what they have on him. We think there's definite potential on that avenue.'

'Servetus, you mean?' said Spitaleri.

'Sorry,' said Peter, breaking in. 'Peter Christian here. A step back—what's the basis for assuming there's a link between KSR and this Servetus character? It's not even clear he exists, is it?'

'He definitely exists, and a lot of the sources we've spoken to within the hacking community say he's behind this,' said Calvin. 'It's our priority to track him down.'

There was silence for a moment.

Peter was undecided about continuing, and again wondered whether he'd be tipping his own hand. He wasn't supposed to be interested in who was behind KSR. But the Servetus thing rankled with him, not least because Calvin had got the name wrong. 'Is there any evidence of that beyond speculation?' he said. He was developing the same feeling as when he'd questioned Calvin about the amusing derivation of Kittehsaurus Rox.

'We think it's pretty well-informed speculation.'

'Is Selvetex a Romanian name? Russian?' came a voice, perhaps Mowbray.

'It's just that based on what we've been hearing in our investigation,' said Peter, 'I'm just not convinced he's anything more than an urban myth.'

Calvin's tone had an edge to it. 'Well, the Americans disagree. They have a full file on him and they're sending it to us.'

'Okay,' said Peter with a shrug. 'Fair enough.'

'All right, thanks for the update, everyone,' said Spitaleri. 'Let's keep in touch. As always, we'll prepare a file note of this and circulate it within forty-eight hours.'

There was a chorus of thankyous and goodbyes and mates.

Spitaleri didn't move from his seat. Peter sensed from the body language that he was expected to leave. He left the office and closed the door behind him. It was a long time before Spitaleri emerged.

TUESDAY
1 DECEMBER

'Shall I leave you two alone?'

Peter looked up from his phone. 'Oops, sorry. I got a bit preoccupied.' He put the phone away and smiled at Kat, who sat down opposite him.

'Drink?' he said.

'Hmmm. White wine, if they've got it. Chardonnay, probably . . . anything that's expensive,' she said.

Peter had picked a bar not too far from the Telstra building on George Street, to give some verisimilitude to Armitage's identity, and invited Kat to come and talk about the planned KSR meeting next week at the Gaelic Club. That, at least, was the pretext. He also liked the idea of developing a closer relationship with her to see if she'd tell him more about KSR, especially if it was inconsistent with this absurd Michael Servetus thing that the ACSC were apparently running with. The phone and internet taps on Kat weren't producing anything useful, but she might be encouraged to reveal more in person.

'Hahn Premium and a glass of the Cockfighter's Ghost, please,' he said to the girl behind the bar.

And the more he thought about it, the more he didn't mind the idea that ACSC were chasing shadows while he got close to the person who might be able to lead him straight to the people behind KSR. He could picture walking into Guy Collin's office. 'What have you got for us?' Collin would ask dourly. 'I've got Kittehsaurus Rox,' he'd reply levelly. 'I know who they are and where to find them.' The subsequent teleconference with ACSC and the AFP would be a thoroughly enjoyable one, especially when he could explain that the Michael Servetus thing was nonsense.

He returned from the bar carrying a beer and a glass of chardonnay and sat back down opposite Kat. She was wearing a short white dress and looked, he thought, very attractive, though she was a little sweaty.

'How are things?'

'Busy,' she said. 'Hot. You?'

'Not too bad. Been busy with the KSR stuff.'

'I saw the site. It looks great.' She sipped her wine and made a face.

'No good?' he said.

'It'll stay down. Did you hear what the Attorney-General said?'

He frowned. 'No? What?'

'Apparently he said just now they were eighty to ninety per cent confident they'd stopped the leaks and that investigations were continuing into the parties responsible.'

'Wow,' he said.

He had not heard that; there had been no mention at work of KSR being shut down, not when he'd left half an hour before. This threw him entirely. He'd have to check. Maybe Kat had misheard, but it was unlikely given it was her job to know what was happening with KSR.

'Weird that they're saying they've shut it down but no one's been arrested,' he mused.

'Yeah, that is odd. You'd have thought the two would have gone together,' she said.

He nodded, trying to think of a scenario in which the leaks would be stopped without identifying those responsible. Maybe they just hadn't arrested them. Hmmm. Focus on the job at hand, he then thought to himself. Don't worry about what's outside your control. Your job is to be Peter Armitage, Telstra employee and budding online activist.

'So how much interest next week?' she said.

'Heaps,' he said, entirely truthfully. 'Heaps and heaps. I've been really surprised by the level of interest. Lots of calls and lots of emails.'

By dint of setting up the website and tapping into existing offline left-wing groups, Peter had indeed managed to stir up quite a bit of interest in a KSR support group, especially with the Politics in the Pub event.

'So did you have any luck finding another speaker?'

Kat had given him a loose commitment to speak, but he had been anxious to find someone else as well.

'Yep, Kim Braddock from the Law Society will be there. He's a human rights lawyer, very well respected.'

Braddock was a pain-in-the-arse civil-rights clown who regularly made submissions to parliamentary inquiries calling for ASIO's powers to be wound back. He was ideal for the gig.

She nodded. 'I think I've heard of him.'

Peter noticed a small mole on her neck. She had long, slender hands, though her nails weren't too flash; Kylie was mildly obsessive about her nails, finger and toes, and currently sported purple toenail polish. Kat's dress was open sufficiently to show a little cleavage. He wondered if she was wearing a push-up bra and, if so, why.

'But you're the main attraction,' he ventured, trying to make sure he didn't look at her chest. 'After that thing on *NVR* last week. That was amazing. It just went totally viral.'

She shrugged a little dismissively. 'You can never plan that sort of stuff. So where do you find all the time for this activism? You must be putting a lot of effort into it.'

Peter thought for a moment about what would sound most plausible, sipped his beer, then hit on the perfect reply. 'Well, if I can be brutally honest?'

'Sure.'

'I had a fairly stressful break-up a month or so ago and this is kind of an activity to keep me busy and distracted.'

She looked at him and nodded slowly. 'And is it working?'

He lifted his hand and wiggled it from side to side. She smiled.

'Have you spoken any more with KSR?' he said, deliberately moving the conversation on. 'Any more interviews?'

'No interviews.'

He couldn't be sure whether she was being truthful or just being guarded in her response, and decided not to press the matter for now. The wiretaps would reveal whether she'd had any contact.

'The media keeps talking about this Michael Servetus like he's real,' he said, drinking his beer. 'They won't let go of it.'

'Ser-vee-tus,' she said.

'It's pronounced Ser-vee-tus?'

'Yeah. It's a Spanish name. I speak a little Spanish.'

'Ah, okay.'

'It's easier for the media to report something complex like this if you can blame a single individual rather than a genuine online movement,' she said, playing with her glass.

'But it's such a cliché,' Peter said, feigning intensity. 'I mean, it may as well be a villain in a James Bond film. And why does it have to be a male? I know most hackers are male, traditionally, but just for once, maybe, why can't it be a female hacker?' He was pleased with that line, knowing it would appeal to a woman.

'Clichés are clichés because they save time,' she said. 'And everyone understands them. They're the lingua franca of journalism.'

He didn't understand 'lingua franca', but let it go. One to look up later.

'So this break-up of yours,' she began, then paused.

Yes! He was inwardly delighted. He *knew* she wouldn't be able to resist coming back to it. It confirmed the benefit of tapping her phone. Even if it didn't yield anything in terms of direct information, it gave him enough understanding of what was going on in her life to manipulate her without her knowing.

'Was it a long-term relationship?'

'Not that long term,' he replied. 'But it was pretty good. At least, I thought it was pretty good. As you can probably guess, I wasn't the one who ended it.'

She nodded. 'I've been through a break-up myself lately. It sucks.'

'Yep,' he said reflectively. 'You hate them and you miss them at the same time.'

He'd heard her say something similar, but longer and with better words, in her phone conversation with Madison Enright, in the first batch of recordings.

'Yes!' she said loudly. 'Get out of my head!'

She drained her wine. 'Thank god I've been busy with all this. It was so perfectly timed. I would have ended up lying in bed eating nothing but cheese sandwiches and drinking cheap wine for a month.'

Peter frowned. 'I hadn't heard about cheese sandwiches. Maybe I should try them.'

'Oh, fuck yeah!' she said animatedly. 'My mum's toasted cheese sandwiches got me through my first broken heart when I was sixteen and Ray English dumped me for Samantha Caligari. Samantha Caligari! Can you believe someone was named Samantha Caligari? Maybe she hypnotised him.'

Peter didn't understand that either.

'I wonder what Samantha Caligari does now,' he said, trying not to lose the thread of the conversation.

'Oh, she's a housewife in Engadine,' Kat said. 'I know her on Facebook. Ray went to America, I think. I hope his skin improved. He was good-looking but had acne.'

'Do you want another drink?'

She paused for a moment. 'Okay, I'll have one more. I'll get it. Then I have to go. What do you want?'

Nathan left work and crossed over to the Hyde Park side of the street, walked up towards Oxford Street and crossed over with the lights. It was 5.45, and outside it was still in the high thirties; there were three or four days of hot weather forecast, before a break on the weekend. He walked down College Street to the Pullman and entered the creatively named Bar Rendezvous. Inside it was mostly empty, and Angela was nowhere to be seen, so he approached the bar and ordered a glass of wine from the youth behind it.

'How's your day been?' said the barman.

'Saved by air conditioning,' Nathan replied, after a pause.

'That's the way to be.'

The exchange was, he felt, almost perfect in its pointlessness, as if neither performer could be bothered making a real effort, and yet both felt compelled to go through the verbal motions. Perhaps he should write a play made up entirely of such banal moments of everyday exchange. Instead of the Pinteresque Pause, there could be the Wellesian Witlessness.

The youth charged him twelve dollars for what looked a very small glass, although to the lad's credit he had pitched out the remains of one bottle and opened a new one after giving it a sniff.

'Bloody hell you walk fast,' Angela said, appearing from behind him. 'I was trying to catch up to you.'

'I thought you'd be waiting impatiently for me,' he said. She was wearing a red top he liked, and a grey skirt he hadn't seen before and didn't much like. She ordered a Corona 'without fruit' and lamented the heat.

'Did you drive?'

'Nup.'

They headed for a couch well away from the bar. She dumped her bag opposite him and sat down, then fanned herself.

'You're from Brisbane, you should be used to this weather,' he said.

'I'm fucking over it,' she said. 'So you want to stop?'

He looked at her. 'What?'

'You want to stop seeing me?'

'How did you know?' He frowned.

'Well, it seemed an odd thing to do, to ask to have a drink.' She smiled at him, pleased she had thrown him with her bluntness. She drank some of the Corona. 'We're kinda past the drink stage.'

'Um, yeah, okay.' He gulped his wine, wondering if she was going to remain as relaxed as this about the whole issue. 'I had a close call the other week, a very close one. It gave me a bloody heart attack.'

'What happened?'

He had a lie ready. 'I, um, well, I got careless. Stupid, really, about where I was supposed to be. And a friend of Ree's saw me in your car.'

She was aghast. 'Shit. So what did you do?'

He waved dismissively. 'I explained it away okay. I said you were a colleague from work, which gets bonus points for being true, and that we were going to a meeting with a New South Wales MP. I went on and on about this terrible meeting we had in Macquarie Street. There's no problem. But just for a little while I thought I was in real trouble and I've been worried ever since. So I think it'd be a good idea if we stop for a while.'

Angela narrowed her eyes at him. 'So you think you can just fuck me and dump me at your convenience?'

He narrowed his eyes back. 'Well, yeah,' he said, and they both grinned.

'Well, it's probably a good idea,' she said. 'I don't want your wife hunting me down 'cos I tried to steal her bloke. Not, of course, that I actually want to steal you—just borrow you for an hour or so at a time.'

He found himself staring at her breasts, and for a moment contemplated the pleasure to be had in kissing her nipples. He looked away. Discipline, he thought.

'We're losing four people in my area,' she said conversationally.

•

He was not particularly happy when he got off the bus, and he was downright gloomy by the time he walked in the front door. There was no pleasure to be obtained from his act of ceasing the affair, and no compensation or reward for it, no gain for the pain, however relaxed Angela had been about it—which in any event might merely confirm that she was fucking that Todd Brown child. But when he walked into his house, he felt even worse, like a wave of domestic banality was washing over him. Sophie was in the bath while Ree, rather grumpily, was making risotto. No sex here, he thought. No girlfriend, no fucks in apartments in Botany, no secret passion. Just coping with a narky wife and extracting a protesting daughter from the bath.

And the best part is, Nathan, he thought to himself as he towelled down Soph, you haven't done anything to deserve any better. Why should he expect any reward for ceasing his infidelity? What a champion you are, mate, what a huge sacrifice you're making, to actually stop cheating on your wife, to stop lying to her, to stop disrespecting her. You merely stopped being a shit and you want some sort of reward for it.

'We'll get some dinner when you've got your PJs on, okay?' he said to Sophie.

'Daddy, I feel sick,' she said.

When Anderson reached his office just before 8 a.m., Crick was waiting, and followed him into the office, closing the door behind him.

'Going to be forty-one degrees out there they reckon,' said Gary as Anderson put his briefcase and phone down.

Anderson nodded as he sat down. 'Like summers in Cape Town when I was a kid.'

'Be baking hot out west.'

'What did you want to see me about?'

Gary played with his fingers for a moment. 'Well,' he began, 'this is a tough thing to do, and I'm not sure if I'm doing the right thing, but I think it's probably important that you know.'

Anderson looked at him. 'What is it?'

'The security guy, Ewan Mazzoni, I think he's having . . . ' Crick stopped, coughed, then resumed. 'I think he's having an affair with your wife.'

Anderson froze.

Crick, watching him, began to turn red. He gulped nervously and continued.

'Um, at the party on Friday night, I noticed your wife go into the house, which of course was hardly, well, unusual. But then Mazzoni went inside after a couple of minutes.' He stopped.

'Go on,' Anderson said, his voice almost a croak.

'I followed. I'm not sure why; after all, he's your personal security consultant, there's no reason why he wouldn't go inside. I guess I got nosey. Anyway, I saw him go upstairs, and then I saw him come back out about ten minutes later. Your wife came back out a couple of minutes after that. They looked . . . well, yeah.'

Anderson rose slowly from his desk, walked over to the meeting table and leaned on it, looking at it.

'It could be innocent,' Gary said.

'But why isn't it?' said Anderson.

Gary directed his gaze out the window, into the clear morning sky beyond.

'Well, I did some checking. Your wife's diary is online here. According to our pass logs, there have been about eight occasions when Mazzoni has left the office during the day and returned around ninety minutes or two hours later. And Vanessa has a blank spot in her diary for exactly the same times. As you probably know, she doesn't have that many blank spots in her diary.'

Anderson put his hands to his head, then pushed them along his forehead, stretching his eyes. For a time he didn't speak, but merely stared at the table.

'The bastard,' he said simply, after a time. He closed his eyes, and breathed out, in a halting, almost sobbing fashion. 'My wife,' he muttered. 'At my house.' Then he opened his eyes and said, 'That's why he was so eager to put in security measures at my place. So he could fuck my wife.'

'I'm sorry.'

'I want him here. I want the bastard here. I want to talk to him.' Anderson was becoming more visibly angry now, breathing harder, his right hand turning into a fist. 'He did that in my fucking house. I want to . . . Get him here.'

'Okay,' said Gary. 'Sure.'

Anderson looked away, then back, struck by a thought. 'But don't do anything until I've spoken to . . . spoken to my wife. It might have to wait till tomorrow.'

'Sure.' Gary stood up, then turned and headed for the door. 'Um . . . anything else you want me to do?'

'No.'

'Okay.' He opened the door.

'And, Gary, thank you,' said Anderson.

'Thank you, sir. I'm sorry, sir.'

Anderson sat down and began to think, breathing loudly.

Ewan had been caught in traffic, and it had taken him a full hour to get home. He'd spent the entire day in the office, not daring to venture out into the heat, the full ferocity of which he hadn't discovered until he'd driven the car out of the basement at work. It was only after he'd dumped his phone on the table that he saw there'd been a number of calls, none of which he'd heard as he'd left it on silent. They were all from Vanessa, five of them. What was she so eager to discuss with him? Just for a moment, he allowed himself to indulge in the thought that she wanted to tell him she was leaving Derek for him.

He hit call, and walked over to contemplate what the city looked like as darkness fell. Her own voicemail was on, so he hung up; there was no point in leaving a message, since she would recognise his number. He went to get changed but she called straight back.

'Hey,' he said happily, smiling as he spoke. 'How are—'

She cut him off. 'Why haven't you answered your phone?' she said loudly, almost hysterically. 'Derek found out.'

His heart skipped a beat. He didn't reply for some seconds.

'How?' he said finally.

'I don't fucking know,' she snapped. 'Someone saw us at the party, I think. I had no choice. I told him.'

He breathed out slowly. 'Okay. Uh, what did he say to you?'

'Nothing much. He's furious. I'm making plans to stay with a friend for the time being.'

'What did he say about . . .' He paused, and then a belated thought occurred to him. 'Vanessa, I'm sorry this happened,' he said. 'I'm really sorry. I didn't—'

'There's no point saying sorry. I did this willingly.' Her tone was becoming more brusque and businesslike.

'Did he say anything about me?'

'No. Look, I have to go, I have to find a lawyer. Everything is fucked up completely, needless to say.'

'Okay . . . Well, I'll talk to you soon, okay?'

'Okay.'

She hung up, and he stared ahead, his mind blank for a time. Anderson knew. Shit. He knew. How? *How had he found out?* He was pretty sure no one had seen him go upstairs on Friday. But it had been a wild risk, a crazy one. They were so besotted, so desperate to fuck each other that they hadn't thought through the risks properly.

Fool. *Fool.* If only he'd played it safe.

There was really no choice, he realised; he had to face Anderson, regardless of what the latter might do. He'd fucked the guy's wife; the guy had a right to be furious, to take out his anger on him, and he knew it would cost him his job, at the very least. The thought of confronting Anderson actually worried him. The man couldn't hurt him, but Ewan had behaved badly towards him. There was no altering that.

THURSDAY
3 DECEMBER

Nathan sat in the doctor's waiting room with a rather listless Sophie on his knee. She had a rash on her back and a fever, and Ree was anxious for her to see a doctor, but had a work appointment; Nathan had readily offered to look after her, given his state of unhappiness at work. Even the purgatory of a medical waiting room appealed more than Veldtech.

'Only if you do me one favour,' said Rachael, when he called to tell her he wouldn't be in until lunchtime.

'What's that?'

'Come with me to the Christmas party. I won't know anyone there.'

'Er . . . fine,' he replied. He hadn't been planning to attend, but he didn't mind the thought of attending with Rachael.

Sophie, displaying a little bit of energy, pushed herself off his lap and went over to the rather desultory collection of kids' books and toys. The old woman sitting next to the toys smiled at her indulgently, then coughed with a definite rattle and lifted the tiny hanky she was clutching in her left hand to her mouth. He looked over at his other colleague in limbo, an old gent sitting three chairs down from the woman, and offered him a smile. The old fellow nodded back. He was dressed in a brown suit and had a walking stick.

A well-turned-out old gent, Nathan thought. Can't wait till I'm so old going to the doctor is my only excuse to dress up.

He flicked idly through one of the women's mags next to him, having located the oldest one he could find (June 2003) and then, on a whim, picked up one of the other, more official-looking magazines, *NSW Obstetrics Quarterly*. The well-turned-out old gent was summoned into a surgery by the other doctor in the practice. He rose stiffly and shuffled out of sight.

Nathan leafed through the obstetrics mag, one eye on Sophie, and then stopped.

Vale Sally Branch, read the small title towards the back, at the head of two paragraphs.

Sally Branch? He frowned and read on.

NSWOQ records with sadness the death in April this year of Sally Branch.

Sally was educated at the University of Sydney Medical School and was admitted as a Fellow of the RANZCOG in 2009. Sally was a dynamic person with a great sense of humour, capable of inspiring colleagues and patients alike with her love of life. She was a keen tennis player, playing for the Sydney University Lawn Tennis Club side, and was recently appointed sub-dean of the Sydney Medical Program.

Sally did not practise in the months before her death, and accordingly her time with the college was relatively short. However, her great popularity with colleagues and her capacity for hard work were reflected in the very great representation of fellows at her funeral. Her premature death was a tragic loss and she will be remembered with great affection.

He looked at the date: June 2013. Then he reread the article, unable to believe it. Sally Branch had been dead for a couple of years and he had not known about it. Sally dead? It had to be her, there couldn't be another, separate Sally Branch who was at uni at the same time as him and played tennis.

Sally was dead.

He was stunned. Perhaps that was too strong a word, maybe not stunned, but he felt deeply peculiar and couldn't quite believe what he had read. He read it yet again, looking for something about how she died, but it said nothing about the circumstances of her death. Was she ill? She didn't practise before she died. Did she have cancer? Or did she have a car accident or some other misadventure? Or suicide? He remembered hearing that Sally's mother, a GP, had killed herself a couple of years after Sally had left uni.

He watched Sophie playing, his mind blank.

Sally dead.

They had been very good friends at uni; not lovers, at any time, but friends, good friends, drinking pals. He had met her in some arts course she did, as med students were compelled to do an undergraduate degree before being permitted to enrol in medicine. She had a quick mind, and moved with a languid elegance; he saw immediately why she was a good tennis player. Her (very wealthy) family had sent her to Women's College, while he flatted, but despite this they moved in somewhat similar circles, had similar friends at uni, had probably seen each other around before meeting. However, their friendship became particularly close because of Sandra Dunkley, a friend of Sally's. He had gone out with Sandra for a few months, until she had dumped him at the end of second year in exchange for Harry; to assist his emotional recovery, Sally had invited him with a select group of friends to her father's winery in the Hunter, a trip that had amounted to approximately seventy-two straight hours of drinking. On the second night, he and Sally had lain under the stars, completely drunk, discussing life, love and the future. They had also discussed Sandra's behaviour in dumping him. 'Stupid girl,' Sally had said, while spilling some wine—quite a lot of wine, actually, but there was always more where that came from. 'Stupid girl. I wouldn't have dumped you.' It was only months later, when he was over the whole thing, that he realised what Sally's words had really meant, and how obtuse he had been at that moment in not understanding them. But by that time, he hardly ever saw her.

And now she was dead.

He wondered how he could find out more. Knowing her family, there would probably be a death notice in the *Herald* which he could look up, but it would not be likely to offer too much detail. He went through a list of people he could ask, but he no longer kept in contact with anyone from uni. There was Sandra, but he hadn't spoken to her since she'd dumped him and he had no idea where she was now; and Matty Tessoriero—hadn't he moved to France? Belgium? Maybe Linda might know someone who might know, but calling people out of the blue did not seem a particularly good idea. He had met Sally's father, an eminent barrister, once, but that was hardly sufficient to call the poor bloke cold and demand details of his daughter's death.

He closed the magazine and continued to gaze at Sophie without really seeing her. This was, he realised, the first death of a contemporary of his, of a person of some (if not much) actual importance in his life beyond family. David had killed himself, of course, and he'd known other people who had died; a couple of people he went to school with or knew vaguely had hit the fence, as he put it. A guy from school had OD'd, one ended up in the army and died in Afghanistan . . . but none with the status of someone like Sally, whom he had known well, with whom he had spent a lot of time, someone the same age as him. It was bizarre; she had been dead for years without him even knowing, leaving him to find out by accident in his GP's surgery. He felt like crying, though he wasn't sure why.

'Sorry to keep you waiting, Nathan,' said Dr Pryor, as she opened the surgery door.

Ewan stabbed the button for the twenty-eighth floor. Gary Prick had, unsurprisingly, rung half an hour before and demanded that he come to 'speak with Mr Anderson'. As he stood in the lift, he felt his pulse. He was, unusually, a little nervous. Still, time to get it over and done with. He would have to take his lumps. Whatever Anderson did to him, it was entirely justified.

Anderson's EA wasn't there. Prick opened the door of Anderson's office, and beckoned to him. Rather than move towards the door, Ewan merely turned away and picked up a magazine, uninterested in appearing to be at Prick's beck and call.

'Are you coming in?' Prick said loudly.

Ewan put the magazine down and walked towards him. 'You didn't say the magic word,' he said.

Anderson was standing by the office windows, looking out. Prick followed him in, to Mazzoni's annoyance.

'What's this guy doing here?' he said loudly. 'I thought this was between you and me.'

Anderson turned. 'Don't come into my office and tell me who can and can't be here.'

Anderson's tone had a restrained, cold anger to it. Ewan indeed regretted trying to dictate to him. 'Suit yourself.' He shrugged.

'You're sacked,' said Anderson, taking several paces towards him. He had turned red. Ewan wondered whether he might be in danger of a heart attack.

Ewan half smiled in resignation. 'Sure,' he said. That, as it were, was that.

'You think it's funny, huh?' said Anderson angrily, clearly looking for an opportunity to lash out at him.

Ewan chuckled in bemusement and shook his head. 'No, I don't. Really, I don't. It's fair enough.'

'Your visa expires with your job,' said Prick. 'You have twenty-eight days to get out of the country. And we'll make sure no one else hires you here.'

Ewan paused. He hadn't thought about that, but yes, he realised he'd have to leave once he'd been sacked.

'And if you check your contract you'll see there's a complete non-disclosure clause. If you ever reveal anything that's happened here, we'll sue you wherever you are and keep on litigating until we've buried you.'

'Is that right?' said Ewan sarcastically. The statement offended him, offended him a great deal. He was fully aware of the non-disclosure clause, but for him it was entirely pointless—it was an important part of his personal code that he would never discuss confidential work matters with anyone other than those directly involved. He didn't need the threat of litigation to ensure he never revealed what happened at work, and was offended they thought he did.

'Yes,' said Anderson. 'If you want to find out what a very large and very powerful company can do to a person, just try us.'

This wasn't going quite the way he'd anticipated. He'd expected some sort of one-on-one with a furious Anderson over Vanessa, not this contractual stuff.

'Look,' he said. 'I'm sorry. I can understand your anger, it's entirely justified. You've every right to be furious. But there's no need for threats. We can all be professional about this.'

Anderson flew at him with a yell, striking him on the side of the head. Ewan didn't defend himself, or even raise his hands, but simply let the man flail at him. Prick strode over and pulled Anderson back.

'Don't fucking tell me to be professional,' he yelled as he broke out of Prick's hold. 'Not you. Not after what you did. I can fucking crush you. You're not shooting kids in Iraq now.'

Ewan stared at Anderson.

'What, you didn't think we knew about that?' Anderson said, almost with a snarl.

'Fuck you,' said Ewan, finding himself growing angry.

'Sore point, is it?' said Anderson, clearly pleased to have struck a nerve. 'Shoot a kid, take his leg off, run away. Big tough guy. Well, tough—'

'I did not run away!' shouted Ewan defensively.

'No, it's okay,' said Anderson. 'You can run away again. Get out of this country. Go back to shooting kids in the Middle East.'

Ewan now wanted to hit Anderson. It took a real effort to restrain himself.

'You'll be accompanied by security back to your office and then escorted out of the building,' said Prick, now anxious to get him away from Anderson.

There was a silence while Ewan stood there, breathing hard.

'I shot a lot of people,' he said, making a supreme effort to maintain self-control. 'That's what you need to worry about.'

'Get out,' Anderson said.

**FRIDAY
4 DECEMBER**

Tom was away for a couple of days, without clear explanation, and had left Em with a pile of work and several meetings to attend. Her last meeting finished at 5 p.m., and she still had perhaps two hours' work ahead of her, despite it being Friday. It was not, however, an option for her to leave it until Monday, not if she wanted to go home with a clear conscience and refrain from spending the weekend worrying what Tom would think. And James wasn't finishing until 6.30 anyway, so he'd promised to wait for her and they could go back to his place together.

It had been a physical effort to come to work, indeed just to get out of bed, and she'd taken her first Panadeine Extra, along with twenty milligrams of Cipramil, with breakfast, to get her functional. She would have far preferred to lie in bed and stare at the wardrobe all day. But having to cover for Tom at least distracted her from how revoltingly bleak she felt. Normally, depression killed her work ethic by preventing her from caring about anything. But having to do a pile of work for Tom had short-circuited that. So, instead, she just felt blackly depressed about being stuck at work late on a Friday, rather than blackly depressed about everything.

At 5.55, she was considering taking half of another Panadeine, having resisted the urge to take one at lunchtime. She left her desk and walked slowly around to the kitchen to use the vending machine. That was when she saw Nathan, walking past the corridor that ran between the offices to connect both sides of the floor. He was wearing a close-fitting black shirt and a pair of dark grey trousers and, it appeared, no shoes, just black socks. She went to the machine and calmly inserted some coins in it, conscious that her heart was beating faster, then decided she needed to use the machine in the kitchen on the other side. She walked around to the other side of the floor, but the pretence of having actual business there was not required—the floor was deserted except for Nathan and his young male work colleague, both with their backs to her. Clearly they were working on something urgent to still be there on a Friday. She craned her neck: Rachael Ambrose's office appeared to be dark.

Em collected her beverage and walked back around to her desk on the other side, sat down and ignored her work and the bottle of soft drink. All thought of Panadcine had vanished. Instead, she was thinking about speaking to Nathan: his lover, that tart Rachael Ambrose, was absent; Nathan was around the other side, working quite late, and there was no one else about, except his colleague . . .

She put the idea out of her head: it was impossible to talk to him without humiliating herself in front of another person. She turned back to her PC and made an effort to focus on work, but found herself unable to concentrate on the document on the screen. In frustration, she closed what she was working on and opened up a short document Tom had asked her to read through and correct. She printed it, and began reading through it, but after a few minutes she got up and walked around to the other side, taking with her some paper so it would look as though she was on a work-related journey. She walked right along the length of the floor, clutching her paper, as if looking for someone. A phone rang, but otherwise there was no movement except for Nathan and his colleague, tapping away. She slipped back to her desk unobserved and sat down.

'Okay,' she said to herself. 'I just have to get over this.'

She made a concerted effort to complete work on the document she had started on, and finished it after several minutes, then got up and put the document on Tom's desk. Then she heard the lift ping. She stood up and craned her neck.

Nathan's colleague was leaving.

She sat down quickly, but her heart had suddenly accelerated. Nathan, unless he too was departing, was alone.

She stood up in her workstation, then strode out into the corridor that ran between the offices, walked right down to the other end of the floor, then walked through another interconnecting corridor and back along the other side.

Nathan was sitting there, typing away, busy. Not going anywhere. Alone.

She inhaled and exhaled slowly, to calm herself, as she returned to her desk.

Okay, she thought. I have a chance to approach Nathan.

I could tolerate it if he rejected me, laughed at me, whatever.

I couldn't tolerate being rejected in public.

He is alone now, no one within miles. I can speak to him and no one will ever know except the two of us.

The two of us.

Her heart was pounding ferociously, *kdoonk kdoonk*, as she sat down in her chair. She stared at her screen, then at the floor, at the carpet and its banal pattern, and put her chin on her hands.

Okay, okay, she thought. Get a handle on this.

I've got to go and speak to him.

And say what?! Dark Voice was sharp, almost vicious. *Say what? You love him? You're obsessed with him? He'll be impressed with that, Em.*

Ask him out, she thought. Simple. Dead simple. Ask him out, he says no, then you know that, amazingly, against all the probabilities in the world, he is not secretly in love with you, that he hasn't been hiding his adoration for you all this time, that it ain't gonna happen.

Or he says yes.

Simple.

Dead simple.

I can handle him saying no, she repeated to herself. At least I'll know.

Enjoy the humiliation, psycho bitch.

She rose from her desk again. She was not going to go and *talk* to him just at this point; she had to check if he was still there, do a recon, work out the lie of the land, understand the territory. *Art of War* stuff.

She walked softly towards the other side of the floor. She could hear tapping. It had gone 6 p.m., so the air conditioning was off now, and you could hear just about anything in the Friday-evening-in-December office silence.

There. She could see him. Busy. He wasn't going anywhere, not for the next few minutes at least. She retreated to her desk and sat down, her breathing shallow.

'Fuck,' she said. 'Okay. This is it.'

She was going in. She stood up.

Those who are about to die salute you.

Fuck—I should check how I look, she thought.

Dark Voice roared. *And let him get away? That's just an excuse! You don't want to do it. You've been served an opportunity on a plate and you're not going to take it because you're too fucking scared.*

Consistency, as she had noted many times, was not Dark Voice's strong point.

She knew from experience that the longer she put the task off, the less likely she was to do it. If you made an excuse to delay for even a second a task that you feared, then you would never do it, you would go on finding excuses, and eventually find an excuse not to do it at all, to sit and wait until Nathan packed up and left. She knew it, better than most people, because she'd studied psychology and behaviour when she was a student, had read studies proving that the human brain was superbly analytical when it mattered, that it could turn even the simplest issue around and around, exploring every side of it, addressing every aspect salient and otherwise, in an effort to chew up valuable time while a feared task went undone. She could stand here rationalising all day, thinking about how her thinking about it was going to cost her the opportunity, and it would indeed be lost.

She almost dragged herself out of her workstation and around to the other side of the floor. He was still there, tapping away. Her heart rate accelerated further, and she felt a tight ball of nerves take shape in her midriff. She stepped forward, and then wheeled around and walked quickly back to her desk.

I can't do this, she thought. He doesn't know me at all, it would be completely out of the blue, I have no right, the guy is obviously busy with an urgent task and who wants to stand around talking at—what was the time now? 6.05?—talking at 6.05 on a Friday night, when they doubtless want to go home or go for a drink or just get out of the office?

You stupid woman, she thought—or Dark Voice thought, the two were now hopelessly confused—how much more of an opportunity do you need? You are so fucking gutless. The ball of nerves in her stomach seemed to be threatening to turn into actual, violent nausea.

Fuck it, I'm going in, she thought aggressively, and this time strode out of her cubicle, down the corridor, and then broke cover and headed towards Nathan.

She was three metres from him, closing in fast, her line prepared and ready for use. She realised he was wearing a collared T-shirt, not a proper shirt. She was nearly on him, when his phone rang. She froze, stopped dead, but it was too late to turn around. He picked up the phone—which, judging by the ring, had an internal caller at the other end—and, in turning to get it, saw her. His face didn't change expression.

'Hello?'

. . .

'Hi. You with Jane?'

. . .

'Okay, I'm just finishing it now. Be ready in a couple of minutes. Five tops.'

. . .

'Yep, I worked in that paragraph—'

Em stood there, totally thrown. He looked at her again. She raised her hand, in a gesture that might have been interpreted to mean that she would be back in a second but which more accurately suggested 'I've just come to act on my obsession with you but by divine intervention I have been stopped by the phone so I'll go away and suicide'. She returned to her desk.

'Fucking fuck!' she whisper-shouted, and put her head in her hands. She would have to stay away now for a couple of minutes, otherwise it would look weird.

Weird?

Weird?!

Fuck, Emma, she thought, it's gonna look pretty fucking weird no matter what you do. You've already been humiliated by a telephone . . .

She went out and around again, and couldn't hear his voice, but could hear his tapping as she walked down the corridor to see that he was off the phone. She was going in again.

You go, girl!

Just as an aside, she told herself, just for future reference, just one to file away for another time, it's amazing how banal and uninspiring inspirational rhetoric can sound when you really need to motivate yourself.

'Hi,' she said.

Nathan looked up and gave her a smile.

That's a good start, she thought. She could see a shoe and one socked foot beneath his desk.

'What are you doing here so late on a Friday?' she said, although it came out a lot more forced than she intended, not so much chatty as terrified. She stopped about a metre from him and leaned on the end of his workstation partition.

'Oh, the state government has some proposals for new software security standards. We're trying to get something together for it.' He gestured at his PC. 'Except we've had some computer problems.'

She rolled her eyes exaggeratedly. Here was common ground! 'Terrible, isn't it,' she said. 'They can sense when you're under pressure.'

He smiled. 'Like photocopiers.'

She nodded. Okay. Well, fuck it, here goes nothing. Here goes my life.

'Listen, um,' she began. She couldn't, she discovered, look him in the eye, not in those hypnotic eyes. She looked down at his desk, at his hands on his desk. 'Um, I was just wondering if, maybe, you'd like to, say, er, grab a coffee some time or maybe do lunch . . .'

May as well keep going, she thought. She finally lifted her eyes to meet his. 'I've wanted to ask you for a while, I've been fascinated by you since I met you.'

Oh Christ, I can't believe you said that.

He smiled—a nice smile. 'Oh, well, that's nice to—'

I CAN'T BELIEVE YOU SAID THAT!!!!!!!!

'—hear, thank you.' He paused. The microseconds ticked by. 'But I'm, um, very attached.'

Em smiled. 'Okay,' she said. 'So am I . . . I didn't quite mean it like that . . .'

Like what? Didn't mean it like what? Mean what? How else could you have meant it?

Fuck logic, I'm trying to save face here, she thought. Or a nose. An eyelash. Anything.

'Oh,' he said uncertainly, rightly confused.

'Anyway, just thought I'd ask. I'll let you get back to struggling with the computer.'

'Okay,' he said, still smiling. 'Thanks.'

Thanks? Thanks for what? For humiliating myself? For exposing my emotions to a complete stranger?

She walked back to her desk, not striding, but not slinking, either.

How do I feel about that? she asked herself, sitting down. Bad? No, she definitely didn't feel bad. Okay, the whole 'I didn't mean it like that' thing was a terrible fuck-up. But she felt sort of good. Her heart rate had returned to something vaguely approaching normal; in fact, she even felt faintly euphoric. There was no need for any Panadeine now.

How come, came Dark Voice, *you're trying to turn a complete, abject humiliation into some sort of victory? You are totally deluded.*

Well at least I tried, she thought. So I'm not going to go out with him.

You were completely—

But at least I asked! Fuck it, I tried.

She watched her desk, not thinking much, for a couple of minutes, and then turned back to her PC and opened the document she had given up on a while before. She glanced at her watch: 6.14.

She worked solidly for forty-five minutes and then decided to leave. She felt exhausted, probably more from the encounter with Nathan (*Encounter? Don't get carried away, girl*) than the long day. She emailed a document to Tom, closed his office door and then walked around and waited by the lift, hoping like hell Nathan wouldn't be leaving at the same time as her.

The lobby was like a mausoleum inside, until she swiped her way out; the main doors slid open, admitting the drone of evening traffic on Liverpool Street. The evening air was still hot, and she closed her eyes. She wasn't thinking about Nathan, or what she had done. She wasn't thinking much about anything. She stopped and checked her bag to make sure she had her phone to text James.

Just as she located her phone, she saw a red Toyota RAV4 pull up, and then from off to her right Nathan walked into her view and over to the car. At the wheel was the woman in the photo on his desk, with a young girl in the back. Nathan got in, they kissed, and she drove off. Whether or not Nathan had seen Em on the way out, she didn't know.

Peter managed to scrape the kerb as he parked. 'Check out my mad parking skills,' he said. 'Well, it was great to see you again.'

'Yeah,' said Kat. 'It was nice. Do you want to come up for a, um, cup of tea?'

'Sure,' he said, after a brief pause.

'I don't really have any tea,' she said.

'Well then I'm not coming up,' he said, undoing his seatbelt.

They got out and she led him inside and upstairs. It was still warm, but there was a nice breeze carrying the smell of jasmine, a scent she strongly associated with spring in Sydney.

Peter was none too bright, she'd decided, and not the most dynamic company. He was by no means relationship material, but he had a nice body, was attracted to her, and it had been longer than usual since she'd had sex, not just because of Chris but because she'd been so busy. She accepted the reality that she'd briefly had the man for whom she was designed—intellectually, emotionally and physically—and then lost him. Or, more accurately, he'd removed himself from her. She might grieve over that for months, but she wasn't going to deprive herself of sex because of it, not when there was a ready source of it close to hand.

'It ain't much, but it's home,' she said, ushering him in and switching on several lamps. 'I've got wine. White wine. Good white wine. Want some?'

Peter was a beer man, to the extent that he drank, which didn't appear to be much.

'Ah, yeah, sure, a little glass,' he said. He wandered over to her bookcase. 'Wow, a lot of books,' he said.

'Most of them are in storage,' she said. 'I haven't got room for them here. I've stopped buying them in book form, though. I'm a Kindle convert.'

She poured wine and contemplated his back as he surveyed her bookcase.

'You speak German?' he said.

'Not really, but I can read it okay. Only if I can't get a good translation. I'm a little better at Spanish.' She walked over and handed him his wine.

There was one small thing about him that nagged at her, a tiny irritant. Every time they met, he asked whether she'd had any more dealings with KSR, often two or three different ways. At first she thought this was his eagerness to be in the know about what was happening, a way of taking advantage of his close relationship with her. After it had happened again that evening, while they were having a drink down the road at Coogee, she'd started wondering if his persistence actually meant he had some sort of agenda. Maybe, she thought idly, he was an undercover policeman, although that wouldn't explain why he was going to such lengths to establish a KSR support group. Still, it made her doubly determined not to tell him much.

She joined him in front of her bookcase and looked at him and then, wordlessly, leaned over and kissed him. He placed his wine on the bookshelf, put his hands on her hips and returned the kiss. He wasn't that bad a kisser, though that would turn out to be the overall standard of his whole sexual repertoire. She liked his boxer shorts and his pecs and sixpack. She was less enthused about his uncircumcised and fairly average cock; she preferred cut—as Chris was, but the preference predated him—but realised she'd just have to get used to younger men who were *au naturel*. Chris, with his large penis, had definitely spoiled her in the size department. Peter also seemed in a huge rush to slide his fingers inside her; she preferred the build-up of kissing and having him caress her nipples with his tongue, which he was reasonably okay at, but he seemed desperate to stick his fingers in her cunt; indeed, he seemed in something of a rush throughout.

As usual for her with first-time sex, he wasn't able to make her climax. That didn't bother her too much; eventually she told him he could come. He wanted to do it from behind her and on her side, which she was fine with. She lifted her left leg up slightly as he slid a condom on and he spooned in behind her and entered her with a little help from her hand, and began thrusting. But after a couple of minutes he did something that creeped her out. He slid his hand beneath her neck and then around and clamped it over her mouth. She was at a loss as to whether to object, and how she might if she wanted to, since he was gripping her mouth tightly, but it seemed to especially excite him, and he came rapidly, breathing loudly—nearly as loudly as she was breathing through her nose—and then quickly released her.

Once he'd withdrawn from her and pulled the condom off, he appeared eager to leave, after a perfunctory couple of minutes lying next to her. Men who bolted the moment they came annoyed her no end. He drained his glass of wine—she'd brought both into her bedroom once they'd adjourned in there—pulled his boxer shorts on, then lay next to her again for several minutes. He hadn't removed her bra, but had pushed it up above her breasts. She undid it and dropped it next to the bed. She was covered in sweat, though Peter's body seemed to betray no evidence of the heat or of his physical exertion.

'It's okay, I'm not after a relationship,' she said. 'And I know you're not either. But you don't have to run out the door pulling the condom off.'

He laughed and apologised, then asked for more wine.

It wasn't Chris.

That was the worst thing, she thought, as she lay there with this male next to her, drinking her wine. It didn't really matter that his cock was too small, or he wasn't too bright, or that, on the positive side, he had a much nicer body than Chris. He was fatally flawed not because he was Peter, and whatever positive or negative qualities that entailed, but because—like all the other humans on earth—he wasn't Chris. She felt strangely alone now, more than before, more even than in the aftermath of learning about Chris's infidelity, because Peter Armitage, or anyone else she might have gone to bed with, perfectly embodied the absence of Chris, perfectly reminded her of what she had had and then lost. Sex with Peter made the Chris-shaped hole in her existence 3D, gave it life, sent it moving around her apartment, kissing her, fucking her, lying beside her, reminding her in exquisite, vivid detail of what she'd once had and would now never have again.

Would it always be this way? Was she doomed to hundreds of post-coital embraces and midnight taxi trips home that only made her think about how they weren't Chris, and instead made her wonder what Chris was doing at that moment, rather than give her any pleasure or satisfaction?

Right that second Chris was probably at home in Five Dock, in bed with Her, his multiply-cheated-upon spouse. Was he thinking about Kat? Was he hurting? Yes, of course he was, she told herself. That's been the whole fucking problem. If he was an arsehole who'd simply exploited her love for him, she could deal with that. Far, far worse was the idea that he really had loved her, and maybe still did.

'This Servetus,' Peter said after a while.

Here we go again, she thought. He can't stop with that. Even after sex.

'Not the hacker one, I mean, but the original one.'

That was a surprise, like he'd sensed her annoyance with the subject.

'Yeah?'

'Interesting guy,' he said. 'He was executed in Geneva by other Protestants because he upset the Catholics and Protestants with his theolology. And he read the Torah and the Koran. Burned at the stake.'

He rolled over and ran his fingers over Kat's breasts.

'Theology,' she said, correcting him. 'I didn't know that.'

'Apparently they couldn't legally kill him, because he wasn't a citizen of Geneva, just banish him. But they wanted to make an example of him because his ideas were so dangerous, so they killed him anyway.'

She reached over and finished her glass of wine, partly out of thirst. 'That's what elites do when they want to stop the spread of dangerous ideas. You can't control what people think but you can make an example of someone if you do catch them thinking the wrong things.'

'Which Servetus are you talking about?'

'Both, probably,' she said, then realised he'd actually made a joke, and not a bad one. It was unexpected pillow talk for Peter.

'It's a nice story. Servetus the hacker, that is. I wonder who thought it up. Maybe Amy Dinh invented it.'

Kat laughed. 'Amy Dinh couldn't invent shit.'

'She looks good in pink panties, though.'

'Okay, you can leave now! Ugh! Men!'

SATURDAY
5 DECEMBER

'Hello, is your daddy home?'

Sophie, who'd recovered and was now pretty much her usual self, was playing in the entry hall. Nathan recognised the Scottish accent instantly; it was etched on his mind after their previous encounter. He rushed from his bedroom, where he was getting dressed, into the front hallway, standing there in pants and no top.

Mazzoni stood at the front door, the sun just high enough to shine over the top of the house next door and past him into the entry.

'Sophie, go see Mummy, this is not for you,' Nathan said. The tone in his voice sent her scurrying, shooting a scared glance at Mazzoni over her shoulder. Nathan turned back to look at him.

'It's okay,' said Mazzoni. 'It's okay.' He raised his hands in the air. 'Friends. Really.'

'What is it?' said Nathan, moving closer.

'I want to give this to you.' He held out a USB stick.

Nathan eyed it suspiciously through the screen door.

'What's that?'

'Remember when you found that Kittehsaurus Rox stuff and we took it off you? Well, I made a copy, just for safety's sake.'

Nathan looked at him in confusion. 'I thought that you were . . .' He trailed off uncertainly.

'I'm no longer working for Veldtech,' he said. 'I was thinking of going to the press myself, but then I thought, well, you're the one who found it and got in trouble for it. So you can use that material any way you see fit. In fact, I'd encourage you to use it.'

Nathan advanced tentatively. He was reluctant to open the screen door, for fear Ewan would do something threatening, or even just mention Angela. After a moment, he opened it, requiring Ewan to step back. He handed the stick to Nathan.

'All yours,' he said, uttering 'yours' with a particularly thick Scottish accent.

'I thought you said you'd . . .' Nathan glanced behind him.

'I'm not gonna to be around anymore,' said Mazzoni. 'So it's all yours. I hope you bring the stupid pricks down.'

Nathan looked at Mazzoni, trying to read his eyes.

'Why?'

Mazzoni shrugged. 'Stuff. There's more, Nathan. There's a reason why this is very sensitive. I got no proof, but the information that Veldtech's been putting out there pretending it's from hackers is actually from a login to the parliamentary system down in Canberra.'

Nathan frowned. 'Hang on, we provided that system. That's our PICS system. That's a Veldtech . . .'

'That's not why it's sensitive. It's sensitive'—Mazzoni lowered his voice—'because ASIO uses the same access to monitor what the politicians are doing.'

Nathan looked at him, amazed. He found himself speaking in similarly soft tones. 'But they can't do that. They can't just spy on MPs. If it comes out, they'll be in huge shit.'

'That's what I figure. See you later.' The Scotsman turned away and then turned back. 'Look, Nathan, I'm sorry. I was just doing my job. But that doesn't make it all right. I apologise. Have a good weekend.'

As Mazzoni strode off, Nathan contemplated the USB stick.

Ree appeared in the hallway as he went back inside.

'Who was that?'

'Ah, just some guy from work,' said Nathan. 'He had something he wanted to give me.'

SUNDAY
6 DECEMBER

Minnie dropped the ball, covered in slobber and grass, at Chalmers's feet. He raised his foot, prompting her to rush backward three steps, then kicked it vaguely in Steve's direction. Steve had the Chuckit. Minnie contested the ball with Steve and the Chuckit until Steve stepped on it and she backed away, watching him intently.

Dalmatian Woman appeared. Minnie and the Dalmatian were friends, and had a chase and a sniff whenever they met up. Dalmatian Woman, who was eternally talking on her phone while walking the Dalmatian, waved to them. Like them, she'd plainly had the idea of walking as early as possible, before it got too hot. He glanced at his watch. It wasn't yet 9 a.m., and it was already well into the twenties. The forecast was now for the heat to end the following day. Steve had suggested they go to Bronte for a swim, a suggestion Chalmers was almost tempted to take up.

Having said hello to the Dalmatian, Minnie was now interested again in the ball, so Steve hurled it away, with the dog in hot pursuit.

'Do you think she's running a bit funny?' said Steve, watching her.

'It might be arthritis,' said Chalmers. 'They're prone to arthritis in the back legs. She's old enough to be a candidate for it.'

'I'll mention it to the vet.'

'There's a dog with a cone of shame,' said Chalmers, pointing. A large dog of indeterminate breed was trotting towards them with a plastic cone around its neck. It appeared to be unaccompanied by any owner. It reached them and, entirely indifferent both to them and to Minnie, kept going, its cone gently bobbing as it strode purposefully along.

'Out doing his own thing,' said Steve, twirling the Chuckit. 'Creepy.'

'What's his agenda?' said Chalmers. 'What does he have in mind? Do we need better surveillance of dogs doing their own thing?'

'And why does he have a cone of shame?'

'Indeed. Who is this sinister hound? Questions without answers.'

Chalmers's phone rang. Or, more accurately, barked. That was the ringtone for Derek. Minnie's ears twitched and she glanced at Chalmers, then returned to chewing the ball and avoiding Steve's efforts to retrieve it.

'G'day,' Chalmers said.

'Hi, Mark. Look,' Derek said brusquely, 'I need a favour. I need a few days off. Maybe the week. Rathbone's spending two days in Canberra and Maria's in Texas till Wednesday. Can you run the show until I'm back? I'll let Ethel and Gary know.'

'Sure. Is everything okay?'

'I've got some domestic issues to sort out. It should be fairly quiet.'

Domestic issues. Chalmers wondered what he meant. Had the cancer returned? Or was there trouble with Vanessa? 'Yeah, that's fine, Derek. I'll let you know if anything significant crops up but take whatever time you need,' he said.

'Okay. I'll talk to you soon.' Derek hung up.

'That's odd,' Chalmers said to Steve, who had managed to secure the ball from the dog. 'Derek wants a few days off. Says he has some domestic issues.'

'He doesn't have any kids, does he?'

'No. No, he doesn't.'

'So who's in charge? You?'

'Allegedly.'

He bent down and scratched Minnie's ears.

After spending an hour looking for an internet cafe that was open, Nathan eventually gave up and drove into the city to find a Starbucks. He recalled one near Wynyard, where parking would be easier. It was just after 1 p.m., and baking hot. He circumnavigated the maze of one-way streets repeatedly until he found a parking spot on York Street, then walked over to the Starbucks, which was inexplicably nearly full. Eventually, he found an empty table with what looked like half a cup of coloured dairy product poured all over it, opened his laptop, then set about establishing a Hotmail account.

He'd dwelled at length on to whom he would send the information. He wondered about the ubiquitous Kat Sharpe, the guru on Kittehsaurus Rox, but decided she probably lacked the capacity to really pursue what he would send to her. This would be serious stuff; it would probably require heavy legal resources to bring such accusations against the company. An established media outlet, rather than some blogger or freelancer, was thus required, one that would be able to cope with legal threats. But he disliked both News Corp and Fairfax, so he decided on the ABC, and set about gathering email addresses for several journalists in different areas—tech, the parliamentary press gallery, business—to ensure the story didn't get lost.

> Dear all,
> I have some information about the company Veldtech.
> Veldtech is behind the Kittehsaurus Rox 'hacking'. They

are using a remote login in a piece of software Veldtech itself designed, the parliamentary email network PICS, to access the emails of politicians.

Attached is an email obtained by someone within Veldtech containing material from the first KSR release. You will see it contains material not released by KSR.

To further confirm, here is the password for the KSRComms Twitter account:

%kcatta%

I am told that ASIO also uses PICS to monitor the emails of politicians, which is illegal. However, I have no direct proof of this.

I hope the ABC will appropriately investigate this.

Regards,

Anonymous

This was it, he thought. An email that might destroy, or at least seriously damage, Veldtech. And perhaps ASIO, if what that mad Scotsman said was correct. Information, he realised, that might see people sent to jail. How high did the KSR conspiracy go? All the way to Derek Anderson? Ewan Mazzoni was Anderson's personal security consultant. Clearly Anderson must have been involved. The more he thought about it, the more remarkable it was: a security company that set out to steal information from the very organisation to which it provided security services. And yet it also made commercial sense as a potentially cheap and effective way to stimulate demand for the company's product. That, after all, was marketing at its purest: convincing people they needed a product when they didn't, selling the consumer a fiction about how much better their life would be if they bought more of something. It was perfect.

How many other companies, he wondered, were doing the same as Veldtech? How many 'Chinese hackers' were actually Larry from Buttfuck, New Jersey or Jeremy from Dickbridge, Gloucesternessfordshire, trying to drum up business for their cyber-security companies? And for that matter, how many government agencies were doing the same, in order to keep politicians pumping money into them to stop Chinese hackers and the cyber 9/11, digital Pearl Harbor or Hackergeddon? Terrorism guaranteed an eternal supply of big dollars to defence and intelligence agencies. Why shouldn't cybersecurity serve the same purpose? A clever intelligence agency would maintain a persistent threat capability on its own government, to be deployed if anyone ever suggested cutting funding.

'Of course,' he said aloud. 'You idiot.' Why else would ASIO have access to PICS? It made perfect sense: the spooks were way ahead of him—and, for that matter, way ahead of Veldtech. They'd been doing to the government for years what Veldtech had only recently begun doing.

Clever, clever buggers.

Moreover, he had to admit, there was something comforting in learning that the company was behind this outbreak of unstoppable hacking that seemed to have shaken the government to its very foundations. Kittehsaurus Rox's apparently freewheeling rampage through the most guarded confines of the government had, to a degree, perturbed him, creating a sense of genuine anarchy. Now, he knew, there was no anarchy, no chaos and disorder, just a greedy, aggressive company prepared to do whatever it took to increase sales. The thought reassured him: all was right with the world; the right arseholes were in charge, the arseholes he worked for, not some other mob.

Nonetheless, he felt little reluctance about trying to bring it all undone. After all, this was the company that had overlooked him for promotion, refused to give him a promised bonus, invaded his privacy and leaned on him when they thought he posed a threat. The stuff about Rachael and the bonus was one thing, perfectly normal bastardry that was infuriating but not surprising. But the rest, that was something else, way over the line. Even the guy who had leaned on him had hated doing it and wanted him to expose the company. He had no compunction in doing what he could to expose Veldtech.

He sent the email. Not with a sense of triumph, or vindication, or satisfaction, but merely with the cold sense of a squaring of accounts.

MONDAY
7 DECEMBER

The temperature must have still been in the high thirties when Kat got the train to Central from Bondi Junction. The heat of the underground rail platform was barely distinguishable from the heat outside, and she'd started sweating the moment she stepped off the train. As she crossed the road and walked up to the Gaelic Club, she noticed it had begun to cloud over, but it was still uncomfortably warm. She climbed the stairs at the club and found what she assumed was the room where the event was being held, and almost panicked at how many people had crammed into it: there must have been two hundred people in the place.

She decided she'd made a serious error of judgement in not preparing a speech.

Peter and Nicola were near the entrance to greet her, but she had the awkward experience of a large number of people in the room turning and looking at her and then turning back to discuss her with their companions; she heard 'Kat Sharpe' several times. She felt like blushing, which would have made a good addition to the sweating.

'Hey!' said Peter. 'Looks like we've got an amazing turn-up. Isn't it fantastic?'

'Awesome,' she said unconvincingly, growing more nervous.

Peter led her through the crowd to the rostrum, on which was a table, three chairs and a lectern. She could hear her name being mentioned as she went past. She went up on the rostrum with Peter. 'Want a drink?' he said.

'Hell yeah. A Corona?'

'Er, I don't think this is the sort of place that has Corona . . .' he said.

'Well, something light, whatever light beer they have,' she said.

A middle-aged woman approached the rostrum. 'Excuse me, Katrina? I just wanted to say I'm a huge fan of your work. What you say is just wonderful.'

'Well . . . thank you very much,' Kat said uncertainly. 'That's lovely to hear.'

'I'll leave you be. I'm looking forward to hearing what you have to say,' the woman said, retiring.

Fucking hell, Kat thought. She had assumed that there wouldn't be a big turnout, and she could give a quick talk about transparency and the need for people to use the tools technology gave them to blah blah blah, the sort of thing she'd used for her book launches. But the sheer size of the crowd unsettled her. Plainly they were expecting something more than a cribbed version of her book talk. It also unnerved her that people were looking at her and talking. She was having one of those moments she used to have before she had become experienced at doing radio, when she wondered why on earth people couldn't see the obvious, or what was obvious to her: that she was just an ordinary person with nothing much of interest to say, like she was an eight-year-old pretending to be an adult in a roomful of grown-ups, shocked that others hadn't spotted her inept masquerade yet.

She looked around; there were some people in the audience with Guy Fawkes masks on, and lots of young men. A *lot* of young men. The room was also quite warm, despite the air conditioning, and she hadn't stopped sweating yet.

She made a conscious effort to dismiss the worry. She'd eventually realised that there was a perfectly good solution to the problem of feeling like she was masquerading as someone more intelligent and insightful than she really was, and that was to realise everyone else was faking it too, and not faking it as well as her. She began trying to mentally put together some points for her speech. She could recycle some stuff from the book, but she'd also need something new.

Peter returned with a beer of unknown type. He was strictly in official mode. 'Have you met Kim?' he said. She realised the other speaker, Kim Braddock, was actually standing next to her and Peter was trying to introduce them. She shook his hand.

'If it's okay with you, Kat, I'll go first and then Kim and then you? Is that all right?'

She sipped the beer. It was foul. What is this, Catpiss Draught? she thought.

'Yep, that's fine,' she said. Better than fine. Far beyond fine. That would give her time to put a speech together. She took another sip. Christ, she thought, this is undrinkable.

Peter headed back to the door, where Nicola was admitting still more people. A gaggle of young men were sitting on the carpet right near the rostrum, more or less ogling her; behind them, standing next to a pillar, a quite tall young blonde woman in a navy suit was staring at her. She made small talk with Braddock, then reached for the pen and paper that Nicola had thoughtfully left on the table, and began putting together some dot points for her speech.

Eventually, Peter went to the lectern to try to get everyone's attention, unsuccessfully, until someone whistled at about a hundred decibels, inducing sudden and almost complete silence.

'Um, thanks for that,' Peter said, smiling. 'Welcome, everyone. I'm Peter Armitage, and I've been organising the Support KSR campaign with Nicola Franks—and many thanks to Simon Berg, who's done a lot of great work as well. First, I acknowledge the traditional owners of this land on which we are meeting. I pay my respects to their elders, past and present, and the elders from other communities who may be here today. Now, just some housekeeping things—as you can probably see from the camera in front, we're livestreaming this so people all over Australia and indeed the world can see this event, and isn't it fantastic that so many people have shown up? This is just an amazing turnout . . . I particularly want to say a big hello to the ASIO agents here . . .'

That got a laugh. Kat ventured another sip of her beer, which almost made her gag. Someone needs to have this beer taken out and shot, she thought, scribbling some notes. She checked Twitter. A good twenty people in the room or watching the livestream were tweeting what was going on, including one who'd declared *@kat_sharpe is seriously fucking hot #supportKSR.*

Yep, she thought. I'm hot. That'd be why I'm sweating like a pig. An especially sweaty pig with a sweat problem, sitting in a sauna. Her dress was clinging to her back, particularly where it was in contact with the plastic chair she was sitting on.

'As you probably know, the government last week announced that they believe they've shut down Kittehsaurus Rox,' said Peter.

One grey-haired man near the bar, in shorts and a tattered Camper Van Beethoven T-shirt, shook his head angrily at that and yelled, 'No!', as if personally and deeply aggrieved by it.

'But,' Peter continued, 'it's important that we show the government that even if they do shut down one outlet, they can't shut down the cause of transparency and . . .'

Kat had three dot points committed to paper by now. She looked at someone nearby with a Guy Fawkes mask and found it disconcerting. Off to the left, by the windows, there was a young woman with cornrows and, a quick count suggested, half a dozen visible piercings; beyond her, Kat could see that it had now clouded over a great deal.

By the time Peter introduced Kim, she had six points and the makings of a reasonable speech. Kim rose and went to the lectern to polite applause. And as he proceeded to speak about the law and leaking and hacking, it became clear that Peter had done her a favour by leaving her till last, because Kim was boring as hell. She locked eyes momentarily with a tall, attractive guy dressed in black and gave him a polite smile, then added an idea for her last line to her speech plan. The tall blonde woman near the pillar was still staring at her. She wondered about the last line and decided to leave the decision on whether to use it or not until the end of the speech.

The audience was visibly bored and distracted by the time Kim finished. Kat had long since tuned out, and hoped she wasn't about to cut across any ground he'd covered while she'd been surveying the room and writing her notes. There was some surprisingly warm applause for him, probably because people were pleased to see him finish.

Peter rose, explained there'd be an opportunity for questions at the end, and introduced her. There was a big round of applause, a few whistles and at least one whoop.

The fuck? she thought. I'm being whooped at? The level of public fandom about her was genuinely disconcerting. Notionally, she supposed she should be flattered by it. But she couldn't be. Didn't these people have any sense or judgement? Didn't they realise she was in no way out of the ordinary, that she had no particular insight or analysis to offer? In short: What. The. Fuck? Even so, it's better than the alternative, she thought.

'Thanks,' she said, adjusting the microphone down to her height. She wished she'd drunk more beer, but it was too late, and the apparent absence of beer not manufactured from the urine of domestic animals made the point moot. 'It's really great to see so many people come along to support KSR, but I think that reflects the amount of concern in the community about the whole imbalance that is now happening between governments and citizens. Bearing in mind that governments are supposed to be the creation *of* citizens, it seems like citizens now exist to serve governments and not the other way around.'

There was a cheer and some applause at that. On with the speech itself.

'One of the things that interested me right from the start when KSR first appeared was it said, and I'm quoting from memory here, that it wanted to subject governments to the same level of surveillance that they now subject their citizens to. And I think this is really, really important. I call this information asymmetry, the way governments always want to know more about us and what we're doing, while trying to stop us from finding out what they're doing.'

The speech flowed surprisingly smoothly given her nerves and lack of notes. She deviated a couple of times into unrelated matters, and found herself giving a short description of how governments themselves leak all the time for official purposes—'governments are in the business of managing information, not keeping secrets'—but once she was on to government surveillance she was on familiar ground, and even recycled old jokes. 'Now, my life is sufficiently uninteresting that the only risk from any surveillance of me is that the people listening die of boredom, but that shouldn't be the point . . .'

Peter laughed particularly loudly at that.

Unencumbered by notes to read from, she looked around the room as she spoke. One of the young men close by seemed to be staring intently at her chest. Towards the back of the room, a muscular man in an Everlast T-shirt appeared to be engrossed in inaudible conversation with a much slighter young man who looked as if he'd just come off a building site. Over by the door, a rather unfortunate-looking middle-aged man with a grey streak and a black leather jacket alternately eyed her and looked around, bored.

'What gets me most,' she said, locking eyes with the tall blonde girl near the pillar, 'is how as an individual I am a relatively innoc-uous threat to society, even if I decide to harm it. But governments can inflict enormous damage even in the process of doing what they think is good. The information asymmetry I spoke about earlier is a reversal of the asymmetry of power—we're the ones surveilled, whereas our governments, which are capable of profound damage, successfully hide what they do.'

Nearing the end, she decided to abandon the conclusion, so she was left with her usual problem of being unable to figure out a nice, climactic way to conclude the speech. She decided to finish, or more correctly trail off, with words about how important it was to support KSR. This drew another big round of applause and a lot of whistling when she finished.

That ushered in question time. She was dying for a drink, but couldn't leave the rostrum; she toyed with the idea of simply asking aloud for a drink and seeing how many of the ogling young men present obliged. In any event, the first question was directed at her; a middle-aged man rose stiffly and said into a microphone: 'We've heard the government say that they've shut down KSR; do you believe that Michael Servetus'—he pronounced it serr-a-veetus— 'will be caught or has been caught already?'

'Go Servetus!' someone cried at the back, also getting it wrong. There was more applause.

This put Kat in a quandary. She remained convinced there was no evidence for the Servetus thing, but a widespread conviction that this one individual was behind the whole thing appeared to have taken hold. Only the previous day, Amy Dinh (Amy Dinh LINGERIE BLOGGER) had run a story at news.com.au that began: *Who is Michael Servetus, the mastermind behind the hack that has paralysed the government?* She decided to answer vaguely.

'I don't know whether there's one person behind KSR or a group. What I do know is that we need to support anyone who is genuinely committed to transparency and correcting the information asymmetry between citizens and governments.'

There was applause, and another 'Go Servetus!'

@kat_sharpe can cybre me anytime, someone tweeted at that point, she saw later. Who the hell misspells 'cyber'? she wondered.

The Camper Van Beethoven man took the microphone, which Nicola was walking around the room with. 'How important do you think KSR is in being able to stop the CIA Zionist plot to control the world's financial system?'

There were groans. The questioner looked around. 'Well, this is what we're dealing with. Everyone knows how powerful the Zionists are . . .'

She exchanged glances with Kim. He rolled his eyes.

'They're using chemtrails to keep the population down,' the questioner insisted, looking a little besieged.

Kat rose to her feet and went to the lectern. 'Look, I really don't mind what conspiracy theory you subscribe to. That's up to you. Personally, I'm a lizard people person myself.' That brought a round of laughter and some applause, though the questioner shook his head furiously. 'But I'm assuming the one thing we can all agree on, whether we believe in global conspiracies or aliens from space or we're simply all concerned about what our government is doing, is that the more we know about what they are doing, the better. Transparency is the key here. There is no one in this room, and pretty much no one outside this room—except in government, and in the security companies that make lots of money working for them—that thinks there shouldn't be more transparency.'

More applause.

@kat_sharpe just owned a nutjob #supportKSR she later saw. That was countered by *@kat_sharpe self-promoting media whore, nothing to say #supportKSR*

Media whore. Well, there may be an element of truth in that, she thought.

The woman who had bailed her up when she first arrived made her way to the microphone. 'I don't have any conspiracy theories, I'm sorry,' she said. There was more laughter. 'What I want to know is, what can I do about this? We all know there's a problem. What do you and I and all of us do about this?'

Kim wanted to answer that, and leaped up to talk about the importance of writing to MPs and supporting NGOs that used FOI laws.

'You want to add something, Kat?' said Peter.

She walked over to the microphone. She felt like she could nail this.

'Here's what you can do. Crypt up. Start using encryption on your computers. If the government has data retention, let them discover that they can't find anything out because we've all encrypted our online traffic and we're sending it through ports in Europe and the US. Don't put lots of personal information online. Don't use Facebook. Don't allow applications to use geodata. Think about using bitcoins for small internet transactions. And harass politicians. Most politicians are on Twitter now. Bombard them with demands to protect your privacy and be more transparent. And most of all, talk to people. Whether they agree with you or not, communicate. Connect. Because when we're together we're unstoppable. Governments and corporations want to herd us back into nice little separate clusters where they can control us more easily. So break down the information barriers and connect up.'

The woman who asked the question was nodding enthusiastically.

'Now, I *really* need a beer,' said Kat, to wild applause.

'You kicked arse, babe,' said Peter at the end. 'That was fantastic, just perfect, and there's been a huge response online. You're okay with me putting the video up online?'

'Yeah, that's fine, go ahead,' she said. She was dying to check Twitter and drink a beer some young man had delivered to her, but there was a queue of people who wanted to talk to her.

'Just on that Servetus thing,' Peter said, 'it's bullshit, isn't it? There's no Servetus. It's a group, isn't it? This whole Servetus thing, I don't know where it's come from.'

Again with his questions about the group.

'It just seems like speculation that has become received wisdom,' she said neutrally.

It took her a full half-hour to disentangle herself from all but one of the people who wanted to speak to her. Early on, she took a sip of the beer and discovered it was the same beer as earlier, so she abandoned it. One of her interlocutors was the attractive guy in black, who asked her out for a drink after a preamble consisting of praise. She declined; all she really wanted to do now was get out of the room. The middle-aged woman came back for a discussion, which she quite enjoyed; the woman was an old leftie but sensible and asked thoughtful questions. The worst had been saved for last: an ostensibly rational middle-aged man who seemed to have an encyclopaedic knowledge of CIA operations, and who proceeded to lecture her about the role of the CIA in Afghanistan. After a few minutes and a couple of efforts to get him to finish, she said 'Okay, thanks very much for that, I have to go,' and simply walked away towards the exit, but he said, 'Sure,' and followed her, continuing to explain what the CIA had been doing in the 1980s.

'Now, you've heard of Milton Bearden, of course,' he said, as Peter waved goodbye to her. The man, creepily, followed her down the stairs, ignoring her efforts to disengage.

There was a huge crack of thunder as she reached the entrance of the Gaelic Club. Outside, the wind had begun to pick up, and there was an unpleasant olive tinge to the clouds overhead. It was apparent there was going to be a storm.

The man continued to follow her, still running his lecture on Afghanistan. She began to wonder how to get away from him.

I need rain, she thought. I need rain to escape from this appalling man.

He segued effortlessly onto the myth that the CIA supplied Osama Bin Laden. 'Simply propaganda,' he insisted, then began reeling off names and dates in an unceasing drone. She had yet to work out what exact point he was trying to get across to her.

On the pavement in front of her, audible even over the sound of the traffic, there was a wet *thwack*, then another, then another. Thankfully, it had begun to rain, and not just average, regulation-issue rain, but huge drops. It rapidly accelerated. 'I have to get under cover,' she said, and ran down the street away from CIA Man, free at last. There was another huge crack of thunder. After a moment, she noticed it wasn't just large drops but hailstones. She lingered under an awning, then bolted across the road with a Walk signal and reached cover at Central, along with dozens of other people.

I must tell Chris about that weirdo, she found herself thinking, then cut the thought off. She pulled out her phone and dialled Maddy's number.

'What's up?'

'It's fucking pissing down. Are you home?'

'Yeah, just got in.'

'I'm down at Central. How about I grab a bottle of wine and come watch the rain?'

'Sounds good. I gotta head out about eight thirty.'

'Done.'

The rain was ferocious in the city, a cloudburst that hurled torrents down onto the streets and buildings and anyone caught out in it. All the streetlights were on, though good only for illuminating the vertical rivers roaring past them; windscreen wipers swished futilely on vehicles trying to creep through the downpour; crowds of people stood in doorways, contemplating the velocity and mass of the rain, staring up into the sky or watching the streets begin to submerge as the drains dammed up. The sound was so intense that the booming thunder of the storm could barely be heard at street level, while flashes of lightning were themselves scarcely visible through the sheets of descending water.

Derek Anderson stood right next to the full-length windows of his office, looking out. His lights were off, all calls diverted and meetings cancelled. He watched the torrents pouring past. At this height, nothing else was visible—the rain obscured the park and the other buildings in a grey fog, with the only change coming from the occasional flashes of lightning that brightened the office. At the moment, he far preferred to be at work. He couldn't stand to be at home—their home—by himself.

The conversation with Vanessa hadn't taken long. She didn't try to deny the affair. They had fucked—made love, as Vanessa ever so politely put it—nine or ten times (she wasn't quite sure), and only twice at the house. She did not love Ewan.

He had found himself asking, 'Why?' A stupid question, he had thought, one he had been determined not to ask; why was not the issue, wasn't relevant, but he had asked it anyway, after listening to her businesslike description of her infidelity. She wasn't sure why, she said; she had not done it before. He thought she was lying, but probably to spare his feelings.

'Did he wear condoms?' he asked, feeling stupid, ridiculous, and angry that he should have to ask such humiliating questions. He could hear that Vanessa was angered by the question, but dared not articulate that anger; of course, she had replied, did he think she was stupid?

He didn't explode at her, didn't rage and yell. He couldn't. His first marriage had ended a few years after he'd moved to Perth—his ex-wife had moved to the UK after that. Back then, he was the rising business star, a man suddenly sought out by investors and the media and even governments. He worked extraordinarily hard, because he loved it, loved growing a company, loved designing software products. Eleanor and home held no interest for him; the real world was Veldtech, that was all that mattered. He didn't particularly mind when she left him, until later, much later, especially after the cancer scare. It took him years to work out what he'd lost.

Accordingly, a part of him considered what Vanessa had done to him to be a simple balancing of his own stupidity, in a different area, towards Eleanor.

Vanessa didn't ask what he was going to do; she knew there was no point, and anyway, she would find out soon enough. He had told her to leave the office, feeling a wretched turmoil of fury, sadness and frustration.

'I'm sorry I hurt you, Derek. Really, I am,' she'd said. He hadn't replied.

He'd never felt older, or lonelier, as he stared out the window into the wet nothingness.

The storm had hit while Em was four stops from her station. She'd caught a train almost as soon as she'd left the Gaelic Club; Kat Sharpe had been brilliant, as she'd expected. She'd become a huge fan of Sharpe. Witty, intelligent, famous, attractive but unglamorous, making a living doing what she really wanted. She had a perfect life, thought Em.

She'd wanted to go up to Sharpe, to say something that somehow conveyed the message that *she* was Kittehsaurus Rox, that she was the person responsible for it all, the person Kat had interviewed. Instead, this Michael Servetus (it had to be a *male*, of course, like the Anonymous figure on the book cover) was being hailed as the responsible party. She didn't necessarily mind that people were convinced some mysterious superhacker—of 'Eastern European origin', according to one media report—was responsible: that just made it even less likely that she or Tom or the leaker would be tracked down. But she felt a kinship with Sharpe that made her want to ensure she somehow knew the truth. Only Kat seemed to get it. She was the only one who deserved to know what was really happening.

But she hadn't been able to think of the right thing to say, and anyway there was a press of people around Kat at the end of the talk. Sharpe, who appeared to be copiously sweating in the crush, might think she was just some creepy fan. Instead, Em had left and headed for Central, realising there'd be a storm, although the cloudburst that occurred was beyond even her enjoyment of inclement weather.

At her station she sprinted from the train doors down the nearby stairs, only to find that the undercover part of the station was flooded; there was a good three or four inches of water in there. Em removed her shoes and picked her way carefully through the water to the exit, where a large crowd of people was gathered, evidently too scared of the torrential rain to make a break for it. The station car park was about twenty metres away from the entrance, and her car more likely about forty or fifty. Most people were just watching the rain hammer down, while a similar, parallel group was located under a shop awning across the road. She decided, after a moment of thought, to bolt to the car. She pushed forward to the front of the group, checked there was no traffic after a car went slowly past, then sprinted across the road.

Why she tripped, she wasn't quite sure. She might have lost her footing from the sheer volume of water on the road, or encountered an unseen obstacle. More likely the former; she felt her right foot go out from under her. It wasn't a full trip, more like a slide, but she still ended up on the road. She stuck her hands out and planted them heavily, while her bag fell to the road, spilling her phone. A man with an umbrella heading out of the car park yelled out above the rain, 'Are you okay?' and came towards her.

She picked up her phone and the shoe she'd dropped, pushed herself up and walked towards the car park. 'Yeah, I'm fine, thanks,' she said to him. She didn't look back at the large group of people who would have seen her fall. But she couldn't bring herself to run again, no matter how logical that would have been. Instead, she trudged through the torrential rain to her car in bare feet and got in to survey the damage as water pooled in the driver's foot well. There was a long, painful graze on the side of her right leg, and both her hands were grazed from where she'd stuck them out to arrest her fall. One of her shoes, which she'd been holding in her right hand, now had a broken heel from where she'd slammed it into the road.

The worst damage, of course, was to her pride, which wasn't so much hurt as ready to have life support switched off. She reclined in the seat and listened to the rain pound on the car. There was a brief flash of lightning, followed after a few seconds by a loud peal of thunder.

'I'm not going to cry,' she said. 'I am not going to fucking cry.' She contemplated her wet, bleeding hands that now stung savagely, and brushed the dirt out of the grazes, wincing.

You are such an idiot. You fell over in front of—

'SHUT UP!' she yelled. 'SHUT UP, SHUT UP!'

She screamed and clutched her hands to her face. Some water trickled onto her lips and she could taste blood.

'I'm fucking Kittehsaurus Rox and I turned the whole fucking country upside down, me, upside fucking down, and there's *nothing* you can do about it, so fuck you. *Fuck you.*'

She reached into her bag and rummaged for her key, then stuck it into the ignition, her hand smarting as she did so. Her wipers, even at high speed, made minimal impression on the windscreen, and her side windows had rapidly fogged up. But she floored it out of the car park anyway. And she didn't cry.

TUESDAY
8 DECEMBER

'So last night was a success?' asked Spitaleri.

'Mate, it was a fucking *roaring* success,' said Peter. He leaned back and put his feet on the desk. 'About two hundred, two fifty people showed, we've got hi-res photos of most of them, we had thirty or forty people using Twitter, and we had, get this, six hundred people watching on livestream, and we've got IPs for all of them. It's a honey trove that's gonna keep on giving.'

'Did our friends from Eastern Europe tune in?'

'That was the first thing I checked. Apparently not. Which might mean they tuned in unprotected.'

'If you're lucky.'

'If we're lucky. Who knows, we might actually have the IP of the real Kittehsaurus Rox people among it all. But, mate, you should've seen it. I have not met such a gallery of freaks and dickheads in my entire life. Every fucking left-wing nutter in Sydney must have been there.'

'Cool. How did your mate Kat Sharpe go?'

'She spoke really well,' said Peter. 'But she's a bloody non-starter on the surveillance front. All I've got from her is calls to her mates and her mum and endless interview requests. She does more bloody interviews than . . .' He trailed off.

'Someone who does a lot of interviews?'

Peter had a vast pile of information to sort through. He'd had a huge array of contacts in the lead-up to the previous evening's event, via email, Facebook and Twitter. All of it would have to be compiled into miniature dossiers for each individual; a researcher in Canberra was going to help him process the information. His immediate goal was to see if there was indeed anything to link people who'd attended or watched the event to KSR. They must surely have watched—how could they not? Frustratingly, however, since the Attorney-General had announced that they thought they'd shut down the attacks, there'd been nothing from them. Worse, no one in ASIO had a clue as to what the basis was for the AG's statement; they had assumed he'd received ACSC advice, until a phone call between Guy Collin and Calvin had revealed the ACSC and the AFP thought ASIO had advised him. So who the hell had told the AG that the leaks were finished?

'Must have been ASD!' Collin and Spitaleri had joked simultaneously, with even Collin laughing.

He still thought he had a chance of identifying KSR before the ACSC did, but Kat wasn't providing anything useful. In retrospect, he wouldn't have slept with her if he'd known she was going to be such a dud on the information front. But, he told himself, he had to take the chance. He wondered whether he should tell Spitto that he'd slept with her, then decided he didn't have to make a decision until she actually produced actionable intelligence. He still hoped to be able to encourage her to be more forthcoming over some pillow talk, so he would give the affair a little longer. He felt only a mild twinge of guilt; he could fairly effectively compartmentalise his personal life and his professional life, and Kylie was aware that the nature of his job meant some unconventional choices. Still, he didn't intend to let her know either.

He went downstairs to check his, or more correctly Peter Armitage's, messages on his mobile and call Kat.

'Hey, it's Peter. Just wanted to thank you again for yesterday, I think it was a big success.'

'No worries,' she said.

'Anything happening that you've heard? It's been pretty dead since they said they'd stopped the attacks.'

'No, same thing here. I'm not hearing anything.'

He decided to try a more direct tack with her.

'I'm really angry about this Servetus thing. I mean, it's just . . . I know for a fact it's a group, isn't it? Not just one person?'

'That's what I think,' said Kat. 'It's a group of people. This Servetus thing has just been taken up by the media. Still, like I said, I guess people need an identity to personalise their support.'

'True,' he said. 'I hope none of the group came along last night. I assume there were ASIO agents there.'

'I don't know. I'm not sure all of them are even in Australia.'

'Yeah, that's what I heard. Anyway, look, do you want to, ah, catch up later in the week?'

'Yeah, sure. I'll check what I'm doing and text you okay?'

'Okay, cool,' he said.

When he checked his messages he discovered a call from a Nine producer wanting an interview for *Today Tonight*.

'*Today Tonight*? Goodness, you've cracked the big time,' said Spitaleri. 'You do that, your days as an undercover officer are going to be over very quickly.'

'Well I did livestream last night's event,' Peter said. 'I considered doing it in an Anonymous mask but couldn't find one.'

'Discretion might be the better part of valour, mate,' Spitaleri replied.

'Red alert,' said Rachael, emerging from her office. 'Level twenty-six. Urgent meeting.'

'What about?' said Nathan, rising.

'Don't know, but there's a major panic.'

He followed Rachael around to the lift, wondering if it had anything to do with what he'd done on Sunday. It couldn't, he decided, be anything but that. He'd been slightly nonplussed when he hadn't seen anything the previous day. Presumably this was now it, and corporate hell was breaking loose in response. They rode the lift to twenty-six in silence. Rachael, unusually, was in a quite summery dress, and looked, he thought, five years younger and very attractive. He led the way from the lift around to the meeting room on twenty-six, where several people were already gathered, only one of whom he recognised, the head of the media area. There appeared to be considerable agitation.

As they approached the door, Mark Chalmers appeared from the other end of the corridor and reached the door before them. He pointed at Gibbo.

'I've just come from giving riding instructions to the lawyers,' he said to him. 'They're rounding up QCs. I want a full denial prepared, a comprehensive denial. And tell them we'll sue their arses off. This is core business for a company like ours and publication will inflict *existential* damage on us. It's the height of irresponsible journalism and we will litigate like hell if we need to. But don't issue it until I clear it.'

'Of course.' Gibbo nodded.

He turned to Rachael. 'I want some briefing notes along exactly the same lines for whoever is going to speak to the government about this, whether it's Levers or whoever.'

Chalmers's manner was his usual brusqueness cubed, all sharp words and blunt instructions.

'But denying what?' said Rachael.

'Gibbo'll explain,' he snapped. He jabbed a finger at Nathan. 'You come with me. You've got an hour.' The last comment, said to Nathan's face, apparently was directed at everyone else.

He walked past them towards the lifts. Nathan, nonplussed, shrugged at Rachael and turned and followed him. Inside the lift, instead of going up to his office, Chalmers pressed a basement button.

'Where are we going?' Nathan asked tentatively.

The lift stopped at eighteen. As the doors began to open, Chalmers stabbed the button to close them. 'Fuck off, it's full,' he said to the woman and man who were intending to get in. The doors slid shut in their alarmed faces.

Chalmers then sneezed, and produced a handkerchief. 'I think I'm getting a bloody cold.' He blew his nose loudly. 'I suspect my EA . . . Right,' he said, stowing the handkerchief. 'It's the fucking end of the world. About twenty minutes ago we got a call from the ABC asking a series of questions about whether Kittehsaurus Rox was actually in this company, using a backdoor access into the Parliament House IT system.'

Has he worked out it's me that told them? Nathan wondered. Were they still spying on him? Had they somehow tracked him to the Starbucks on the weekend? Or had they put something on his laptop at home? Christ. He should have thought of that. And if Chalmers knew, where was he taking him?

'So we've got a relatively short period of time to try to save the company.'

That comment seemed to suggest Chalmers didn't know. Or, for the moment, was not dealing with that particular issue.

'Where's Mr Anderson?'

'He has some personal issues to attend to. I left a message for him.'

That hadn't actually sorted out where they were going. The lift reached the basement. Chalmers strode out quickly and headed down a row of cars to a Lexus and gestured for Nathan to get in. Nathan slid into the passenger seat and Chalmers began backing out. 'I hate this parking spot,' he said. 'Lexuses . . . Lexii, I suppose, are so big, it's like I'm trying to steer the fucking *Titanic*. After it's sunk. I'm always scared I'm going to lose a thousand-dollar mirror on the column.'

The mirror was left intact, but as Chalmers clunkily shifted gears and began spinning the wheel, Nathan winced as his side of the front of the car barely missed the rear of the BMW on the other side of the column.

Chalmers drove out onto Clarke Street, turned right, turned right again, and then accelerated quickly to get onto Liverpool Street ahead of an oncoming wall of traffic. Nathan didn't know whether to repeat his question about their destination. He wondered darkly if Chalmers knew he was the one who had contacted the ABC, and was driving him off to some unpleasant fate.

'Fuck!' Chalmers yelled suddenly.

'Ah, what is it?' said Nathan.

'I forgot my phone. You got your phone?'

'Ah . . . yeah . . . I need to turn it on.'

'Call my office.'

'Sure,' he said, turning his phone on. 'What's the number?'

Chalmers squealed the tyres accelerating down Liverpool Street. 'Um . . .' His tone softened somewhat. 'I've no idea what my number is. I never ring it. Sorry.'

What sort of person doesn't know their own number? Nathan thought to himself. His phone came to life and he dialled his own desk. Eve answered.

'Hi, Eve, it's Nathan,' he said.

'Hi, Nathan,' she said. 'What are you doing ringing your own phone?'

'Can you put me through to Mark Chalmers's office, please?'

'Sure, okay, let me just . . . let me just find the number.'

The line went silent. Chalmers swerved around a car pulling out from a parking space. 'Out of the way, cunthead,' he snapped. 'Fuck, I hate people who do that.'

'Hello?' said Nathan, to silence.

'What are they doing, running a fucking string and some cups up the wall?' Chalmers said.

Eve returned. 'Okay, Nathan, I'll just put you through.'

'Thanks.'

There was further silence. After about thirty seconds, she came back on. 'Sorry, I can't work out how to transfer the—'

'Just tell me Mark's number then, Eve,' he said patiently.

'It's . . . oh wait, Brian's just showed me. Putting you through.'

'Mark Chalmers's office?'

'Hi, it's Nathan Welles here, I've got Mark to speak to you.'

'Hold it up,' said Chalmers.

Nathan held the phone near his face.

'Mary, it's Mark,' he called. 'I need you to book the secure video-link line to Marshall and tee up a meeting with Mike Armstrong ASAP, okay? Tell his office it's very urgent, and it'll be me and Derek, maybe, if I can get Derek. It needs to be as soon as possible, preferably tonight. And can you call Derek again and leave another message saying it's urgent.'

'Okay,' came a tiny voice.

'Also, I need some Codral or something for my cold. Can you have something when I get back? Thanks.'

He glanced at Nathan. 'It's okay, you can hang up.'

Tom closed the door behind Em. It was clear there was some sort of crisis, and thus, Em assumed, it had to be about Project X.

'What's the disaster?' she said.

'A media outlet has found out about Kittehsaurus Rox.'

It was the first time Tom had ever said the name.

'How?' Em's instinctive thought was that it must have been her fault, somehow. Had she made some sort of mistake? Or maybe it was Nathan Welles.

'We don't know, but they have proof.'

The word 'proof' panicked her a little. 'Like what? They know the leaker?'

Tom looked at her for a moment, then he sat down. 'Em, I'm sorry, I'm really sorry, but there was no leaker. No whistleblower. It was me. I was using some software we sold to the parliament, to steal material.'

She stared at him, stunned.

'I'm sorry,' he repeated.

'I knew it,' she said after a moment. 'I knew it.'

That was completely false. She didn't know it at all. She had believed Tom, had automatically believed him, as if it were impossible for him to lie. But it seemed like the dignity-saving thing to say. Tom had lied to her. Easygoing, straitlaced Mr Family Man, boring, process-obsessed Tom, had lied to her. God.

'I said it was a whistleblower in order to protect you, so if it ever got exposed, I could say I misled you, that I lied to you to secure your cooperation. That way none of it comes back to you. Just to me.'

Em felt herself tearing up. 'Fuck, Tom. You lied to me. Over something as serious as this.'

Tom ignored her. 'The media knows about the software, so there's no denying it. And when the government hears about it, they'll realise everything that Kittehsaurus Rox released was obtained through that software.'

She felt a tear roll down her cheek.

Crybaby.

'Look, Em, I'm so sorry about lying to you. But this is now a deep, deep crisis. Something that could destroy the company. They know how we got the stuff.'

She spoke, her voice breaking slightly. 'But we had that Cabinet submission. That wasn't something that gets emailed around Parliament. They protect that shit.' She didn't know why she was arguing with Tom about what he was saying, since he was the one who had done it.

He sat back. 'Some idiot sent a copy of the submission to an MP because he was chair of a committee. That's how I got it.'

Em leaned back in her chair and put her head in her hands.

He fooled you completely, said Dark Voice. *Used you.*

'I'm gonna go to jail. I'm going to fucking go to jail.'

'Calm down,' Tom said. 'Calm down. We need to think clearly. It's okay. I'll take the fall. None of this need affect you, at all.'

She didn't reply.

Tom had stolen the material *himself*. Of all people. There was no whistleblower. He'd actually stolen the information. Him.

'Em, look at me,' he said. 'Look at me. You are not going to jail. I will go to jail if anyone does, and I'll make sure nothing happens to you. And it will *all* be the truth, because I kept what was really going on from you.'

'There wasn't even a whistleblower giving us information. We just stole it.'

'Yes,' said Tom. 'And we've been found out. *I've* been found out,' he corrected himself, after a moment.

This was worse than being found out, Em thought. It was one thing to have been involved in leaking a whistleblower's secrets. But now it was like KSR was going to be revealed as a joke, a scam. People would know it was an elaborate con. The thing that had shaken the government and stunned the country, revealed as a poor con job by a security company, to drum up business.

It was a wretched, awful, humiliating way to end KSR, something she'd been so proud of.

'I'm sorry,' Tom repeated.

She stared at Tom's perfectly clean desk. Why on earth had she been arguing with him about being found out? Then a thought occurred to her.

'What if something else got leaked that wasn't obtained via that software?' she said suddenly.

Tom looked confused. 'I don't understand.'

She spoke slowly, not bothering to think through what she was saying before she said it. 'If the proof that KSR is us is that everything that's been leaked was got through the software that you used, what if we leaked something that you can't get with that software? What if KSR released something else?'

'But that's not going to change anything if the media already knows how the other stuff was obtained.'

'Isn't it worth a try?'

'But where can we get something like that?'

'I don't know.'

He thought for a moment. 'Fuck it, it is worth a try.' He put his phone on speaker and dialled a number. Mark Chalmers's EA answered, then put him through after a moment. A strange voice answered.

'Um, who's that?'

'Nathan Welles. Who's this?'

A shock went through Em, making her stomach churn.

'Tom Dao. I was looking for Mark Chalmers.'

'Ah, yeah, I've got him here,' said Nathan. 'He's driving. Hang on.'

'Put him on speaker, can you?' they heard Mark say.

'Tom,' called Mark.

'Hi. Look, we've had an idea, might be worth thinking about.'

'What is it? Make it quick.'

'What if KSR releases something that's not available via PICS? That might throw—'

'FUCKING IDIOT!' Chalmers yelled, causing the phone speaker to distort slightly. 'Hey, dickhead, what the FUCK are you doing?'

'Er, sorry?'

'Sorry, Tom, wasn't talking to you. Go on.'

'It might throw suspicion off PICS if something that can't be got through PICS is released.'

'Like what?' Chalmers snapped.

'I don't know. A Cabinet document, if you could get one. A letter from the Prime Minister with her signature on it. Something you definitely couldn't get via PICS.'

'Okay, let me think about it. Gotta go.'

'Nathan,' Chalmers said, once Nathan had ended the call, 'I gather that when you found out about the KSR thing, you had an . . . a, um, interview with our Scottish friend.'

Nathan shifted uncomfortably in his seat. 'You could say that.'

Chalmers slammed to a halt rather than go through a yellow light to turn onto Pier Street.

'Did he threaten you?'

'Yes.'

Chalmers was silent for two minutes, until he pulled away from the lights, glanced in the left-hand side mirror and changed lanes. 'That was an . . . error of judgement on his part. A serious one. Mr Mazzoni is no longer with the company. And we're eager to rectify his errors of judgement, including in relation to you. We need all your expertise right now, Nathan.'

Well, thought Nathan, I guess that means I'm not going to be shot. Clearly he doesn't know that I know Mazzoni's left.

Chalmers went on. 'This KSR thing could kill us, Nathan. I mean, the whole company. The, um, mild panic you currently see might shortly give way to a general fucking stampede for the lifeboats. We need some fancy footwork to prevent that from happening. And there're not too many people I can trust, currently. You at least know about what has been going on.'

He went silent again, then resumed. 'So I need to know that I can trust you, Nathan. Trust you completely. Because otherwise, Veldtech might be shutting down. We won't survive this.'

I don't fucking believe this, Nathan thought. Is this actually happening? He had to stop himself from smiling. As the author, the sole proprietor, the man behind the turmoil that was engulfing the company and threatening its very existence, he was delighted at the chaos he had wreaked. But to have Mark Chalmers begging for his help, apparently unaware of his role in causing it all, was bizarre and astonishing.

The car in front of them took several seconds to begin moving when the right-turn arrow went green. 'Oh, COME ON, mate, you need a written invitation?' Chalmers said loudly. 'We've all got places to be. Go waste some other prick's time.'

'You can trust me, Mr Chalmers,' Nathan said finally, having checked to make sure there'd be no minor traffic inconveniences to set him off. He felt like laughing at himself as he said it. *You can trust me, Mr Chalmers. After all, I'm the bastard who shopped you.*

'Oh fuck, call me Mark.'

He was silent for another couple of minutes as he drove into Pyrmont. 'Shit!'

He braked violently. Something on the back seat fell off with a distinct thud and mild *tink* sound. 'Oh no, I think that was a bottle of something. Sorry, I just spotted a park I can actually fit into.'

Nathan looked into the back. A bottle of red wine had fallen into the foot well.

'It's okay, it's not broken.'

Chalmers turned around and reversed back. Within seconds, he had completely botched the reverse park. He pulled out to start again. At least three cars were now banked up behind him. One of them sounded its horn, but Chalmers didn't react. He proceeded to bugger up the park a second time, although the cars behind had managed to get around him. He sat there, the car stuck out into traffic at an odd angle, thinking.

'Question is,' Nathan ventured, 'can I trust your parking?'

'I'm so shit at reverse parks.' He accelerated back out.

Nathan pointed to the rear-view camera right in front of him in the centre console. 'Don't you have one of those reverse-park cameras?'

'It's no fucking good to me. Can you get out and guide me?'

'Ah . . . yeah, sure.' He undid his seatbelt and got out. Another car had stopped behind the vehicle. Chalmers jerked forward. From the kerb, it seemed there was plenty of room. Chalmers began reversing. Nathan wildly signalled to him to start turning. The wheels belatedly turned and the car began actually entering the space. The car behind him managed to slip around, its driver giving Nathan an odd look. Nathan crouched and reversed his waving motion, gesticulating even more dramatically, but despite actually making eye contact with Chalmers within the vehicle, to no avail. The back wheel of the Lexus hit the kerb with a slight squeal.

The car jerked forward, almost hitting the car in front, then reversed as jerkily, then accelerated out of the spot, only barely ahead of another car that had to brake and sounded its horn. Chalmers went forward about one hundred metres and stopped in a loading zone. Nathan began walking up to the car.

'If I get a ticket, I get a ticket,' said Chalmers as he got out. 'Let's go.'

'Go where?'

'GaySIO. You should think about what Tom Dao suggested.'

He led Nathan into a nondescript office block. A young woman and a male security guard were at the front desk, in front of some train station–style security gates with glass panels. The young woman frowned at them. The security guard smiled.

'Mark Chalmers to see Guy Collin, please.'

He turned to Nathan. 'You've got to leave your phone here. No mobile devices allowed.'

They each had to fill out a form and sign it, and the young woman handed them passes to hang around their necks. They were then permitted to swipe their way through the security gates, which led around to the lifts. Access to the lifts themselves required going through another security station, this time with three guards and a metal detector. One of the guards languidly picked up a phone and called someone. They were then given a second pass to go with the first and directed through the metal detector. After several minutes, one of the lifts opened and two young men appeared to escort them. On exiting on the eighth floor, one of the men accompanying them went ahead while the other walked behind. Nathan froze, because the moment they stepped out of the lift several lights in the corridor ahead began flashing.

'It's fine,' said Chalmers.

'Unsecured visitor,' called the first man as they walked down a corridor merrily flashing with red, amber and green lights.

'I think insecure visitor would be more accurate,' Nathan muttered.

They turned left into a meeting room, where a nondescript middle-aged man, rather hangdog in expression, awaited them with another, younger, man. The two men accompanying them left the room.

'This is Nathan Welles,' said Chalmers. 'He's been helping us on the Kittehsaurus Rox issue. Guy Collin, Deputy DG.'

'I see,' said Collin, by way of greeting. They shook hands.

'Sorry we're late,' Chalmers said as they sat down. 'Nathan's a hopeless parker. So, you blokes certainly are up shit creek.'

Collin frowned. 'How do you figure that?'

'Well, you're about three hours from it being revealed ASIO's been spying on MPs,' Chalmers said.

Nathan couldn't help but admire his chutzpah.

'And you're three hours from the government learning Veldtech has been stealing information from it,' said Collin.

Chalmers shrugged, as though he was entirely indifferent to the subject. 'There's no direct evidence of that. And we have a couple of Sydney's best silks working on an injunction application that will prevent it from getting out.'

Collin laughed suddenly. 'Then why the panicked call for a meeting, Mark?'

'Well, it wasn't so much panic as, perhaps, concern, serious concern, at the mutual problem we face, Guy.'

'Created by your company.'

'Well, as I said, there's no direct evidence of that. But we both have an interest in making sure that the back door into PICS doesn't become the centre of attention.'

Collin eased back in his chair. He was a man, Nathan noted, of limited, even sparse, body language, like he'd trained himself to stay absolutely rigid during meetings, giving nothing away. 'How long is your injunction going to last? You said they've got the first email and know about PICS and the Twitter account. It can only be a matter of time. And who knows what might filter up from the ABC to government?'

'As I said, we need to find a way to shift attention elsewhere.'

'Well as *I* said recently, Mark, if only you'd come to us before all this started.'

'There's no point discussing what might have been, Guy. We have a suggestion. Nathan?'

Nathan wasn't expecting to be pitched into the discussion. Again, the thought occurred to him that Chalmers somehow knew it was he who had caused all the turmoil. It appeared to be a kind of test, a demand for a demonstration that he could be trusted and was worthy of Chalmers's confidence. He assumed Chalmers meant for him to run with the idea put forward by Tom Dao in the car. It perhaps also meant Chalmers didn't directly own the idea, so could afford to ditch it if it encountered resistance.

'Well,' Nathan began, clearing his throat, 'if Kittehsaurus Rox leaks something that can't be obtained by PICS, it would discredit the idea that PICS is at the heart of what's been going on. And Veldtech could,' he continued, shooting a glance at Chalmers, 'state that the, er, back door is a perfectly ordinary admin login for administering the system, just like any significant software system has.'

It wasn't bad, he thought, given he'd invented it on the wing. His lying skills were coming in handy.

'Leak what?' said Collin.

Nathan thought for a moment. 'A Cabinet minute, maybe? They're never distributed on PICS, are they? In fact they can't be. They're CABNET only. I've not worked in the public service, so I'm not a hundred per cent sure, but you blokes have—that's the case, isn't it? And people already think the first KSR leak was obtained from CABNET.'

'It wasn't. Someone emailed the cab sub to an MP,' said the other man with Collin.

'Yes, but not many people are aware of that distinction,' said Chalmers. He had begun rubbing a red spot on his chin. 'It would demonstrate that PICS isn't the problem.'

'How are you going to leak a Cabinet minute?' asked Collin.

'I think that's a question for you to consider. ASIO receives Cabinet minutes, surely?'

Collin was silent for nearly a minute. After about thirty seconds, he drummed his fingers on the table.

'AGD gets them. We only get ones relevant to us.' He paused for a moment, then resumed. 'We couldn't leak an electronic copy. We'd have to get one from our Corporate people, who have the access to the CABNET terminal. But I've got a paper copy of the minute from this week's meeting about KSR in my in-tray.'

'The minutes have watermarks,' the other man said. 'They'd know it was our copy.'

'We'll just give them the text,' Collin said. 'They only need the text, surely?'

'It would be better to have the document, but the watermark is a problem. The text would be okay,' said Chalmers. 'Of course, we're open to more conventional suggestions.'

'The other problem is how we get it to you, or should I say, for the sake of not having an argument, to KSR,' Collin said. 'I'm sure as hell not emailing the text of a Cabinet minute to you.'

'Well, we have our own guy,' said the other man to Collin quietly.

Collin looked at him and nodded. 'Of course, he could send it. He's all set up to do it.'

'It's a breach,' the other man said. 'We might need to make it a special intelligence operation.'

Collin shook his head. 'God no, we'd need the Attorney-General to approve that.'

'Well, we'll do whatever we can to make sure KSR is receptive to whatever it might get,' said Chalmers, keeping a perfectly straight face. He scratched his chin.

The other man leaned in to Collin and spoke to him too quietly for either Nathan or Chalmers to hear. Nathan heard the words 'special intelligence operation' again. They spoke for about a minute. 'True,' Collin said eventually. 'We still have a problem with ACSC. They want to look at the whole usage of PICS by IPs outside Parliament. When they do that, they'll find that login has been used regularly, even though there'll be nothing to connect us to the source addresses.'

Nathan was enjoying this. Clearly what Mazzoni had told him was true. ASIO were big users of PICS as well. He decided to venture his hand. 'Why don't *we* put our hands up for that? It's our software. And we have the contract for administration and upgrades, as I recall. We can say it was just a regular system check to make sure there were no bugs or security flaws.'

Collin gave him a sour look. 'ACSC won't believe that. They understand this stuff. At the very least there'll be criticism of Veldtech.'

'We can wear that. And what evidence is there to contradict it?' said Chalmers. 'That login doesn't leave any evidence of activity, just login, logout and source location data. There's no evidence it's been used for anything . . . just a lot of logins. Entirely consistent with the product manufacturer checking to make sure the software is working okay, without looking at the content.'

Collin looked dubious, but eventually said, 'All right. Think of it as a quid pro quo. You can take responsibility for routinely accessing the system. It isn't too much of a price to pay for the garbage you've been up to.'

Chalmers looked out the window for a few seconds. 'Okay,' he said. 'We all have our homework to do. Shall we get started?'

Collin sighed. 'Sure. I want a word in private before you go.'

Nathan hovered uncertainly while Chalmers and Collin had a short but animated discussion at the other end of the room. Chalmers then turned and signalled to him. They headed back to the lifts, accompanied by the two men who'd walked them to the meeting room, complete with flashing lights and cries of 'Unsecured visitor'.

'The Director-General wants to meet with Derek. This could be ugly,' Chalmers said. He waited until they exited the lift and had left the building before speaking again. 'Guy Collin is the reason I left ASIO.'

'Did he, erm, fuck you over or betray you?' said Nathan.

'Oh god no,' said Chalmers. 'I was just terrified of ending up like him.'

Inevitably, when they reached the car, he had a parking ticket.

Peter sank onto his couch and inserted the USB stick Spitaleri had given him into his laptop. On it was a PDF with three paragraphs of text.

> *The Cabinet agreed that, concurrent with consideration of a proposal to establish a national cyber-intelligence agency to be brought forward by the Attorney-General at the first meeting of 2016: –*
>
> > *a) the Minister for Defence should bring forward options for better integration and coordination of Australian cybersecurity, information security and cyber-intelligence operations with those of the United States of America, the United Kingdom, Canada and New Zealand; and*
> >
> > *b) the Attorney-General should bring forward options for amendments to the Criminal Code, the Telecommunications (Interception and Access) Act 1979, the Australian Security Intelligence Organisation Act 1979 and related legislation to strengthen the capacity of law-enforcement agencies and agencies of the Australian Intelligence Community to prevent and detect cyber-crime and cyberterrorism.*

Spitaleri had requested that he send the PDF to KSR. As a trusted supporter of KSR, Spitaleri said, they'd assume the document was from a genuine source; only, there was code embedded in the PDF that would permanently 'mark' the computer it was used on, even if they deleted the PDF. This would make proving the case against them easier once they were tracked down. It was a smart play, Peter thought.

Only . . . 'Don't send it from here. No way. Send it from somewhere else.'

All of that was cool as far as Peter was concerned, because Kylie had a day off too, and he was keen to spend some time with her, given what was happening with Kat Sharpe. He'd received some more recordings from Sharpe's phone, and again derived nothing from them; a number were his own conversations with her. She'd briefly mentioned him to her friend Madison Enright, but in fairly neutral terms.

He watched Kylie over at the dining-room table, working through some bills. She was wearing a singlet top and sweat pants but still managed to look gorgeous. I was smart to put a ring on that, he thought.

He'd DM'd @KSRComms, and they'd responded with a temporary email account. He'd uploaded the file to a Hushmail account, attached it to an email and dispatched it. His only other task for the day was to go through some material the area monitoring WikiLeaks had given him on prominent supporters of the group.

'You still up for lunch?' said Kylie.

'Yeah, yeah. Where we going?'

'I was thinking somewhere in town. Down by the water.'

'How about Aqua?' said Peter.

'You shitting me? That's massively expensive.'

'Fuck it, let's do it. We can get the ferry.'

'Hang on,' she said. She went over to a drawer and produced a ferry timetable, unfolded it and consulted it. 'I think you gotta change at Birchgrove for Milsons Point outside peak.'

'So if we go round eleven thirty, we could get there by one. We can get the train back.'

'Okay.' She grinned. 'Let's do it. I'll book.'

Peter's phone rang distantly. It took him ten or twenty seconds to find it. It was Kat.

'Hey! How are you?' He stood up and walked over to the window.

'I'm good. So you free Friday evening?'

'I am. Do you want to meet up?'

He wasn't worried that she might want to come to his place. The organisation had a flat he could use.

'Yeah,' she said. 'Come to mine? We can go from there. I'll pick a place in Randwick or Coogee.'

'Sure, that'd be good.'

'Yep.'

'Okay, cool.'

'See you.'

For a moment he felt sorry for Kat, sorry that she was completely fooled by him, that she was unaware he was listening to her every phone call and reading every email she sent. 'Eyes on the prize, mate,' he told himself. 'She's just another whingeing activist and she knows KSR.' And with the email he'd just sent, it would make it easier to nab them in the end.

'I've got to work Friday evening,' he said to Kylie.

'Lunch is on you then,' she said.

THURSDAY
10 DECEMBER

A light drizzle had started when the taxi arrived at the Sheraton. It had been threatening to rain all afternoon—the early-morning warmth had been replaced by grey clouds and sticky air—but it had not been hot enough for a repeat, even on a less-biblical scale, of the deluge earlier in the week. Jayde, Tim and Em had shared a taxi; this was Em's first Veldtech Christmas party, while Jayde and Tim were veterans. The party was a dinner at a function room at the Sheraton overlooking Hyde Park, which would be followed by excessive consumption of alcohol, dancing and then dispersal to various points of the compass: the senior executives to drinks at another, still more expensive hotel (they would pick up the tab themselves, a change from previous years); mid-level managers to pubs in Balmain; and the rest to one of several designated kick-on points around the city. The venue had been booked months before the current round of cuts, but in deference to the company's current circumstances, the price of the tickets had gone up to eighty dollars.

Em had gone for red, and was beginning to regret it. It was not that red was not her colour, but she would normally have gone for something black, and was now wondering why she had decided to be bold, even if it was hardly fire-engine red. The dress had a diagonal hem and a neckline that plunged (well, more like glided); she had matching shoes, black stockings, a thin black necklace and black handbag. Jayde, who had gone for black, had already told her several times she looked great, but Jayde looked better, Em knew, even if it was slightly odd to see her in heels.

'Santa Claus is Coming to Town' was playing as background music inside the function room, where Em and Jayde wandered about looking for their table, until Tom waved them down. They were nominally seated at tables corresponding with the areas in which they worked, although Tim had arranged to sit with the self-styled 'gay mafia' only two tables away and Craig, thankfully, was off with some engineers across the room, where five or six tables were clustered with perhaps two or three women in total at them. Three other people from the area next to them were at their table, as well as Adriana, who was already there when Em arrived. Jayde's boss David, a woman named Kris and some guy called Mick, who had been away for quite a while in mysterious circumstances, were also on the table. As they sat down, Tom lifted a bottle of sparkling wine from a cooler in the centre of the table.

'Champagne?' he said. He poured glasses for Em and Adriana. Em had a strong sense that he was still trying to make up for his lying. 'Raining yet?'

'Just starting to,' said Jayde. She leaned over. 'Look, Em, there's your boyfriend.'

Em gave her a savage look, and then glanced over: Nathan and Rachael were approaching another table, both clutching glasses. Rachael was in blue, and looked very, very good. She turned and looked at Nathan and laughed. Em looked away instantly. She was not going there, not going to let that mess with her. She was there to have a good time. A good time consisted of having probably five or six drinks over the course of the event, tops, having a dance when everyone was sufficiently drunk that they wouldn't remember, then going home. It did *not* consist of getting drunk, or of going on somewhere else. She had done wild Christmas parties before, and was determined not to repeat them here: not the drinking to the point of vomiting, not the drunken groping with some guy she only vaguely knew, not the yelling and throwing of objects.

This was reinforced by the fact that she was in a much-improved mood, despite the doubts about red. Kittehsaurus Rox had been reactivated. At lunchtime, she had dispatched an actual Cabinet decision, causing yet another firestorm. The Attorney-General, who'd boasted only last week of how the hacks had been stopped, was humiliated and there were calls for his resignation. A Senate inquiry was about to commence. And the mooted media story about the company and its backdoor access to the Parliament House system hadn't appeared. Tom had made passing reference to the company's success in obtaining an injunction.

'It is a nice outfit,' said Jayde, sipping and staring at Rachael. Em resisted the temptation to look back again.

'I like that suit,' said Em. 'Is that the guy from Legal?' Adriana turned around. A man was standing nearby wearing a shimmering silver suit, attracting admiring looks and comments. 'Yep,' she said. 'Matthew . . . I can't remember his name.' She sipped from her glass. 'God, I hate this song. I hate it more than any other Christmas song. Look at the twins.'

The twins were two girls from Accounts, although their actual jobs were a mystery, and they weren't twins. They looked quite different—one was much taller than the other—but they had been christened thus on the basis that they were never observed apart. The taller one was wearing a bright blue outfit with a segment missing from her midriff; the other a mostly see-through lace outfit, with her hair up.

'My god,' said Jayde. 'I can't believe she's wearing that. Not to a work function.' She tutted primly: Jayde could be conservative in such matters.

'I don't know,' said David, overhearing her. 'I'd hit it.'

And the first inappropriate comment of the night is away, thought Em. She spotted Craig, wearing a suit, across the other side of the room, and instantly thought of him snorting a line of coke in the toilets.

Sniff.

Sniff sniff.

'What happened to your hand, Em?' said David. She had a skin-coloured bandage on the heel of her left hand from where she'd grazed it when she fell. Her right hand had only a minor abrasion.

'Got it trying to hang on to my job,' she said almost automatically, without thinking. Tom laughed.

She hadn't really been angry at him, on reflection. She understood what he'd done, and why he'd done it. In retrospect, she was now pleased the material had all come from an actual back door into the government's email system, rather than a whistleblower; it made it more . . . well, legitimate as a hack, more real, than if it had been parcelled out by a disgruntled public servant or political staffer.

'Nice ring, Kris,' said Tom, eagle-eyed. 'Are congratulations in order?'

She smiled. 'Yes. Engaged earlier this week.'

'Wow,' said Adriana enthusiastically. 'Congratulations!' She leaned forward to examine Kris's hand.

'What's his name?'

'Phillip. He's a lawyer.'

Em, unable to resist, stole a glance at Nathan and Rachael. She was again laughing at something he was saying, gazing at him almost rapturously, chatting animatedly to the other people at their table. She looked a little in love.

There was a change in the overall noise level, and they all looked towards the front of the room, where there was a raised platform. The lights dimmed slightly and a figure emerged behind a lectern. It was Maria Campanella, dressed a little severely in black but with a Santa hat on.

'Good evening, everyone, and Merry Christmas,' she said in her usual scary soft tone, as if she was revealing everyone in the room was about to die. 'It's been a very exciting and productive year for Veldtech and I'm looking forward to celebrating our achievements with you tonight. We thought this year we'd get the speeches out of the way early in the piece and get to the enjoyable part of the evening. So without further ado, I'd like to call on the executive chairman, Mr Derek Anderson, to say a few words.'

There was a round of applause—strangely generous, Em thought, although perhaps everyone appreciated the strategy of completing the formal part of the evening quickly.

Anderson appeared behind the lectern. He wore a dinner suit, and looked almost intimidatingly serious. A hush fell over the guests.

'Thank you, Maria. I have to say I agree with this policy of getting the speeches out of the way first, because I'm pretty keen on having a drink myself.'

He paused.

'Look, I'd love to be able to say that this has been a year of unalloyed success for Veldtech, and to a great extent it has been. But of course, as you all know, we're celebrating the festive season in the shadows of some job cuts, and it would be silly if I didn't address those straight up.'

This was an unexpectedly sombre note to commence with. For that matter, Anderson himself seemed rather downbeat.

'We are a successful company, and we're part of a successful group of companies right around the world. We're outstanding at what we do, and our customers know it. But we're all operating in difficult times, at a point when our main customers are cutting back on spending. As one of the ETS board members said to me recently, there are a lot of good people cleaning out their desks around the world currently.

'I'm fairly confident that, given our strong performance this year here in Australia and in Asia, we can keep the number of our people—dare I say it, my people—doing that, clearing their desks, to a minimum. We've increased sales and revenue and are now moving to meet the targets we set ourselves earlier in the year, we've rolled out some outstanding products, genuinely innovative products, and we've further enhanced our reputation as the best cybersecurity firm in the country.

'So let me thank you all for your efforts this year, they've been truly splendid, and I know I speak for all of the senior management team when I say that Veldtech *is* its people, it is you, we feel that very strongly, and we are working hard to make sure that next year is one of growth, not of retrenchment. I'm not looking for Veldtech to hold its ground next year; I want us to move forward, to expand again. Please have a happy and safe festive season, enjoy your break, do recharge your batteries, and come January we'll see you back refreshed and ready for the new year.'

There was a round of somewhat tepid applause.

'And I think that's enough from me—let's enjoy ourselves!' Anderson said with surprising enthusiasm.

Some vague, jazz sort of music started up, and the level of sound in the room immediately surged back to what it had been several minutes before. Waiters appeared with bottles of red and white wine, and Tom poured again for Jayde and Em, who resumed examining outfits around the room. At one point, Em heard Rachael giggle, sufficiently loudly that she could be heard above the noise, and she couldn't help herself: she stared for a full twenty seconds at Rachael, suppressing the urge to rise from her seat with an item of cutlery, walk over to her and gouge out one of her eyes. Jayde, who could demonstrate surprising sympathy in the most unusual of circumstances, grabbed her arm and they headed for the bar to get cocktails: a Cocksucking Cowboy (predictably) for Jayde and a Sex on the Beach for Em, both eagerly ordered by Jayde. Two tables full of IT men were right near the bar. Most of them looked like they had been stuffed into their suits, which were already in the early stages of disarray. One of them was clad in a dress and was wearing make-up, which, judging by his grin and animated conversation with his mates, was considered to be an act of unprecedented comic genius by his colleagues. Proximity to the bar meant not merely rapid access to alcohol but an opportunity to survey their female colleagues, which they weren't making any effort to disguise. Standing at the bar, where she was taller than any of the women and many of the men, Em felt like a piece of meat on a barbecue.

Tim joined them as they waited. He was dressed in a grey Nehru jacket, a black shirt to go with it and black trousers. Em had already told him he looked amazing.

'Plenty of eye candy at your table, Tim,' said Jayde.

'And not a one of them available,' he said, examining the drinks available behind the bar, 'for you. We're having a drinking competition a bit later if you want to join in.'

On the raised platform where Campenalla and Anderson had spoken, a group of four men from Corporate, all dressed alike, were gathering. These were the Paranoids, an a cappella group who annually provided a humorous take on the year's events within the company and without, usually to much chortling at the not-particularly-daring mockery of the company executive.

'I'd shame you all,' Jayde said, paying for their drinks. She stopped to exchange badinage, less flirtatious than outright pornographic, with the IT boys on the way back. 'God they're hilarious,' she said, rejoining Em.

'They're all arseholes,' Em replied flatly, and a little too loudly as the room quietened and the Paranoids began to sing. Despite her best efforts, she'd allowed Rachael to put her in a foul mood. She decided more alcohol was the least worst answer to that.

> *Chalmers they say is charming*
> *But we've observed he's not*
> *If something is alarming*
> *He will cause a shock*

'You're all sacked!' yelled Chalmers, to a bigger laugh than the verse itself.

> *Derek's made his riches*
> *Securing PCs*
> *Now he's owned by creatures*
> *From Washington DC*

'I could do better than that,' said Em, leaning over.
'You already have,' whispered Tom.

> *Our highly effective malware*
> *That catches activists*
> *Is beloved by tyrants everywhere*

To put together torture lists

There was shocked laughter and hoots at that—had the Paranoids *gone too far?*

Now we need retrenchments
DC wants job cuts
Just forget about sentiment
All those who make peanuts

It was not long afterwards, just as the not-especially-nice meal was being served, that Mark Chalmers, dressed in a dinner suit, advanced on their table.

'Hi, Tom,' he said nasally. 'I wanted to meet Emma.'

'Sure,' said Tom. 'Emma Thomas, this is Mark Chalmers.'

Emma lowered her drink, surprised, and stood up and extended her hand.

Chalmers extended his and then withdrew it. 'Sorry, I don't want to give you this bloody cold I've come down with. I wanted to thank you for your good work this week. And before that, too.'

'Thanks. I hope everything's going to turn out okay,' she said, adopting his lack of detail. She tried to avoid staring at a red patch on his chin.

'Well, you've given us a fighting chance. We were in a lot of trouble and your idea really helped. If we do get out of it, it'll be partly because of you, so I wanted to say how much it was appreciated.'

He looked at Tom. 'She's good value, Tom. We'll be making more use of her.'

'I hope so,' Tom said.

'Have a good evening, guys.'

'Fuck me dead, mate,' Jayde said as soon as Chalmers was out of earshot. 'The whole room just saw Mark Chalmers come up and talk to you. What did you do?'

Em shrugged. 'This and that.'

I'm just going to let this moment slowly wash over me, she thought. Dark Voice was silent, unable to offer anything, struck mute by Mark Chalmers, the Devil incarnate, singling her out for praise, as if one malignant force had been banished by the arrival of another, vastly more powerful dark deity. She knew she wouldn't be happy for long, that something would come along shortly to annoy or depress her, but for the moment, she was going to enjoy being happy. Happy? Perhaps not happy, but content. That was it—she was content.

Chalmers headed back to his own table, and encountered Theo T. on the way. Theo was wearing a grey suit and, unusually, a tie, a pink one already well on the way to coming undone. He was clutching a beer and swayed uncertainly when he locked eyes with Chalmers.

'Evening, Theo,' said Chalmers. He was dosed up on large amounts of flu medication and pain relief and wasn't drinking, but felt a little light-headed and somewhat distant from everything going on around him.

'How are you, Mark?' Theo sounded less drunk than he looked, but wasn't entirely sober.

'Shithouse. I have a nasty cold.'

'Bummer. Listen, I've been meaning to ask how that tender went—the one you and that Tom guy were going to lodge after the deadline.'

'Well, I might have pushed my luck a bit there,' replied Chalmers, 'but we might still get a good result. Thank you for your help with that, by the way, I really appreciated it.'

'Can I get that in writing?'

'Of course. I must be infected with Christmas spirit as well as this cold, I seem to be being uncharacteristically pleasant to people this evening.'

'Heh. Can I get you a drink?'

'No, I'm off the grog till I get rid of this lurgy. Have a good evening.'

'You too.'

Back at the executive table, Derek was in conversation with Baz. Derek hadn't eaten anything and appeared to be drinking water. He was clearly very unhappy. He hadn't contacted Chalmers about the KSR crisis until very late on Tuesday night, listened to how he had handled it and what the lawyers had to say, pronounced himself satisfied and cancelled the planned secure conference call with Armstrong. Chalmers knew he'd received what he called 'a frightful bollocking' from the Attorney-General mid-afternoon after the new leak had happened; Chalmers hadn't been present, but gleaned from Anderson's account that he'd borne it with equanimity, which was the only sensible approach. Plainly his mind was on other things—in particular, Chalmers had learned, his collapsing marriage. In that context, abuse from a government minister probably didn't matter as much as it normally might.

What was important, as Chalmers had pointed out, was that neither the Attorney-General nor anyone else in the government yet knew the real story about either them or ASIO; the injunction on the ABC was in place and now the whole rationale for the ABC story had been undermined by KSR releasing a Cabinet decision. Still, there was more work to be done. The whole matter was to be sorted out at a meeting with the Director-General the following day. Anderson had long planned to attend a cricket match that evening, and insisted that everyone come along to his box at the SCG.

Anderson broke off from talking with Rathbone. 'I might head off,' he said to Chalmers.

'Sure. I understand.'

'So I'll see you around seven tomorrow, and we can have a chat before the ASIO mob arrive. You'll have some options for me.'

'Yep.'

'Good.' Anderson rose. He looked like a tired old man. Very tired, and very old.

The issue of the moment in the ladies was who was having a break-down in one of the cubicles. Someone was sobbing, just loud enough to be heard, but her identity was not apparent from the expensive-looking black heels visible from outside. Em, who had just got her period, was manipulating tampons when a particularly earnest sob broke free from the distressed woman two cubicles down. The sound had a faintly familiar ring, but she couldn't place it until, finished up and with make-up restored, she had gone back out and noticed that Rachael was no longer at the table with Nathan, nor at the bar. What had happened to Rachael? she wondered. Was she the sobber? If so, why had the fits of giggles dissolved into wailing? Was there, to use Jayde's frequent refrain, 'trouble in paradise'? Nathan was sitting chatting with someone else from his area. Their eyes briefly met, and then Em sat down as Adriana poured herself a small amount of wine. Adriana had been awestruck ever since Mark Chalmers had come over to speak to Em.

'Who's having hysterics in the toilets?' said Adriana. 'Did you hear?'

'Bit hard not to hear,' she said. 'I think it's Rachael Ambrose.' She nodded towards the next table.

'My god, it could be,' said Adriana, looking over and almost spilling her drink. 'Do you think?'

Tom had also vanished, but that was unsurprising; he was a reluctant socialiser who preferred to be home with his family. Em figured he'd gone home already. Jayde returned with another cock-tail, apparently after an extended period of 'flirting' with the IT boys, possibly about anal sex—'back doors' being one of the topics of conversation she'd heard earlier at their tables. Periodically, the tables erupted in calls of numbers, uncertain in origin but presum-ably ratings of the attractiveness of female colleagues.

There was raucous laughter nearby. Two of the Paranoids were performing some sort of feat with cutlery. The IT guy in a dress was beside them, chanting and clapping.

Kris came back to the table and stood next to the chair beside David as waiters began serving coffee. 'Have you heard?!' she half yelled excitedly.

'What?'

She closed in on them, anxious others wouldn't hear.

'Maria Campanella was in the ladies and got stuck into Rachael Ambrose.'

'What?' shrieked Em.

'She said she saw her sitting with Nathan Welles and didn't she realise office affairs should be kept out of sight, that she should get her act together.'

'You are fucking kidding,' Jayde said, excitedly.

'Nope. One of the twins was in the stalls and heard it. She must've thought no one would hear. Now everyone knows.'

'That's why she's having a breakdown in the toilet!' Em gazed at Kris in fascinated delight, resisting the urge to turn around and look at Nathan.

'Well, it's understandable,' said Jayde. 'I mean, they've been pretty blatant about it.'

'But still, getting told off by an executive—shit,' said Kris.

'Fuck, there she goes!' said Jayde in a loud whisper.

They all looked over to see Rachael heading for the exit, looking reasonably composed but not happy.

'I'd be leaving, too,' said Jayde.

'Funny how she's the one who gets told off,' said Kris. 'He doesn't get told off, and no one thinks badly of him.'

This profession of a contrary viewpoint to the prevailing narrative seemed to stifle further discussion. Kris had a point, Em thought, frowning, although Rachael was Nathan's boss. Still, her loathing of Rachael made any sympathy for her impossible to maintain. Her enemy had been sent packing. How could the evening get any better?

'Why didn't you get me another drink?' she said to Jayde.

'So what's with the dramatics?' said Nathan cavalierly.

Rachael was standing behind one of the pillars on Elizabeth Street, not far from the Sheraton entrance, looking a forlorn figure. She had left to go to the bathroom half an hour before, and then suddenly called him from outside on the phone, urgently seeking his presence. Nathan had instantly thought she wanted to fuck him. She turned and looked at him, then looked away again. It was clear that she had been crying.

'Whoa, what's the matter?' he said, worried.

'I just got accused of having an affair with you.'

'Affair?' he said incredulously. 'What?'

'Maria Campanella.' She stared out at Elizabeth Street, the Friday-night traffic going past in the rain. A horn sounded for several seconds across the road from them.

'Campanella?' he said, aghast. 'What . . . why?'

'I don't know!' she said angrily. 'She just told me she'd seen me sitting with you and I should be much more discreet about office affairs and I should watch myself.'

'But . . .' He trailed off.

'Do you know anything about this?' she said, in a faintly accusatory manner.

'No!' he said, loudly. 'An affair? That's ridiculous.'

'You sure?' she said, looking at him.

'Rachael,' he said, in a low tone, 'I don't know anything about it.

For real. I'm as shocked as you.'

'Well apparently a lot of people must think I'm sleeping with you. So no one has said anything to you?'

There was a whoop from across the road, from within Hyde Park.

'No!' he said quickly. 'I'd have told you if anyone said anything like that. Told you instantly.'

He turned and leaned on the column, shaking his head. He was unsure what to say to her. She was clearly devastated.

'You know that this completely fucks me,' she said. 'I've been here for, like, a month, and a senior executive tells me off. There's no way I can have a future in this place.'

'But . . . it's not true!'

'Doesn't matter,' she said, shaking her head. 'Doesn't matter that it's not true, it's what people think. What important people think. She would've talked about it with the rest of the executive. I'm here a month and I'm sleeping with a married co-worker, they reckon. Shit. They probably told her she should warn me.'

'Okay, hang on,' said Nathan. 'What you should do is go and see her tomorrow, tell her that whatever she has heard, you are not having an affair with anyone and you're deeply distressed that people think you are. And I will back you all the way.'

'And what good will that do?'

The rain was starting to get heavier.

'Well, it might change her mind.'

'Doesn't matter, Nathan,' she repeated flatly. 'It's too late. The damage is done.'

'I'll go. I'll tell her that it's bullshit and ask her to apologise. It's blatantly false and can't be allowed to—'

'Nathan, you're not getting it. It doesn't matter that it's not true. All that matters is the powers-that-be think it's true, and act accordingly.'

She stood there, ignoring the rain. Nathan couldn't tell if she'd started to cry again. He stood there in silence for a minute, listening to the passing traffic. A car rolled past from the Sheraton entrance.

'The last place I worked, there were hardly any women,' she said. She was definitely crying again, but her voice wasn't cracking, instead she sounded angry. Nathan wanted to hug her, to offer her some form of comfort, but didn't dare touch her. 'It was like a giant boys' club. I thought this place might be different. At least there were some women working here.' She shook her head.

Nathan felt a deep, deep shame inside, but was pleased he had never thought to act on his attraction to Rachael.

'Well,' he said, after a time, 'sure is a great Christmas party.'

She smiled sadly, without looking at him.

FRIDAY
11 DECEMBER

Chalmers nodded to the security guard as he was admitted to Anderson's private box. His cold had developed into full-scale man flu and the only thing he currently wanted was to lie down and sleep under the influence of some especially powerful pharmaceuticals. The SCG was about one-third full, but the match had only just commenced, and the ground would probably be mostly filled by halfway through the first innings. He was dressed in black jeans and a polo shirt that covered a bulging stomach usually hidden beneath a suit jacket.

The suite consisted of two large rooms with cheap-looking, though thick, sky blue carpet; each room had a balcony with upholstered armchairs that looked directly over fine leg at the Randwick end. One of the rooms contained an extensive bar and kitchenette, and both had large television sets, showing the match that had just commenced, in slightly overcast weather.

Along with a couple of catering staff, Gary Prick was there, dressed in a suit. Chalmers had gleaned that Prick was the one who'd told Anderson about the Scotsman and Vanessa having an affair, which was the reason they were now in the shit, given Mazzoni had promptly gone out and leaked the information about Kittehsaurus Rox. Mazzoni, who'd survived Iraq at its worst, had always faintly unnerved him; he struck Chalmers as someone you would not want to get on the wrong side of. Hope she was a good fuck, he'd thought, given the price everyone was now paying for it.

Still, what was done was done. Or, in this case, pretty fucking well undone.

Prick offered him a beer, which he declined. Anderson, dressed in trousers and a short-sleeved shirt that fitted him poorly, already had one in his hand. In fact, given Prick was the only other person there, it seemed that Anderson was on to his second one. Maybe this was Anderson's coping mechanism: drinking more than his usual minimal amounts, in the company of his young spear-carrier. An Asian woman in a uniform appeared and removed the empty.

'Options' Anderson had wanted from him. The options, he knew, were about how to restore the company in the good books of the Attorney-General, who'd been humiliated by the release of the Cabinet minute, after he and Anderson had assured him all was well. And about how to settle things permanently with ASIO. 'Options' meant a scalp, to placate the angry gods. Ideally, that of someone behind Kittehsaurus Rox.

That meant two options, Tom Dao or him. There were no third options within the scope of normal human possibilities.

'I don't even know who half these bloody players are,' Chalmers said, looking away from the large TV in the corner of the suite and through the glass doors. He stifled a yawn and pointed. 'Who the bloody hell is that guy?'

'I think he's the captain,' said Anderson. 'So what's the game plan?'

'Well, I imagine they'll try to bowl them out for as low a score as possible,' Chalmers said, continuing to look out at the pitch.

'With ASIO.' Anderson was not his usual self by any stretch.

'Look, Derek, I don't want to cough up Tom Dao for them. I approved all this. If there's a need for a scalp, it should be mine.'

'That's very selfless of you Mark, but . . .' Anderson paused. 'Lovely shot. But not very helpful. What about this other chap, the one who spoke to the lawyer?'

'Nathan Welles? No, he knows too much. We need to keep him and look after him. It's me or Tom Dao. And preferably me. I know you don't like the choice, but it's the only one you've got.'

'You've got a . . . red spot on your chin,' Anderson said.

'I'm trying it out to see how it looks,' Chalmers said tiredly.

Guy Collin and the Director-General of ASIO arrived. Both of them were dressed almost identically in dark jackets with open-necked shirts. Anderson rose to greet them effusively.

'Wonderful view,' said the Director-General, immediately walking over to the glass.

Chalmers knew, as of course Anderson did, that the DG was a cricket tragic. He declined to shake their hands, pleading the cold.

'Vanessa shopping?' the DG said to Anderson, turning back.

Chalmers flicked a brief glance at Collin, who rolled his eyes and shook his head.

'She's visiting relatives,' said Anderson distantly.

They took seats around the television set, something that Chalmers found inexplicable given the game was going on right in front of them outside. Someone below the box screamed excitedly. Prick joined them, but sat slightly away from them, with a tablet.

'Who's the captain?' said Collin. 'I've never heard of him.'

Both men had accepted a light beer.

'We need to sort out this Kittehsaurus Rox business, Derek,' the Director-General said. 'We're very unhappy. And I think you know the Attorney-General is too. You've put us in a very awkward position.'

'I appreciate that,' said Derek. 'And I also know that you guys have been very—'

There was a roar from outside as the opener clubbed a six over long on.

'That's the new kid. Geez, he's strong,' said the Director-General.

'You guys have done the right thing by us,' Anderson finished.

'I think we need to give the Attorney-General something—something public,' said the Director-General, after taking a swig from his bottle. 'Something that will bring this business to an end. And something that will make the Americans confident our whole bloody system isn't insecure. I'm under a lot of pressure on that front, Derek. You understand that better than anyone. There's a lot of concern within the government and, I've got to say, within the intelligence community.'

'We've had a number of calls from US contacts; they are very worried,' Collin added. 'Much more so than they're saying in public. And of course I haven't been able to tell them why they needn't worry.'

'Anything that links Veldtech to something public is going to kill us,' said Chalmers. He stumbled over his words slightly due to the cold.

'Not if it's a rogue within your company,' said Collin immediately. 'Not if it's something that you were unaware of.'

Anderson glanced at Chalmers.

'You want us to offer someone up, then?' said Anderson.

There was another roar.

'Bloody hell!' said Collin in amazement.

Anderson frowned and pointed at the television. 'That's gone completely flat,' he said. 'I haven't seen a flat cut shot go for six since the days of Lance Cairns.'

'Gee, he's given him a gobful,' said Prick.

'They don't know how to sledge anymore,' said the Director-General. 'Not like the old days.'

'They should have a specialist sledging coach,' said Chalmers.

A uniformed waiter brought in a tray of salmon barquettes.

'So just putting that issue to the side for one moment,' Anderson said, 'this new cyber police force—we need to know we'll be in the running for the contracts for that.'

The Director-General shrugged and took some food. 'As you know, Derek, that's out of our hands. It won't have anything to do with us.'

'Well, it's not really worth our while giving someone up if the end result is the same as . . .' Anderson stopped as another waiter presented a tray of truffled quail eggs. He took one. 'Do you have any pies?'

The waiter nodded. 'I'll bring those next.'

'They do the best pies here.'

'Sausage rolls are good too,' said Prick helpfully. 'Very gourmet.'

Derek continued. 'If the end result is going to be the same as if we don't cooperate, then there's no incentive for us to really work with you on this. We're not in the business of commercial suicide. Free hit! He's overstepped by a good two inches there.'

'What we can guarantee,' said the Director-General, 'is that if you don't give us something, there'll be enormous trouble. The government won't cop it. You heard how angry the AG is.'

They waited while the free-hit delivery was bowled. It only went for well-run two down to long off.

'But you can talk to the department and the Attorney-General about the new agency,' said Anderson.

'We can offer advice if asked,' said Collin. 'We won't have input to the tender process. And to be frank, Derek, that's the least of your problems at the moment.'

A roar went up outside. 'That was a shocker of a shot,' said the DG. 'Hit it straight to him.'

'What do you think, Mark?' said Anderson, as the batsman trudged off.

Chalmers sniffed. 'Bit of a leading edge.'

'About what the DG said.'

'We may need to offer up a scalp,' he said noncommittally. He wished he'd brought some more pain relief.

A waiter entered with a tray of pies and sausage rolls. All five men helped themselves.

'Mark's got a point,' said the Director-General, dropping some pastry from his mouth and pointing at the television. 'Definitely looks like a leading edge.'

'These *are* good,' said Collin to Prick.

'What's the bet he plays a ramp shot first ball,' said Anderson.

'Or a reverse sweep that completely misses and he gets bowled,' said the DG, mid-pie.

'Well,' Anderson began, 'we think we can—'

'Whoa,' said Prick loudly.

Chalmers thought Prick was 'whoaing' over the quality of the sausage rolls, until the screen suddenly flicked over to ABC News 24. Anderson and the Director-General both frowned and turned around. Prick had the remote control.

'What are you doing?' said Anderson incredulously.

'Watch,' Prick said, with pastry on his lips.

They watched. There was a host sitting at a desk talking to someone about mining.

'Watch what? Put the bloody game back on.'

After a few more seconds, the scroll at the bottom of the screen read *Sydney man arrested over Kittehsaurus Rox hacking.*

Both the Director-General and Collin put down their beer and their pies and reached for their phones. Chalmers did too, discreetly, retiring over to the glass doors.

He rang Tom Dao, who didn't answer. He thought it wise not to leave a message. He was convinced, and deeply worried, that it was Dao who'd been arrested. There was no other possibility, given it had said 'man'. That ruled out the blonde giantess Emma Thompson, or whatever her name was. He felt mild panic at the thought of what would happen once it was revealed a Veldetch employee had been arrested.

There was applause for a two to square leg outside.

The Director-General appeared engrossed in a conversation to which his contribution was a series of 'yes' and grunts. Collin had retreated into the other room. So, after a moment, did his boss.

'Do we know who they've arrested?' said Anderson softly.

'No. But I can't get hold of Tom Dao.'

'Oh Christ,' said Anderson, putting his beer down. 'Oh fuck. This is a disaster.'

A waiter appeared with more sausage rolls. Anderson and Chalmers ignored him, but Prick helped himself.

'But if they were going to arrest him, they'd tell us, wouldn't they? Why would we be having this meeting?' said Prick, before cramming a sausage roll into his mouth.

'ASIO's not investigating KSR, remember?' said Chalmers impatiently. 'The ACSC is. Their AFP officers would go arrest him.'

'Who else could they have arrested?' said Anderson quietly. 'This Welles fellow? But you'd think they'd still know. Clearly they don't know, or didn't expect it.'

Chalmers went searching through his phone for Welles's phone number, and couldn't find it. He was partway through dialling Rachael Ambrose's number when Collin and the Director-General returned. The five men stood in a tight circle.

'Okay, we've got a problem,' said the Director-General, in a particularly grave tone. 'It appears the AFP have arrested our undercover bloke.'

Derek, Chalmers and Prick stared at him disbelievingly, in silence.

'Your undercover bloke? Where was he?' Chalmers asked finally.

'He's the one who leaked the Cabinet material on Wednesday to your crowd,' said Collin, highly agitated. 'The AFP officers working for the ACSC had a wiretap on him and saw him send the document. They think he's behind the whole thing.'

Chalmers was trying to process what had happened. 'But they must *know* he's your guy?'

'The bloody ACSC have got their wires crossed,' said the Director-General. 'We kept them in the loop but they don't seem to have paid attention because we weren't working on the same thing as them. This is a disaster. And there was press there.'

Collin, showing remarkable animation, turned to his boss. 'They leaked it to the media? For Christ's sake.' He returned to the other room, dialling someone else.

'Well, there's an upside,' said Chalmers, 'you've got your KSR scalp. The ACSC have their man.'

The Director-General turned to him angrily, but it was Anderson who got in first. 'That's not going to work, Mark,' he said, shaking his head. 'If it comes out he's an ASIO officer, there'll be hell to pay.'

'A rogue ASIO officer,' pressed Chalmers, wiping his nose with a tissue. 'Maybe one who had access to an administrative back door in the Parliament House information system.'

'We are not dropping one of our own officers in it,' said the DG. 'Absolutely not. We'll clarify with the AFP that there's been a mistake.'

Chalmers persisted, despite sensing Anderson wanted him to drop the issue. 'Think about it: we've already got half of a workable story here,' said Chalmers. 'The ACSC and the AFP think he's the guy. The media already think he's the guy.'

'It's not going to work,' said the Director-General. 'Once he goes on trial, all of this will come out. All of it. And why should he keep his mouth shut if we abandon him?'

'Simple—you don't have a trial,' said Chalmers. 'Give him to the Yanks.'

'Why would the Americans take him?' said Anderson sharply. He was visibly unhappy that Chalmers was pushing the subject.

'Wasn't he responsible for the leaking of some confidential information about US military spending? Isn't he reputed to be a superhacker that fled America?'

'That's all nonsense,' said the Director-General. 'He's not this Servile-us character. The ACSC and the feds have been fixated on Servile-us and there's never been any evidence he exists.'

There was a huge roar from outside. The Director-General reflexively looked out through the glass. The roar appeared to be for an enormous six that had landed not too far below them. Chalmers turned and took a sausage roll.

'Yes, but if this guy—what's his name?'

'Peter Christian.'

'If Peter is handed to the US, they can spend six months investigating and interrogating him out of sight, then they'll discover it's bullshit and let him go. By that time, everyone's forgotten about Kittehsaurus Rox.'

'But the *Americans* will know it's one of our guys,' said the Director-General, frustrated.

Collin rejoined them.

'One of your rogue guys. Who knows what other activity he's been up to inside ASIO, apart from using the PICS access? What other information did he deal in?' said Chalmers, warming to the idea. He was beginning to see a clear path to the lowest-cost solution. He just had to get the rest to follow the steps he'd already taken in his head. He turned to Anderson. 'And when this Peter Christian comes back, if he decides he doesn't want to remain in ASIO given how you treated him, we'd be very happy to secure his highly valuable skills. In fact, we'd remunerate him generously, isn't that right, Derek?'

Anderson thought for perhaps thirty seconds, then looked at the Director-General. 'It could work. I know some people in the US who could smooth the way for this.'

'Look,' Chalmers said, spreading his hands and prompting a bit of pastry to flake off his sausage roll, 'I'm not averse to sacking someone in Veldtech. It's easy. Okay? I'll go. Me, all right? Or we'll find someone else. You can have your scalp. But that doesn't address your longer-term problem.' Due to the cold, the last words came out as 'lonnerturprolem'.

'Which is?'

'ASIO has been breaking into the PICS system for years. Now that the ACSC has discovered that someone's been doing that, how long until they work out that it was you all along, before Peter Christian appeared on the scene?'

'There's nothing to connect us to those logins,' said Collin, with an air of affront.

'But how widespread was the use of that access, Guy? What if someone from ASIO who's at the ACSC knows about the login? My point is, you can't guarantee they won't find out, and in fact there's a good chance they will.' Chalmers's sausage roll was shedding flakes in time with his hand movements. 'And you can't guarantee a politician won't find out. What if someone at ASD hears about it? You know what those pricks are like. They'll take it straight to one of their journalist mates and make sure it gets out. And in that case, there's no point having a Veldtech scalp. What you need is an ASIO scalp. The scalp of someone who has been using that login.'

Only the crowd noise could be heard for a few moments.

'So we can give you a scalp,' Chalmers continued. 'But the percentage play is, give someone up. And you've got a candidate right there.'

'It could work,' repeated Derek. 'Look, I'm willing to take responsibility for this whole thing. This is the humblest day of my life. But Mark makes a good case.'

'We'd of course make sure anyone who might have been responsible for Kittehsaurus Rox was no longer employed at Veldtech,' said Chalmers. 'We understand there can't be a cost-free solution for us.'

'That's a given,' said the Director-General. 'But it would be completely inappropriate to let one of our staff take the fall for this.'

Chalmers shrugged. 'Fair enough. But once the politicians find out you've been using the back door to spy on them, there's going to be some massive damage to the organisation. This would be a way of minimising the chances of that happening.'

'That'd be a tragedy,' said Anderson. 'A real tragedy.'

The Director-General reached for a sausage roll. 'Bugger it,' he said.

It was shocking—and frightening—at the time, but Peter's arrest also had, Kat admitted to herself later, its weird side. The plan was to go down to the Royal for a drink, probably get something to eat, then go back to Kat's place for sex. Peter had arrived at about 6.30 and come upstairs. She'd been tempted to fuck him there and then after they'd kissed. He looked nicer than he had previously, for some reason, and was wearing a tight black shirt and jeans. She kissed him hard and he placed his hand on her arse and pulled her closer, till she broke the kiss. 'Okay, okay,' she said, with an effort. 'We're going out for a drink first.'

'Cool,' he said, then pulled her back and kissed her again.

They headed downstairs, with him in the lead.

The first people she spotted were the photographers: a middle-aged man with a beard and baggy shorts with numerous bulging pockets, and a short woman dressed similarly, both taking photos of Peter from the kerb as he exited the building. Then she saw the rest of the group: a uniformed police officer, a man in casual clothing filming with a small camera and two men in suits.

Peter had stopped halfway between the doorway and the footpath. She turned with a start: another uniformed officer had appeared behind her, in the corridor that led to the back entrance to the apartment building.

'Peter Armitage, you're under arrest for offences under divisions four seventy-seven and four seventy-eight of the Commonwealth

Criminal Code in relation to the accessing, possession and supply of restricted information,' said one of the uniformed officers.

Peter looked at them uncomprehendingly. 'What?'

'Are you Miss Sharpe?' said one of the men in suits, looking at Kat.

She didn't think to correct him. 'Yes,' she said reflexively.

'I'm Sergeant Steve Rizk. I work for the Australian Cyber Security Centre, we're Australian Federal Police officers. Mr Armitage is being placed under arrest.'

'You're kidding,' said Peter. 'You're fucking kidding me.'

'It's not a joke, sir. You'll have to come with us,' said the uniformed officer.

'No, no, you need to check with your supervisors,' he said. 'You're making a mistake. A really bad mistake.'

'Mr Armitage, we're concerned that you may attempt to destroy evidence and therefore will be placing you in restraint until we can process you,' said the first suit officer. 'Arrangements will be made to transport your vehicle to AFP headquarters for forensic inspection. Would you please give us your phone and any other mobile devices you have on your person for safekeeping.'

'Look,' Peter said, sounding increasingly panicked, 'you need to call your supervisors right now.'

'Mr Armitage,' began the second suit guy.

'I can't be arrested. This is a huge mistake. Not here,' he said.

One of the uniformed officers stepped forward with handcuffs. 'Please place your hands behind your back, Mr Armitage.'

'Look, my name's not Armitage,' Peter yelled. 'I'm with ASIO. I'm fucking with ASIO. Call your supervisors. They'll tell you.'

'We're aware your name is a pseudonym, sir. Our warrant covers all your names.'

'Look, I work for ASIO. Surveillance Officer Peter Christian. Call them.'

The officer with the cuffs pulled Peter's hands behind him.

'We're supposed to be working with you guys,' he yelled.

He was walked over to a police vehicle and the AFP officer actually did that thing of protecting his head as he was pushed into the back seat. It was all over within thirty seconds.

During the entire time, up until the second suit guy said, 'Thank you, madam,' and they left, Peter did not look at her or say anything to her. That he was an ASIO officer, or claimed to be one, did not come as a surprise. She'd resolved previously that she wouldn't tell him anything about KSR, no matter how often he asked, because she'd decided there was something downright odd about his obsession with the topic. She was quite happy to sleep with him, but only because she had no intention of sharing anything with him.

But what puzzled her, once she'd calmed down, was why on earth they'd arrested him if he was ASIO agent. Surely they would have known. It mystified her.

Unless the stories about Servetus were true.

Maybe, she thought, after she'd retreated upstairs and rung Maddy—who was on her first date in two months and thus only available to speak briefly—the stories about Servetus were true. The whole affair had taken on a Kafkaesque air: she was convinced there was no Michael Servetus, and yet the rest of the universe insisted there was; indeed, the only other person who apparently 'knew' there was no Servetus was, allegedly, Servetus himself.

She recalled the story about Servetus creating a fake FBI identity good enough to fool that agency. Maybe he'd done the same here with ASIO.

It was all too ridiculous, that Servetus existed and that Peter, of all people, was him. This rather boring guy with a great body and an interest in online activism? And yet, it didn't otherwise make sense that they'd arrest him.

She poured herself some wine and gazed out the window. No sex tonight, then.

SUNDAY
13 DECEMBER

Ewan rose from the table, went to his apartment door and admitted Vanessa wordlessly, closing the door behind her. She walked ahead of him into the lounge room. The table was covered in piles of documents, many of them IDs.

'Sorry,' he said, going around her. 'I'm just getting my stuff together.'

'Your stuff?' she said, examining the contents of the table. 'You got enough driver's licences?'

'Yeah, well, I told you I had a thing about IDs. Want a drink or something?'

'Um, yes . . . Yes please,' she said. 'I do actually.' She went over and contemplated the view, then came back and sat down. She was wearing jeans and a loose shirt.

'I've got wine or beer.'

'Beer's fine,' she said. 'What happened between you and Derek?'

He opened the fridge, removed a Kirin and poured a glass.

'It wasn't too bad,' he said. He spilled some of the beer on the bench, said 'oops' and mopped it up. 'He got angry. I got angry. Then I left, escorted by security—aptly, given my job.'

'Shit,' she said, taking the glass from him. She looked around the room. 'I never wanted to come here. For some reason that *really* felt like cheating. Weird, isn't it? Like it was somehow worse if I was in your bed.'

She looked tired, and her eyes were a little red. She wasn't wearing make-up, which he actually preferred. He was torn between wanting to touch her and being worried about what he'd done to her life, even if he wasn't unhappy she would be leaving Derek.

'What are you going to do now?' she said.

'I've got twenty-eight days, unless I get another job. So, I'm thinking about what to do.'

'Do you want to stay in Sydney?'

'Yeah, I do. But there's plenty of work overseas if I want. I—' He stopped abruptly. 'What about you?'

'Well, I've got to work through the divorce and the settlement. I don't actually want much money from him. We had a pre-nup, of course, which was very generous. I just want it over and done with.'

'You're not going to try to patch things up?'

'I don't think so. I haven't fully decided.'

There was silence.

'If you . . .' Ewan began awkwardly. He wasn't sure how far he wanted to go. 'If you don't patch things up . . . I was thinking, about us.'

She looked at him. 'You and me?'

'Yeah.' He was struggling to meet her gaze, but forced himself to.

'Ewan, I'm in the process of fucking up one relationship. I'm not thinking about another at the moment.'

'I know that,' he said rapidly. 'I understand that. Shit. Of course. Of course. I just wanted to, well, make sure you didn't think that just because of what's happened, I no longer felt the same way.'

'Which way?' she said softly.

'That I love you,' he said eventually.

She didn't reply. After about thirty seconds, he walked back over to the kitchen bench and wiped it again.

'I'm sorry I fucked everything up for you,' he said.

She eyed him, then shook her head. 'It was already fucked up, Ewan. I just didn't know it.'

They went silent again.

'I'd better go,' she said, after a moment.

'Okay,' he said resignedly. He watched her rise from the chair, noticing her figure beneath her clothes. She walked over to the door and he followed her. Then she stopped beneath the bright halogen light of the hallway and looked at him. Wordlessly, unselfconciously, they kissed. It started as a brief touch, but Ewan found himself consumed by her proximity, by his lust for her, and she responded, but then she pushed herself away, without looking him in the eye, and opened the door.

The first phone call about Kat's involvement with Peter had been on Saturday afternoon. Clearly the AFP or ACSC or Run DMC or whoever the fuck it was had tipped off the press about Peter, given the photographers present at the arrest. There had also been TV cameras at the AFP headquarters in the city when the car carrying Peter had arrived there, judging by the footage she saw on television later that night. Amy Dinh had been handed the 'exclusive', doubtless by the AFP—'Romanian superhacker Michael Servetus has been finally tracked down and brought to justice,' the Australian Cyber Security Centre and the Australian Federal Police were happy to reveal, 'bringing his reign of online terror to an end.' 'Peter Armitage', the police claimed, didn't exist; he was an invented identity, a prop devised by Servetus—pronounced four different ways on TV, none of them correct—to shield his identity. 'Amazingly high-quality ID forgeries,' according to one anonymous police source, 'virtually indistinguishable from the real thing.'

The actual basis for the arrest was the most recent release, of a Cabinet minute, which they'd found on a USB in his possession. 'Allegedly', of course. He lived in Parramatta, with his wife.

Great, Kat thought. I was fucking another married guy.

But on Saturday afternoon she'd gone for a swim down at Coogee, and when she'd returned there were three separate messages from journalists wanting to speak to her about 'Michael Setevus'. She turned her phone off and left it off. Fuck them.

471

On Twitter, things were a lot less circumspect. An anonymous account was claiming Kat was Servetus's girlfriend. Or 'Severetus's slut' as it eloquently termed her. Some confused her and the wife of 'Peter Armitage'. Another suggested she was a hacker groupie, yet another that she'd been charged as well. She ignored them.

She couldn't work Peter out, and it nagged at her. What if he *was* Servetus? How did she really know, anyway? Why was everyone else so convinced Servetus existed? What was wrong with her that she didn't share in the universal belief in this mysterious superhacker? She was losing her grip, she thought. Maybe he *was* Servetus. She of *all* people should have known—well, apart from his 'wife' in Parramatta. And yet . . . that didn't make any more sense than that he actually was an ASIO agent. Why would some master hacker, someone never even photographed in a long career of wreaking havoc online, adopt a public profile in relation to his own hacker group? That, presumably, was how they had started monitoring him. Had they tapped his phone and internet? Were they tapping hers? A cold sensation overcame her. They would have heard all her conversations with him. For that matter, all her conversations full stop. Then again, that didn't overly fuss her: nearly all of her conversations on the phone at the moment were with media editors and producers and her mum and Maddy. But did they know about her and Chris?

Shit, she thought. What if they saw me breaking into that girl's account? She suddenly felt incredibly relieved she'd decided not to post that picture of Claire.

Smart move to wimp out, Kat, amirite?

That was the point at which she realised, with some pleasure, that she hadn't yet thought about Chris finding out she had been involved with 'Servetus'.

'I must be recovering,' she said aloud.

On Sunday morning there'd been a photographer waiting for her down on the street. At least, she assumed he was waiting for her, in the absence of any other figures of public notoriety living in the building. Purely by chance, she'd glanced out the window and seen him lingering on the nature strip downstairs. When she'd left, she'd gone out through the back and clambered over a fence to get onto Stewart Street, wearing a cap and sunglasses, stepping past the cheery red and green sign in the front yard of the duplex next door that read: *Our place has Santa's elf surveillance*. The photographer was no longer waiting when she returned.

Hell of a way to finally get a photographer interested in me, she thought.

The other problem was a more pressing one, but she was determined to address it. She needed to restore her place at the top of the Kittehsaurus Rox heap. Lingerie blogger Amy Dinh and her little police helpers needed to be kicked off, along with any other pretenders. She was the apex predator of the KSR food chain, and it was time to demonstrate her ascendancy. That was one thing she had control over. This wasn't a story that she spoke to other journalists about. This was *her* story, the one she controlled. Whether Peter was Peter, or Servetus, or some ASIO agent mistakenly arrested, didn't matter a great deal. Indeed, it didn't matter at all for the media.

She'd begun to realise this as the Servetus delusion had taken hold—that being right, or having evidence, or being well-informed on the subject, wasn't relevant to the media; all they wanted was interesting stories. She'd known that in a standard 'they just make shit up' kind of way before, but now she knew it first-hand, knew it via lived experience. It didn't matter that the stories didn't make any sense, and it certainly didn't matter if they weren't true. Truth, actual real-world information that was verifiable and provable, was simply one type of raw material for media content.

But she had lots of raw material, true or not. She opened a blank document on her MacBook and typed: *On the internet barricades with Servetus.*

MONDAY
14 DECEMBER

The first thing Em noticed was that Tom had two large cardboard boxes on his desk.

'Hey,' he said, giving her a smile. She closed the door behind her.

'That doesn't mean what I think it means, does it?' she said, gesturing to the boxes.

He nodded. 'It does. I'm moving on.'

'Because of Project X?'

Even at this late stage, Em still didn't like saying the words 'Kittehsaurus Rox' inside the building.

'Yep. They need a scalp. I'm it.'

'That's awful,' said Em, although her first thought was about her own status.

'No, no,' he said. 'It's fine. Really. I was looking for an opportunity to go. This way I get a payout. They'll make sure I get a glowing reference if I want a job with someone else. So it's all good.'

'Really? Or are you just saying that?'

He smiled. 'Nope. Really. The kids won't starve. And, even if I wasn't relaxed about it, it was always a risk. Anyway,' he said, changing the subject, 'what I wanted to talk to you about was you.'

Em braced herself. If they were sacking Tom, then surely she would be going as well. If anything, she'd been more heavily involved than Tom. Who had uploaded all the releases and written all the accompanying boasts? Who had been Kittehsaurus Rox?

476

'I've told Chalmers, and he fully agrees, that you should replace me. He's spoken to Corporate to clear it. So they're promoting you immediately.'

'What?' She was numbly incredulous.

'This is now your job. Congratulations. Chalmers will want to talk to you at some point.'

Em looked around the office. 'Why me?'

'You heard how impressed Chalmers was with you.'

She sat down in one of Tom's chairs. Which were now her chairs. In the office that was now hers.

Some day, all this will be yours, said Dark Voice. It seemed almost . . . impressed.

'But I've only been here for a year. I'm not . . .' She trailed off.

Tom waved dismissively. 'You'll be great, Em. It's a big step up, but I know you can handle it. Just as long as you don't give the wrong USBs to people.'

Had Dark Voice actually said something non-critical?

No, how the fuck do you deserve this? You're not up to doing a job like this. You'll be found out very quickly.

'Well, I don't know what to say. Thank you. I know you always made sure that I got credit for things.'

As if you, of all people—

She tuned out Dark Voice.

'The job comes with a hefty sign-on bonus.' Tom bent down and pulled the cord to his lamp out of its wall socket. 'You will, of course, have to sign a new contract. And it will come with a confidentiality agreement. A fairly . . . comprehensive confidentiality agreement.'

She nodded slowly. 'I understand.'

'You'll do great, Em,' Tom said. He stuffed a large pile of documents into one of the boxes. 'I know you will. You deserve the job.'

'Come on in, Nathan,' Chalmers said, beckoning.

Nathan sauntered in, and Chalmers gestured towards the sofa on the other side of the office, with the view down Elizabeth Street.

'So,' Nathan said with just a touch of familiarity, 'how is everything vis-a-vis the excitement of last week?'

Chalmers sank into the armchair at right angles to the couch. 'We think it's under control. We arrived at a mutually beneficial solution with our friends from ASIO. And we've agreed to lift the injunction on the ABC. They're no longer running the story, and indeed agree that it was incorrect, now that the culprit has been arrested.'

'That's . . . a good outcome,' said Nathan, a little nervously. He still wasn't quite sure whether Chalmers knew the truth.

'Which just leaves us with you,' he said, as if reading Nathan's mind. He sat and watched Nathan for a moment.

'You have a law degree, don't you? I dug your CV out from some godforsaken part of the IT system, after an epic battle.'

'Ah, yes I do. Sydney Uni,' he added involuntarily.

'Mary?' Chalmers called.

His EA appeared. She was a redhead, and in her thirties, Nathan guessed. Nice, he thought.

'Do you want a coffee?' Chalmers asked.

'No, no, I'm fine,' he said, anxious to get to the part of the conversation about him.

'Can you get me one?' Chalmers requested, looking over at her.

'From downstairs?'

'Yeah . . . not Antonio's, Canopy.'

'Sure.' She disappeared.

Chalmers looked back at him, satisfied. 'Good. Well, we'd like to offer you a new position as Chief Regulatory Counsel, overseeing the company's regulatory responsibilities and ensuring we have a culture that meets our high standards of transparency and account-ability. How does that sound?'

Nathan nodded slowly, not sure what he was being offered.

'Naturally you'll report directly to the executive group. And obviously it's a significant promotion, so you'll be remunerated accordingly. It's a new position that exists outside the current struc-ture, so we're thinking around two hundred thousand to start off with.'

'Those sorts of things are hard to judge,' Nathan found himself saying. 'But that sounds good.'

'And given your role, clearly legal privilege will attach to your activities,' Chalmers continued.

'Sure. Sounds fine.'

'Good,' Chalmers said, smiling. 'That's settled then. We'll go find an office for you. You might have to spend time in the US, of course, talking with ETS's regulatory area. Would your family object to spending a few weeks in Washington? We'll give you some pocket money so they can spend time sightseeing. Head up to New York, perhaps, if you like that sort of thing. Or go visit New England . . . although of course there's nothing but bloody snow there currently. Actually,' he mused, 'it'd be nicer heading south this time of year.'

'No, they'd be delighted with that,' Nathan said.

Chalmers rose. 'Good then. Oh, there's just the issue of timing.' He sat back down again, catching Nathan in the act of rising. He followed Chalmers back down onto the leather sofa.

'Um, look, Rachael's doing a fine job. Well, I don't deal with her directly, but I hear good things about her. But, in retrospect, we think it was something of a mistake to bring her in rather than promote you. So just to make everything tidy, how about we post-date your new role from when she commenced.'

Nathan cottoned on to what he was getting at straight away. 'And presumably the legal privilege attaching to my work would commence from that point as well.'

Chalmers frowned, as if that had not occurred to him. 'So it would. Indeed.'

'That all sounds fine.' Nathan stood up. 'Look, um, just on Rachael.'

Chalmers frowned. 'Mmm?'

Nathan paused again, unsure how to proceed. 'She's been outstanding, an amazingly quick study. She'll be fantastic. And she's totally, one hundred per cent professional. Totally.'

Whether Chalmers took his meaning or not wasn't clear. He gave a noncommittal, 'Good.'

He walked to the door and paused before opening it. 'That play of yours with ASIO was quite impressive, if I may say.'

Chalmers allowed himself a rare half-smile as he returned to his desk. 'In this business, Nathan, it's doesn't matter what's true— what matters is what suits the needs of important people.'

'Good advice,' he said.

Chalmers glanced at him. 'That's what I give.'

He went around to the lift to return to his floor. He waited a long time for the lift to arrive; when it did, Mary, carrying a cup of coffee, said a warm 'hey' to him as she walked out. I wonder what she looks like naked, he thought idly.

A well-dressed man, short and with a neatly trimmed beard, waved to Kat as she entered the QVB Tea Room, where an awful jazz version of 'Santa Claus is Coming to Town' was playing. She walked over as he stood up. He was wearing a jacket and a black skivvy, despite the weather.

'Hi, I'm Matthew. Lovely to meet you. This is Susan Schopenhauer.'

A woman with steel-grey hair, who couldn't have been more than forty, rose and shook her hand. 'Great to meet you, Katrina.' She was dressed all in black.

Susan Schopenhauer. All in black. Gone grey before forty. Kat marvelled at the name. It was almost as good as Samantha Caligari. She was like someone's stereotype of film producers. Susan Schopenhauer.

Matthew—Matthew Wilson, an unfortunately plain name to accompany Ms Schopenhauer—was a producer whose company had just had a series on online activism greenlit by the ABC. There would be four episodes looking at different aspects of cybersecurity, the role of social media in politics and online activists. Wilson had called her out of the blue and asked if he could meet with her.

He was also oddly hot, Kat thought. She normally loathed beards, and had never been interested in short men, but there was something faintly courtly about his manner that appealed. She liked the way he turned the palm of his hand to the chair opposite them.

Peter must have reignited my libido, she thought.

She ordered an Assam tea and waved off Susan's offer of a pastry. Susan Schopenhauer.

'Look, Katrina, thanks very much for taking the time to meet with us,' Matthew began. 'We appreciate you're obviously very busy.'

Susan Schopenhauer.

'As I explained in the email, we're producing *Cyberwar*, and yes I know the title is problematic, but anyway, we have a contract for four half-hour episodes to be screened on the ABC—not quite sure whether ABC1 or ABC2 yet—next year.'

'Sure,' said Kat, nodding. It was a very well-trimmed beard. Indeed, Matthew was very well turned out. His suit was blue, a little lighter than your usual business suit, and the black skivvy was matched with a plain silver chain of some kind. She wondered if he had a big cock.

'We had some discussions with the ABC last week, Katrina, just to nail down details.'

He was the sort of guy who used your name every couple of sentences. Did he use Susan Schopenhauer's name every few sentences?

'They're very happy with how we've planned the four episodes, and the research we've done for each of them. But they've asked us to think about getting you, Katrina, to host them.'

Kat stopped thinking about little Matthew's possible penis size.

'Hosting them?'

'Yes,' said Susan—Susan Schopenhauer. 'We were thinking Amy Dinh, but hadn't approached her yet. There's a strong view at the ABC, and it's one that Matthew and I share, that you might be even better than Amy, particularly given much of episode three is going to be reworked to incorporate Kittehsaurus Rox. You're the expert on that, of course.'

'And obviously, Kat, you've got a lot of media experience and credibility in the sector,' said Matthew.

'Especially after that rant of yours went off on YouTube,' Susan added.

'Um, well, that's great, but I've only done panel work on TV. Is that a problem?'

Susan shook her grey head. 'No, not for what we have in mind.'

'So we were wondering if you were available in February? We're probably looking at a week of filming links, voiceovers, intros and conclusions, plus some preparation time.'

'My diary for February is fairly clear,' said Kat. 'I'm mainly a freelance writer and consultant.' She knew she had a contract for a course with a government department at some point, but wasn't sure which week.

The tea arrived, borne by a very thin Indian waiter with a smile. 'Santa Claus is Coming to Town' was reaching a kind of strangled climax in the background.

'Well, we're currently looking at the third week of February. We're happy to accommodate you, Katrina, and move the schedule around, but that would be ideal for us. We'll be shooting some more material on Kittehsaurus Rox at the end of January. We'd also like to consult with you on that material.'

'Okay.' She nodded.

'So there'd be two contracts between us,' said Susan. 'One for consultancy work, and you can advise us what your hourly rate would be for that, and then there's one for the on-camera work, which we'll negotiate separately.'

'That makes sense,' Kat said. She added milk to her tea and sipped it.

'Just on that, Katrina,' said Matthew, rubbing his beard momentarily. 'On the Kittehsaurus Rox thing . . . You knew Michael Servetus, didn't you? The guy behind it?'

She'd decided to quit holding out against the Servetus myth, having done the article on how she'd known Michael Servetus, and worked with Michael Servetus, and, Senator, you are no Michael Servetus. Her main objection, she realised, was that Servetus wasn't *her* narrative. It was, she'd always thought, the Official Narrative, the one handed to Amy Dinh arse-of-the-year by some police source, when the narrative she preferred, which just happened to be more accurate—as if that was what mattered—was that it wasn't at all clear who was behind Kittehsaurus Rox.

She far preferred the narrative in which the perpetrators behind it remained unknown and at large, ready to strike again whenever they chose. But her personal preference, she realised, was getting in the way of her commercial judgement. Important people preferred to believe the myth of Servetus, so that was where the money was to be made. It didn't matter who Peter Armitage, or Peter Christian, or Michael Servetus, or whatever he was called, was. Maybe he was the fall guy for KSR. Some innocent wrongly identified by the police. Or maybe he was the real thing. The idea that Peter was a superhacker who had manufactured his own espionage identity was another example, indeed the silliest yet, of the Servetus mythologising—a superhacker so powerful he could create an entire official identity as a spy as yet another confusing layer to obscure his real identity and purpose.

But it didn't matter. She was now running with the herd.

Thus she'd rung Nicola, who was a full adherent of the Servetus myth and in a fury over Armitage's arrest. 'We need to establish a Free Servetus Group *now*,' she told her. And Kat was going to be the head of it. 'Fuck Christmas. We start right away.'

Simon Berg would be involved, but Nicola was the competent one, who could get things done. Kat knew Nicola could organise things like rallies and meetings, having set up the Support KSR group with Peter. Berg could be given some other role he might be better at, whatever the fuck that might be. Maybe he could keep out all the wingnuts, conspiracy theorists and lunatics.

'Yes, I knew him,' she said to Matthew.

'What was he like?'

She shrugged. 'Well, nothing remarkable. He was just a guy who said he worked in IT and was concerned about online stuff.'

Matthew nodded. 'I guess he had everyone fooled, didn't he?'

She nodded and raised her eyebrows. 'I guess he did!'

'Hey, Dad.'

'Hey, Ewan. Good to see you.'

'You got the heating turned down?'

His father was wearing what, despite the lack of clarity of the Skype picture, was clearly two jumpers.

'Saving a bit of money.'

'A true Scot. But you don't need to save money, Dad.'

'Ah, it's fine. How are you?'

'I'm okay. Listen, I got good news. Assuming I can get a flight, I should be back for Christmas.'

His father grinned, revealing his awful teeth. 'That's wonderful! When are you arriving?'

'I don't know, but I'll try to get a flight on the twenty-third. Hopefully I'll get there on Christmas Eve.'

He was dreading Christmas back in Glasgow, absolutely dreading it. It would be freezing cold, and his father and he would run out of things to talk about within twenty minutes of his arrival. He'd much rather fly his dad out to Sydney for a holiday, let him enjoy the warm weather and have Christmas somewhere decent. And Christmas Day itself would be hideous; even though Dad was now living in Kelvinside, in a place Ewan had bought him after he'd returned from Iraq, everything there reminded Ewan of his mum. But now, he figured, with his dad getting old and his own unemployed status, he didn't have an excuse, although he still wanted to stay in Australia.

He'd thought about simply staying past his visa expiry and using one of the fake IDs, but had decided against it. The employment situation would be a problem. All his contacts were either in the Middle East or in the US, and Anderson was quite capable of putting the word out that he wasn't to be trusted.

And therein lay another problem. He'd expected that Nathan Welles character to drop the Kittehsaurus Rox stuff on the company, but he'd heard nothing about it. Moreover, some person he'd never heard of had been arrested for it, which confused him no end, since as far as he knew the debacle had been entirely run from within Veldtech. He'd vaguely fantasised that Anderson would be forced to resign in disgrace over the matter, but that hope appeared to be receding rapidly. It grated with him, especially after Vanessa had made it clear they had no future together. He wanted Anderson to pay. Pay what, pay *for* what, he wasn't sure, given he was the one in the wrong.

After ending the call with his father, he sat and stared at the screen. His email pinged. He opened it, wondering who was emailing this late at night. It was only his work email. He was about to close the laptop, then stopped.

There was a gentle tap at Anderson's door, and Crick opened it. 'Vanessa's here,' he said quietly, then to Vanessa: 'Go right in.'

'Yeah, thanks,' Anderson heard her say, a little tartly. She entered the office, while Crick retired and closed the door behind him. Anderson was sitting at his desk, with a number of documents lying about it. It was nearly 7 p.m., but he'd only been in at work since 4. He glanced up at Vanessa, trying to appear casual.

'Hi, take a seat,' he said, clearing his throat. He placed the document he was holding down while Vanessa went over to the meeting table. 'How have you been?' he asked her, walking over to the table. He pulled out a chair and sat opposite her.

'Not too bad,' she said. 'You?'

He smiled sourly. 'Tired.'

She nodded. 'You do look tired, really tired.'

'So you're off to the US for Christmas?'

'Yes, Greg's coming over to New York,' she said, referring to her brother.

'I'll go to Vail, I think.'

She nodded. 'Lovely.'

There was an uncomfortable silence. Eventually, Vanessa spoke.

'I've just got something to say, and then I'll go. Being unfaithful to you was an appalling thing to do, and you have every right to be extremely angry with me. If you'd done it I'd regard it as unforgiveable, but there I was doing it myself, and I know I did something terribly wrong, and I'm sorry for that. And I know it's hard to hear when you're angry at someone, but when I say I'm sorry, I really mean it.'

She watched him, then switched her gaze from his face to the table, and remained silent for a time.

'Okay. Well, I want a divorce, on the basis of the pre-nuptial agreement,' she said at last. 'You probably want a divorce as well, but either way, I can't live with you.'

It was Anderson's turn to look at the table. But after a while, he half smiled and shook his head slowly. 'You can't live with me? So this is my fault?' he said, almost sneering.

She watched his face. 'It's my fault, Derek. Completely my fault,' she said.

'If you want a divorce,' he said, 'that's fine, there'll be no difficulties, we've got the pre-nup, it will all be fine. But I don't want a divorce.'

She looked back at him.

'Why not?'

'Well, when I say I don't want a divorce, I mean, if what I think is true, then I don't want one. I've made mistakes before. Bad mistakes, ones that hurt people I cared about. It seems, I guess, *wrong* if I just . . . if I just acted as though I'd never made a mistake.'

'What do you mean by "if what you think is true"?'

He studied his fingers, interlocked on the desk in front of him. 'I'm assuming you regard what you did as a mistake, as an error of judgement . . . however you want to describe it. If that's how you feel, then I'm unwilling to simply end the marriage based on that, because god knows I've made mistakes myself.'

She was silent for a long time, looking out the window into the Sydney evening. It was still bright, though the shadows stretched across Hyde Park.

'It was a mistake, yes. But . . . I don't know if I can stay married to you.'

He shrugged, rose and walked to the windows. 'I've been looking a lot at this view lately. So pleased I've got it. Anyway, if you want a divorce, as I said, that's fine. But I don't. I'd like to try to get through this.'

'You seem . . . almost relaxed about it,' she said.

He turned sharply and looked at her, though he could see she was regretting the words almost immediately. 'Oh, don't mistake this for being relaxed, Ness. Don't mistake it for one moment. But I want to try to overcome this.'

'Okay,' she said, after a while. 'I'll think about it over Christmas. It's . . . more than I deserve, after hurting you like that. I'll think about it.' She exhaled slowly. 'I'd better go.'

He didn't look at her, and after a moment of waiting for him to reply, she left, closing the door behind her.

Anderson stood there for several minutes, ignoring Crick, who opened the door after Vanessa's departure, then closed it again after several seconds' silence. He looked at Hyde Park for a while, then at the Law Courts building down the far end of the park, the top part of which was still in sunlight. When he'd first been in Australia he'd spent a solid part of a year in that building, attending a Federal Court intellectual property case, which he'd eventually won, a key moment in Veldtech's history. Back then, the company was only around twenty people and run from some fairly squalid offices in Ultimo. By 2000, the company was worth $100 million.

He returned to the papers on his desk, but was unable to work.

Em stretched her hands as far as possible above and behind her head to try to get rid of the soreness between her shoulder blades. Then she suddenly jerked forward and switched her PC off, without even bothering to close anything. It was 7.40 and she'd had enough, especially given she'd arrived at 7.30 that morning. This week she'd worked longer hours than ever, despite it being on the verge of Christmas, for which she hadn't even done any shopping yet. She slammed her office door shut and carried her bag and jacket over to the lift. The silence indicated that there was no one left close by, and she didn't feel particularly tempted to go around to Nathan's side and check if anyone around there was still slaving away. She'd managed to completely avoid him since the Incident, and didn't feel like tempting fate or, more particularly, down-right goading it. She also remained uncertain about what role he'd played with Mark Chalmers in resolving the crisis the other week.

The lift doors opened, and she was confronted with Chalmers himself and Maria Campanella. They appeared engaged in close conversation, which made her pause, unsure whether she should join them, but she figured she'd look stupid for stopping the lift for no reason, and got in.

'Here's our new Tom,' said Chalmers brightly. 'You going to the basement?'

'No, just the lobby.'

He stabbed G for her. 'You're working late,' he continued. 'Given Santa's almost here.'

'Well,' she said, adopting a tone of professionalism that stopped just short of martyrdom, 'there's a lot to be done with Tom gone.'

Chalmers nodded. 'I expect so. Do you know Maria? This is Emma Thompson, she's replacing Tom Dao.'

His mistake plunged Em into a horrible dilemma. Should she correct him? Would he take it badly? Would it look embarrassing for them both? Of course it would, to the extent that Chalmers could ever be embarrassed about anything.

'Ah,' Campanella said, bringing to a close any opportunity to correct Chalmers. 'Pleasure.' She looked severe, Em thought, even when she smiled. Perhaps she implicitly disapproved of her, or her promotion.

'Have we formalised your promotion yet?' said Chalmers. 'I know technically no one's being promoted, but we're making an exception for you. Keep that to yourself, of course.'

She nodded vigorously. 'Sure. I hadn't heard anything yet.'

He'll probably promote someone called Thompson by accident. You should check if there are any Emma Thompsons in the company.

Dark Voice was plainly struggling. Until recently, Chalmers calling her 'Emma Thompson' would have induced ferocious mockery that such an important person didn't even know her name. Now it was reduced to a kind of helpful sceptic.

'I'll sort that out in the morning,' Chalmers said. He turned to Campanella. 'I've got two bloody Christmas parties tonight and tomorrow. I can't do it anymore.'

'Not if they're as boring as Derek's,' she said.

'At least he has a nice view.'

The lift slowed to a halt and the doors opened. 'See you later, Emma,' Chalmers said to her and then extended his hand, ushering her out.

'You too.' She smiled. She walked across the lobby and swiped her way out, then stood on the steps leading from the entrance down onto the street. The cafe was shuttered, and there was less traffic than she was used to. There was a group of people walking across the road, talking animatedly. Some had Christmas hats on; they were evidently heading to a festive function. But it was the least Christmassy Christmas period she could remember.

You see, the problem, she said to herself, the real, absolute bitch of a problem, is that I have nothing really to be unhappy about. There is, annoyingly, very little that is actually wrong with my life. That is what hurts worst of all.

I got paid to move from crappy Adelaide to Sydney, one of the more wonderful cities in the world. I have an okay boyfriend, even if he's a little wanting in the sex department. I've managed to lose two kilos in the last month. My current employers love me and they're paying me a huge whack to keep my mouth shut, and for a little while at least I got to be at the centre of the biggest thing in the country.

She walked over to the lights on Elizabeth Street, intending to head up to Town Hall.

. . . And just because some male, about whom I know nothing, some male with a cute arse and nice eyes and bad taste in women is sleeping with someone else, I feel like slitting my fucking throat. So what the fuck is wrong with me? Where is the problem?

Maybe the grass is always greener, that cliché. Yeah, fucking right. What I'd like to do is get the bastard with the spray can of green paint and shoot him.

See how green the grass on the other side looks when it's been stained red with his blood, chimed in DV.

. . . Or maybe I'm just a selfish bitch who doesn't know the value of what she's got. Uh-huh. That could be it. She stabbed the button at the crossing.

The phone rang and rang, until Ewan was sure it was going to voice-mail, but then a groggy voice answered.

'Gary?' Ewan said.

'Who's this?'

'You don't recognise my voice? It's Ewan Mazzoni.'

Silence.

'It's fucking nearly midnight, Ewan. Is this your idea of a prank call?'

'No, no, not at all, Gary. You and I have business to discuss.'

Another pause. 'Well call back during business hours. You've woken my wife up too.'

'I don't think so, Gary. You know that horrible feeling when you begin to realise that you've fucked up very badly?'

'What?' Prick was clearly still not up to complex thinking.

This was a moment that Ewan intended to savour. 'That . . . I guess, gap, between blissful ignorance and realising that you've really fucked up big time. That's where you are, Gary.'

'Look, Ewan, I don't really care what you—'

'You know when Derek dispensed with my services? Understandably, given what happened. But you fucked up.'

The moment could only be more perfect for Ewan if he was actually there to see the look on Prick's face when he told him. After the encounter with Anderson, he'd been escorted downstairs by a uniformed private security officer to the lobby, where he'd handed over his pass. But, presumably because his sacking was a private decision by Anderson, no one had thought to delete his company login or reclaim the work laptop he had at home. Nor had Corporate removed his details from the payroll—he had received his usual salary in his bank account (one of his few genuine ones) that day.

'You didn't delete my login. You didn't delete the login of Derek's personal security adviser. Who had access to Derek's emails.'

More silence.

'Are you wide awake now, Gary? Have I got your full attention, mate?'

'Yes, you've got my attention,' said Prick slowly. He did, indeed, sound a whole lot more alert.

'By the way, Gary, did you know that everyone in the company calls you Gary Prick?'

'I've been getting that since school, Ewan. Do you think it means anything to me?'

'Even Derek calls you that behind your back. Fancy that. Anyway. I've spent most of the last twenty-four hours downloading Derek's entire inbox.'

'Go on,' Gary said after a silence.

'Who knows where it might end up? Those Anonymous hackers have a history of breaking into security companies and stealing executives' emails, don't they? This has all sorts of things. ETS board papers and financials. Lobbying stuff about the US and Australia. How they wine and dine politicians. Appraisals of people in government.'

He paused to let it sink in. 'It'd be a real treasure trove. Another addition to Anonymous's storied history of amazing hacks. All because of you.'

'If you release any of that stuff we'll get you thrown in jail,' said Gary. 'And we'll sue you.'

'You can sue me all you like, Gary Prick. But there are some impediments. I've already left the company's employment, and it's just your sloppiness that has given me this information. You'll find I have no assets. My dad, on the other hand, is a very wealthy man.

As for putting me in jail, good luck there. I'm just a whistleblower revealing what really goes on inside a defence company. And you're about to kick me out of the country, remember? I can release it all from Scotland.'

Silence.

'Do you know Scotland has a different legal system to England, Gary? You'll have to hire some Scottish lawyers.'

'No I didn't, Ewan. Why are you telling me this? Oh, I get it. How much do you want?'

'I'm very offended at that, Gary. I do not blackmail people. But what I can assure you of is that when a company employs me, I give one hundred per cent unconditional loyalty to that company.'

'We've seen how loyal you are.'

'Well, that was a little different. That wasn't business. But I'd never do anything to harm the company that employed me.'

He paused.

'It'll be cold and miserable in Glasgow, Gary. I will miss Sydney. And I've not sold my apartment yet. And you haven't even stopped paying me.'

'We're still *paying* you?' Prick sounded appalled. 'Christ on a fucking bike. All right, give me forty-eight hours. Everyone's packing up for the break. It can't be your old job.'

'Well obviously it can't be my old job, you fucking idiot. I took that as read.'

'What's your number there?'

'I'll call you, Gary.'

'Yes, well, not in the middle of the fucking night, all right?'

'Nice doing business with you.'

THURSDAY
24 DECEMBER

Rathbone and Campanella were having a beer when Chalmers walked in. It was just after 2 p.m., and most of those people who had actually come into work that day had now left. The company would close down over Christmas–New Year, although some technical bods were on alert in case there were any major incidents involving the company's products. Derek had left on the weekend for the US, where things were looking less dismal for ETS. The CBIS contract had been announced, but the share price had only fallen seventy-five cents. It was now just above a hundred and sixteen dollars, and analysts were suggesting it was good value given the company's aggressive commitment to managing costs.

Rathbone handed him a beer and Chalmers slumped in the chair next to him. 'Thanks, Baz. What a fucking end of year,' he said. 'Jesus.'

'We were just discussing whether Vanessa went with Derek,' Campanella said.

Chalmers shook his head. 'Prick said she's going to New York. Derek's going to Colorado by himself. They're travelling separately as far as I know.'

'I don't know who's worse,' said Campanella, 'that bloody Scotsman for throwing a leg over Vanessa, or Prick for telling Derek.'

'It was perfect fucking timing too,' Chalmers said. 'The company was nearly killed.'

'I was having a chat with Levers,' said Rathbone, putting his feet up on the desk. 'He was saying they're going to spend up big on this new cyber agency. Separate legislation, ongoing funding, external appointee to run it.'

'We'll have to wait till May to find out how much. There'll be no contracts till July at the earliest,' said Campanella, who'd stood up and was looking out the window. Rathbone's office faced west.

'Well what did they fucking expect when they asked us to generate more revenue?' said Chalmers. He didn't go further and express his real concern: that the company would miss out on contracts for the new agency because ASIO would thwart them in Canberra. Or, worse, some politicians might actually hear about what had happened, although the chances of that seemed to recede when the Attorney-General signed off on Peter Christian being sent to the US. Christian hadn't appealed the decision; someone in ASIO must have had a word with him to play along. It had all gone smoothly, from the moment he'd convinced the Director-General to make use of his own bloke being arrested.

On reflection, in fact, he realised Christian's arrest was almost preordained. Collin had found out the AFP officers working for the ACSC had placed him under surveillance several days before, without telling the officer who was liaising with ASIO. They had a record of his uploading the Cabinet document courtesy of the malware they'd placed on his home laptop.

'Silo thinking,' Collin had said, genuinely aggrieved at the way events had panned out and how Chalmers had been able to convince the Director-General to sacrifice one of his staff. 'Terrible. An absolute bloody balls-up.'

Chalmers figured that if anyone was going to cruel the company's hopes in Canberra from now on, it would be Collin, who could inflict a lot of damage on them, especially given the Attorney-General was still angry at being made to look a fool.

A tall blonde woman appeared in the doorway, clutching a sheet of paper.

'Ah, Ms Thompson,' said Chalmers loudly. '*Entrée.*'

She appeared nervous. 'I have that document you asked for.'

'Excellent,' he said, sitting up. 'Bring it forth, minion, for my perusal.'

She came in and handed the piece of paper to him and then hovered there.

'Well,' said Campanella, 'don't just stand there, woman. Have a beer and a pew.'

Rathbone produced a bottle of beer and handed it to her. She obediently sat down on the seat in front of her.

Chalmers's hand reached out for something as he read the document. Unsatisfied, he eventually looked around for what he was reaching for.

'Chuck us a pen, Baz,' he said. Rathbone lobbed a pen in his direction. Chalmers continued to read the document, the pen poised. He went to make a correction, then held back, finished reading it and signed it.

'All done. Thanks for turning that around so fast, Emma,' he said.

'It's what I do,' she said.

'Well, cheers,' he said, raising his bottle to Emma and the others. 'When I was in the public service, I don't know if they still do it, but hardly anyone showed up on Christmas Eve, and the Secretary of the department would always issue an email at two o'clock telling everyone they could leave early because people had to travel. And the only people who'd be left at that point anyway would be the SES officers. So I always made a point of coming to work and sticking around, because they'd all get on the grog in the afternoon. "What are you still doing here, Mark?" they'd say. "Come have a beer." Marvellous networking opportunity.'

'And there'd be the thing about pulling down all the blinds,' Rathbone said. 'Did you have that? At Defence, we'd get told to pull down all the blinds before we left to keep the temperature down over the break.'

'Oh fuck, yes, that's right,' Chalmers said, laughing.

'Even though we had triple-glazed windows to thwart eavesdropping.'

'Would you like me to go and close all the blinds?' said Emma.

Chalmers glanced at his watch. 'Well if you start now you might be finished by Boxing Day.'

The Kittehsaurus Rox girl, he thought, whether by acquisition or coincidence, seemed to have the same deadpan sense of humour her former boss had. It might be worth shifting her a little closer to him in the new year. Her talents might be applied more fruitfully in other roles.

'Welcome to Vail,' said Derek, extending his hand.

'Great to see you, Derek,' said Steve Lydecker. 'This is Major Forrest.'

Lydecker was accompanied by a tall man in an air force uniform. He shook Anderson's hand. 'A pleasure to meet you, sir,' he said briskly.

'Come on through,' said Derek. He was wearing jeans and a thick black shirt. 'How was the flight? The weather's gorgeous and clear.'

Lydecker followed Anderson through into a cavernous, double height room with a chandelier and enormous, columned fireplace.

'Wow,' said Lydecker. 'No wonder it's called the chateau.'

'Bit too much wood for my liking,' said Anderson. 'They really went a bit overboard with the polished wood.'

'Yeah, flight was good. And we'll be able to get back to Washington by early evening, weather permitting.'

'I do appreciate you coming out on Christmas Eve like this. The airport busy? It gets a little busy around this time.'

'The road in was busy,' said the major. 'Airport was fine. The virtues of corporate jets, I guess.'

'Can I get you fellas a coffee, or something stronger?' said Anderson.

'We were fed and watered on the plane,' Lydecker replied. 'But a coffee would be great.'

'I'm fine, thanks, sir,' said the major.

'Sara, can you get Steve a black coffee—make it a strong one—and I'll have tea, please,' Anderson said to a short uniformed Latino woman, who appeared momentarily from behind him, then vanished again.

'I know it's a little cool, but let's talk out here,' he said, leading them out onto a stone terrace bathed in full sun. It had a sweeping view of the nearby ski slope, with a healthy covering of snow. 'The view's great.'

'Sure is,' said Lydecker.

'No snow on your terrace,' said the major.

'Well spotted,' said Anderson. 'Well spotted. It's heated.'

The terrace, at least that section of it, overlooked a chairlift about four hundred metres away, over a slope that was liberally dotted with skiers.

'So you have an info terrorist problem,' said Lydecker, slipping on a pair of sunglasses.

'More like a blackmail problem,' said Anderson. 'A former employee whom we separated recently, a former British soldier—he was my security adviser. My assistant didn't delete his access immediately when we sacked him. And he used his access to my emails to steal information.'

Lydecker nodded. 'This is Ewan Mazzoni.'

'Yep.'

'And he's threatened to use the information.'

'That's right: contacted my assistant and said he'd use the information unless he was given his job back, or some other job. Talked about doing what Anonymous did.'

'And this was your Veldtech account?'

'That's right.'

Lydecker gazed out at the mountain across from the building, then stepped closer to the terrace wall and looked at the skiers below.

'What sort of information did he have access to?' said Lydecker.

'My diary,' said Anderson. 'ETS financial papers and other board documents that had been emailed to me ahead of meetings. Personal emails, emails with public figures.'

'Any ETS material that shouldn't have been on your email system?' said Lydecker. 'Material from our confidential servers?'

'No, just board papers. I don't normally access the ETS system from Sydney. I don't trust the connection.'

Sara appeared with a tray, and set it down on the stone table around which they were gathered. She handed Lydecker a tall cup and gave Derek a teacup.

'The board papers are bad enough,' said Lydecker. 'That sort of financial information could be enormously damaging.'

Anderson nodded. 'That's the main problem as far as ETS goes, yes.' He sipped his tea. 'The other stuff, though, can potentially cause us—or me—difficulties in Australia.'

'And this guy threatened to shoot you, sir?' said the major.

'It wasn't a direct threat. But he alluded to his background,' Anderson said. 'Something about having shot a lot of people.'

'We've got a file on him from when he was with Safeguard in Iraq,' said the major. 'There was an incident involving civilians.'

'So where is this guy now?' said Lydecker.

'He left Australia. We think he returned to the UK. He's a Scot.'

Lydecker glanced at the major, his breath shooting out from his mouth in a puff of steam.

'Oh, we can find him, no problem, sir,' the major said, knowing exactly what Lydecker was thinking. 'Won't take us long. Be straightforward.'

'Will there be any problem given that he's in the UK?' said Anderson.

The major gazed reflectively across the valley for a moment, then shrugged. 'Shouldn't be. We'll have to talk to GCHQ, but there shouldn't be a problem. We have a strong relationship, as you know. The mention of shooting is good. We can use that. Clearly makes him a threat.'

'Experience,' said Lydecker, 'tells us you've got to deal aggressively with these sorts of problems early. If you leave it, it just gets worse. So we'll handle it. You can leave it to us from here.'

'Have you thought about giving him what he wants?' said the major.

Anderson's mouth twitched. 'I did, but of course there's no guarantee that his demands will stop there. And ultimately he may choose not to release the information, but someone else might get it from him, and that would double the problem. Once information's out of your control . . . well, you know.'

'Sure,' said Lydecker, sipping his coffee. 'We just wanted to check that you'd covered all bases.'

'Look, Steve,' Anderson said, turning around and taking a step towards the wall. 'This Mazzoni fellow . . . he was the one responsible for my, well, my current domestic difficulties.' His breath swirled around his face for a moment in the breeze. 'But that's not the reason for this. In fact, I thought that had all been resolved. This came out of the blue afterwards.'

Lydecker took two steps over to Anderson and patted him on the shoulder. 'Thanks, Derek. I appreciate your candour. I know it's tough. It's a hell of thing to go through. Particularly given the time of year. But you've covered off my final question. You can leave it to us. We'll handle it from here.'

'Thanks, Steve. I do appreciate it,' Derek said.

'Well, now, if you don't mind, we might head back to the airport and see if we can get home for Christmas Eve.'

'Sure,' said Derek. 'With clear weather, you'll be sitting down to bad Christmas Eve television with your family by seven.'

The major came over and shook Derek's hand. 'Great to meet you, sir.'

Derek walked them back inside and through to the entrance. 'I'll see you at the January board meeting, Steve,' he said. 'I'm staying in the US until then.'

'Great,' said Lydecker. 'If you're in Philly, give me a call, we'll have you over for dinner. Katie always loves to entertain.'

'Love to,' said Derek.

They paused before the entrance.

'I'll let you know how it goes,' said Lydecker. 'Happy holidays, Derek.'

'Happy holidays,' Anderson replied.

'Happy holidays, sir,' said the major.

'Happy holidays.'

FRIDAY
8 JANUARY

Tom rose and, unexpectedly, hugged Em as she approached his table. He was dressed casually—she had never seen him in anything other than a suit—and had a pair of sunglasses perched on top of his head in a most un-Tom-like fashion.

'It's lovely to see you,' he said. He gestured at the plate of pancakes in front of him. 'I'm sorry. I didn't have breakfast. I was starving. I only got up an hour ago.'

'It's fun being unemployed, evidently.'

He grinned. 'Oh yep. It's great having a summer break without worrying about when I'm going back to work.'

A waiter appeared and Em ordered coffee.

'It's a little better than Antonio's.'

'Noisier, too,' she said.

'You look fantastic,' he said, continuing to smile. 'Love the short hair. How's the job?'

Em assumed Tom was referring to her obvious weight loss; she'd lost another five kilos since Christmas, a time of year when she usually gained a couple.

'It's good. I'm liking it. I like the extra responsibility. I don't like the meetings.'

'Well, you just have to accept the meetings. But you look great. Did you have any time off?'

'Just between Christmas and New Year.'

He nodded. 'And has there been any fallout from Project X?

I haven't heard anything except that guy agreed to be extradited to the US.'

'No, nothing. Who was that guy anyway?'

Tom shrugged. 'I have no idea. Wasn't it bizarre? I guess it was faked up.'

'You think?'

'I really don't know,' he said. 'I know my leaving was part of some deal. I'm guessing ASIO had something to do with it. Anyway.'

'You look pretty relaxed.'

He nodded. 'I am. It's good. But look, I didn't just want to catch up; I wanted to have a talk, a confidential talk, about whether you were interested in some other work.'

She frowned, partly at Tom's odd choice of words. 'What do you mean?'

'Well, okay,' he said, glancing around. 'I haven't been *entirely* unemployed lately. I work for an intelligence firm.'

'Which one?'

He spoke softly, and she could barely hear him above the noise of the coffee machine. 'Well, you won't have heard of us. We're very low profile. Anyway, if we can speak on a strictly confidential basis?'

'Sure.'

'We think that Project X would be a valuable asset in the sort of space our client is interested in.'

It took Em a moment to process what he'd said.

'Project X? Are you kidding? Who's your client?'

'We have a special partnership with only one client. A government client.'

'Which government?'

'A friendly one.'

Em was already mildly suspicious of why Tom wanted to 'catch up'. They had never been close enough to socialise. She'd vaguely wondered if he was desperate for a job and wanted to pitch his consultancy wares. Now, what he was saying suggested she'd had good reason to be suspicious. But the thing about Kittehsaurus Rox, which had now been in abeyance for nearly a month, was wholly unexpected. A 'valuable asset'?

'How long have you been working for this firm, Tom?'

She didn't know where the question came from, but it suddenly made sense to think that Tom hadn't necessarily been only working for Veldtech.

He paused. 'Well, if I'm going to be honest, quite some time. We think there are some good opportunities to collaborate with you in your current position.'

'Quite some time?'

'Yep.'

She was surprised at how calmly she made the realisation. It explained why he'd occasionally disappeared from work for 'meetings' which were not held within the building. He'd been working for someone else all along. Someone bigger than Veldtech, or at least allied with someone bigger than Veldtech. An intelligence agency.

Funny. The more she learned about Tom, the more it was clear she had formed completely the wrong impression when she'd worked for him. He'd been spying in Veldtech the whole time. And now he was trying to recruit her to do the same.

'So,' she said, 'you want me to remain in my current job and spy for you, like you were doing?'

'I wouldn't put it as crudely as that. We're not a commercial rival of Veldtech's, we're in no way or area in competition with them on any product. But we're always on the lookout for worthwhile intel for our government client.'

Suddenly she recalled the day he'd packed up his—now her—office, and how he'd taken a large amount of paperwork. Another thought struck her. She knew Tom had been at ASIO before joining Veldtech. 'Quite some time.' Did that extend back to his time as an intelligence officer too?

'And who's your client, Tom? The CIA? Homeland Security? The NSA? FBI?'

He didn't reply for a moment. 'One of those, yes.'

She wanted to get out of there, immediately. She knew, deep down, the only sensible thing was to get out of this interaction as quickly as possible. She didn't particularly care that she'd offend Tom by doing it. He'd just tried to recruit her to be an actual spy. And to do something more with KSR.

Which he'd got her to set up in the first place.

That thought made her breathe in sharply. The whole thing had been his idea. KSR was Tom's idea in the first place. He hadn't just lied to her about where he was getting the information from. She'd joked about stealing government secrets, but he'd gone ahead with it. And now he wanted to use what he'd got her to set up.

I need to get the fuck away from Tom right now, she thought. Right. Fucking. Now.

She stood up. The waiter appeared with her coffee.

'I'll let you and your client know, Tom.'

He frowned, then rose with her. 'Um, please do, yes,' he said.

'I've got to go. It's been nice seeing you.'

His napkin fell from his lap onto his pancakes. She didn't offer her hand to him, but walked out.

She crossed the road and walked up to Macquarie Street, then headed for the top of Hyde Park. She felt better now she was out of Tom's presence, felt like she could breathe more easily. And she was pleased with the way she'd handled him.

It was an overcast day, cool, with a chance of showers later, and the walk would be pleasant. The path from the top of Hyde Park would take her straight back down to the office at the other end, past the War Memorial, where she'd launched Kittehsaurus Rox onto an unsuspecting world. KSR was hers, and she wouldn't be sharing it with anyone.

The temperature must have been around zero, but Ewan couldn't bear being inside anymore, and had left his father's flat to go for a run. His route would take him out onto Cleveden Gardens and around behind the apartments that had sprung up on Bellshaugh Court since he'd last been back, then up to Winton Drive and then Cleveden Road. The trees were midwinter bare and the sky, while clear, had that pallid British lowness that, having lived elsewhere, he could never get used to again. It was like living under a lid.

His dad had moved to the Kelvinside flat four or five years ago; a decent three-bedroom flat on Cleveden Gardens, a nicer area than over the road in Wyndford. But it was still Glasgow, and still winter, and Christmas had been as depressing as he'd feared. All he'd been able to think about was the fact that, only a few weeks before, he'd been fucking Vanessa in a harbourside bedroom in Sydney, an event that might as well have occurred in a science-fiction novel for how remote it now seemed. The depressing greyness of Glasgow had only sharpened his profound sense of dislocation, of being exiled from heaven. But Prick had promised him a job, to start in late January. He'd renew the visa or, more correctly, not cancel it, because Prick hadn't got around to that, either. It would be on less pay, and it was to be offsite. Prick didn't want any chance of Ewan accidentally encountering Derek. All of which was fair enough.

But he missed Vanessa dreadfully.

He wondered what she was doing right now. She was in New York, probably. Or had she gone back to Australia already? Maybe he could fly to New York and try to meet her, if he knew where she was. He had her number, but dared not call it, although he'd texted her a Christmas greeting, which she'd either ignored or never seen.

A car with two men drove past, one of them talking on a phone, but otherwise it was quiet, except for the buzz of a light aircraft somewhere overhead. He stopped on Winton Drive, the steam of his breath jetting out into the cold air, and stood next to some bins positioned in front of a neatly manicured hedge. The car pulled into a driveway up the street and turned around and headed back past him, the two men now talking and gesticulating, as if debating directions. He'd dreamed about meeting Vanessa again, the other night, about waking up with her in, of all places, New Zealand. He'd never even been to New Zealand, but there they were, together. The dream had left him profoundly sad and unsettled, wishing he'd stayed asleep, next to her, in her life rather than exiled from it.

Still, fuck it. He checked his watch. He'd mapped out the route for his run, and had a good idea of where he should have been, which was rather further along his route than he was. Plainly he was lacking enthusiasm. Still, those were the days when you had to tough it out, he thought.

'Fuck this. I don't want to be here. This isn't where I belong,' he said aloud, conscious of how silly he sounded. He still had another five kilometres to run. He resumed runn—

**WEDNESDAY
13 JANUARY**

Nathan sauntered across the lobby of the Hay-Adams and up the steps to the concierge's desk, where a middle-aged man in a waistcoat was engrossed in conversation with two guests, neither of whose first language appeared to be English.

This was Nathan and Ree's second visit to DC, and by far the more comfortable. Despite the air of austerity in Veldtech, he'd asked for, and been given, a suite at the Hay-Adams, albeit only a St John's Church view, not a White House view. Yesterday he and Ree and Sophie had walked down to the Lincoln Memorial; today was a walk to the Jefferson Memorial and, depending on how Soph was faring, maybe a visit to a Smithsonian on the way back. His meetings with ETS wouldn't start till Friday; snow was forecast for tomorrow.

He'd wanted the Hay-Adams because he knew something of John Hay from his Lincoln research, but hadn't found out until they'd actually checked in that the Hay-Adams was only built on the site of Hay's house and was not the original residence itself. Still, he was more than happy, and Ree was delighted with the trip.

'Well, Nathan,' she'd said over dinner downstairs the night before, 'sometimes you're not such a bad husband.'

'Sometimes,' he'd agreed with a smile, pleased she was so happy.

While he waited for the concierge, he opened the copy of the *Post* that had been left by their door and, ignoring the presidential primaries news, opened it to the World section, seeing nothing of interest, except for a small item at the side of the page under the headline CAMERON PLEDGES CRACKDOWN ON JIHADISM.

> *British Prime Minister David Cameron has said further steps will be taken to monitor extremist Muslim groups in Britain after the murder of a former British soldier.*
>
> *Ewan Mazzoni, a former British Army lieutenant who worked for US contractor Safeguard in Iraq, was gunned down in Glasgow on Monday. A hitherto-unknown group, the Justice Jihad of the Iraqi Genocide, claimed responsibility on Twitter. British officials have declined to comment on speculation Mazzoni may have been killed in retribution for a civilian shooting incident in the Iraqi town of Al-Wahda in 2007.*

Wow, Nathan thought. Guess the Scotsman finally found someone even scarier than himself.

> *Mr Cameron said his government would consider what further steps needed to be taken to ensure authorities could effectively track what he called 'lone wolf groups' who operated without direct connections to established terror networks, including online surveillance.*

Nathan made a mental note to email work back home and alert them to a potential opportunity in Britain, though presumably ETS's people in Birmingham would be on to it as well.

A uniformed African American woman walked behind the concierge desk. 'I'm so sorry for keeping you waiting, sir. How may I help you?'

Nathan looked up. The woman must have been in her thirties, and was very attractive, with a lithe elegance that she managed to convey merely standing there. 'That's fine,' he said. 'I was wondering if you could give me some advice about cruises on the Potomac?'

'Oh, I can organise that for you, sir,' she said, smiling. 'Were you thinking of a lunch or dinner cruise? Or just a sightseeing trip?'

'Probably a sightseeing trip for tomorrow morning. Hopefully before the snow arrives.'

'Of course,' she said warmly. 'The boats are usually glassed in. There are several that we would recommend. I'll write down the times, prices and marina locations for you, and if you want to select from those, I'll make a booking for you.'

'That would be very kind of you,' Nathan said, his eyes flicking downwards to her nametag. 'Thank you, Naomi.'

Kat adjusted her Free Servetus T-shirt slightly and waited for Simon Berg to finish. The weather was ideal, probably no warmer than twenty-five degrees. There were at least two and a half thousand people standing in the Domain, clustered around them. She'd designed the Free Servetus T-shirt (and, yes, a wristband; I can't believe we're doing fucking wristbands, she thought), with quotes from KSR's releases littering them. They were trying desperately to get more than a handful printed so they could put them on sale. But the group had received pledges of more than fifteen thousand dollars already for a fighting fund, and not just from Australia, but the US as well.

This, however, was Free Servetus Group's first big rally.

Peter/Servetus seemed to have disappeared entirely before Christmas. There had been no court appearance, no bail hearing; it was as if he'd been swallowed up by the criminal justice system. Kat's attempts to get an answer from the federal police had drawn a blank. Then, during the Christmas–New Year lull, when the entire country was somnolent, it had been quietly announced that Servetus was the subject of an extradition request from the United States and had waived his right to appeal against it. The government stated that he had been extradited on the basis that he would not be subject to the death penalty, and that the government's main concern was that he be subject to 'due process'.

'He'll receive full consular support,' averred the foreign minister.

Peter was thus now, as far as anyone could determine, in the United States.

Berg was going on about exactly that right at this very moment, about habeas corpus and how 'this could happen to any one of us'.

The vanishing of Peter/Servetus had planted further seeds of doubt in her mind about her original narrative. It was appalling that he'd disappeared, of course, but if he really *was* some superhacker, it would make sense. God knows what they'd do to him. Send him to Gitmo, perhaps.

Maybe Servetus was real after all.

It salved her conscience about peddling the Servetus narrative somewhat, that and the fact that she felt partly responsible for Peter being arrested. Whatever the objective reality of Free Servetus Group, it would help Peter.

Berg was now playing into the microphone the audio of a message from Seamus Hannon, the Irish American net guru, in support of Servetus. It was, Kat had to admit, quite a get for the otherwise banal Berg—Hannon was a big name in internet circles, known even to the mainstream media. Free Servetus Group—handle @Free_Servetus—had taken off online immediately; the arrest of Peter, whatever else it may have done, had turbocharged the whole Kittehsaurus Rox thing. She didn't need to see Twitter to know it would be trending at the moment.

'Okay, after that amazing message of support from Seamus Hannon, I want to present the head of Free Servetus Group—I don't need to introduce her; you know how important she's been—Kat Sharpe.'

There was a roar. There was no other word for it. A *roar*. Two thousand people cheered her enthusiastically. She adjusted the hat she was wearing against the sun and pulled her T-shirt down a little self-consciously—she didn't normally wear T-shirts in public—and stepped onto the fold-up stage they were using. Simon handed her the microphone as he stepped off, and there was a brief moment of feedback from the speaker on the stage, but it was lost in the noise of the crowd. She had to wait for them to go quiet enough for her to speak. She noticed two TV cameras at the rear of the group. A number of people were holding up placards with Peter's face on them, and the words *Free Servetus!*

'Hey,' she began. She didn't have any notes, but knew exactly what she wanted to say.

'So here we are, and we're all angry, and we're all frustrated. Because we all know what's going to happen from here. They're going to make an example of Servetus, like they always try to make an example of those who challenge them. He'll be charged with hundreds of offences. He might even be in Guantanamo Bay right now, held incommunicado. The government will claim that what he's done could cause immeasurable damage. He'll face spending decades in jail. We'll see the full display of state power.'

She felt good. The crowd didn't make her nervous—quite the opposite: its energy was transferring itself to her. Their confidence in her, and their expectations of what she would give them, weren't a burden at all, but rocket fuel. She knew exactly how to use it.

'But what this really is,' she said, speaking slightly more quietly, 'is weakness.'

There were a few *yeah*s and a whoop. One of the placards with Peter's face waved about excitedly.

'It's an admission that they don't know how to cope with what the internet gives citizens: the power to connect, the power to share, the power to hold them to account.' She raised her volume again. 'They think it should just be a device for them to spy on their citizens. They hate that we can use it against them, to expose them. So they lash out at whoever they can get their hands on, hoping that they'll make an example of them and deter the rest of us.

'But sorry, guys, I've got some news for you: the reverse is going to happen. Deterrence? Look at all the people who've gathered here this evening.'

They began cheering, but she kept going. 'I'm pretty sure that strategy isn't going to deter us—it's going to energise us. You can lock up Michael Servetus, but every time you do you create a thousand more people determined to do the work of Michael Servetus.'

There was another roar from the crowd. Then a chant broke out. It started over on her left, then it spread, rippling across the crowd, swelling in volume second by second. The placards with Peter's face began rising and falling rhythmically. There was no need to continue speaking. The crowd was speaking for her.

'Free Michael Servetus! Free Michael Servetus! Free Michael Servetus!'

Kat smiled. Naturally, they were mispronouncing it.